THIS BOOK DONATED BY

The San Antonio
Express-News

Avenue E and 3rd Street
P.O. Box 2171
San Antonio, Texas 78297
(512) 225-7411

KINGPIN

KINGPIN

by
BURT HIRSCHFELD
and
EDWIN FADIMAN

DONALD I. FINE, INC.
New York

Copyright © 1988 by Burt Hirschfeld and Edwin Fadiman

All rights reserved, including the right of reproduction in whole
or in part in any form. Published in the United States of America
by Donald I. Fine, Inc., and in Canada by General Publishing
Company Limited.

Library of Congress Cataloging-in-Publication Data

Hirschfeld, Burt, 1923—
  "Kingpin."

  I. Fadiman, Edwin.   II. Title.
PS3558.I67K55   1988   813'.54   87-46356
ISBN 1-55611-091-X

Manufactured in the United States of America

10   9   8   7   6   5   4   3   2   1

For Francine. Without her
this book would never have
been written.

THE PRESIDENT, CHATTING AMIABLY, LED JACK KE-
veney out of the Oval Office. On the lawn behind the White
House, a hundred or so invited guests began to applaud. The
president took up his position in front of the microphones set up
for the occasion. In the press section, flashbulbs began to explode
and television cameramen switched on their equipment.

Keveney, ill at ease in these unfamiliar surroundings, glanced
over his shoulder. A cluster of White House officials, a senator or
two, the minority and majority leaders of the House of Represen-
tatives, the secretary of the interior and a youthful army lieutenant colonel complete with decorations watched him with obvious
approval and veiled curiosity. The secretary of the interior, a
large-bodied man with a long, dour face, gave a slight nod, and
Keveney could hear his irascible rumble of a voice commending
him: "You've done well, my boy. Very well indeed."

Keveney could have disputed that, could have made a strong
case for failure—his and theirs alike. But the president had summoned them all to the White House to boast of glorious victory
and to honor an American hero. Keveney was that hero; the president said so.

"What we have here is a true hero of the republic," the president declared in that warm, homey way he had.

Despite his unease, Keveney appeared unaffected, very much
his own man. Nothing showed on his face, a face composed of
angles and shadows, of aggressive thrusts, of a ridged brow. His
eyes, the color of green glass, were solemn and steady, his lips

7

sealed against the by-now-familiar anguish. The once bright red hair was laced with silver, falling in gentle waves; he had neglected to get his hair cut for the ceremony.

"What we have here," the president went on, "is a man who, against formidable odds and enemies, has triumphed in the cause of the nation. More than anyone, Jack Keveney has turned the tide in the war against drugs, and in so doing, has spared the lives of thousands of our young people who would otherwise have been corrupted."

The president draped a large gold medallion on a red, white and blue ribbon around Keveney's neck. "Thus does the nation and its people honor you, Jack Keveney, with its highest civilian award. It's men like you who make this country what it is."

And Keveney, thirsting for a long pull on the bottle of Jack Daniels in the bottom drawer of his office desk, muttered under his breath, "God help us all . . ."

Almost sixteen hundred miles to the west, the tall man sat listening to the president's words on a small handheld radio through tiny earphones. The presidential voice was thin, without weight, the tinny words a mockery of what the tall man knew to be the truth. He heard enough and put the radio aside.

Even at rest, he gave off a nervous energy. He set himself against frustration and a mounting resentment. And something more, something worse. The fear scratching at his insides. Freezing his guts, causing him to question his strength, his manhood. The fear was the worst of it all. The fear left him naked before his enemies, helpless and vulnerable.

The Americans had done this to him through Keveney. And through Keveney he would have his revenge. He would find Keveney and kill him, destroy him and destroy all that was good about his country. Yes, he would do these things. He, of all men, was able to do them. With a word, a gesture, a single command.

Adios, Keveney.

His mind circled and swooped around one obsessive thought. Soon his friends would complete their arrangements and he would once again be able to assume his rightful place in the world, to reclaim his riches and his power.

His friends. His companions. All those he had raised up, even as he had raised himself. How much they owed him. How much they needed him. How much they admired and respected him and, yes, loved him. Where were they now? What had happened to them? His handsome chin came to rest upon his chest and he considered his plight. How alone he was, how utterly alone. No human being had ever been so alone. No one.

"Madre de Dios," he muttered. "Madre de Dios . . ."

ONE

FROM A DISTANCE, THE VILLAGE OF EL ARBOLITO glittered like a tawdry jewel in the almost tropical sun. From the window of an approaching plane, the corrugated tin roofs of the houses glistened in yellows and reds and greens. The houses were on stilts. The beach upon which they sat was an astonishing white. It was all a technicolor fantasy, unless you lived in El Arbolito. Then you knew that the houses were shanties, barely livable. There was no running water. There were no toilet facilities, no doors, no glass in the windows. The beach was littered with human and animal offal. Pigs, goats and chickens ran wild through the twisted dirt lanes of the village. Every night beneath the houses the addicts injected themselves, murmuring softly as they borrowed a golden rush from the cocaine and heroin they spent their lives hunting. The constant search for chemical surcease swallowed their days, their nights and their hopes, shredding the fabric of their time.

In a half dozen years, this El Arbolito would disappear, to be replaced by a string of luxury hotels catering to vacationing *gringos*.

But not yet. Now life was grim, nervous, and dangerous. For 15-year-old Napoleon Cruz life was especially nervous this early afternoon. He was slim and quick, with the beginnings of an athlete's body, his movements graceful and alert. He possessed the boneless grace of boyhood just beginning to be formed with the sinews of early manhood, and there was a fluid suppleness to his movements. His smile was a quicksilver flash; his eyes were black,

11

liquid and enormous in his small, tight face. His bones were well-defined, a trifle flat and overheavy—the bones of a *mestizo*, declaring his Indian heritage.

Now, outside the hovel of Teresa Valdez, he rubbed his tattered sneakers together in the brilliant early afternoon sun; there was a flash of brown leg through a tear in his jeans. He passed his hand through his black hair. His hands were large and strong, with square fingers and dirty fingernails. He would grow into them, but not for another few years.

He made a loose fist, and knocked. He knocked again, with more power, and blinked his eyes uncertainly. His legs made small movements of anticipated flight, but he held his ground. The door opened at last, and Teresa peered out into the sunlight. Like Napoleon's mother, she was a creature of the night. And unconsciously, she made a face at the glaring light and the fetid air. She was a tall, large woman who would be Rubenesque two years from now, a harridan at thirty.

Teresa was one of Flor Cruz's best friends. They often visited each other's houses and spent a part of their working time together, sharing long, boring hours sitting at the bar of the local *cantina*, drinking the weak tea that looked like beer and tasted like cooling urine, waiting for some man to come who would choose one of them.

"Welcome to my house," Teresa said formally and stepped aside. Napoleon darted in and stopped just beyond the door. It was relatively cool here, and dark. For a few seconds while his eyes adjusted he could see only dimly. Then Teresa's face swam into his vision. She was made up like an enameled doll with a huge crimson bow of a mouth, fiery red cheeks, white powder over her throat and bare shoulders. She wore a pink nylon negligee, all blue furbelows and strategically placed open mesh, perfumed beyond imagining. But to Napoleon she was the essence of sexuality; and in a dim part of himself, he realized just how much effort this woman of twenty-five had gone to, to make herself beautiful today in his eyes.

"My house is your house," Teresa said grandly. "Will you drink?"

The boy looked around. There was only one room, furnished with a couch that had seen better days and a bed occupied by a row of dolls staring at him from its ornate headboard. There was a battered breakfast table, a rusty kerosene stove, a large enamel washbasin and some stained towels. Dominating the room was the inevitable *Cristus* on a filigreed plastic cross, shedding glistening tears of crimson from his wounds. To Napoleon it all looked a little less shabby than his own home—and why not? Teresa was younger than Flor, and made more money.

Out loud, he said, "No. I did not come to drink." He looked at Teresa. "Take off your clothes," he said flatly.

Teresa smiled. "There's plenty of time," she said. "You hurry too much."

Napoleon frowned. He didn't understand all this. He had come to fuck, after all, and she was delaying everything.

Teresa sat down on the couch. "Come here," she said softly. "Come little one, kiss me."

She shrugged her shoulders, the negligee falling away, baring her breasts. The boy touched his mouth to her nipples. How soft they were. Soon they grew hard and he felt Teresa's hand at the back of his head. Her fingers curled in his hair. Under her guidance, his mouth trailed over her breasts and the hollow of her throat. The mixture of dried sweat and powder caused her skin to smell stale and unappetizing. The people of El Arbolito did not bathe often; there was little water to spare for that. And the bright blue sea fifty feet away was indescribably fouled.

"Such a little man," Teresa murmured. She worked at his trousers. Soon he was naked and he felt the woman's fingers on his hardness, pulling, while her other hand caressed his buttocks. Her finger probed his anus and he let out a grunt of surprised pleasure. Teresa put her lips to his ear, and said, "I want to feel your mouth on me."

Napoleon pulled back. "I came here to fuck," he said in his flat voice. "Let's get to the bed and do it."

"Here," Teresa said.

"No. In a bed, properly." This was his first time and it must be done right.

She positioned herself on the bed, legs spread, and with thumb and forefinger guided him inside her.

She began to move, and instinctively he followed her rhythm. How soft she was, warm and wet inside; how much better this was than jerking off.

Teresa began to moan, and her legs locked round his waist. He began to move faster, and much sooner than he expected, it happened. He grunted loudly in pleasure while the woman screamed and writhed beneath him. Suddenly it was over.

The boy's back began to sting. He explored and his fingers came away stained with blood. She had scratched him, the bitch. He spoke to her closed eyes, "Whore of the world. You hurt me." He reached out and pinched her nipple.

The woman gasped and opened her eyes. The mascara beneath them was smudged, and a long tear rolled from the inner canthus. She said, "I didn't mean it. It was during the moment of wonder. I didn't know what I was doing."

Napoleon, hard again, began to pump. "And be careful with your nails," he said between clenched teeth.

"You are a tiger," Teresa said when he finished. "Or perhaps just a little boy eating cake for the first time."

"This tiger has teeth," he boasted, wheeling off the bed and into his clothes.

The woman watched him, admiring his movements. "Do you have a present for me?" Her tone was wheedling, practiced, informed by generations of stolid Indian ancestors.

In response Napoleon slapped her hard across the face. "You asked me to come here. You wanted this. I owe you nothing." The quicksilver grin wiped the anger off his face. "I think you should pay me, no? After all, how many cherries have you plucked?"

"Bastard!" she snapped back. "Mariposa! I know what you do with the other little boys. I shall tell Flor about today," the woman said in an ugly whisper, her cheek turning red from where he'd hit her. "How we'll laugh!"

"You will tell no one," Napoleon said. "No one will know about this—ever. If you tell I will kill you."

Teresa stared at the boy. She saw the petulant face of a fallen angel. His tone was hard as flint, the tone of a man rather than a child. She closed her eyes, suddenly afraid. "Get out," she said. "I don't want to see you again."

Napoleon let himself out of the hovel. He glanced at the sun. It must be after five; he'd spent over two hours with the whore. He sighed. It was time to go home, to face Flor and her despair. Someday, he vowed to himself, someday soon I'll get myself out of this. And never, never come back. He could sense what it would be like to know El Arbolito only as a vague and fading memory— the feeling would be good. At any rate, he thought, I've done it. I'm a man now. As for the woman calling him a queer, it meant nothing. Hadn't he just proved he wasn't?

Yet on the way home to the misery he knew would be waiting, he felt an unaccustomed wetness on his cheeks. He was crying. Afraid he might be seen by someone he knew, Napoleon ducked into a deserted alley and sobbed bitterly, unable to come up with a reason for the sudden outpouring of emotion. After a while the seizure passed and he wiped his eyes with his sleeve. He made a silent vow, that he would never cry again. And he did not—until many years had passed.

TWO

TANNENBAUM PUT KEVENEY IN MIND OF SISTER Asumpta. Both of them owned the long, powerful jaw of a natural predator. Both of them possessed a prim, disapproving mouth and small bright eyes that moved quickly and constantly. Each of them inspired awe, fear and a grudging respect in Keveney. He admired people who knew who they were and who believed in the correctness of their views.

Sister Asumpta, of course, would have disapproved of Tannenbaum. Not so much because he was a Jew, but because he was a *lapsed* Jew; an *unbeliever*, as she used to call such persons—people without faith, unable to give themselves to God and his truth, unwilling to accept the miracle of the Holy Trinity.

"Why did God make you?" Sister Asumpta used to ask, putting the third question of the Baltimore Catechism in a voice that brooked no nonsense. She expected a firm, precise answer. The only true answer.

And she would receive it. "God made me to know him, to love him, and to serve him in this world, and to be happy with him forever in heaven."

Tannenbaum, in his way, was no less dogmatic. He allowed his students in Senior History—World Wars I and II—very little leeway. Tannenbaum claimed that he taught *facts*, and from his students he expected *factual* answers. With this in mind, Tannenbaum gave examinations salted with complex questions; and he graded each student with a cruel exactness.

17

"Right and wrong," Sister Asumpta used to declare. "There is a difference. Ignore it at your peril."

They were soulmates, Keveney was convinced, the aging nun and the atheist historian. The school bell interrupted his thoughts. Four minutes to the next class. But not for Keveney. He gathered up his books and headed for the door. Tannenbaum's harsh voice drew him back.

"I want you, Keveney!"

He presented himself at the teacher's desk, avoiding that penetrating glare. Tannenbaum was stocky, with thick shoulders and powerful hands. Once each year, on the first day of class, Tannenbaum would remove his jacket, folding it neatly across the back of his chair. He would roll up his shirtsleeves to reveal massive forearms, corded and swollen with muscle. Next he would raise a copy of a Manhattan telephone directory so that it was level with his shoulders, holding it in both hands. Very deliberately he would tear the thick volume into two separate parts. Without a word he'd roll down his sleeves, put on his sportscoat again and begin to teach. There was never a discipline problem in Tannenbaum's classes.

Sister Asumpta used to obtain similar results with a disapproving stare behind rimless glasses and a yardstick that she wielded like a saber, inflicting pain and shame with total righteousness.

"You disappoint me, Keveney."

Tannenbaum expected no reply; none was given.

"You're smarter than most of these thugs, but you're letting it slip away."

"I thought I did okay on the last test."

"Okay is failure for you. I expect better. Where's your head, boy? Not in this classroom. Not on your work, where it should be. Your concentration stinks, I can see it in your eyes. What the hell are you thinking about when you should be paying attention? Smarten up, kid. Don't let that good brain of yours go to waste."

"I'll try to do better, Mr. Tannenbaum."

"Don't try, just do better." Tannenbaum hesitated before continuing. "You going to college?"

"No sir."

"Too bad, you've got what it takes. You may go now."

In the corridor, Keveney picked his way through the flow of students. Someone fell into step beside him. Sophia Bondi was dark-haired perfection in a cotton blouse and tight jeans. Her smile revealed gleaming teeth and she gazed up at Keveney out of eyes moist with longing.

"You never said if you were coming to my party on Saturday?"

"Oh, yeah, I'm not so sure I can make it."

She made a face, her voice low and full of promise. "It's your loss."

"I guess it is." Sophia Bondi and all the girls around the school made him edgy with their blatant sexuality, their forthrightness, the nonchalant way they displayed themselves. The sisters at Our Savior School would never have tolerated such behavior. Perhaps there was something to be said for the sisters and their parochial view of life.

"Not afraid, are you?" Sophia Bondi did not give up easily.

"Hell no," he said.

"Just a few of the kids," Sophia said. "We'll drink some beer, smoke a little grass, fool around. You do fool around, don't you, Jack?" She put her hand on his arm. They were a study in contrasts. Sophia was lush and voluptuous, with a skin that shone with good health in the yellow overhead lights. Keveney was slightly taller, with a pared-down body drawn taut, all muscle and bone. Even at rest he seemed poised for flight or action of some kind, a natural athlete who had yet to choose his sport. His head was graceful and round, topped by shining red hair that was thick and curly and in need of barbering. His upper lip seemed too long for his sensual mouth, and his chin was rounded softly, masking off a strong jawbone. His eyes, a strange washed green, seemed sometimes to lose their color, giving an oddly ominous expression to what would one day become a remarkable face. There was a scattering of freckles across his strong, short nose, and his cheeks were lean and smoothly pale.

"Another time," he said in a voice that echoed roughly of the city's streets. "Okay?"

Sophia shrugged, and her breasts rose and fell in counterpoint.

The hell, he thought. A prize for the plucking. He watched her depart, hips swinging slow and easy. He wet his lips and headed for the staircase that took him to the second floor of Vandenheuvel High School.

A second bell sounded, and the corridors and stairwells were emptied of students. Classroom doors were closed and a misleading quiet spread throughout the building. In years past Vendenheuvel had been a training ground for students with a talent for mathematics and engineering. No longer. Now it boasted a citywide reputation as a holding pen for malcontents and troublemakers, an academic desert in what had once been an intellectual garden. Constructed in the shape of a capital letter *B*, Vandenheuvel had a clear view of the Hudson River from the athletic building at the rear of the *B*. It was to the second floor gymnasium, unused at this early hour, that Keveney hurried. He ducked unnoticed into the men's room.

Felipe—no last name given—lounged against the cold radiator, sucking a joint. Light from the tall, wired window at his back put him in shadowy profile. "Hey, man," he muttered in greeting. "I been waitin' on you."

"Yeah," Keveney said. He went along the row of stalls, kicking the doors open, making sure each was unoccupied. He turned back to Felipe. "Yeah, my man, how's it goin'?"

Felipe laughed and extended the joint. "I like it, you bein' so careful. It shows you a smart kid." His narrow face was without expression and his lidded eyes were shining and lively.

Keveney refused the joint. "I still got classes to go to. What about you?"

Felipe grinned. "You got pretty big ambitions for yourself, ain't it so?"

"How else I'm gonna get ahead, I'm not ambitious? Okay, I get a diploma from this place, it's gonna make me rich and famous alluva sudden? No way. I got better plans."

"You think it's easy, it ain't easy."

"Never said it was. I can do it is what I said. Make good money for me, for you, for whoever else is involved."

Felipe gave him a hard stare. He brought a switchblade out of his pocket and flashed it in a quick jittery sweep.

"Hey," Keveney protested. "You don't need that with me."

"I dunno. I ain't that sure about you."

"What is it you ain't sure about?"

"Maybe you don't got what it takes."

"Which is what?"

"Which is a major case of balls."

Keveney laughed. "Except for brains, what I got more've than anything else is balls."

"Maybe." The switchblade disappeared.

"Don't let this baby face fool you, Felipe. Balls and brains, I got 'em both, and I also got what counts most."

"What's that?"

"The grease. I got bread, my man."

"So you say. On'y I ain't seen shit."

"Time comes, I'll show it."

"How much bread you got?"

"Enough."

"I don't know, a kid like you. Where you get any kind've real money?"

"I got a source. A backer."

"Who's that?"

"You think I'm dumb, I tell you that? Thing is, I need the dough, my man gets it up."

Felipe thought about it for a while. "How much you wanna spend? And for what?"

"Some grass, some heroin for the hard cases." He paused for effect. "Let's say five big ones. At wholesale, naturally."

Felipe seemed impressed. "You doin' okay, Jack."

"Does that mean we got a deal?" Keveney felt his heartbeat quicken.

"Tell you one thing for sure, nobody pushes in this school except Felipe. Otherwise he gets his guts sliced up. You understand that?"

"Sure, man, I understand. I'm a customer, not your competition. I got a territory all staked out."

Felipe nodded. He squished the coal on the joint and dropped it into his pocket. "Yeah. Well. Maybe. Lemme nose around, I'll see what I can do for you."

"Right on," Keveney said, "you let me know. . . ."

Riverside Park at night. Not an inviting, gentle place to be. Keveney strolled along the promenade, the Hudson River lapping noisily at the retaining wall. To his left was the park itself, dark and quietly frightening. That would really do it, Keveney thought with suitable irony, to be jumped by a team of teenage muggers out for an easy score. Surprise, boys!

Advancing south from the boat basin, Keveney squinted into the night. Felipe. Where the hell was he?

There was a noise and a scurrying shadow up near the wall that separated the park from Riverside Drive. A pair of half-wild street cats were enacting their own mating dance, screeching at the moon. Violence of one kind or another had reduced the parks of the city into jungles. Keveney grew skittish.

Felipe and Keveney. How easily he could have changed places with the dealer. Felipe from Spanish Harlem, as they called it these days; he from Hell's Kitchen. Gangs had prowled both areas, protecting their turf, looking for easy ways to make a buck. The Black Riders, the Westies, the Brass Hundreds, the Night Crawlers—Irish, Italian, Puerto Rican gangs, each preying on its own people while claiming to be their protectors. No good-hearted Merry Men in those ranks.

Keveney had grown up with guys like Felipe. Kinds bent out of shape by age eleven or twelve. Precocious street hustlers, gamblers, thugs. Killers, some of them. Adept at break-ins, stickups, dealing, whatever turned a buck. Anxious to impress the wiseguys who hung out at Timmy Gavin's Shamrock Grill on Ninth Avenue.

Damn Felipe, where are you?

As if in response, a shadow detached itself from the line of trees and floated onto the promenade, taking up a position alongside a vandalized park bench.

Felipe, at last.

Keveney made no effort to conceal his displeasure. "You were due ten minutes ago."

"Hey, man, here I am."

Keveney glanced around. "Where's your man? Parading around down here in the dark, it's not my idea of a good time. A sitting duck for every spaced-out junkie on the West Side."

Felipe giggled. "You bring the bread?"

Keveney put a hand to his jacket pocket. "I told you, I make the deal with the man, direct."

Felipe put two fingers between his lips and whistled. Two figures came forward. Sammy was a willowy black man in leather and Wellington boots. Slightly to the rear of the tall man marched Dokie. He was a stocky white man with a pigeon chest, long, thick arms and a wary manner. The brains and the brawn, Keveney remarked to himself, hoping his people were within hailing distance.

Sammy checked out Keveney. "You just a kid," he said. "How you gonna come up with the kind've bread we talkin' about here?"

"Don't worry about me."

"Fact is, first, last and always, I worry only about me." He gestured and Dokie moved behind Keveney. "My man there, he's got to give you the once over. Just to be safe. You don't mind."

Keveney planted his legs apart and raised his arms to shoulder height for the frisk. Dokie missed two good places. Amateurs, Keveney thought when the search was over.

"Clean," Dokie said.

Sammy grinned. "Didn't hurt at all, did it?"

"So now we stop playing games and do business, okay?"

"Let's see your money."

Keveney brought forth the envelope from inside his jacket, displaying the contents. "Now the goods."

Sammy chuckled. "You got a suspicious nature, my man. Dokie, fetch the stuff."

Dokie hurried to a trash basket chained to the safety railing of the promenade. He returned with a plain brown paper bag from which he removed a brick of marijuana.

Keveney accepted it, sniffed it quickly. "Green," he snarled, retreating a step, setting himself so that he confronted Sammy, pointing in Felipe's direction. "Acapulco Gold, you told me. The best, you said. This stuff is green."

Felipe started to protest but Sammy broke in. "The kid knows merchandise, and that's a good thing. This is for this time, next time I'll do better for you."

"What about the horse?"

Dokie offered a plastic bag filled with white powder. Keveney tested the powder by rubbing the residue on his gums. Almost at once the gums grew numb.

"Nice," he said.

Sammy giggled. "First-grade shit."

Keveney hefted the bag. "No more'n half a kilo here."

Dokie moved around uneasily. Felipe shuffled his feet. Sammy giggled and leaned Keveney's way. "Come up with ten grand, and next time it's quality merchandise, I guarantee it."

Adrenaline pumped into Keveney's bloodstream. His voice rose half an octave in direct ratio to the excitement he felt. "What am I, some kind've a virgin! We had a deal, and here you're jerking me around on quantity and quality."

"Step on the shit, kid. Step on it four, five times. You'll make back your investment and a lot more. And not so loud, kid, don't wanna wake up the whole neighborhood."

Keveney back away, dropping the brick and the plastic bag onto the bench. His eyes were wide and bright, working around from one man to the other, never still. His voice began to climb again. "You're hustlin' me. You deal like I never been there before. What am I, a kid? I'm a man. Treat me like a man, like a *man*. You don't think so? Take a look at this I'll show you I'm a man . . ." In one swift motion, he unzipped his pants, reaching inside, hand sliding into the pouch of his Jockey shorts. "Here's how much a man I am!" His hand reappeared, clutching a Smith and Wesson .25 caliber with a two-inch barrel. "Freeze, motherfuckers! I'm a cop and you're busted! Every goddam one've you!"

Dokie cursed, crouched and made a practiced move. Keveney shot him slightly east of his navel. The stocky man went over backward, spitting and coughing, blood spurting, crying out in anger and agony. "The bastard shot me! He shot me. Jesus Almighty God, I'm gonna die."

Hearing the gunshot, Keveney's men came rushing down the hillside, weapons in hand, making intentional and professional noise. After a while, somebody said it might be a good idea if they sent for an ambulance.

As for Keveney, he stood to one side, gazing out on the river. In the night it glistened, looking as pure as when Indians roamed the land. But Keveney knew that with daylight you would be able to see the floating turds, the empty cans and the yellowing rubbers. Garbage was everywhere, he reminded himself, and he was on his way to becoming one of the city's finest garbage men.

THREE

POVERTY IS BOTH UNORIGINAL AND IMITATIVE. NAPO-
leon's home was a duplicate in most essentials of Teresa's tin
shack. The exception was Flor's "boudoir," which consisted of an
upturned packing case upon which she had arranged her various
creams and lotions. The single room was divided longitudinally by
a checkered sheet hung by wooden clothespins to a rotting string
line that sagged perilously in the middle.

The floor was tamped earth.

Two mattresses served as beds, one in each "room." The mattresses were covered with guinea cloth stolen from the potato bags
that piled up in the back of Pablito's *bodega*. Upon this sacking,
Napoleon had spent the long nights of his childhood.

When Napoleon entered, his mother was sitting on a discolored
stool, her top bare but for a stained bra, preparing her face for her
nightly prowl. Two candles blazed, even though it was still quite
light. Christ looked down from his great agony upon Flor's small
one, and he wept at what he saw: Flor trying to apply eyeshadow
with a trembling hand.

From across the room, Napoleon could see the fine sheen of
sweat that covered his mother's body. Occasionally, and unbe-
knownst to her, she uttered an animal moan of pain. But she was
unaware of her agony, so much a part of her life had it become.

This late in the day, the sun had lost its ardor. Soon there would
come cooling breezes, laden with intolerable smells, but better
than the fetid heat of the day. When she heard her son, Flor said
harshly, "Where have you been?"

27

Napoleon didn't bother to answer.

"Do you have any money?" Flor asked him. Her voice was weary and sad. Her hand shook. Napoleon said nothing.

She turned her face to him. She had been a pretty girl in her youth. There were still traces; age and disease could not hide the fine structure. But her face was hollow, her eyes dazed and dull. At thirty-two, she looked fifty. Flor had always been clean, as clean as this place allowed her to be. But now Napoleon noticed the dirt in the creases of her skin. Even from a distance the faintly sour scent of his mother filled him with distaste. She made him recall the smell of Teresa Valdez and her soft, powdered flesh. He felt soiled and vaguely guilty and averted his eyes.

She said, "Little one, I must have some medicine." She swung around on the stool, her legs spread, and Napoleon had a flash of reminiscence, seeing Teresa on the tattered couch, her legs positioned in just such a fashion. He averted his eyes. "I must have it," Flor said. "I can't go on without it."

The boy spread his hands in protest. "There is no money for medicine," he said, "no money for food, unless you work."

"I can't," Flor said, shaking. "It hurts, my son. It hurts terribly."

The boys' face twisted momentarily in sympathy. "There is no money," he said flatly.

"You might have worked this afternoon," Flor said shrilly. "You might have brought enough home for what I need."

"There is no work in El Arbolito. You know that. Only what you do."

"Everyone does it here," Flor said. "In one way or another we are all in La Vida. There is no other way for us." The boy said nothing. It was true. His mother spoke softly. "Go. Go to Orlando."

"I talked to him yesterday and the day before."

"You must convince him. Otherwise I will die."

Napoleon shrugged. "I'll try," he said. "All he will do is laugh."

Napoleon ran his fingers through his hair and went out into the dwindling sunshine. Orlando, like so many of the people in El Arbolito, lived at night. He would not be ready to receive anyone until sunset. And even then, he would not be ready to see Napo-

leon unless he had some money in his hand. The boy clenched his
fists. It would be unpleasant, and Orlando would be unwilling to
extend any more credit. But the boy had to try. He walked the
tortuous dirt path that led to the cantina. He walked slowly, filled
with dull rage. He would take Flor away from this place some day,
away from the life they lived, away from the stench and the dirt
and the eternal poverty. He would take her away from her "medicine," away from her syringe and her battered tiny spoon. He
would bathe her in hot water and perfumed soap; he himself
would run a comb through her tangled hair; he would smooth her
and polish her and make her again beautiful. He would set her
down in a magnificent *hacienda* to live in splendor and safety for
the rest of her life. And no one could touch her, no one would
ever again laugh at her. She would have a toilet of her own, and
running water; and she would kiss his hands and call him the best
son in the world.

The sun had almost set when he arrived at the cantina. The bar
was built of wood, solid and cared for. There were windows of real
glass, and a pole with a sagging cable attested to the fact that there
was electricity here.

He could feel the luxury of the cantina's wooden floor through
the thin soles of his sneakers; he wriggled his toes against the
smoothness. Paco, the bartender, was polishing the top of the bar
with an oiled rag. He jerked his head at Napoleon and put a coke
on the bartop. He and the boy were friends though they had
scarcely exchanged a dozen words in as many months. The place
was cool and dimly lit. A half dozen men sat in the back at the
shadowed tables. They sat in silence, and in silence they observed
the boy as he lifted his glass. Everyone knew what he had come
for. Everyone knew Flor, for it was here she earned her living.

Orlando owned the bar, as he owned the souls of most of the
people who lived in El Arbolito. He was the richest man in the
village. If you wanted anything: whiskey or *pulque*, a fix, a girl,
even a small boy if that was your inclination, Orlando would supply it. He was a man of respect, and for a while, until Flor ran out
of money, Napoleon had wished desperately to be like him. Now
he hated Orlando, hated his hiccuping laughter and his high-

pitched voice. Orlando laughed a great deal, mostly at his customers. But then, he was the only person in El Arbolito who had something to laugh about.

After a while, Napoleon spoke in a whisper. "He is in?" Paco inclined his head. The boy understood that Orlando would shortly appear.

Soon he felt a hand on his shoulder. The high voice he had come to detest said, "Did he pay for that drink?" Paco nodded. The boy knew the price of the coke would come out of Paco's pocket. Orlando sat on a stool next to him and said, "What are you doing here?"

He wore a spotless white suit, a black silk shirt and a red tie with gold stripes. His shoes were gray lizard skin, shining and pointed. His fingernails were buffed to a high gloss. His complexion was sallow, his skin tired under the dim light. He had small eyes, hard and black as obsidian. He smiled with thin lips and said, "The sun sets, and the little black flies come out. I asked you, why are you here, little black fly?"

"My mother is sick. She sent me for medicine."

"Have you brought money? Money buys medicine."

Napoleon looked at him.

"On your way then. Come back when you have money. Your mother should work harder, to make more money to cure her sickness."

He laughed his high-pitched laugh.

"There is no work," the boy said. "If there were work, I would earn money to pay for the medicine."

"Go to the capital. There is plenty of work there. Or to Chiriqui. In Chiriqui you can pick coca in the fields and sell it for cash at the market. You are right. In El Arbolito, there is no work."

"I could work for you, Orlando." The boy forced the words through the dense hatred in his throat.

"I am Perez. *Señor* Perez to you."

"Señor Perez. I would work well."

"I do my own work," the man said mirthlessly. "I take care of my own business."

"I would work *very* hard. I could run errands, deliver the medi-

cine to whoever you say. I am a fast runner. I am smart and I have
cojones. I am dependable."

"Those who buy from me come to me."

"Let those who come to you continue to come. But those who
cannot—a fast boy, brave, dependable, would be a help, Señor. I
could add to your business. In time, I would double it."

"And those who owe me? You would take care of them too, little
fly?"

"Whatever is necessary, Señor," the boy said. Paco, who never
talked, abruptly spoke.

"This boy, Señor, he has wings on his heels."

Orlando stared at the boy. Napoleon stared back, his face impassive. Orlando felt a small chill. There was something about the
boy's look. It was the look of a man, not a child. He said at last: "If
you do not do what I say, *exactly* what I say, I will beat you. Cheat
me once, I'll have your legs broken. Betray me, I'll have you
killed."

"I understand, Señor."

"I will make you a deal. There is a man, a mestizo, out in the
country. He farms a little, does odd jobs. He owes me. He owes
me for six months. His name is Carlos. You collect from him, and
I'll try you. I will pay you one hundred pesos a week. If you
collect."

"And medicine for mama, every day."

"Fifty pesos and the medicine."

"I'll be back. How much does the man owe you?"

"Six hundred."

"You will have the medicine ready when I return?"

Orlando laughed and shook his head. "Surely," he said, "when
you hand me the six hundred pesos. I will have the medicine
ready for your mama. Flor will be proud of such a son." He snick-
ered again. "Let me give you directions."

"Not necessary," the boy said. "I know where this Carlos lives."

Orlando looked at Paco. "Give him two hard-boiled eggs," he
said. "He'll need his strength."

Napoleon walked out into the tender young night, munching.
The food filled his belly. From his back pants pocket he took out

an oil-soaked rag. Inside there was a curved fisherman's knife, the blade shining and vicious. Satisfied, he put the knife back in its nest and set out at a steady lope that would devour the miles. He had often run this way. Carlos would have to pay, as he had to pay. It was fate.

The dim lights of El Arbolito fell behind him as he ran, and then winked out. He ran now on grass, and there was enough moon to see by. It was a silver world he ran in; the night scents pleased his nose, and he breathed deeply. Within a few minutes, he had his second wind, and then it seemed to him that he flew through the scented air. Everything around him was mysteriously beautiful, everything seemed to glow. He felt a rush of impossible happiness and he put his purpose behind his mind, where it waited while he enjoyed his happiness.

Carlos's small house was only a few miles out of town. He grew maize, and he distilled pulque from a field of cactus. The boy approached silently, moved up to a window, and peered in.

Carlos sat at a homemade table, the remnants of his supper spread about him. His head was bowed to the table top, and there was a half empty bottle of pulque near his crossed hands. He slept deeply, half drunk with pulque and his usual inhuman day's work.

The boy worked the door open and entered. A kerosene lantern flickered on the table top.

Napoleon approached slowly. He kept his weight on the balls of his feet and the earth floor made no sound. Carlos slept on, snoring lightly, his matted, graying hair obscuring his face. With his crossed hands he looked as though he were praying.

The boy came closer until he was staring down at the sleeping mestizo. He took a slow, deep, careful breath and held it. The knife was in his hand. He reached out to the kerosene lamp. The light flickered. With all his strength, he drove the knife through Carlos's crossed hands, deep into the table top. With the other hand he extinguished the lamp.

Carlos screamed. The room was pitch black. He began to sob with the pain. The boy spoke in a hissing, unnatural voice.

"Your hands are pinned by a knife. Don't struggle, or you'll make it worse. Are you listening, man?"

"I am listening. You have hurt me seriously."

"You won't die. I come from Orlando. You owe him money."

"Who are you?"

"That is a stupid question. Do not ask it again. Where is the money you owe Orlando?"

"I owe him nothing. On the innocence of the Virgin, I owe him nothing."

"I have another knife," the boy lied. "Pay me now or I will use it. It will not be your hands this time."

"But I have no money."

"Last week you sold corn for three thousand pesos. Do not lie to me. Your brother, Enrico, boasted of it in the village."

"That cabrone." The mestizo choked in pain and anger. "Release my hands and I will find the money. Put the light on."

"No. Just tell me."

"Under the mattress," the man said. "This hurts. It hurts terribly. I am dying of the pain."

"It will soon be over." Napoleon moved to the bed and felt under the thin mattress. The sour odor almost made him vomit. He located a sheaf of bills and held them up to the moonlight.

"I am taking what you owe," he said. "Orlando is not a thief. One thousand pesos. The rest is still yours."

"But I only owe six hundred," the peasant said. His blood darkened the table top, almost ebony in the moonlight.

"There is interest. Do not argue."

Carlos said nothing.

"I will remove the knife," the boy said. "You will sit quietly. Put a cold bandage on your hand till the flow stops. Then bandage them tightly at the wrists.

He leaned over the man and tugged with all his strength at the knife. To his dismay, it didn't move. He considered leaving it, but it was his prized possession. He pried back and forth until it loosened; the mestizo screamed in pain. At last the knife came free and Carlos screamed again.

The boy wiped the stained knife on Carlos's shirt and ran.

Orlando was waiting when he entered the cantina.

"So, little fly, you are back."

"It is done," the boy said. He held out some bills. Orlando counted them with the swiftness of a bank teller.

"Seven hundred pesos?"

"I told Carlos he owed interest."

"And he paid you?"

"He is an honorable man."

There was a long silence. Finally, Orlando sighed. "You begin work tomorrow," he said. "Be here at five."

"Thank you, señor."

There was another pause. "Well," Orlando said impatiently, "what is it now?"

"My mother's medicine."

Orlando looked at the boy's flat face and his large, still eyes, and he felt again that curious shiver. He held out a small packet wrapped in tinfoil.

The boy took the heroin silently. He backed to the door, saying, "Until tomorrow, Señor," and vanished into the night.

Napoleon headed home, moving without haste. Today's events filled his mind. In his pocket were three hundred pesos. In his hand was heroin for Flor to soften her pain. Tonight she would not have to sell herself in the cantina. And he had a job. What a fine day it had been. He knew there would be many more good days, for he had indeed become a man. He straightened his shoulders and lifted his chin and walked with that graceful prowl that would forever mark him.

FOUR

"YOUR TURN, SERGEANT."

The hooker called herself Tiffany. She was tall and lithe, with fine round breasts and buttocks to match. Bleached hair cascaded across her shoulders, and she wore an abundance of drugstore makeup. She was nineteen years old, and if it weren't for the makeup she could have passed for sixteen, which a certain number of her clients wanted her to be. She came from a small town in Idaho and had been on the streets for two years. She'd been with Louie Carbone before and found him gross and offensive; she didn't like a man who wasn't personally clean. She would have turned down his invitation to accompany him and his partner to the Great Urban Hotel for a party, but Carbone had given her no choice. Cops seldom did, she had discovered early in her career.

Carbone had put it straight: "You can do six months on Riker's and go cold turkey. You won't like that, Tiffany, not with the habit you got. So what's a couple of hours fooling around?"

"I get paid for fooling around," she complained, and went along.

So they checked in to the Great Urban, Jack Keveney, Louis Carbone and Tiffany. Carbone arranged for a room on the cuff and brought along a bottle of Black Label. He ordered ice and soda sent in, poured drinks for the three of them and took off his clothes. For safety's sake, he put his gun on the floor alongside the bed.

"This," he said, stretching out, the drink balanced on his deep, hairy chest, "is the life." Carbone had been married for sixteen years. He had three children, a mortgage on a row house in Queens and a burning desire to put in his time and retire to one of Florida's

35

Keys. He wanted to fish, get sunburned and fat and read about the blizzards and the crime waves in New York. He liked to say, "Fuck the city. Fuck everything about it, fuck alla you guys, also."

Louis Carbone was not the most popular man in the precinct house. But he was considered an okay cop, reasonably honest, good under cover and dependable under pressure. He announced to Tiffany and Keveney that he would go first. "Slippery seconds ain't my style."

The hooker began to strip.

Keveney took off his leather jacket, filled his glass with Scotch and withdrew to the bathroom with a copy of that morning's *Daily News*. He made himself comfortable in the tub, his legs dangling over the side, and read the sports pages, the crime stories and the entertainment section, in that order. Through the closed door he could hear Louis Carbone advancing through the various levels of sexual excitement toward his usual asthmatic climax. Carbone fucked noisily, giving off truncated snorts and roars as loud as anybody Keveney had ever listened to.

Tiffany did her best to keep him on track, matching him dirty word for dirty word. She displayed, Keveney admitted to himself, a fine working vocabulary. At last Carbone popped his cork in a succession of hoarse exhalations, extended cries and gaspings of "Oh, God!" and lapsed finally into a silence broken only by an occasional groan of satisfaction.

"Your turn, sergeant," Tiffany called through the closed door.

Keveney allowed his eyes to close. Two weeks since last he had had his pipes cleaned. Remembering brought tension back to his limbs and a tightening in his loins. Though long overdue, he was reluctant to walk the path Carbone had taken. Even with the hookers he frequented, Keveney preferred the illusion of affection and concern.

"Be right there," he answered without enthusiasm.

He raised himself out of the tub and examined his reflection in the mirror. His beard, sparse and gold-red in color, failed to make him look older than his years. With his red hair shaggy, he could easily pass for a drug-infested street creep, and that was what mattered. He was reaching for the doorknob when he heard Carbone's enraged cry.

"I'm a cop! You're busted!"

Three shots at regular intervals. Swearing under his breath, Keveney yanked his gun from its holster and pulled the door open, plunging ahead, finger squeezing down the trigger . . .

Eight men, experienced in such matters, reliable, obedient, dressed in plain clothes and working rapidly, cleaned up the mess. Tiffany the hooker was whisked away, given an acceptable supply of money and a bus ticket to Chicago and told never to show her face again in the city.

"What happened didn't happen," a burly deputy inspector muttered in her ear. "What you saw you never saw. How could you have? You weren't here."

Tiffany, happy to escape with her life, her clothes and her savings, understood. But Chicago . . . ?

"What about Miami?" she found nerve enough to say at the bus station. "I'm sick and tired of the cold."

The commissioner issued a statement: "Working undercover, Detectives Jack Keveney and Louis Carbone broke up a multimillion-dollar heroin ring last night to climax a long, arduous and dangerous assignment. In a shootout precipitated by drug dealers, Detective Carbone was killed and Detective Keveney shot one of the dealers. Two others escaped. Drugs in the amount of two million dollars street value were confiscated plus a number of weapons.

"Detective Carbone will receive an inspector's funeral and Detective Keveney has been awarded the Distinguished Service Medal for heroism beyond the call of duty.

"The investigation is ongoing and additional arrests are imminent."

"I don't wanna do it."

The deputy inspector, magnificent in his custom-tailored uniform, examined his buffed fingernails. His hands were square and pale and soft. He had never walked a beat or patroled in a black-and-white, he had close ties to City Hall and he hoped one day to become police commissioner.

"You don't seem to understand, Sergeant. You've become a hero."

"Let's forget it," Keveney said.

"These are rough times, lots of criticism of the blue, Sergeant. The department can use a certified hero."

"Let me go back to the street."

"You're a valuable asset."

"I didn't do anything."

"You broke up a major drug ring."

"That's crap, Inspector. The perp was a small-time hotel burglar. He caught Louis with his mind on his dick, otherwise . . ."

"I read all about it in the papers, Sergeant, so it must be true." He glanced at a slip of paper on his desk. "The lady's name is Rose Tierney, and she does features for the *Daily News* Sunday section. A little conversation, some pictures taken, and that will be that."

"I don't need my name in print. I don't want my picture in the paper."

The deputy inspector shook Keveney's hand briefly. "That's a fine career you've got ahead of you, son, make sure not to fuck it up . . ."

"You don't like women, is that it?" Rose Tierney said.

Keveney drained his glass of wine and filled it up again. "Which women?" He made a point of not looking at her. She reminded him of somebody. That creamy skin, those crisp blue eyes, the dark hair that fell across her shoulders in waves. The nuns, he told himself, all those damned disapproving Irish nuns in those forbidding black and white habits. Scurrying around like human prowl cars, searching for evildoers among their young charges. What he didn't need in his life was a civilian version of Sister Asumpta, full of disapproval and disdain. Not now, not ever.

"For example—me." She smiled his way, taking the sting out of the words, watching him closely.

He shrugged. They were having dinner in Arcudi's on West Thirty-eighth Street, where the food was Northern Italian and the wines were excellent and inexpensive.

One look at her and Keveney knew it had been a mistake, agreeing to this interview. It was certainly a mistake to meet at night over dinner, as if they were friends or lovers, or about to become one or the other. There was too much of the familiar in that face of hers. Too much that brought back troubling memories, too much that stirred his interest. She was, he conceded grudgingly, a damned good-looking woman. The face of a madonna, he told himself. Or was it the face of an Irish slut? Whores and madonnas, Catholic confusion, inextricably entwined.

He answered around a mouthful of veal rollatine, delicately flavored and precisely cooked, thinking that at least he was getting a decent meal out of this. No diner food when the department picked up the tab. "Whataya want me to say?"

"The truth."

He swallowed a half glass of wine and waved to the waiter for another bottle. "I don't know you well enough to like you."

"But well enough not to like me."

"I never wanted to do the interview. I said that when we began."

"You think I'm going to write a story that will hurt you?" Most of the men she met talked readily about themselves; it was frequently their only topic of interest. Not Jack Keveney. He functioned from around corners, out of mysterious pockets of personality that she was unable to investigate. Added to that was his prototypical Irish face, with those remarkable green eyes, faded and unblinking. Freckles and white skin emphasized his youthfulness. He was one of the most attractive men she'd ever encountered. But not her type, no.

"Maybe it'll hurt the department," he said.

"Why would I do that?" Was she making more of him than he was? He had the look, the hard demeanor, the background; just another street cop with a fast trigger finger. The story of that hotel shooting, it matched almost word for word the official departmental version. "What," she said watching his eyes, "really happened at the Great Urban that night?"

He stared at her until she looked away. "What you got, that's all there is."

The waiter uncorked the new bottle and refilled Keveney's glass. Rose Tierney indicated that she had enough.

"I think there's more," she said.

He shrugged and cut off some rollatine but left it on his plate.

She rolled the wine in her glass around. "Tell me," she said with an artificial lack of concern. "How does it feel, shooting somebody, another human being, killing another man?" She raised her eyes to his and they were bright and unforgiving.

The question made him gag and bile rose up in his throat. With the bile came the fresh, crimson memory of that night. That frozen instant when he came plunging out of the bathroom. Carbone, already dead, hanging over the side of the bed, eyes round in disbelief and rage; the hooker Tiffany, her back against the headboard, mouth agape in a silent scream, hugging herself against the expected volley.

Keveney, crouched low, shooting. Three shots, they told him later, enough to do the job. Squeezing them off by reflex, watching the perp's body jerk and twist on impact, hearing him cry out and grunt—a thick, gurgling protest as the blood filled his throat. One of the slugs struck an artery and as he crumpled to the floor, a long red glistening arc of liquid burst out of his chest. The fear, the horror of it, would remain with Keveney for a long time, and though he would use his weapon again and again, he would always carry the burden of that night. How does it feel to shoot somebody, he repeated to himself, and in answer he almost went to his knees, weeping, praying for God's grace to enlighten his mind and move him to shun evil and do good. He brought his napkin to his lips in a strangely dainty gesture. But his face remained hard and immobile.

"That's a dumb question."

"That's your answer?"

"It feels good," he said presently. "Good that it was the other guy and not you."

She looked into his face, trying to peer behind the bone mask, to find her way into the fissures and convolutions of his brain.

"I'm trying to discover the truth about that night. Is that so wrong?" Was that all it was, she wondered. Or was there something more, the desire to force him to confess some unnamed guilt, to break through that complex construct of cop defenses behind which he functioned? What in God's name was she after?

"We both ask questions," she continued. "Cops and reporters. That's all it is."

He longed to be rid of the questions. Hers and his own. To put the guilt away. What had gone down in that room—Louis dead, the burglar dead, Tiffany sent on her way and he, Keveney, turned into a paper hero—he appreciated none of it. He had not joined the force to become part of a coverup, to erect a public deceit, to pretend to be something he wasn't. But being a cop meant you played by the rules of the job. This reporter—though that face of hers could turn his resolve to jelly—was one of *them*. Outsiders. Departmental critics. The enemy.

"Stop asking," he said. "Believe me, Miss Tierney, you know all there is to know."

"Most people call me Rosie," she said. She smiled, and it was the kind of smile that made his skin shift, his eyes blink.

"Sure, Rosie." Were they supposed to be pals now? Kissing cousins with no secrets from one another? No way he'd allow her to soften him up with a smile and a name. He recalled a childhood rhyme: Ring around the rosies, pocket full of posies. All fall down. No way he was going to take a fall, not for her, not for anybody. "You can call me Keveney."

"Okay, Keveney, tell me about yourself. What made you become a cop?"

He did his embarrassed young man act, ducking his curly red head, producing a sheepish grin, massaging his chin, providing his prepared answer. "Where I grew up, it was either the cops or the firemen. Whichever list you could get on, whichever job came up first. It was the pension, you see, the security."

She wasn't impressed. "You still feel the same way?"

Smart dame, he said to himself. Knew a lie when she heard it. If not for the cops he'd've been bent like the other wiseguys around Gavin's Shamrock Grill. He'd have become a cheap hustler, maybe busted or dead by now. The cops kept him straight. Maybe it was the blue with a buzzer on his chest and a police special on his hip. Maybe it was simply belonging to something bigger and more important than himself. Maybe it was the excitement, the danger, doing a job that *mattered*. And chasing bad guys, catching them, taking them off the streets. The pride it provided and the sense of personal worth. And always there was the Big Blue Secret, the secret seldom talked about: that police work was more fun than anything else he'd ever done. Except for dipping his wick, naturally.

"Ah," he said, "I'm just a guy with his finger in the dike."

"Isn't that heroic?"

"Not when there's too many holes and not enough fingers."

"Why not build a new dike?"

"That," he said, emptying his glass, "ain't my job." He called for the check.

"I'm not finished," she said. She was amused by this man's rough edges. Her father—a professor at Boston College—would not have approved of Keveney. "An unreformed Irishman," he would have said. "All muscle and balls, without sense enough to use his head." Rosie Tierney didn't agree; there was more to Jack Keveney than that and she intended to draw it out of him. What, she wondered, would it be like to live with such a man, love him, be married to him? What an outrageous idea!

"I'm a cop," Keveney said brusquely. "I got work to do."

"I'll go with you. We can continue our conversation."

She was full of surprises, and the more dangerous for being so, he thought. "Stick to your job, Rosie, and I'll stick to mine." He left her sitting at the table in Arcudi's.

He headed straight up Tenth Avenue, thinking he would walk back to his apartment and let the night air clear his head. He was disoriented and full of subdued rage at the way he'd acted with Rosie Tierney, letting her get under his skin that way, responding to her questions like some rookie a week out of the academy. It wasn't smart; worse, it wasn't professional, and he prized professionalism above all other qualities in a cop. It made for reliability and trust and kept casualties to a minimum. That's what had gotten Carbone killed, thinking with his cock instead of remembering he was a cop and acting like one, no matter the situation.

The streets were empty at this hour, except for an odd dog-walker, and no one noticed his unsteady, wine-induced gait. A block or two above Forty-sixth Street he spotted the car thief. No doubt about it. A young black man industriously at work on the door of a Chrysler sedan, dark green with lots of chrome and tail fins. Engrossed in his labors, the car thief failed to notice Keveney until he was only ten yards away. Keveney reached under his jacket for the pistol holstered at the small of his back, automatically assuming the firing position, feet apart, knees slightly bent, both hands supporting the weapon in a strong, steady grip.

"Freeze, motherfucker! I'm a cop!"

The car thief came around in slow motion and as if by magic a pistol materialized in his right hand, pointed Keveney's way. The two men stood without moving, mirror images in the dim glow of a street lamp.

Keveney's brain tipped and yawed, unbalanced with shifting images, all the possibilities flipping swiftly into view. Shoot the gun out of the perp's hand. Order him to put his weapon down, give himself up. Better yet, put a bullet between his eyes, take him off the streets for good.

He concentrated hard, trying to make sense out of a senseless situation. Two men about to kill each other over a damned automobile. He thought about Louis Carbone, dead in that grubby hotel room, and the perp he, Keveney, had shot to death. He thought about Rosie Tierney. Damn that woman! If not for that madonna face of hers, if not for all that red wine, for all that talk of him being a hero, none of this would be happening.

The Smith and Wesson grew heavy in his hands and his elbows seemed to lock in place. Damn, damn, damn. What would the sisters say about this? Nobody was going to walk away from this one. And Keveney wasn't ready to die. His eyes rose to the car thief's face. A sheen of sweat glistened on the man's upper lip. His eyes were wide, his expression fearful.

"Tell you what," Keveney heard himself saying. "I'm gonna put my weapon away."

The car thief was a man of little faith. "I'm no fool."

"You do the same."

"Oh, sure."

"I walk away, you walk away."

The car thief thought it over. "You're a cop. How I know you're not jerking me around?"

"What choice do you have?"

"Sweet Jesus . . ."

"You see?"

The car thief spoke slowly. "If I go along, how's it gonna work?"

"I'll count to three. On three I'll put my gun away. You do the same."

"Then what?"

"Then we both leave. Face it, man, this is stupid."

"Stupid, yeah. Okay, I'm gonna go along."

"One . . . two . . . three . . ."

Very deliberately, smoothly, Keveney lowered his arm and put the pistol away. The car thief did the same. Keveney breathed a sigh of relief. He walked past the car thief and continued on his way uptown, not daring to look back.

When he arrived at his apartment, he was shivering, his shirt soaked through with perspiration. He peeled off his clothes and showered, hot and cold, and brushed his teeth vigorously in an attempt to wipe away the metallic taste of dread that lined his mouth. It didn't work.

"Holy Mother of God," he said aloud, "Holy Mother of God . . ." Still shivering, he'd climbed into bed and pulled the blankets up to his chin. It was a long time before he fell asleep, and when he did he dreamed he was back in Our Savior School and Sister Asumpta was after him, yardstick ready, aiming to administer a good Catholic punishment. And just as she caught up with him, he recognized Rosie Tierney under the wimple, her full mouth gaping as if about to devour him.

FIVE

COCAINE, HEROIN AND MARIJUANA WERE, TO THE IN-
habitants of El Arbolito, what a salt lick was to a herd of cows—
always there, so omnipresent that they were not even thought of
as special or necessary. These substances formed their lives. They
used them almost subconsciously when they were available. They
were important only when they were absent. Then, everything
stopped until the flow resumed. Only with the help of these narcotics were the people able to support the daily horror of their
diminished, hopeless existence. While eighty percent of the in-
habitants took dope, the very cost of the product was so out of line
with their income that few were able to become truly addicted.

Flor was an exception. Every day, she received her medicine.
Every day, she went over the scarred, pitted surfaces of her body
to find a clear space in which to inject her syringe. Every day, as
she poisoned herself, she became older, slower, more dependent.
And every day, Napoleon hated her and loved her more.

She adhered to her routine. Every night she entered the cantina at six-thirty and took her accustomed place at the bar. There
she would sit, sipping tea, her eyes vague, slowly and volup-
tuously scratching herself, talking to the other whores. When the
men entered, she would cajole them into buying drinks, caressing
them almost primly as they drank, squeezing their thigh muscles
and occasionally leaning her face for a kiss. She knew most of
them; they had been customers for years. The talk was almost
familial. But when they were sufficiently drunk, she would ease

45

them over to one of the other girls, something that she did quite skillfully. At the end of the week, she would collect a small commission for clients found. The girls always paid her what they owed her; they cheated the world, perhaps, but never one another.

Whenever Napoleon had to go to the cantina, he would studiously avoid his mother; and Flor acted as though he were not there. But every afternoon, she would kiss his hand when he presented her with the foil-wrapped dose of "medicine."

One night he surprised her as she sat at her dressing table making herself ready for her purposeless journey into the night. He took one of her hands in his and examined the creased skin on the back of her hand, the slight malformation of her fingers that heralded a future arthritis.

"Why? Why do you go out at all?"

Flor shrugged. "What else should I do with myself? And besides, I am lonely. You are always out, you do things in the night and I do not know what they are." She paused. "I do not want to know what you do . . ."

"What I do, I do for us," Napoleon said angrily. "For your medicine." Flor said nothing. "Your medicine is not cheap."

"I must have it," Flor said, her voice shrill. "You see I must have it."

"All right," he said. "But one day the medicine will kill you."

"I know."

"We must leave El Arbolito."

"How could I do that? This is my home. All my friends are here."

"I want to buy a house, a proper house, where you can live like a *gringo*."

"Such talk makes me afraid," Flor said. "To leave my home, that makes me afraid."

The boy let go her hand. "You have no pride."

"I have been in the life for twelve years. That does not leave much pride." Flor finished her toilette and said abruptly in a child's voice, "Would there be a proper bathroom in the fine house you'd buy us?"

"Yes," Napoleon said firmly. "There would be a bathroom inside with running water."

"That would be wonderful," Flor said dreamily. "But where would you get so much money?"

"I will get it," he said. "Somehow." To himself he said, "Like shit, little friend." For all his greed, his cleverness, he was unable to scam more than three hundred pesos a week. That was all Orlando allowed him to steal. It was an unwritten, unspoken agreement, for every fish must eat, and Napoleon was the best collector Orlando had ever hoped to have. But Napoleon honored the parameters. He was afraid to transgress them; had he stolen more than three hundred pesos a week, Orlando would have broken his legs and Napoleon knew this.

By now the boy was on familiar terms with every shady character in El Arbolito and the surrounding countryside. He knew every one of Orlando's customers, knew which of them could be trusted and which could not. Like a first-class secretary, he made his employer's life easier. Orlando's accounts receivable were in excellent shape. No one now owed him money for more than two weeks. Despite his youth, Napoleon had earned the respect of the villagers. He had grown taller, and his body had firmed out, and his constant running (he did everything at top speed) had provided him with the muscles of a man. He was afraid of nothing, and few men dared trifle with him.

Sitting at the bar of Orlando's cantina, he sipped a coke and watched the old bartender wipe the bar top. Back and forth he went, exerting no pressure, the movement mechanical. It contributed to the odd peace that Napoleon felt sitting in the quiet semigloom, unspeaking, waiting until Orlando had need of him. His muscles and his mind were at rest; and out of somewhere deep within him there emerged the beginnings of a plan. He thought about it for more than a week, inspecting it for flaws, honing it in his mind until he was certain. Until he knew he could follow through, the boy bided his time. But no one knew the splendors that unrolled behind his flat, black eyes. At fifteen, he had learned the value of discipline. Everything he did, everything he thought, was motivated by his dreams of glory.

He made friends, deliberately. But he loved no one except perhaps himself, and himself not that much. But his customers never knew it. He was popular. The whores mothered him, the men moved uneasily in his presence but respected him nevertheless, and some feared him. After a while he became the respository of many secrets, for he never talked—about anyone. Among his many acquaintances, he picked a few as intimates; or, perhaps, he made them think they were intimates. No one really knew Napoleon.

The day Orlando sent him to meet Juan-Manuel Negrete was an important day. It started ordinarily enough, with Orlando beckoning him to his shadowed booth, which was reserved exclusively for him and from which he did all of his business. Napoleon stood, deferential and courteous, until his boss magnanimously waved him to a seat. Orlando looked well, he had developed a small, neat paunch over the months, and there was a blurring of his jaw line. The dealer's life was now peaceful and prosperous, and he knew that he owed much of his peace of mind to Napoleon.

"Little fish," he said, "I have a job for you."

"I am ready."

"But this is different," Orlando said. "This is a supplier. And he is not a man to be trifled with—not in any way. He would eat you up alive." He paused. "And me."

"He sounds formidable," Napoleon said. His voice had deepened into that of a man.

"Do not joke," Orlando said. "Juan-Manuel Negrete is not one to joke about."

Napoleon made no reaction. Obviously, this man was special. Orlando was not truly a coward, and yet the boy could smell his fear. "Eight miles out," Orlando said, "to the northeast. There will be someone waiting for you who will take you to Juan-Manuel. You won't see him, but he'll see you."

"Will he blindfold me?" Napoleon said, and Orlando caught the irony in his tone.

"No. He doesn't need to. He changes his camp every week. No one ever knows where he is for more than seven days."

"He is careful."

"He is a *bandito*. You've never heard of the Ché Brigade?"

"A little," Napoleon said. "Very little."

"People do not talk of the brigade. Or of Negrete. But occasionally, he has some merchandise for me. And he sells cheap."

Orlando chuckled. "It costs him little. So he eats, and I eat." Orlando handed him a sheaf of bills. "There's five thousand there," he said. "Negrete has a third kilo of pure. In return for the merchandise, you give him the money. Simple."

"Simple," Napoleon agreed.

It took the boy two hours to cover the distance to Negrete's camp. He was not even breathing hard when a voice called sharply. He stopped immediately.

From behind a rock a youth approached. He had the beginnings of a scraggly beard, and beneath it a bad case of adolescent acne. He wore baggy blue pants and a blue shirt; the clothes fell from his scrawny body and yet, perhaps because of the self-importance in his eyes, he looked vaguely military. He was cradling a Czech machine-pistol in his arms. These were curious weapons — unfinished, with machine-tool marks still on them. But for all of their crude appearance, they were among the most efficient portable tools of destruction ever created. They fired and kept on firing through bad weather and enormous abuse, when the American and Russian equivalents, finely machined and gleaming in their ferocious perfection, jammed from heat and overuse.

"You are the 'little fish,' " the youth said.

"I come from Orlando."

The youth gestured with the barrel of his weapon. "Follow me." He led the way, and the belts of ammunition with which he was festooned swung like strange jewelry from his shoulders and waist.

Negrete had pitched his camp behind a U-shaped formation of rocks that reached up almost twenty feet. He was vulnerable only from the air. The camp consisted of ragged tents and ragged men, most of them pitifully young. There were girls and women too, all somehow the same: humble, with large, liquid eyes that saw little.

Negrete was sitting a little apart, blowing into a magnificent mouth organ, which blindingly nickeled and at least a foot long.

He played well; and as Napoleon approached, he swung into "La Palomita." The romantic strains of the popular love song were incongruous in these grim surroundings. Negrete was dressed like his followers, in ill-fitting blues, but two silver stars were sewn to his shoulders, and he wore a bestarred cap besides.

Negrete looked up and smiled. His teeth were very white. Napoleon crouched on his haunches beside him. "You play well," Napoleon said. Negrete smiled again. His face was narrow and bearded. He appeared to be in his early twenties. His eyes were bright and his fingernails were manicured. The clear polish shone through the streaks of dirt on his fingers.

"Will you drink?"

Napoleon nodded. There was a stack of paper cups to Negrete's right. He plucked one and filled it from a filthy bottle. "Pulque," said Negrete.

"I prefer water."

"You drink pulque. Water is scarce here."

Napoleon took a spare mouthful of the stinging liquid and coughed behind his hand, spitting into the sand. Negrete said, "You have money for me?"

"You have the merchandise?"

"Roberto. Bring the stuff," Negrete yelled. A stocky man hurried to his side with the inevitable plastic bag. Napoleon reached into his pocket for the portable scales he always carried, and then thought better of it. "This is the agreed amount," Negrete said, watching him. "Do you want to check the weight?"

"No. I am satisfied." Napoleon handed over the sheaf of money into Negrete's dirty hand.

Not to be outdone, the bandit put the money away without counting it. Then he said, "Now, you may have water." A leather bag of water was brought, and Napoleon drank thirstily. It was lukewarm and smelt of the hide in which it was contained.

Negrete leaned back against a low outcropping of stone, measuring the boy.

"Napoleon," he murmured, "you are well named."

He took a sip of pulque and continued. "You have worked for Orlando long?"

"Long enough," Napoleon said.

"I have heard of you," Negrete said. "There are stories. It is said you have cojones. Are the stories true?"

Napoleon shrugged.

Negrete clapped him on the back. "Stay for supper," he said. "I like you."

"And I you," Napoleon said, discovering to his surprise that he meant what he said.

Supper was roasted goat, refried beans and pulque. Napoleon ate too much, drank too much. He felt ponderous and sleepy.

Night had fallen, and the stars were out in the deep black sky. The fire was warm on his back. Negrete lay with his head in the lap of a pretty girl and began to talk.

"My father was a doctor, in Chiriqui. He had a large practice among the poor. The poor in Chiriqui are poorer than the poor in the country. They are dirtier too, and they have diseases. My father was a saint. He treated people for nothing. He rarely collected his fees. Still, he tried hard to pay his bills. He was the greatest man I have ever known." Negrete paused and his drawn, narrow face stared into the fire.

"He worked in a military hospital. At the time, the military had the only hospital in Chiriqui. My father was well known there. The nurses loved him, the other doctors admired him. He worked long hours, and at night he did his rounds among the poor. I don't remember his sleeping, but he must have. He had a small German car, I remember, with a strange snub nose. But it never failed him, and everyone knew the sound of his engine.

"My mother had died when I was very little. We were brought up by Mathilde. She cooked and cleaned and blew my nose. I can remember my father falling asleep over his soup, his head nodding, until he would have put his face in the bowl if I had not held up his head." Negrete sighed. "He was a great reader. But he was always too tired to open his book. He was a great man."

"You are a great man," the girl said softly but fiercely. Her name was Desiree.

Negrete shook his head. "In some ways," he continued, "Chiriqui is a small town. Somehow my father became involved in politics. Even then, there were men who wanted to change things in Sixaola. They were intellectuals. They had the ideas, but they were not capable of action. They weren't even organized. But they met occasionally and discussed conditions and drank wine and talked of a better future. My father joined them. It was all theory." Juan spat into the fire. "They were only words. They played with words instead of women. They were harmless. Even I knew that, and I was only fourteen. My father would bring books home. More and more books about the Soviet Union and the successful revolution there. About Cuba. He had no time to read, but I did." Negrete glanced over at Napoleon. "They did an extraordinary thing in Cuba," he said. "They gave the land and the government back to the peasants, the *peons*. And when we win, we will do the same."

Napoleon said nothing. To himself he thought, Who cares what the reasons are? Sixaola is a poor country. I will go where the money is. And that is the only politics I need to know.

"One day they raided the place where they met, those futile intellectuals. My father was taken along with the others. I didn't hear from him for a week. And then, they arrested me.

"In the prison they did not feed me for three days. Then the prison commandant took me and led me to a dark place well underground, and told me I was free to go and take my father's body with me. It was the first I knew of his death."

"Stop now," Desiree said. "That's enough."

"He was lying on a stone table," Negrete said. "They had torn out his fingernails and his toenails one by one. They had burnt his intimate parts. And they had forced him to swallow water until his belly burst and he died. They gave me a sack and I put my father into it and I dragged the sack for two miles, back to our home, and buried him the next day.

"My friends came to the funeral. My father's colleagues were too afraid. After the funeral, I talked to some of the boys. And that's how the brigade started. Now you know."

I don't know why he is telling me all this, Napoleon wondered. The answer was plain; already a special bond existed between them. Juan-Manuel and he would be friends. Sooner or later, Negrete would be valuable. He was a man of action, Napoleon judged, and would eventually become a precious tool.

"It is a small band," Napoleon said.

Negrete looked up. "We have not the food or the money to buy arms for a larger group. But soon, perhaps, we will make a real killing. Then we will buy more arms, and I will have more men. In five years..."

"In five years?"

"We will be thousands," Negrete said. "And we will take the presidential palace."

"And then?"

"And then we shall have a true democracy in Sixaola. The people shall rule. There will be no oligarchy to exploit the *campesinos*. No crooked politicians to line their pockets while the workers go without food. There will be work for everyone. We will bring water to irrigate the high desert and electricity into the villages. Sixaola will become a good place to live."

Napoleon's natural cynicism, refined and sharpened in the dirt streets and alleys of El Arbolito, came into play. To his ear, Negrete sounded very much like the men in Orlando's cantina, drunk on pulque and giving voice to their most fanciful dreams, which would never come to pass.

"What about the gringos?" he asked without emphasis. "Will they allow this to happen?"

"To hell with them!" For the first time, Negrete displayed the force behind his words. His eyes went round, points of angry light boring into Napoleon, fixing him in place. "There are those who will help us. The Soviets. The Cubans. We have friends in Managua. I do not fear the Yanquis."

Napoleon nodded and fell silent; let Juan-Manuel wallow in his dreams. He, Napoleon Cruz, would confront reality and, in time, bend it to meet his own requirements. And at such time perhaps Negrete and his grandiose dreams might be of some use to him.

SIX

IT WAS A RIGHTEOUS BUST. CORRALES WAS THE BIG-gest distributor of narcotics on the West Side, his turf running from Seventy-second Street north to Columbia University. Corrales himself was a sort of American success story. He was born poor into a broken family, and his mother had given birth to seven children by five different men, none of whom remained with her for very long. Early on, Corrales knew he wanted out of such a no-win situation. Poorly educated, his absences from home hardly noticed, he roamed the streets of Spanish Harlem seeking oppor-tunity. He was bright, perceptive, ambitious and eventually ruth-less; had he been born in an earlier time, he would have made a marvelous *conquistador*, a man geared to take risks, to exploit the smallest opportunities that came his way. Drugs offered him his opportunity. Not yet thirty, he was a millionaire many times over, with a large, faithful organization and with a burning desire to become the biggest narcotics dealer in the metropolitan area.

He had no way of knowing that Jack Keveney was working long hours to stop him.

The bust came only after a year of careful planning. Keveney had placed one of his men inside Corrales's group to feed out information about the dealer's various activities and work his way up to a position of trust. Then the hook was put out, expertly baited, appealing to Corrales's greed and rising ambition. Ke-veney presented himself as a small-time operator with a ravenous appetite. Finally he'd been able to convince the department to risk enough buy-money to tempt Corrales to come out of his shell and put his own hide on the line—a quarter of a million in cash in return for an appropriate amount of heroin, the exchange to be made in a bar Corrales owned on Upper Broadway.

They met at four in the afternoon. Only a handful of lonely drinkers were at the bar, lost in their own alcoholic reveries. Corrales and Keveney sat in a back booth while the dealer made a quick count of the briefcaseful of cash Keveney offered. Satisfied, Corrales handed over a shopping bag with the Bloomingdale logo on it; it contained the agreed-upon amount of heroin.

Corrales said, "I like the way you do business, man." He extended his hand.

Keveney took it, squeezing down hard. "I don't think so, man. I'm a cop and this is a bust."

Four men faded away from the bar, flashing both their shields and their weapons. There was a certain amount of shouting and protesting as they rounded up Corrales's people, until at last a reasonable quiet prevailed once more.

Corrales appraised the situation with calm appreciation. "Hey," he said to Keveney. "You're pretty good at what you do."

Keveney snapped the cuffs on the other man. Corrales frowned.

"Whataya think," he said, mild disapproval creeping into his voice, "I'm gonna run? I ain't gonna run."

"Let's go," Keveney answered, getting to his feet.

Corrales slid out of the booth. "Ever heard of Marcus Carter Guest? He's my lawyer, cop. Best criminal lawyer in the city. He'll have me back on the street in a couple of hours."

He was wrong. Four hours passed before he was back in his favorite booth in his Broadway bar, boasting of his triumph, insisting the case would be thrown out of court because of police entrapment. "The cops can't hurt me," he told anyone who would listen.

Keveney agreed. "Everything turns to shit," he said somberly to his boss. Captain Neil Xavier Holahan, chief of the Narco Division, tried to soothe the ruffled feathers of his best man. "Ah, Jack, let's not get your water hot."

"I've had enough, Captain. I want out."

Holahan, a large man with a large head and features to match, had never been one to control his temper. It had cost him two wives and the affection of his five children. His already bulbous nose seemed to swell, pumped up by rage, painted a livid purple by broken veins and enlarged pores.

"Fuck that noise," he growled. "What've I got here without you, Keveney? A bunch of slobs that can't think their way out've a paper bag. When I put in my papers, you'll take over this desk."

"And the bad guys will still get away."

"You want justice, go into another line of work. You wear the blue, you just try to keep up. Maintenance work is what we do. Keep things going is all. Somebody's got to do it, Jack, and you're the best."

"I wanted Corrales so bad. I almost had him."

"Grow up. The big fish always gets away, it's the law of the sea. Corrales is no exception."

' "There's got to be a way to take them all out, street pushers, smugglers, the top guns. Otherwise . . ."

"When you figure out how to do it, let me know." Holahan tapped a file on his desk, putting a satisfied grin on his wide mouth. "My spies downtown found out the scores of the lieutenants' exam. You came in number three, my boy. The way people are retiring you'll have your bars inside've a year."

"I don't know, maybe I should give it all up."

"And do what?"

"There's a security job . . ."

"Not you, my boy. Let go of the tin and all you'll do is sit around waiting to croak. People like us, we were made to be cops. It's God's will. Now lay off bitchin' about what you can't do and get on with what you can . . . Go out, get drunk, get your pipes cleaned, and we'll just go on, you and I. Okay?"

But it wasn't okay. Not by a long shot.

"How do you feel?"

Jack Keveney dragged on his cigarette. Smoking after sex was inevitable and necessary, as if closing the circle of satisfaction.

"All right," he muttered.

Next to him, Rosie Tierney traced the outline of his rib cage with one slender finger. She wondered if Keveney ever knew true, deep satisfaction, if he ever completely relaxed, gave himself over to his emotions. Certainly she had yet to see any such signs; always there was an undercurrent of tension and unrest, as if he were expecting some imminent attack. She tried to lighten the mood.

"See, Holahan was right, about getting your pipes cleaned."

The words coming out of her mouth left him uneasy. "Holahan's never right, not about anything. The man is a brown-nosing fool marking time till his pension comes through. He's scared shitless I'll make waves."

"Maybe he's right."

"The man is a hack, just putting in his time. He wants me to be the way he is, to sit back and wait for promotions and the pension."

"You can't do that, can you?"

"No way. I hate cops like Holahan. I'd like to strip 'em of their guns, their badges, kick 'em off the force . . ."

"You'd like to kill Holahan, isn't that it?"

"To be rid of him is all. They disgrace the badge, they corrupt the job, they disgust me."

"Ah, Keveney, you're a modern-day Quixote."

"Yeah, who's that?"

"You're a true romantic . . ."

"Romantic—me? You must be kidding."

"I'm not. There you are, believing that by your own efforts you can make things better."

"What's wrong with that?"

"It's the impossible dream." She envied him his noble dreams, and at the same time she was distracted by his innocence, his almost persistently ignorant vision of the real world. He was a tough cop, yes, but he was also a naive cop, and she was afraid for him. She didn't want him out there by himself, tilting at windmills, being hurt, eventually getting ground down and defeated. All that nobility, that dedication, that supreme innocence! No man by himself could put things right, not even Keveney. Why couldn't he be like the rest, accepting and passive—ordinary? "It's futile," she bit off.

"Don't try to change me, Rosie."

So that's what he thought. Well, he was right. She wanted to change him, to keep him safe, so that she might cherish and nurture him. "My love will transform you," she wanted to say aloud, but dared not give voice to the words for fear of his reaction. Instead she said, "What happens if you do make waves?"

He laughed, pleased by the idea. "Maybe a big fish will be washed ashore."

She squeezed his thigh. Even in his darkest moods, Keveney was an optimist. "If you want to catch big fish," she said, "you need a bigger net."

He ground the cigarette out in the glass ashtray that sat on his chest. He lit another cigarette. "You smoke too much," she said, wishing she hadn't said it. He didn't belong to her, he wasn't her responsibility. He was entitled to do whatever he wanted to do.

"Say that again."

"Forget it."

"Go ahead."

"All right—you smoke too much."

"Before that."

"I don't know—oh, that maybe you need a bigger net to catch the big fish."

"Right. A bigger net."

"A bigger net might be more difficult to manipulate."

"But worth it if you could land the big fish. The thing is, how to design such a net."

"You'll find a way." She rolled nearer, her breast warm against his side. "Put out that damned cigarette and make love to me."

"You never get enough screwing."

"I never get enough of you making love to me. There *is* a difference, you know." He was unlike her previous lovers. Where they had been sensitive to her needs, to her feelings, he was intense and demanding. The pleasure and satisfaction she experienced was incidental to his own needs. He attacked her body as if it were an obstacle to be overcome, a perpetrator to be subdued and busted. Always when the lovemaking was ended she felt radiantly content yet vaguely annoyed for surrendering some essential part of herself. Yet since their first time together, she could not get enough of him.

His hands on her flesh were rough, spreading, probing, and she turned herself over to him each time with the sure knowledge that he would fulfill her. He never disappointed her.

"Words," he said, and put the ashtray aside. "You're a writer, use the right words for things." He brought her hand onto his genitals. "Give it a name . . ."

"Your penis."

"It's a cock. A dick. A prick. Go ahead, say it."

"I know all the words, Keveney." She pulled her hand away.

He laughed, sensing her annoyance. "Go ahead."

"Fuck you, Keveney."

"Good, very good. That what I want, for you to fuck me. For me to fuck you."

"Bastard."

He laughed again and rolled onto her, forcing her legs apart. "This is what you want, to get fucked."

"Make love to me, Keveney."

"I'm going to fuck you."

She felt him sliding into her, the swollen power, the force of his body pounding at her and she wished she could become the woman he wanted her to be. Her arms and legs went round him and she cried out in her rising excitement, her flesh in harmony with his, her needs transcending everything she'd ever believed about herself, everything she'd ever felt. With him, she knew at last what she wanted.

"Oh, yes," she whispered against his cheek, "fuck me, my darling, fuck me."

Keveney barely heard the words. There were no dirty words when he was with her, no soiled images, no sense of loss afterward. Her freely given love had opened a locked door to a private and beautiful garden in which Jack Keveney felt at home. He was falling in love.

Willie Hatcher was a round man with a hard muscularity developed as a distance swimmer while in high school in suburban Philadelphia. He presented a deceptively soft appearance due to an amiable, fleshy face with perpetually pursed lips and moist brown eyes. His clothes were nondescript and rumpled, and the knot of his faded knit tie was never quite in place. While in New York, he stayed at the Hotel Carlisle for a few days, then moved over to the Waldorf. He spent a great deal of time in his room or walking the city streets or dining alone in good but moderately priced restaurants, displaying a penchant for Szechuan food. Two or three times he went to a movie and one night he saw a play. He had no guests, entertained no women and spoke to no one other than the desk clerk at the hotel and the people who attended his needs in restaurants. Amidst the city's millions, he went unnoticed, attracted no attention.

Except for Keveney's people, who kept him under a twenty-four-hour-a-day watch. Wherever he went, two of them were not far behind, tracking him around midtown Manhattan. Five days of this and the men of the Narco Division were becoming discouraged.

"Stay with him," Keveney insisted. "His name keeps showing in all our intelligence reports. The guy is dirty, and wherever he goes a deal is in the works."

"Whatever he's doing," Ted Greenberg said, "he's a pretty slick operator." Greenberg, short and heavily muscled, owned a pug's face, scarred and lumpy, his nose bent out of shape. "The dude's got no yellow sheet."

"So he's smart," Keveney said. "Only we're smarter. When he moves, we move with him, and quick."

Late the next afternoon, Hatcher moved. He boarded a limousine for Kennedy Airport. Detectives Walsh and Bradley followed in an unmarked car. They raised Keveney on the radio and reported their destination.

Keveney checked his listing of plane arrivals from various key locations in South and Central America. "Flight 452 out of Mexico City. Arriving six-fifty this evening. That's Latin American Airlines. There'll be a shipment on board."

Walsh, a veteran of eighteen years on the job, was dubious. "What we know about Hatcher, his people have never used a Mexican flight before."

"So this is the first time," Keveney snapped irritably. "Two hours till arrival. I'll meet you there."

Willie Hatcher went directly to the LAA arrival building, settling down with some magazines in the arrival area. Flight 452 arrived forty minutes late.

Keveney took up a position across the room from Hatcher, keeping watch on the round man. Walsh and Bradley went off to check on the flight crew. As the passengers from Flight 452 began exiting the customs area, Hatcher rose and watched them, as if waiting for someone. When the last of the passengers had passed through, Hatcher strolled away without urgency.

Outside the terminal building, Walsh and Bradley were standing together, trying to look innocuous. They saw Hatcher hail a cab and drive away. Walsh hurried to where their car was parked and brought it around, following from a distance.

"Know what I think?" Bradley said. He was a tall, well-built black man who looked more like a Certified Public Accountant than the hard-nosed detective he was. "I think the sucker is jerking us around."

"Maybe he's clean," Walsh said. "Maybe he's just a citizen."

"Who likes to spend his time waiting for planes to unload?" Keveney said caustically. "No way. What've we got on this guy?"

"Practically nothing. A model citizen. No record. He works for the Bergstrom Travel Agency..."

"Yeah," Bradley added. "Only one thing ain't right..."

Keveney completed the sentence for the other man. "Nobody around Bergstrom knows the man or ever heard of him."

"Right."

"So something's going down with this guy at the airports. Let's not lose him." Walsh pressed down on the accelerator, closing the gap between the two cars.

Keveney studied his timetable. "Worldwide's got a flight out of Sixaola in an hour from now. Number 67. Let's meet it . . ."

Once again Willie Hatcher settled down in the arrival area, reading his magazines. To Keveney he looked no different from the many other middle-class American men waiting the return of their friends and families.

When all the passengers from Worldwide's Flight 67 had disappeared into the baggage area from where they would enter customs, Willie Hatcher made his way without haste to the public corridor lined with ticket counters. He took up a position against the opposite wall, staring at some point in space.

Some fifty feet away, Keveney placed himself behind an architectural pillar with a clear view of the other man. Whatever the deal, it was going down now; he was sure of it.

Presently a painted door alongside the Worldwide ticket counter opened and the crew of Flight 67 appeared. Two pilots, a navigator, a covey of neat and almost pretty flight attendants—all chattering, carrying their personal luggage. From the tarmac, they had passed along a long corridor that allowed them to bypass customs, Keveney knew. This then was how it was done.

The navigator placed his black leather overnight bag on the counter and motioned to one of the clerks. Without a word, the clerk swept the bag out of sight and went back to work. The flight crew went on.

Keveney signaled to his men, most of whom went after the crew. Two others headed for the ticket counter. Keveney fell into step a dozen yards behind Willie Hatcher, who left the terminal building and boarded a Carey limousine for the ride back into Manhattan. Ten seconds later, Jack Keveney lowered himself into the seat next to the round man.

"Tight squeeze," he remarked conversationally. "These seats don't give a man much sliding around room."

Hatcher delivered a half-moon smile, saying, "Not bad for

somebody your size. But nobody makes seats big enough for my bottom."

"Diet and exercise, that's what it's all about."

"Genes," Hatcher said. "I don't eat much, really." He looked out the window as the limousine began to move into traffic.

"Took me a while to catch on," Keveney said. Hatcher's head came back around, the brown eyes empty, the half-moon smile still in place. "You're a watcher, Willie. Just making sure it all goes off as planned."

Hatcher blinked. "Mister, you got me mixed up with somebody else."

"Come on, Willie. Level with me."

"My name's Frederic Bryan. I'll show you my passport. You've got me confused with somebody else."

Keveney flashed his shield. "Sergeant, Narco Division. Jack Keveney's the name."

Hatcher faced straight ahead.

"Where do they deliver to, Willie? Not the hotel, certainly. That's too risky and you're a careful man, I can tell that. How about a locker in Grand Central? Or maybe through a messenger service to the Bergstrom Travel Agency." Hatcher never flinched. "Oh, you are good, Willie, real good, but it doesn't matter. The operation is terminated. We're picking up your people. The guy on the plane, he'll talk, Willie, provide lots of names. That kind always does. We've been watching you for a long time now."

Hatcher said, "I don't know what you're talking about."

"Drugs, Willie. Oh, nothing truly big. A little here, a little there, enough for a nice, steady income."

Hatcher laughed and his cheeks quivered. "If I had that kind of money, would I be riding a public limousine?"

"Why were you at the airport, Willie?"

"I like airplanes."

It was Keveney's turn to smile. Hatcher was easy to like, unfazed and cheerful, as if he underwent such confrontations frequently and almost enjoyed them.

"Ah, you're not really a cop," he said to Keveney. "More like an Irish choirboy."

Keveney had to laugh. "Used to be an altar boy," he confessed. "Even thought about becoming a priest for a while."

"Your mother would've loved that, right?"

That drew another laugh. "You must've known her."

"Or someone very much like her. All mothers have romantic dreams."

Romantic dreams. Rosie Tierney had called him a true romantic. All so much bullshit.

"And your mother," he said. "What did she want for you, Willie?"

It was Hatcher's turn to laugh, a loud extended roar that drew attention from the other passengers and made them smile.

"That dear lady's favorite fantasy was that I would attend the Harvard Law School, become a respected attorney, a defender of the poor, a loud voice for justice and equity against the entrenched powers. She saw me seated on the Supreme Court. Chief justice, no less. How's that grab you, Keveney?"

"The law and the priesthood—we're coming from the same place, Willie."

"The only true vocations, as far as mothers are concerned."

A flash of understanding passed between them and their eyes locked. Keveney experienced a momentary affection and a grudging admiration for the cheerful round man at that moment, as if they were friends or something more than friends. Indeed they had come from the same place; they were in certain ways a matched pair, interchangeable parts in some medieval pageant unfolding at its own pace. He liked the way Willie displayed no fear and remained true to his own code.

"You're not going to arrest me, are you." Willie said. It was a statement, not a question.

Keveney resented the assumption and admired Willie's perception at the same time. "Don't be too sure," he said.

A slight smile turned the corners of Willie's mouth. "Oh, sure, Keveney. You can hassle me, roust me around, even. Put me on the grand tour for a few days, precinct to precinct, maybe have some goon work me over in the men's room. But I don't think that's your style. You play by the rules, Keveney."

"You're guilty as hell, Willie. Both of us know that."

Keveney wondered how he would act in Hatcher's place. Even more, how well would he do at Willie's job, buying, selling, transporting dope. He knew he would be at least as good as the fat man. No, better than that. Better than Willie—Keveney was convinced of it.

"I like you too," Willie said out of the blue.

Resentment settled in Keveney's chest, resentment that he'd allowed Willie Hatcher to become a human being in his eyes, that he'd allowed him in some strange way to slither past the protective barriers behind which Keveney functioned. He put on his best, hardest cop's face and spoke from between clenched teeth. "I can still take you, Willie, send you away for a long time."

Hatcher started to reply but thought better of it. Keveney had changed the rules of the game so that all control passed back into his hands.

"My people have been tracking you, Willie. Into Central America, into Colombia, into Paraguay, into Sixaola. You know certain persons in whom I have an abiding interest."

"If you travel a lot, like I do, you meet people."

"You're chin high into dope, Willie."

"I'm in the travel business. Bergstrom Agency..."

"Nobody knows you there."

Damn, Willie thought. This Irish cop did his homework. "A silent partner. It's on the record. As for drugs, I don't even use aspirin."

Keveney spoke as if reading off the list. "Jose Luis Medina in Bogotá. You deal with him. Tito Gonzales in Medellín. You work frequently with Tito. Gabriel Todaro in Mexico City. Half the goods he ships come into your hands. And in Chiriqui..."

A nervous spasm tightened Hatcher's belly and he wondered if he was going to be sick. This Keveney was too smart, he knew too much. Willie felt as if he were dancing precariously on the edge of disaster.

"I don't know these guys," he managed.

"Come over to my side, Willie."

Hatcher slumped in on himself. So that was it. Keveney meant to turn him. Maybe he wasn't as smart as he seemed. "No way," he said flatly.

"You lead an uncertain life, Willie."

"Life is never predictable."

"You're in danger. You could die at any time."

"I buy things," Hatcher said after a while. "Strictly small-time. I don't hurt people. I give my word, I stick to it. People like me. They trust me. I got no problems."

"From now on, you do." A threatening note in Keveney's voice brought Hatcher around in his seat. "A word in the right place about you, Willie. Word that you've come over, that you talk regularly to me. How long would it take for that word to get back to your *compañeros* in Medellín, in Chiriqui? How would your pals take the news, Willie?"

For the first time, Hatcher displayed emotion. His jaw flexed and his eyes jerked away and back again. "I'm an errand boy, is all. An arranger. A watcher, like you said. Strictly minor league. Why do you wanna get me killed?"

"It's the nature of the business, ain't that right? I like you, Willie, and I don't particularly want to see you hurt. You want me to save your butt—well, you give me this, I'll give you that."

"I'm not a snitch."

"Of course not. I buy snitches for twenty bucks a pop. What I am looking for is a friend, Willie. A man who functions outside the law in the service of the law. An intelligent man, a source of intelligence. Somebody shrewd and ballsy. Somebody just like you. Whataya say, Willie? Come over to my team."

Neither of them spoke again until the limousine pulled into the terminal. Hatcher followed Keveney off the bus, facing the cop.

"Am I free to go?"

"Consider what I'm offering, Willie. Next time the wrong cop may bust you and I won't be able to help. It'll be too late, Willie, and you'll go away for a very long time."

"Goodbye, Sergeant Keveney."

"Think about me, Willie. Wherever you go, I'll have my eye on you, watching, waiting for you to make a mistake. So take care, Willie. You don't have a lot of time left."

SEVEN

FOR MANY MONTHS, THE PLAN TOOK SHAPE IN NAPO-
leon's brain. It was altered, modified, refined, yet never proved to
be exactly what he wanted. Until his mother moved Porfirio into
the ramshackle hut near the beach to live with them. Tall and
well-muscled, with a neatly barbered mustache and sleepy brown
eyes, Porfirio began to function as Flor's lover and keeper, guiding
her behavior day and night. It was Porfirio who insisted that she
work longer hours at the cantina. It was Porfirio to whom she
brought every penny of her earnings. It was Porfirio who dis-
pensed Flor's daily dose of heroin, which Napoleon continued to
supply. And it was Porfirio who claimed authority over the young
boy.

"If you wish to continue living in this house," Porfirio announced, "you must pay for the privilege"—ignoring the fact that
Napoleon's earnings helped support them all. "You eat too much,"
Porfirio accused. "You drink too much Coca Cola. All these things
cost a great deal. So each week you will hand over to me two-
thirds of what you earn." When Napoleon protested, Porfirio
knocked him down with a single blow. And when the boy tried to
fight back, Porfirio beat him down again. When Napoleon turned
to his mother for support, Flor sided with her new lover.

"Porfirio is the man of the house now. You will treat him as a
member of the family. As your father."

The boy protested and Porfirio smiled down at him with reptil-
ian satisfaction. "It is true, I am not your father, nor do I wish to
be. You may call me Uncle."

"Uncle." The word stuck in Napoleon's throat.

"Say it again," Porfirio demanded, and in emphasis he drew a gravity knife from his pocket. He grinned again at Napoleon. "In case you get any ideas in the middle of the night, little one. Understand what they will come to, how they will end, how you will end."

So it went. With Porfirio sending Flor and Napoleon out to make money while he remained at home gambling with his friends, drinking beer, and, whenever he was dissatisfied, expressing that dissatisfaction with his fists. More than once he struck Flor, and when Napoleon came to her defense, he was knocked down in turn.

The plan festered in Napoleon's brain along with a growing hatred for Porfirio, and soon he could not separate one from the other—until finally Napoleon understood precisely what it was he had to do.

Andreas, the pawnbroker, was the second most successful businessman in El Arbolito, a distant second to Orlando, not nearly as rich nor as powerful. Andreas, a man of gross proportions with a huge head sunk deep between great round shoulders, envied Orlando his wealth and power but knew that given the natural order of life in the village, he had arrived at the level of accomplishment God wanted him to have. So he had convinced himself that he was a happy man, satisfied with his lot, getting exactly what he deserved. But always a small voice in him cried out for more, for some of the rewards that seemed to flow so easily in Orlando's direction.

Thus he listened with interest when Napoleon came to him, saying he had a way to make both of them rich, or at least richer than they were. He offered the boy a warm Coca Cola and drank beer out of a long-necked bottle. He wiped sweat off his high brow and nodded wearily, saying, "How much money will it cost me so that you can make me rich?" He chuckled shortly at his little joke.

Napoleon did not laugh. "Do not treat me like a child, Andreas. I come to you as one businessman to another with a proposition."

"Why do you come to me? Why not to Orlando whom you work for?"

Napoleon blinked slowly and the fat man was struck by the boy's long lashes. How beautiful he was, almost as pretty as a girl. Yet he had already established his reputation as someone not to be dealt with lightly.

"Orlando is part of the plan," Napoleon said. "But he doesn't know it. He will never know it, until it is too late."

Andreas took another swallow of beer. He was anxious to hear what Napoleon had to say; he was also afraid to hear it. But greed overcame his fear. He indicated the boy was to continue.

Napoleon began to talk in a flat, emotionless voice. First he outlined his plan. Then he broke it down into its various elements, providing time and place, indicating the equipment that would be needed, the personnel, covering every logistical question. He made sure Andreas knew what would be demanded of him, what provisions for his personal safety were built into the plan, and that the fat man understood how large would be the rewards of his action and for how long they would accrue to him.

"You will become the richest man in El Arbolito," Napoleon concluded. "The most powerful. The most respected."

"Unless," Andreas replied, "your greed should mean the end of us. In this pond, Orlando is the biggest fish. He could devour us all."

"We are smarter than he is. He could never imagine we would dare to do what we are about to do."

"I am not so smart," Andreas said. "Also, I am fat. I swim slowly, and it is easy to attack me. Do what you must do, and leave me to my business."

"I will make you rich, very rich."

"You will make me dead."

"Trust me," the boy said earnestly. "All will be well, if you trust me."

The fat man stirred uneasily. "It seems a good plan," he said warily, "and I will be there all the time?"

"All the time," the boy assured him. "Nothing will be done

without your knowledge. You will be informed about everything. You know exactly how much money this will make."

"It could be thousands," the fat man said. "Many thousands."

The boy was silent. The fat man belonged to him now and envy had been the bait. Andreas's enormous ambition had done the rest.

Once again Napoleon was made aware of the power within him. People responded to him, followed his lead, did his bidding. Grown men and women deferred to him, as if he had some natural authority over them. They listened when he spoke and acted when he commanded. This inner power grew stronger each day. Soon it—and he—would be unstoppable. He would manage men, control women, direct events, turn the world around him into a place of his private design. And he would become rich. Rich as a conquistador. Rich as one of those gringo millionaires. It had to happen. It was the way things were meant to happen; it was woven into the fabric of his destiny.

He rose to go and Andreas heaved himself to his feet in a silent indication of his respect.

The change in Andreas's attitude was so subtle that it took time for the boy to realize what it meant: He was being treated as an equal, as a man of power. It was Napoleon's manumission into spiritual manhood. And as the boy trod the narrow path homeward, the sweet smell of power rose in his head with the dizzying effect of the most powerful of narcotics.

No one was at home. Napoleon sat at the small round table, his eyes half closed and a curious peace upon his face. He would wait now until Porfirio returned. His plan swam like a large shark through the seas of his imagination, and the more he thought about what he would do, the more certain he was that everything would work as he planned. He balled his hand on the tabletop, and then relaxed it. He would wait for Porfirio, the last piece in his puzzle. And Porfirio would listen to him, and come along.

They sat at the table while Flor snored on her bed, her restless sleep audible through the curtain that formed the wall of her room. Porfirio was sober this late afternoon, sober and drug-free. His face was suffused with blood as he listened.

Napoleon spoke softly: "With your help, it can be done. We will all be rich."

Porfirio grinned. "You need a man with cojones," he said.

"That, and the weapons."

"Can you not get those?"

"I am too young," the boy said. "They would never take my money."

"True. You have the pesos?"

"It is all arranged. Go to Andreas tonight. He will have the merchandise."

"You are one smart boy," Porfirio said. "You have made a good plan."

Napoleon said, "It will go smoothly, I promise you."

Porfirio examined the boy as if trying to penetrate to his psyche, to read his thoughts, to isolate his motives. But Porfirio perceived only what he chose to perceive.

"I will do it," he said, the bullying edge out of his voice. "I will do it for you, for mi mujer." He jerked his thumb in the direction of the sleeping Flor. "A man must take care of his family, no? Otherwise he is not a man."

"That is true," Napoleon agreed gravely.

"Yes," Porfirio said, suddenly uncomfortable, as if he had lost his position in the household, as if some vital part of his being had been stolen away. There was, he conceded to himself, something about this boy he could not understand, something that made him uneasy and afraid.

"I will go to Andreas tonight," he said, as if to satisfy some unspoken demand by Napoleon. Then he smiled sheepishly. "But now I will celebrate our new partnership with a few beers at the cantina."

"Don't get drunk," Napoleon said. "And don't speak of this to anyone."

"You can depend on me," Porfirio assured him. "I am a man of honor."

When he was alone, Napoleon bared his teeth in satisfaction and in hatred. Everything was proceeding according to his secret plan. Everything would come out as he wanted it to. Of that there was no doubt.

EIGHT

IT WAS TO BE A SPECIAL EVENING, AND IT TURNED out to be. But not in the way Rose Tierney had planned.

They dined at Angelina's on West Fifty-fourth Street, near Ninth Avenue. They shared an antipasto, followed by thinly sliced scallops of veal in a delicate wine sauce and a house salad. They drank a dry white wine and declared their love for each other.

Afterward, they decided to walk back to Rose's apartment. Near Forty-fourth Street, Keveney's hand closed tightly on her elbow, bringing her to a sudden stop. His voice was low and urgent.

"It's a stickup. Get in that doorway and stay out of sight."

"Jack, please . . ." Her heart had begun to race and her mouth went dry.

"Do it," Keveney snapped out with a practiced authority she'd never before encountered. She watched him glide silently across the street in the direction of an all-night grocery. Two men were backing out, turning in swift, jerky movements, hurrying toward a car parked at the curb.

"Hold it!" Keveney shouted. "Police! Drop your weapons and put your hands on top of your heads!"

One of the men cried out in alarm, the other one began to shoot. Keveney dived to the sidewalk, returning fire. The two men broke for the car, which had begun to roll ahead. One of them stumbled and went down shouting that he was hit, asking for help. His companion never looked back, leaping into the car, which had picked up speed.

Keveney, on one knee, took careful aim and snapped off three

shots in rapid order. The car swerved, tires screeching, and continued in a long, wide arc, crashing into a lamppost.

Keveney pulled the driver and his passenger out to the street.
He frisked them expertly and called out to the owner of the grocery, who appeared in front of his shop.

"Phone the police. Say an officer needs assistance."

Nearly three hours passed before the men were booked and
hospitalized. One had a bullet wound in the hip; the other two
suffered various cuts and bruises. Keveney was unhurt.

"A good shoot," Captain Holahan assured Keveney. "You'll get a
commendation for this, Sergeant."

"Garbage work, I hate it."

"Cut it, Jack."

"I'm a guy on a treadmill, running as fast as I can in order to
stay in place."

"Keep up the good work." Holahan almost smiled.

It was a little past two in the morning when Keveney presented
himself at Rose Tierney's apartment. Wrapped in a long woolen
robe, her hair flaring across her shoulders in a dark fall, she admitted him without a word. She offered him coffee and they sat in
her kitchen facing each other across the old oak table.

"Does that sort of thing happen often?"

"It was a fluke," he said. "Probably never happen again." He
remembered the car thief he had encountered, remembered the
image of their deadly stand-off. It never ends, he almost said
aloud.

"Cops," she said in a voice larded with disdain.

"It's what I do."

"I was frightened."

"It seemed worse than it was. They never knew I was there."

"I thought I was going to get shot."

"Ah, Rosie, I wouldn't let anyone hurt you."

She brushed his hand aside and stood up as if to put distance
between them. "Cowboys and Indians, but it's real."

"It doesn't happen often."

"You love it."

"Ah, no . . ."

"It excites you."

He started to reply but reconsidered and began again. "Don't make more of it than it was. A one-in-a-thousand roll of the dice, that's all."

She shook her head stubbornly. "Jack, you're a magnet for trouble. There's something about you, a force field that draws danger and criminals, puts you in the middle of the action."

A sudden sense of impending loss took hold of him and he set himself against it. To display weakness, to allow his fears to become known, to be less a man than he was expected to be, all this was unacceptable. He knew he had reached a critical point with Rosie, that she had come to know him in ways no one else ever had; and that knowledge might drive her away. He took her hand.

"I love you, Rosie," he heard himself say, standing off on some spectral platform watching and listening, failing to make sense of the words. He was fond of her, yes. Even more, she extracted a profound affection and concern from him. He had respect and admiration for her accomplishments—she was a fine journalist with a great future, if she wanted it—and she had passion. Oh, yes, passion. With her face and figure, she came close to some vague ideal of perfection. But where was the driving love that would overcome all obstacles, that would defy family and society, that would cost friends and fortune—the kind of love men like Keveney imagined but never truly believed in? For a moment he longed desperately for such high and intoxicating emotions. He took her hand in his. "I love you," he said again, as if insisting.

She removed her hand. "I love you, too, Keveney. But tonight scared me, Keveney, and you scare me."

"Don't be afraid. I'll protect you." What the hell was he saying? What purpose existed for these declarations, toward what goal was he galloping?

"I can't tolerate the fear," she said to herself. She smiled wanly in his direction.

He saw it as an invitation and went round the table to where she sat and drew her to her feet. He kissed her lips, the corners of her mouth. She failed to respond.

She walked into the living room. He trailed behind her, chas-

tened and uncertain, as if Sister Asumpta had scolded and embarrassed him in front of the entire class.

"Dammit!" he said. "Don't do this to me, don't push me away."

She turned around, looking up into his washed green eyes, so
pale and lifeless, as if frozen in plastic. She saw nothing in them.
No hope, no anger, only the opaque barrier behind which she'd
seen Keveney take cover on more than one occasion. What he
couldn't deal with, what triggered the uncontrollable fear in him,
what turned him from a sweet and considerate friend and lover
into a dangerous, unpredictable creature, was hidden behind
those almost white eyes. Keveney came out of a strange and often
distressing world, a world of callouses and blue collars, of beer
bellies and Saturday night drunks and bar fights. It was a world
peopled by hard men who were blunt and often crude, who
viewed the world without sentiment and looked upon the System,
any system, as their enemy, a construct designed to contain and
control them. Keveney was able to enter her world, to understand
it and compete in it, but she would always remain a stranger in
his.

"What the fuck do you expect me to do?" It was all in those
words: the suppressed rage, the underlying threat, the always
vulgar small boy's challenge to do battle, all the more dangerous
coming from a grown man.

She summoned up her courage. "Quit the cops, Keveney."

He stared at her as if seeing her for the first time. "Being a cop,
it's what I am."

"You hate the bureaucrats, the inefficiency, the politics."

He brushed her words away. "That's everywhere. You learn to
live with it. To deal with it. Or else—"

"Or you go under. Isn't that so? Try and understand me, Keveney. I don't want you to be hurt or killed."

"Ah," he said, suddenly tender, embracing her. "Those guys
tonight—they were nothing special."

"But tonight is special, Jack."

"Did I forget your birthday or something?"

She touched his cheek. "Jack, I'm going to have a baby, our
baby."

"Matthew, Mark, Luke and John!" he burst out. "Are you sure?"

"I'm sure," she said softly. "This is no immaculate conception."

"You let this happen deliberately?"

"Would you have made me pregnant otherwise? I don't think so. Relax, Keveney, you don't have to marry me."

He looked at her for a long time. "What's going on inside your head? That you're gonna get an abortion, kill my kid? No way, Rosie."

She laughed. "I'm as Catholic as you are." Then she shook her head rapidly. "Oh, no, I want this baby. I intend to have it."

He chose his words carefully, speaking without hesitation or doubt. "Just like that. Bring a bastard into the world. Well, forget it, Rosie. Not Jack Keveney's kid. I'll tell you what you're gonna do—you're gonna get married, is what. You're gonna marry me. Okay?"

"Okay," she said, almost sadly. "Okay."

NINE

THE FAT MAN TWISTED IN HIS SEAT. ORLANDO'S booth was too small for him. Almost all of Andreas's time was spent in his house, where things were big enough. The outside world was a misery to him, a torture chamber in which he moved awkwardly, always uncomfortable. He sipped the horse's piss that passed for beer in Orlando's cantina and said: "I want to buy."

"Good, my friend," Orlando said. "I am holding six ounces of the finest..."

"Not enough."

"How much then?" Orlando said.

"A kilo."

Orlando made a small placating gesture with his hands. "That's an awful lot of shit."

"One kilo," Andreas said, more firmly this time. He was beginning to enjoy Orlando's discomfort.

"I can go to Chiriqui," Andreas said. "I can find a kilo in Chiriqui."

"And pay twice my price."

"Perhaps not." But it was true. Orlando took a fair profit. Not like those city bastards.

"When do you want it?"

"Within three days."

Orlando whistled lightly between his teeth. The small sound echoed oddly in the shadowed spaces of the booth. "I will try," he said finally. "It will cost you fifteen thousand."

"Seven."

81

Orlando said. "Go to Chiriqui. Twelve."

"Ten and done."

"Done."

The two men spat on the palms of their right hands and shook. So, too, had the peasants sealed deals for corn for a thousand years.

"I need a down payment. In Yanqui dollars."

The fat man nodded, reached into his pocket and drew forth a sealed envelope. "Twenty percent," he said. "Two thousand dollars."

Orlando pocketed the envelope. "I will not bother to count it," he said. "How did you know what price we would agree to?"

"Because," the fat man said and laughed, "we have done business together for many years. I know you." Andreas rose. The deal was concluded. "I will be back with the rest of the money in three days," he said. He was perspiring even though it was cool in the cantina. "I will see you then."

Orlando nodded. "Until then," he said. "Go with God."

"And you."

Outside in the heat, the fat man breathed heavily. How frightened he had been! Had Orlando noticed? Probably not. He shrugged his shoulders and moved off toward his house.

The next day, Napoleon went to Juan-Manuel Negrete's camp. He bought a half kilo of cocaine, paid, and hurried back toward Orlando's cantina. As he ran, he smiled. For one still so young, he was rapidly developing a sense of irony.

The weapons lay on the table, each equipped with its own sound suppressor. There was a certain gracefulness about each of them, a utilitarian beauty, each perfectly designed to perform its lethal function. When he put fingertips to the cool metal, a thrill of excitement went through Napoleon and he shivered at the touch.

"I've done well?" Porfirio said, clearly proud of himself.

"Very well," Napoleon answered, eyes fixed on the two revolvers.

"They are old, but in fine condition," Porfirio boasted. "They came from a person who lives some distance from here, and so they can never be traced to him. Or to us. They are safe, no? Just right."

Napoleon raised his head, his dark eyes impenetrable and still. "Just right," he agreed. "They will do the job."

"Exactly," Porfirio said happily.

The two men and the boy faced each other across the plastic-topped table. Andreas's buttocks overflowed the small chair which cut into his flesh. They spoke in whispers, though Flor was sound asleep, her snores rattling in her throat. Porfirio had given her her "medicine" just a few minutes before. It was agreed among them they wanted her out of the way and sleeping.

"Now," Napoleon said. "I must leave. He wants me there as bodyguard." He hefted his pistol. "He paid for this, gave me cash. Congratulated me upon finding it." He chuckled, his dry, chilling chirrup. "So, I go first. I will enter by the back door. He has closed the cantina for the evening. You two come in the usual way. Understood?"

Porfirio and Andreas nodded.

"It will be over quickly," Napoleon said. "You must not be afraid."

He rose. "Start in ten minutes. I must go now."

The two men sat, waiting. Flor's stentorian breathing in the background was the only sound. Andreas checked his watch at thirty-second intervals. Finally he rose. "We go," he said.

They left Flor behind, secure in her golden dreams.

They walked into the dimly lit cantina. It was deserted, smelling of stale beer and dried sweat. Napoleon's disembodied voice called to them.

"The door to the left of the bar. Orlando and I await you."

They stepped into a small room that Orlando used as an office and the dealer immediately came to his feet, pointing at Porfirio. "I was expecting only you, Andreas. Why is this one here?" His body had stiffened and one hand lingered at his waist.

The fat man spread his hands placatingly. He gestured toward Napoleon. "You have this one with you. Why should I, too, not have a friend, a protector? For a man of my fatness, it is a sensible precaution."

Orlando glanced at Napoleon who nodded agreeably.

"Very well," Orlando said, sitting back down. "Let me see your money."

"Ah," Andreas said. "First the goods."

Napoleon opened the straw bag he had dangling from his hand. The packet of cocaine glistened in the light, wrapped in its transparent plastic envelope. "It's all there," Orlando said. "And you?"

Andreas withdrew a bulky envelope from his pocket, tossed it onto the desk. Napoleon deposited the straw bag next to it. Orlando counted the money swiftly. Satisfied, he returned the stack of bills to the envelope and put the envelope into his pocket. Orlando sat back smiling, assessing the men he had just done business with; it was a most profitable evening and there was no reason not to repeat the transaction from time to time. He opened his mouth to speak when he saw Napoleon bring forth his silenced revolver, the muzzle swinging his way.

"What are you doing! Don't point that thing at me, it is dangerous . . ."

Napoleon shot him in the chest.

"*Madre de Dios!*" Andreas wailed.

Napoleon jerked around and squeezed the trigger again. The shot caught the fat man in the belly and he staggered backward, a look of shock spreading across his broad face. "What . . ." he managed to get out before Napoleon shot him a second time. He went down on his back, staring sightlessly at the ceiling.

Porfirio laughed. He knew a good thing when he saw it. "Oh, you are clever. Now we have it all between us, the dope and the money. I will tell Flor what a clever son she has spawned."

"*Chingara su madre,*" Napoleon said in a thin voice and fired at Porfirio. The slug caught the man in the throat and he went down, blood gushing forth, eyes wide in terror. Very calmly, the boy finished him off with another bullet in his head.

After making sure that all of them were dead, Napoleon

scooped the envelope containing the money and the cocaine into his straw bag and left by the back door, never looking back. He hurried through the silent night, heading home, filled with an almost sublime sense of accomplishment. How easily it had all gone off. How well he had planned and managed men and events. How efficiently he had performed at the moment of truth. He would never, he decided, run errands for any man again. From this day forward, he was his own man. Indeed, he was a real man who could do anything any other man could do.

Now he would put into force the second part of his plan; he would leave El Arbolito with Flor and they would never return. Soon all of his dreams would flower into reality. He would buy a fine house for himself and Flor. It would have indoor plumbing and electricity and they would live in comfort and safety. Charged by his triumph, he walked faster, anxious to share the glorious future with his mother.

Once home he parted the curtain that separated Flor's bedroom from the rest of the house and said, "Mamacita, it is time to wake up. We are leaving this place finally. There is much to do."

She did not respond. He shook her. She was rigid and her skin was cold. He rolled her onto her back and her face stared up at him, her mouth set in a rictus of agony. She was dead.

He moved across the room to the makeshift dressing table. On it lay the syringe she had used and three empty packets of her "medicine." He understood at once what had happened. Porfirio —that son of a whore—had wanted to make sure she would sleep and cause them no trouble. He had tripled her normal dosage, and the cocaine had killed her. Napoleon thought back to her strange breathing when he and Porfirio had sat and talked. Even then she had been dying and he had not known it.

He sat on the edge of Flor's bed for a long time, staring dry-eyed at her lifeless body, thinking that if he had known this earlier he would have killed Porfirio much more slowly. Slowly and painfully. At last he stood up, telling himself that it was better this way. Flor was finished with this foul existence, her miseries terminated, her pain relieved.

He went back into the night, ready to begin his journey into the future. He would go to Chiriqui where, he was certain, he would become a great success. Why not? The kilo of coke, the stolen money, the pistol tucked into his belt under his shirt; he had everything he needed. He stepped briskly into the darkness, anxious to get on with his life.

TEN

"GUNS PUT ME OFF."

Charlotte Wilson had been a secretary at the *Daily News* when Rose Tierney worked there. A month before Rose had left the paper to have her baby—the boy, Patrick, was now two years old—Charlotte had moved on to another job at a local television station. Charlotte was slender and hipless, apparently breastless, but with large round eyes that gave her a look of perpetual wonder.

"Me too."

Arthur Wilson, her husband, had the neat, practiced moves of a man who was good with numbers. A leather case in his jacket pocket contained pencils and ballpoint pens of various colors. Many of his acquaintances were convinced Arthur should have been an accountant. But Arthur was a dentist.

"Don't they you?" Charlotte said to Rose.

The two couples were seated around the small oval English table in the dining room of the Keveneys' apartment, picking at the shepherd's pie and salad Jack had prepared. The Wilsons' attention was drawn to two holstered pistols on the mantle.

"You get used to them after a while," Rose said, wishing they would change the subject.

Charlotte was relentless. "I could never touch them, not even for a second."

"Tools of the trade," Keveney said, bored.

"I could never be married to a policeman," Charlotte said with a bright smile.

Keveney gave her his most awful expression, all clenched teeth and a fixed stare. "Neither could I."

Arthur Wilson laughed and fingered the pens in his pocket. "I could never be a cop."

"Absolutely right," Keveney said.

"Arthur's too sensitive for a job so full of violence."

Keveney was about to say exactly how sensitive he thought Arthur was, when the phone rang.

"Will you get that, dear?" Rose said, a look of relief on her face.

Keveney took the call in the bedroom.

"Congratulations," a faintly familiar voice said.

"Who is this?"

"It's Lieutenant Keveney now, that's what I heard. Before you know it, you'll end up commissioner. Willie Hatcher, that's who."

Keveney filled his lungs with air. For two years, Hatcher had disappeared, lost in the Byzantine back country of the Latin American drug trade. Occasionally word of his activities surfaced, but Willie had remained tucked out of sight. One report had it that he was in Medellín, the drug capital of Colombia, heading up a smuggling ring. It had proved to be false. Then word of his death by gunshot reached Keveney; a slight exaggeration, obviously. Rumors and false leads, those were the currency of Willie Hatcher's existence.

"I figured you were dead, Willie."

"Not yet, Lieutenant. Wanna get together?"

"What's the point?"

"Come on, Lieutenant. Am I free to talk on the telephone? Meet me for a drink."

"You buying?"

"Sure. You know the Cozy Nook?"

"On Third Avenue?"

"In fifteen minutes."

"I'll be there."

In the dining room, Keveney snapped the .38-caliber pistol with the short barrel into place on his belt at the small of his back. "I'm going out," he announced.

"Shall I wait up for you?" his wife said.

He shrugged, kissed her cheek and bid the Wilsons good night.

"Was it something I said?" Arthur said, after Keveney was gone, trying to be funny.

"The phone call." Rose attended to her dinner.

"Just like that, he gets a call and walks out into the night." Charlotte was clearly agitated. "I don't understand that kind of behavior, Rose, I really don't.

"Jack's a cop."

"Doesn't it frighten you? The gun and all? I mean, what if something happens. What if he doesn't come back?"

Rose arranged a wan smile on her pale face. "I try not to think about it . . ."

City Island was connected to the rest of the Bronx by a bridge and separated by an insularity based as much on custom as on geography. The Italian immigrants who settled there raised goats and cattle and grew potatoes on their small farms. But, essentially the island was supported by the sea: shipbuilding, boating and a number of fine seafood restaurants. On any day or night, boats large and small plowed through the waters surrounding the island, their white sails and shapely hulls adding a luster to the scene.

So it was that the Chris Craft attracted no attention as it floated into the slip at one of the island's many marinas. Two young women, lithe and pretty, stood on the forward deck. At the wheel stood a well-built man in his twenties, brown from the sun and muscular, with the easy stance of someone who swam a lot during the summer and skied at Vail during the winter months. According to Willie Hatcher, his name was Roger.

A second young man leaped to the pier and tied down the lines. This done, Roger cut the engines. He called to the girls, and all four young people went below deck. Twenty minutes later they reappeared, appropriately dressed. Each of them carried hand luggage and a shoulder bag, all finely made and clearly expensive. Laughing and talking among themselves, they headed up the pier toward the shore and the parking lot beyond.

They were only a few yards from the silver Jaguar before any of them noticed the man leaning against the car. He wore stained khakis and his tennis shoes were soiled and in need of replacement. He watched them approach out of weary, washed green eyes.

Roger halted at arm's length away. "Hey, man, that's my car you're on. Move it, huh?"

The man glanced admiringly at the Jaguar. "Nice wheels."

"I think so," Roger said.

"Rog," one of the girls said, "let's get out of here."

"Get in gear, old man," Roger said, a slight tinge of menace in his voice.

"Bet it cost a lot," the man in the stained khakis said. He stroked the silver flank of the car. "Let me introduce myself—I'm Jack Keveney."

"Yeah, sure. Now off the car, Jack."

"Thing is, how's a young guy like you make money enough to buy wheels like these?"

"Business," Roger said, unlocking the door on the driver's side.

The girls giggled.

Roger opened the door, and at that moment Keveney slammed him into the side of the car. Roger gasped. "What the hell is this?"

The second young man charged forward to help his friend. Keveney gave him an elbow to the belly, doubling him over. One of the girls cried out in alarm.

Abruptly the group was surrounded by four men with drawn pistols. Keveney flashed his shield, identified himself and informed the young people that they were under arrest. Roger cursed and the girls began to weep.

Detective Greenberg ordered a search for the Chris Craft while he and Detective Bradley began examining the luggage the four young people carried. Soon he displayed a number of plastic bags filled with a white powder. "Eight kilos," he announced. "Cocaine, of a very good quality."

"You guys have no right . . ." Roger began to protest.

"Take them," Keveney ordered.

Roger, being led toward an unmarked police car, swung back. "How did you know?"

Keveney said, "Just dumb luck is all. You know how it is."

Roger nodded agreeably. "Well, it'll take more than luck to keep us in jail, y'know."

He was right. By noon the next day, all four of them were out on bond, in the custody of their stylishly dressed parents and equally stylish lawyers.

"Ah, Keveney," Captain Holahan drawled from behind his neat police-issue desk later that same afternoon. "This one could've been handled more smartly, my lad."

"It was a good bust."

"Not a wise one, considering."

"Considering what?"

"Those citizens are connected."

"And that gives them license to make a score, I suppose? Buying up Sixaolan coke with daddy's money and moving it in Harlem, in Bed-Stuy. Rich kids," he snarled. "Spoiled rotten. I hate them. More than I hate the street pushers or the smugglers because they don't *need* the dough, they have other ways to go."

"Let it alone, Jack."

"They should do twenty years, every one of them."

"Forget it. They'll cut a deal with the D.A. Some lesser charges will be levied. Some friendly judge will be contacted and the case thrown out of court. They'll never do a day's time. You can see it, can't you, Jack?"

"I see it."

"Then where's the sense of such a bust? Look upon it as a mistake, Jack. A learning experience. Forget it."

"Fuck that noise. I'm a cop."

Holahan's face grew flushed and he stood up. "There is a deficiency in your character, Jack. Want to know what? You are simple, Jack, that's what."

"Bullshit."

"Politically simple. You want to screw up your career? Smarten up, my boy. Go with the flow, as they say. You won't make a dent in things anyway."

"If that's how it is, what are you doing on the job?"

"That's the way it is and always will be. As for yours truly, I'm putting in my papers come September and it's off to Florida for me and the missus for some fishing and letting myself get fat. Think on it, Jack. Consider the pension, the future, the rewards you can pick up along the way. When I go, I'll be recommending you for this desk. If you don't fuck things up." He smiled paternally. "You're a good man, Jack, better'n most. But the job eats good men alive. Don't think too much about things. In the long run, you'll be better off."

"No matter how it makes me feel?"

"No matter..."

Keveney got home after midnight, reeking of whiskey. He fell into bed, head spinning, willing himself to fall asleep. Next to him, his wife came up on one elbow, staring at him as if at a stranger.

"Where have you been for two days?"

"The job..."

"I didn't know whether you were dead or alive."

"I'm sorry. I—"

"You're not sorry. You love it, being out there with thieves and murderers, with those druggies of yours."

"There was something going down."

"You could have called."

"You don't understand."

"I understand this—Patrick was sick. I had to take him to the doctor..."

Keveney sat up and felt as if he had left his head on the pillow. "Is he all right?"

"Yes, he's all right, Jack. Which is more than I can say for us..."

ELEVEN

NAPOLEON SAT ON THE EDGE OF HIS BED. THE BED
sagged under his weight, even though he was very thin. Perhaps
the bag of cocaine taped to his waist made the difference. He was
inclined to doubt that; the springs were shot.

The room was small and dirty, alive with cockroaches and bold,
bright-eyed mice. Outside, the small city of Chiriqui hummed
with life. He told himself to go out, to learn the smells and sounds
of Chiriqui, to assimilate the rhythms of these new streets. Instead, though he was hungry and thirsty, he remained in the tiny
room, uncertain and uncharacteristically afraid. He had no idea
how to proceed. He longed for El Arbolito, where he was known
and respected, where he knew people and knew what was expected of him. But the village was dead to him forever, and the
future waited for him to take hold of it.

He rose and made himself descend the rickety stairs into the
night. He walked slowly, jostled by the crowds, a tall, thin youth
with eyes of obsidian, his trousers hanging from his thin hips. He
turned into a cantina. There was a jukebox and soft lights and a
number of small tables where people were eating. He found a
place at the bar and ordered a beer, glancing around. A man and a
woman, engrossed in one another, were at the end of the bar. Two
seats away a corpulent man sipped tequila, eyes watching Napoleon in the mirror behind the bar.

The plump man said, "Your first time in Chiriqui?"

Napoleon gave no answer, sipped his beer.

"No offense meant. Just your clothes."

93

"What's wrong with them?"

"Nothing. Oh, perhaps they're a little old fashioned."

"I will get some new clothes, when my business is done." The fat man smiled, and moved to the stool next to Napoleon. "Business," he said. "Business can be very profitable in Chiriqui. Or very painful." He smiled again. "My name is Willie Hatcher."

"Napoleon Cruz."

"Good. Now we know each other."

As if to drive home that conclusion, Hatcher began to talk. A torrent of words such as Napoleon had never before heard. Hatcher spoke of his desire to become rich and powerful, his abiding need of and affection for beautiful women, his willingness to take risks when the rewards were great enough. He prodded Napoleon, provoked him into talking about himself, until the boy realized that he was providing more information about himself than the fat man, for all his talk, had revealed. He studied Willie Hatcher with rising interest and greater intensity, amused by his verbal pyrotechnics but no longer deceived by his verbosity. Napoleon was amused but wary, and began to choose his own words with considerable care. He wondered what his new companion was after; was robbery his motive? Or did he perceive Napoleon as some kind of fool, just off the *campos,* ready to be swindled? Or was this pale, amiable man a butterfly, thinking he had found a pretty young boy to make love to? Whatever his aim, Napoleon was curious. No, more than curious—interested in seeing where this encounter would lead. Then Willie Hatcher said, "You really must get yourself some new clothes, something stylish, but not too flashy."

"Perhaps you are right."

"Oh yes. In a town like this one, making the right impression is everything."

"Tomorrow. I'll find some clothes tomorrow."

"No, no. We'll do it now. I know a place."

It was nearly ten o'clock at night. "At this hour?"

Willie laughed, a reassuring chuckle. "Nothing worthwhile ever closes in Chiriqui. And after the clothes, we'll get you a decent meal . . ."

An hour later, Napoleon admired himself in the full-length mirror of the clothing store that had appeared, as if by magic, only steps from the cantina. The gray suit he wore, with its narrow lapels, the alligator shoes, the white shirt and the red tie had transformed him. He saw a young man with a narrow face and black, hard eyes and a shock of black hair. A young man dramatically handsome with the stony, impenetrable look of his Indian ancestors. It occurred to Napoleon that he had truly entered into another world, a world about which he knew very little, a world in which he intended to survive and eventually prevail. His eyes shifted and came to rest on Willie Hatcher seated behind him in an awkward, anachronistic posture. His hands were crossed over the silver-headed cane he carried, making him look like a character out of the world of an earlier century. He rested his round chin on his knuckles and smiled at Napoleon in the glass.

"A dramatic improvement," he remarked.

"I would like to buy one of those."

Hatcher straightened up and fondled the cane. "Nobody uses a cane these days."

"Except you."

"This is a special stick. I've had it for a long time. Besides, you are much younger than I and a young man doesn't need the help of a walking stick."

Napoleon noticed that Willie Hatcher brandished the stick in a flamboyant manner like the prized possession it seemed to be, or tucked it under his arm. But never did it serve as a support for the fat man who moved with a casual elegance, a grace that defied his bulk.

The clothing salesman presented his bill. It came to more than seven hundred American dollars. Napoleon retreated to the men's room where he extracted eight hundred dollars from his money belt. He returned to the front of the store. The salesman took his money with an impassive face and made change. Napoleon waved it away. "For you," he said softly, and turned from the man's incredulous face.

The salesman bowed him out of the store, thanking him repeatedly, inviting him to come back any time. Money, Napoleon noted, here as in El Arbolito, brought instant respect. On the street, he waited for Willie Hatcher to catch up. The fat man strode along, an enigmatic smile on his soft mouth. "A word of advice..."

Napoleon felt himself stiffen, as if he were about to come under attack. He said nothing.

"The money belt," Hatcher said. "You do a disservice to your new suit with that unseemly bulge." Again that fleeting smile.

When Napoleon said nothing, Hatcher went on. "I've got to go now."

"Will I see you again?"

Hatcher shrugged. "Adios, amigo..." He hurried along the street in that curiously elegant way of his, disappearing around the corner.

At once Napoleon was made aware of how alone he was in this city, how uneasy and vulnerable. He was a small fish in an endless, dangerous sea, and he had so much to learn. Willie Hatcher, for example. Why had the fat man approached him in the first place? What was he after? Why did he spend so much time with Napoleon, helping him to buy a new wardrobe? Surely he had sought some personal profit from all this; yet he had departed without any suggestion of what he was after.

Napoleon started back to his hotel. He walked for a block or two before he realized that he was hopelessly lost in the busy streets of Chiriqui. Deep in his own thoughts, he failed to notice the two men who fell into step a few yards behind him.

He turned into a narrow street that looked vaguely familiar. Here there were no pedestrians and the night closed in, still and threatening. He walked faster. Behind him, footsteps were closing fast and he jerked around in time to accept a rock-hard fist to the temple. The blow sent him stumbling against a building wall. He made a move to fight back until he saw the unmistakable gleam of a switchblade in the night.

Napoleon cursed the bad luck that had brought him to this place, to confront these two men who he perceived as not too different from himself. He vowed that if he survived this moment he would never again leave himself unarmed. He considered launching himself at the two men as they advanced, knives held low, slicing the night air with a silent deadliness that told him they had done this many times before.

"The clothing," one of the men hissed. When Napoleon failed to respond, he spoke again, hotly, his voice full of menace. "We want the suit, everything."

Napoleon remembered the money belt, the kilo of cocaine taped to his body. In a moment, everything would be lost. He braced himself, knowing he had no chance against the two of them, but convinced he had no choice but to fight back. They intended to strip him of all that he owned—his dreams, his future, his dignity and his manhood.

"Chingara su madre!" he bit off.

"You crazy, you bastard!" one of the men said, his knife now still and coming closer.

Napoleon set himself to strike the first blow when he heard the voice, pleasant and conversational. "Let's break it up, boys. No reason for anyone to get hurt..."

Poised in the darkness, less than ten feet away, Willie Hatcher, using his silver-headed cane for emphasis the way a teacher might use a harmless yardstick as a pointer. A faint smile traced his lips. "Go ahead, boys. Take off while you can."

"They have knives," Napoleon warned.

"El Gordo," one of the thieves muttered. "A fat gringo. Tell me, gringo, what good is that stick? Put the stick down, gringo, or I will cut a hole in your fat belly and shove the stick all the way in." His partner laughed. "Do it! Slice some belly off El Gordo..."

The taller of the two took a step toward Hatcher, and in that fragmented moment the fat man made his move. A quick step to his right brought him out of range of the knife. The cane rose, still pointing, and a brief metallic whirring sound filled the night air. A long steel blade flashed out of the cane and Hatcher wielded it as if it were a fencer's foil. A quick thrust sliced the man's knife hand and the weapon clattered to the pavement. A second movement was directed to his throat. He fell back against the wall, Hatcher's blade beneath his chin.

"Is that it," Hatcher said, still mild of manner and tone, "you want to die?" He leaned forward and drew a dollop of red. "See how easy it would be. First you, then your friend. So you see, it is time for you both to leave."

"Mother of God," the boy against the wall said. "You hurt me, you hurt me *bad*."

"Next," Willie said sharply, "I'll pin you through the heart. Just don't move . . . anything, that is, except your legs. Move those. *Rapido, si!*"

The boy who wasn't hurt shrugged and looked at his partner. Then both of them were running, soon out of sight.

"Discretion is usually the better part of valor," Willie said cheerfully to Napoleon.

Again there was a metallic whir and the blade withdrew into Hatcher's cane. He turned to go. "Coming? We can talk as we walk . . ."

They went a few blocks before Napoleon broke the silence. "You were following me. Why?"

"I thought we might be able to do some business."

Immediately on guard, the youth said, "What business is that?"

"There is more than a money belt around your middle. You're lucky somebody hasn't slit your throat by now and lifted your goods."

"What do you know of my goods?" Napoleon challenged.

Hatcher shrugged. "What is it, a brick of marijuana? It's a small way to start . . ."

Napoleon resented the patronizing tone of voice. "It is more than marijuana. I have the highest grade cocaine. That is no small thing—"

"No," Hatcher said presently. "No small thing. But there is no reason for the world to know. Speak softly, for my ears only."

"You saved my life and for that I am grateful. But I think I have spoken too much already, even for only your ears."

Hatcher grinned. "You looking to sell?"

Napoleon chose his words carefully. "I am looking to buy a gun . . ."

"Yes, of course. All in good time. How much are you carrying?"

"A kilo," Napoleon answered slowly.

"And you wish to move the stuff? Naturally. But you know no one in Chiriqui except me and you aren't sure you can trust me. But then, who else can you trust except me?"

Napoleon made up his mind. "I will trust you for now. But if you betray me, El Gordo, I will kill you for sure. I wish to sell, can you help?"

Willie looked at him. "You'll look considerably thinner when you're rid of it." He laughed. "A small deal. Easy."

Napoleon thought, A small deal? What quantities was the fat man used to? He said nothing.

"We'll get rid of it tomorrow," Willie said, swinging his cane as they walked. "You'll find out about me. I take twenty-five percent. I get you a fair price—not the best, far from the worst. And I guarantee payment, in cash, on the spot."

"How much?"

"For what you're carrying, figuring top quality merchandise, not stepped on, maybe seven thousand. More likely six thousand dollars. American, that is."

Napoleon allowed his disappointment to show. "That's all?"

"You expected to become rich overnight, is that it? Every third man in Chiriqui seems to be a dealer, which makes you not so special. Your goods are not worth so much here. If you would rather not sell . . ."

Not so special, Napoleon reflected. The fat man was mistaken; he was the most special of men and in time he would prove it to Willie Hatcher and to the world. "I wish to sell," he said quietly.

"Good. We'll do our business tomorrow. Meanwhile, go to the bus station and put what you're carrying into a locker. Tomorrow we'll have lunch, you and I, and make our deal. And I'll put you into a decent hotel."

Napoleon nodded slowly, with an odd, remote authority. "You are a good man to know. Continue to be useful to me and one day I shall make you rich."

Hatcher grinned at the tall, slender youth. No doubt about it, this kid would go far. If he lived, that is. There was about him . . . a power that would not be denied. A power, he assured himself, the boy was not yet aware of. Hatcher perceived in Napoleon unfulfilled promise, unshaped gifts, a cunning and wisdom far beyond his years and a ruthlessness that caused him to shiver. Even more—he sensed a primordial quality, hard and chilling, as if all men existed only for his use, their lives little currency meant to contribute to Napoleon's pleasure and profit. Hatcher made himself a silent vow never to openly challenge Napoleon, never to cross him, certainly never to betray him. It was a vow beyond his ability to keep.

"About your cane," Napoleon was saying. "I have never seen anything like it before."

"You'll never see another one," Willie said. "It was made for me by a friend."

"Could he make me one?"

"He's dead. Died three years ago." Willie frowned, then handed the cane to Napoleon. "Keep it. To seal our bargain. Let me show you how it works." He pointed to an inset button hidden in the ornate filigree of the silver top. "Press this and the blade springs out. That blade is backed by a spring of tempered steel. It'll go through just about anything. What you have is a spring-loaded knife, eighteen inches long. To sheath it, you twist her, below the handle. It snaps back into place. Keep the blade sharp. It's better than any gun ever made because nobody thinks of it as a weapon."

Napoleon hefted the cane in his hand. "I thank you," he said with enormous dignity. "I shall treasure such a special gift."

"If you really need a piece," Willie said, "I'll get one for you tomorrow. A thirty-eight. Short-barrelled. Inconspicuous, easy to carry. Two hundred dollars. All right?"

"All right."

That night Napoleon did not sleep. Visions of glory danced through his head so fast, so furiously, that they made little sense. In a secret part of himself, he could feel his power swell—tumescent like a huge cock—an additional organ somewhere inside him that irradiated his body with a constant, sexual glow.

The following morning, he was early at the bar. He sipped a Coke. He had always been patient, and now he deliberately emp-

tied his mind, creating in his head a screen so white, so dazzling
and pure, that he drifted into it until time ceased to exist. His
breathing slowed, his pulse dropped, and yet, it was all secret.
Mechanically he took a tiny sip of his drink every minute or so.
No one would have known he was not truly present. If anyone had
spoken to him, he would have answered monosyllabically but
courteously enough. And all the while, he was awash in his white
dream.

At one-thirty Willie Hatcher sat down beside him and ordered
tequila on the rocks. Silently, he handed Napoleon a small box
tied with a ribbon and a tinsel flower.

"Happy birthday," he said.

Napoleon awoke from his dream of peace and fingered the gift.
"What's that?" he asked.

"Whatever you want it to be," Willie said. "A two-hundred-dol-
lar orchid, perhaps."

"An expensive flower," Napoleon said gravely.

Willie finished his drink and said, "Let's go to a booth." They
sat in a shadowed corner on peeling leatherette.

"You've got the stuff?"

Napoleon pushed a cheap vinyl case toward Willie.

"Pure?"

Napoleon nodded.

Willie reached in his pocket and handed over a bulging envelope. "Six thousand American dollars," he said. "That's net to you.
The flower is a gift."

Napoleon hefted the envelope. "You're giving me the money
before your connection sees the goods?" He could not mask his
surprise.

"Why not?"

"How do you know what's in the briefcase?"

"You said it was there—a kilo of pure."

"And if there was a mistake?"

"No mistakes allowed. If it isn't there, if the quality is off, I'll
return the money." Willie spoke cheerfully. "And you'll be dead
within two days."

"Who's buying?"

"Wrong question," Hatcher said. "Until I know you better. A lot better."

Napoleon felt giddy. This was the kind of dealing he hadn't known existed. Obviously, this new friend was not merely connected, but connected on a high enough level so that he could do business with grace, in a graceless business. By reflex, he tucked the envelope into his inside pocket. It made an unsightly bulge, but to him it was the prettiest sight he had ever seen. "Good," Willie said approvingly. "You didn't count it."

"Not private enough," Napoleon said. "I'll count it later, I promise you. And if there's something wrong—" he shrugged an eloquent threat.

"Understood." Willie rose.

"Let's get to your hotel, pick up your things."

"There is nothing there I want," Napoleon said. "I checked out this morning. Everything starts now," he said firmly. "Everything new. My clothes. My friends. My business. And only the best."

Settled at last in his room at the Hotel Isabella, Napoleon had time to go over all that had happened to him. Already he had come far from the alleys of El Arbolito. Already he had made more money that his mother had ever earned in all of her miserable existence. Still he felt no sense of achievement, no feeling of satisfaction. He yearned for so much, for victories of a magnitude he was unable to imagine, for wealth beyond his ability to conceive, for the kind of life he barely knew existed. His yearnings left him depleted, deserted, and he wished Willie Hatcher had not left him alone in this place.

The fat man seemed to offer a solid, reliable base in an otherwise unstable world. He missed the approbation that Willie lavished upon him in manner and in word. He missed his warmth and friendliness. One thing was certain, he intended to make Willie a part of any organization he was able to construct. Willie was a man of experience, with many contacts in various places; from him Napoleon would learn and grow stronger and eventually prosper.

Soon he would begin his war against his enemies, all those who would prevent him from overcoming his poverty and the lingering pain of his life in El Arbolito, those who would keep him from achieving the great power and wealth he longed for. Those who would deny him his slightest, most transient desire. Oh, yes, he would make a war against all of them, wherever they were, and in the end he would win. He would always win.

TWELVE

JACK KEVENEY SLUMPED IN HIS CHAIR, FEET UP ON the police-issue desk—the same desk that had once been used by Captain Neil Xavier Holahan, now four years retired. He wished he were someplace else. Any number of places would have satisfied him; warm places with palm trees swaying and a sparkling ocean nearby were his preference. He fancied himself in the shade of a tall palm dozing, reading, sipping a cool drink from a tall glass. Without responsibility, without job, without wife or child, without the burdens life had heaped on him.

He tugged at his short nose and gazed around the office, still Holahan's office: Holahan's institutional gray desk, Holahan's walls, painted a faded, peeling green, with tubes of neon lighting pinned to the ceiling. Keveney's eyes burned and teared under the neon; was it time for glasses? The years were chipping at him, body and mind, and he resented the changes.

Time on the street was what he needed. On the job, in the action. Busting dealers and pushers. Raiding a shooting gallery. Setting up a fake buy. Nature hadn't intended him for the passive, sedentary life of a desk cop. That had been Holahan's way. That was Deputy Inspector Brian Corrigan's way; Corrigan, currently his boss, spoke frequently about police work as a career, as a means to an end, as an opening to the good life.

"It's the American way, m'boy," he would declare expansively, gazing benevolently at Keveney. He viewed Keveney as the son he never had, his connection to the future, his belief in the eternal verities as handed down by Holy Mother Church and the

105

N.Y.P.D. Corrigan had appointed himself Keveney's rabbi and intended to guide and advise his protege to a long and successful career. "No telling how far you can go, m'boy. Why not the Commissioner's office itself, you keep your nose clean and watch your Ps and Qs. Keep the mistakes to a minimum, m'boy. Yessir, to the absolute minimum."

Taking the Captain's exam had been his first mistake. Holahan was the man for the job, or someone like him. A slothful cop intent on squeezing out tranquil years in comfort and safety, growing fat on the pad, and taking the pension. That was not Jack Keveney's way. Not yet, anyway.

Officer Nicholson materialized in the doorway. Denise Nicholson administered the Narco Division for Keveney. She took care of interminable paperwork, made sure reports were submitted on time, that work schedules were maintained, that overtime was kept to a minimum.

Beyond her uncommon competence, Officer Nicholson was a sight to behold. In her careful tailored blues, she presented the full, rounded figure of a woman, strong and imposing, secure in her person. Officer Nicholson was also black, actually the color of cork, her skin satiny and shining with good health. Her eyes were large and bright, and her fine, full mouth moved with a hint of salacious good humor. She was, Keveney conceded to himself, one hell of a piece of work.

"What?" he said.

"Here's Vargas's report." She handed over a buff-colored folder. It contained a single page of three short paragraphs. "Not much," he said.

She shrugged. "Anything else you want with me, Captain?"

He stared at her and rubbed his cheek. He needed a shave. "Later," he said.

"Later," she answered, with a faintly mocking grin.

He watched her leave, pronounced insouciance in the roll of her hips. Officer Nicholson, he said to himself, that is one hell of an ass.

He turned to the report. Tom Vargas was what Keveney had

been ten years earlier. Or was it longer than that? Time had fled past him like a mountain river, in one swift, seamless rush. Vargas worked the streets undercover doing real cop work. He was smart, he was aggressive, he was tough. His reports were concise and accurate and almost always resulted in a good bust.

This report said:

A shipload of Acapulco Gold departed Tampico this A.M. headed for N.Y.C. Cargo may be as much as 25 tons. Destination, the old Navy yard piers in Brooklyn. Off-loading to commence at 1100 hours on Thursday.
Shipper: The Sixaolan Connection. The Regents, they've been called: Raphael Salazar, Rene Vega, Pablo Uribe. A loose confederation, designed to eliminate competition and maximize profits. This one's sponsored by Vega.
Shipment to be covered on-site by a gringo freelancer who drifts in and out of local scene. Good luck. I await your pleasure.

Keveney leaned back in his chair. The Regents. The name conjured up visions of pomp and circumstance in his mind, unloosed pulsating images of light and darkness. The Regents were ruthless men charged with greed and an overweening lust for power. Functioning on their own, they were removed from society's restrictions, superior to ordinary men, scornful of those who worked the system. Keveney had known such men all his life. Certainly he had come out of a background similar to theirs, violent and deprived. Half the boys he had grown up with had served time and three of them were dead already—two shot, one killed in a knife fight. He, Jack Keveney, could have been one of them. He could've been one of the Regents.

If only he could penetrate the Regents' defenses, learn all there was to learn. To gaze into their eyes and see—what?—himself reflected there, perhaps. He shrugged away the thought. Such notions were unsettling, made him question his worth, his reason for being. No, there were differences between them, vast and profound differences. He, Keveney, was a decent man, fueled by his desire to uphold the law and protect the good citizens of the city. He wanted only to help wipe out the drug plague before it destroyed the nation. He, Keveney, was one of the Good Guys.

He was a Righteous Man.

But Jesus, the Regents and all drug dealers, they were an itch he wanted desperately to scratch.

The apartment was on the second floor of a renovated brownstone on Jane Street in Greenwich Village. Denise Nicholson lay in bed, naked under a sheet, studying for the sergeant's exam coming up in a month or so. She intended to do well, place her name high on the list, put her career in gear. It was a time for women on the force, a time for black women, and Nicholson meant to take advantage of the changing social order.

She put down the softcover book of sample tests when she heard his key in the lock and glanced over at the clock on her night table. It was nearly eleven o'clock. She tugged the sheet over her breasts and lay back to wait.

He came into the bedroom, his tie hanging loose, unbuttoning his shirt, undressing with the casual certainty of a man convinced of his place in the order of things.

"It was a mistake," she started out.

"What was?"

He arranged his clothes neatly on a straight-back chair. His shoes were lined up alongside the bed, the right sock across the right shoe, the left sock across the left shoe. Jack Keveney had always been an orderly man. Next he drew off his jockey shorts and with an almost cavalier disregard, tossed them to the floor. There was that about Keveney, Officer Nicholson thought; once you thought you had him figured, he broke the pattern. It was his personal charm and his genius as a cop. Nobody ever knew what the hell he might do.

"Giving you a key to this place."

He faced her squarely, a running hedge of fine orange hairs scoring his solid chest. His muscular arms hung loose and his ridged belly was tucked in. A slight roll had begun to work its way

around his hips, the mark of the years and too much time spent
behind that damned gray desk.

"You want it back?" There was a teasing glint in those pale
green eyes. He pulled back the sheet. "I was thinking about the
way you look in the office this afternoon."

"I know."

"You do know, don't you?"

"I was thinking about you, too, Jack. Hoping you'd come
around tonight."

He was on his knees on the bed, enjoying the soft gleam of her
tawny skin, the play of light and shadow as she shifted slightly his
way. "Christ, you really turn me on."

She made a soft, agreeable sound. "Saying your prayers, Jack?
Asking for forgiveness beforehand? One way or another you'll
burn in hell for your sins, Jack."

"Bitch."

She laughed, soft with pleasure. "Well, look at you, Jack. Up at
attention and I've yet to lay a finger on it."

They shared a laugh. "You know what I want."

"We ain't in the office here, Captain." She drawled out the title,
giving it a special meaning. "You don't give orders here."

"But you do."

"Bet on it."

"Maybe not."

"Then fuck off, Jack."

"What . . . ?"

"Make me happy."

"Hell," he muttered, and he lowered his face between her legs.
"It's what I came for." She maneuvered slightly and the opulent
flesh of her thighs closed against his cheeks and the heavy female
smell of her spread into the cavities of his skull. He shuddered
and responded to the urgent and muffled commands she gave.

"Do it, Jack. Do it now. . ."

It was past midnight when he arrived home. He was weary,
slow-moving, annoyed with himself and guilty over his transgressions. Why couldn't Rosie be more like Nicholson? More alive to
his unspoken needs, to the compulsions of his flesh and fantasies

alike? Once their lovemaking had been vital and demanding, a nearly violent exchange of needs and satisfaction; all that was gone now, replaced by an occasional joining of their flesh, mechanical and empty, leaving both of them dissatisfied afterward. As he climbed the stairs to the second floor bedroom they shared, Keveney hoped his wife was asleep.

She lay propped up on her side of the bed, reading her Bible. Rosie had become increasingly pious as the years passed, more Catholic than the Pope, he liked to say, and he felt himself being drawn back into the world of Sister Asumpta and the rest of the nuns at Our Savior School.

"I thought you'd be home before this," she said in a voice benign and accusatory at the same time.

"It's the job." He undressed quickly and donned his pajamas. He slid into bed, keeping to his side, not touching her.

"You said you'd phone."

He glanced her way, as if seeking for hidden intent; her expression was bland, lined with Christian understanding and charity. "I was busy."

She put the Bible aside and appraised him calmly. All girlishness had been wiped away and her face seemed bonier, tighter, without sensuality or warmth. It occurred to Keveney that it had been a long time since they had talked to each other about something other than Patrick or money or that the house required a new heating system. She was a stranger he happened to live with. They were strangers to each other.

"Marvin Newton called this evening."

He frowned, as if trying to remember, not really caring.

"He was features editor when I was at the *Daily News*. He opened his own PR agency a couple of years ago. He's doing very well, thank you."

"Good for Marv." A vision of Marv Newton came rushing up at him. Twenty-five dollar haircuts and custom-tailored suits. Too clever and too sleek for Keveney's taste.

"He offered me a job, Jack."

Keveney folded his arms across his chest. To his surprise, he was pleased. A job would keep her occupied, keep her off his back, put an end to the constant complaining about the demands of his work. Maybe . . .

"You've got a job. You're a wife, you're a mother." He clamped his mouth shut, determined not to influence her too much, fearful of making her change her mind.

"Oh, Jack, I've been so unhappy . . ."

"Unhappy?"

"Very well, frustrated then. As if I'm wasting myself, the time of my life. I was a good journalist, here's my chance to get back to it."

"Publicity is hack work, that's all you'll be."

"Marv thinks I'm a good writer. He'll pay me fifty thousand dollars a year, for starters."

The amount of money startled him; it was more than he would ever earn wearing the blue. Marv Newton, he was smart, going where the money was. It certainly wasn't in police work, not unless you went on the pad, something Keveney refused to do.

"Turn Newton down," he said, in a still, flat voice. "Stay home. Be here when Patrick needs you, when I need you. Be the woman I married."

"We have to talk about this."

His eyes swung toward her. "You told Newton you'd take the job, didn't you?"

"Yes," she said defiantly. "As soon as I can find a housekeeper, I'm going back to work."

Keveney rolled over onto his side. "I'm tired. There's a long day tomorrow."

"That's it, then? That's all you've got to say?"

No, he almost said. There was so much to talk about, to explain, to try to understand. There was his job, his increasing involvement in the work, as if there he could discover the answers to all those unspoken questions that plagued him. There was the growing separation between them, a separation rooted in changes that had affected them both. There was her deepening religious belief, the daily attendance at Mass, the daily prayers, those interminable phone conversations with her fellow believers, discussing God-only-knew-what. As if there were in fact a God, a living Jesus who had been born, lived, died and been resurrected. So much superstitious nonsense. Even as the thought rolled around his mind he felt a spasm of guilt and remorse, as if Sister Asumpta had reached out from the grave to chastise him with her yardstick.

What, he wondered, would Rosie say if he told her about Officer Nicholson? What would she do? Pray, he supposed. Hit the nearest church and ask for divine intervention to separate her husband once and for all from sin and degradation. No use, he wanted to tell her; he had fallen too far from grace. He was denied forever that exalted state of being.

"I'm very tired," he said aloud. "Let's talk about it another time."

"No," she said with surprising force. "It's all settled. I'm going to work for Marv, starting next week. And nothing you say will change my mind."

He was neither shocked nor angered by her response. Husband and father, he had not played either role too well. Gradually, he understood, and unspoken agreement would come into being between them, an agreement that would permit the marriage to continue, each of them attending to his or her needs, laboring to keep from rocking the marital vessel to extremes.

It began to go sour an hour before the ship was due to dock. A telephone call from Tom Vargas came into Keveney's office, but he was already out in the field, observing the operation.

"Patch me through to him or to Zeke," Vargas insisted. Zeke was Zeke Grissom, two years older than Jack Keveney and still a lieutenant. Grissom lacked the flash of his boss, the ability to make the department take notice of his good work. He was a good field leader, plodding and dependable, a man who knew how to take orders and transform them into acceptable police work. It took nearly thirty minutes to make the connection.

"What is it, Vargas?" Keveney said, anticipating that something was wrong.

"A change in plans. The mother ship is lying offshore, offloading at sea. They'll run the shit in on four different power boats."

"To the naval yard?"

"That's just it. It's Staten Island now. Nervous characters, these guys. Changing plans at the last minute."

"Smart."

"Yeah."

"You got a locale for me?"

"The Holland Canal, you know it?"

Keveney glanced at Grissom, who nodded. He lived on Staten Island and had walked a beat there for many years. "About a quarter mile inland," Grissom said. "It intersects with the north branch of the Oanoke River. A piddling little stream," he ended.

"Not much more'n a stream," Keveney added.

"These guys don't make mistakes. They're using flat-bottom boats. Zeke, you know where the river narrows down, swings west to where it almost touches that old dirt road?"

"The one used to service Greens Farm? I know it."

"That's the rendezvous point."

"How much time we got?" Keveney said.

"Forty minutes and that's cutting it fine."

Next to Keveney in the unmarked police car, Grissom began to swear. Keveney waved him silent and said, "This may not go down clean, Vargas. Watch your butt."

"Bet on it, Captain."

"Awright," Keveney growled to Grissom. "This is still your show. Get on the horn and put your people into place, unless you want them to bring that shipment in."

Grisson, reaching for the radio microphone, said, "That'll be the day..."

All units were in place less than five minutes before the first of the trucks pulled up on the dirt road, parked, rear ends facing the river. The drivers dismounted, along with their helpers, and waited, smoking cigarettes. They were expecting no trouble. Abruptly a light flashed across the narrow river, two longs, one short, fading quickly to blackness.

"What the fuck is that?" Grissom muttered.

"A watcher," Keveney answered. "We're lucky he didn't make us. I want that guy."

"I don't have enough men to cover the trucks and the boats when they come in . . ."

"I'll take him myself."

"I don't like this, it's screwy. If something goes wrong . . ."

"Do your best, it'll be good enough."

"Yeah. Cover your ass, Captain."

"You too, Zeke."

Keveney began his move through the trees, advancing silently, staying out of sight of the truckers. A pulse began to beat in his temple and he wiped his hands on his thighs. Upstream, at a bend in the river, he waded across. Once in the woods, he doubled back toward the spot where he had seen the signal light. Some sounds to his left caused him to freeze in place, his pistol a reassuring presence in his right fist.

He paused to listen. In the distance, the gutteral sound of power boats running slow, engines muffled. Again that signal light. Two longs, one short. Hoarse voices drifted across the water and soon he was able to see the boats heading in toward shore. The waiting men guided the boats into place, using low-wattage flashlights, and the unloading process began, bales of marijuana carted up to the waiting trucks and packed into place. A single bale remained on each boat when Grissom's men broke out of their cover, identifying themselves as policemen. One of the smugglers began to run and a shot rang out. He stopped and raised his hands.

A movement in the brush along the riverbank caught Keveney's eye and he hurried forward. "Freeze!" he called in a strong voice. "Or you'll die where you stand."

The man reacted instinctively, ducking away, snapping off a shot in Keveney's direction. The slug tore through branches overhead, sending Keveney to the ground. When he looked up the watcher was gone, crashing through the woods. Keveney went after him.

He stumbled into a tree trunk, bruising his left shoulder. He kept on. He told himself he was gaining, closing the gap, when he realized he could no longer hear the watcher. He pulled up, sucking air into his mouth, listening. He took a single forward step.

A shot rang out and then another. Keveney dived for cover. No more than twenty yards to his front, the watcher was on the run again. Keveney followed.

The watcher made it out onto a dirt track that led from a garbage dump to the main road. Cursing his luck, Keveney went on. In the night, he heard a car engine rev up and roar as the watcher sped away. At the edge of the dirt road, Keveney choked on a thin cloud of dust, wondering who the watcher was and trying to ignore the throbbing of his damaged shoulder.

Officer Nicholson sat curled up in one corner of the contemporary sofa, wrapped in a Navajo blanket, alternately nibbling apple slices and Vermont cheddar, watching the news on Channel Four. Her eyes remained on the screen when Keveney appeared.

"It go down okay?"

"Shut the TV."

"They shot a cop in Brooklyn. He may buy it."

He hit the power button and the picture faded to black. He sat next to her on the couch, looked her over.

"What've you got on under that blanket?"

"Would you believe nothing?"

"Show me."

She did, shifting around to make herself available, watching him as if from a distance. "I figured you wouldn't be able to stay away. It's the action turns you on, the excitement. Isn't it?"

He was unable to answer.

It was past three when Keveney arrived home. He undressed and got into bed. Next to him, Rosie stirred and he realized that she hadn't been asleep.

"I was worried," she said, without emphasis. "I phoned your office. They told me it all went down before ten o'clock. Where have you been until now?"

He started to speak and she cut him off.

"Never mind, it doesn't matter, I know. I can smell her on you, Jack. You might've had the decency to take a shower before you got into your bed."

"It isn't like that."

"Don't lie to me, Jack. It won't work this time."

He started to answer, changed his mind, and said only, "I'm tired."

"Yes," she said quietly. "So am I."

THIRTEEN

DAY AND NIGHT, NAPOLEON EXPLORED THE STREETS of Chiriqui. He counted seven hotels, fifteen banks, three identifiable whore houses, and over two hundred bars. Chiriqui was a city bent out of shape. Prostitution, murder, drugs, all had been a part of life in El Arbolito; but here there was an added factor. What was missing in El Arbolito was intentional, deliberate evil. In a way, the little village was so poor, so close to the land, that it was innocent. The Devil had passed it by; profound ignorance, peasant cruelty and desperation, all were present in abundance. Chiriqui was another matter. Chiriqui was the Devil's own handiwork, an ugly and evil city growing swiftly. Here you had choices; and people seemed to have made all the wrong ones. Napoleon loved Chiriqui; it was his kind of town.

His love went unrequited, unnoticed. He was ignored, mocked, scorned, rejected. No matter how hard he tried, he could not get connected. He was met by a conspiracy of silence, almost of apathy, everywhere he went. And yet, under its skin of stolid calm, most of Chiriqui was involved in illegality of one sort or another; mostly a rising, thriving trade in drugs. Napoleon began to feel that everyone in the town was a player, except him. And he was being kept out of the game.

All around him, people were assembling fortunes. How else to account for the dozen or so ultraexpensive restaurants, the stylish shops, in a town of this size? And the auto dealers, and the whores—a man could get laid in El Arbolito every night for a year

117

for what these *putas* charged for an hour of their time.

He grew increasingly annoyed with his failure to connect. He was angry and short-tempered from the constant rejection he encountered. Yes, he was young and recently out of the back country, clearly unskilled in the ways of a city. But surely the special qualities he was convinced he possessed should be apparent and valuable to someone in Chiriqui. Still, they gave him no encouragement, opened no doors to his swelling ambition. Each day found him growing more irritable, more desperate, his always active mind seeking some way to break down the walls of indifference. Added to that was his dwindling money supply. To him it had been a small fortune; here in Chiriqui, it was merely pocket money, going fast.

He felt trapped, immobilized, stuck in one place. Unless something happened soon, he would be chewed up, drawn into the gullet of Chiriqui eventually to be spit out as garbage. Dreams of glory danced in his head, but his stomach was cramped with uncertainty.

On this particular afternoon, he sat alone at a small table at a small street cafe on the western edge of an unimportant plaza not far from the center of town. Long shadows began their reach across the plaza, and swarms of grackles began to settle for the night in the carefully pruned and shaped trees that were the pride of the neighborhood. He sat tall and seemingly proud in his beautiful new clothes, and sipped a Coca Cola that seeped bitter as gall down his throat. No one spoke to him and he spoke to no one.

Without warning, the tranquility of the plaza was shattered when a large, canvas-covered military truck came roaring out of a side street, circling the plaza and braking to a lurching stop in front of an old stone colonial building, with a facade streaked by bird droppings and rust-colored streaks. A canvas flap was pulled aside, and out of the back of the truck came a dozen uniformed men—soldiers—each armed with an automatic weapon. They formed a double line from the colonial building to the truck, facing outward, weapons at the ready, militarily grim. Napoleon was impressed with the precision of the maneuver; this was obviously a much-practiced exercise.

As if on silent signal, four men came out of the building, each struggling under the weight of a large green duffle bag. They passed along the lane formed by the soldiers, heaved the duffles into the truck and climbed aboard. Only then did the soldiers break formation, one by one disappearing into the dark void of the military vehicle. The canvas flap was yanked back into place and the truck roared off in the direction from which it had come, spewing exhaust fumes, alarming the grackles and putting them to flight, protesting noisily. When the truck was gone, the grackles settled back into the trees, and a familiar silence and lethargy descended again on the unimportant plaza. It had all happened with a kind of surreal swiftness, as if in a dream, the entire affair lasting only a few minutes.

The waiter materialized out of the cafe. "Another Coca Cola, Señor?"

Napoleon stared at the now still, empty street. "What was that all about?"

The waiter shrugged and swiped at the tabletop with a damp rag. "Oh, that. Twice a week at this hour the soldiers come to take away the money, on Tuesdays and Fridays. Each time, four bags of money. Not that I notice such things."

"Money? From where?"

"The bank. El Banco Grande de Chiriqui. There." He indicated the soiled colonial building.

"That is a bank?"

The waiter nodded once. "A very busy establishment."

"It is unmarked. How is one to know it is a bank?"

"Those who need to know, know," the waiter said flatly. "Another Coca Cola, señor?"

Napoleon paid for his drink and left a generous tip. "Always at this time?"

"Always. It is our special entertainment, to watch the soldiers. Come another day and you will see."

"Perhaps I will," Napoleon said, reflecting on what he had seen, on what he had learned.

The next morning, carefully barbered, perfumed and shined, Napoleon entered *El Banco Grande de Chiriqui*—which was anything but grand. The bank looked old and smelled old. The crystal chandelier that hung from the vaulted ceiling was dusty, the paint on the wall was peeling and a musty odor rose up from the stained carpet.

Six tellers worked in cages, and one of them wore a green visor, making him look like a gambling hall croupier.

There were no customers, but there was a fat guard in a worn green uniform. He directed Napoleon to an office at the rear of the bank.

Riccardo Diaz sat behind a small desk. The sign on his desk proclaimed him a vice president. He was a small man with the face of a ferret and a sullen mouth. His nails were unclean and well-bitten. He acknowledged Napoleon's appearance without enthusiasm.

"You wish to open an account?" He fed a form into his typewriter.

Napoleon signed the form with a flourish. Over the years, he had perfected his signature. It was ornate, indecipherable and self-consciously unique. Diaz smiled when he saw it. "You're from the country?" he asked.

"Why do you say that?"

"No special reason." He smiled, showing broken teeth. "One campesino to another, friend." Napoleon said nothing. "How much do you want to deposit?"

"Two hundred dollars American."

Napoleon pushed two one-hundred-dollar bills across the desk, and received his checkbook.

"Let me show you," Diaz said. He ripped a check from the pad. "First you date it," he said. "Then you write in the name of the payee on this line. You put the amount here, and then write it out on this line. Last you sign it. Understand?"

All this was said in a supercilious tone, and Napoleon repressed an angry response.

"Perhaps you can use a safety deposit box," Diaz said.

"What is that?"

"It's a small safe," Diaz explained. "You can put your valuables in it. Your diamonds, your cash, your will, anything important."

Napoleon shook his head. "Not now." He decided he disliked this man immensely. "Will you take coffee with me?" he asked. "One campesino to another."

Diaz looked at his watch. "Why not?" he said. "I take a break about this time anyhow."

Sitting at the cafe across the street, Diaz drank coffee with tequila on the side and talked. He talked about his wife, whom he did not like, and his mistress, who did not like him. He mentioned his two children. He talked about his job, about the bank. Napoleon listened and urged him on.

By the time Diaz had walked unsteadily back across the plaza and into the bank, Napoleon knew a great deal about how business was conducted in the old colonial building. He knew enough, now, to begin formulating a plan that could be the solution to all his problems.

Back in his room at the Hotel Isabella, he sent for a porter he had befriended. Like his father, and his father, and his father before him, Luis was a peon. He seldom bathed, shaved only when management of the hotel insisted he do so and could not read or write. Unlike his ancestors, he had left the land seeking a better life in the city, where he had hoped to make his fortune. Neither hardworking enough nor clever enough to make much money, he was always on the lookout for ways of earning an extra peso or two. Thus, he listened with considerable attention to the young señor who had summoned him.

"How would you like to have fifty dollars American?" Napoleon began.

A wily grin turned the wide mouth and Luis's eyes gleamed. "You wish somebody killed, señor?" Luis was not making a joke.

"I want you to carry a message for me."

"Sí, señor."

"To a man named Juan-Manuel Negrete, you have heard of him?"

Luis shrugged. He cared nothing about names. "Where is this Negrete, señor?"

"Outside of El Arbolito, in the hills, away from the sea. I will make you a map."

"That is some distance from here . . ."

"Can you take the time off? Can you rent a truck? Can you drive?

"Sí, señor. And I can drive, señor. But a truck costs money."

"I will pay for the truck."

"And I shall deliver your message, señor."

"Tell Negrete I wish to talk to him. He must telephone me at the hotel right away. You understand, telephone right away."

"Sí, señor."

"His camp may be moved, deeper into the hills possibly."

"I will find him, señor."

Napoleon gave two twenty-dollar bills to Luis. "One is for you and one is for the renting of the truck. When you return, after I have spoken to Negrete, you will get the rest of the money."

Luis backed out of the room, bowing, grinning cheerfully. A day or two and he would be rich and he would get drunk to celebrate and stay drunk for a week.

Alone in his room, Napoleon warned himself to be patient. To be thorough. To make his plan carefully. This was the chance he'd been looking for and he intended to make sure it worked.

The telephone rang and Napoleon eyed it warily. It was a device of the modern world with which he had yet to feel entirely comfortable. Nevertheless he lifted the receiver with a certain acquired authority.

"Sí," he said.

"Little Fish, it is you?"

Only Juan-Manuel would call him that. "We must talk," he said. "It is very important. Is it possible for you to come here? To Chiriqui?"

"If it is necessary."

"Yes, necessary. And bring three men with you. Good men, men with cojones who know how to follow orders. I want men who, if it rains, will not be frightened."

There was a pause. Napoleon's euphemism for "wet work," for the possibility of murder, caused Negrete to think for perhaps ten seconds. "Perhaps it will be fair."

"Perhaps. One never knows about the weather."

"I will choose them myself." Juan-Manuel chuckled suddenly.

"Why do you laugh?"

"You will see, Little Fish. I will bring my very best."

"Good. Come here to the Hotel Isabella. It is a gringo hotel so dress like a gringo."

"I will need two days," Negrete said solemnly.

"Two days," Napoleon repeated before he hung up. He would use the time to perfect the plan.

Forty-eight hours later, at ten-thirty in the morning, there was a knock at his door. Napoleon went to the door and admitted Juan-Manuel Negrete, resplendent in a suit the color of dusty bark and a shirt with a starched collar and a wide tie decorated with red and blue flowers. The two men exchanged an *abrazo,* clapping each other on the back before separating and shaking hands. Negrete touched the lapel of his jacket self-consciously.

"My father's suit," he explained. "His second suit. He was buried in his best suit. Do I look like a gringo?"

A laugh burst out of Napoleon. "You will never look like a gringo, my friend. Neither of us will." He sobered quickly. "Where are your men?"

"Downstairs. I thought we should talk first."

"A good idea. You still buy and sell a little cocaine?"

"Like everything else, a revolution costs money. I deal a little, when it is in order."

"How would you like to expand your operation? Make a lot of money?"

"I am not trying to get rich, you know that."

"More money means more men for the revolution, more arms, more equipment."

Negrete considered what his friend had said. "Exactly what is going through that brain of yours?"

"Cocaine. Each day the demand for the White Lady becomes greater. Each day the demand in the United States becomes greater..."

"I am not a drug dealer."

"This revolution of yours, once you told me that it is aimed ultimately at the Americans, to end their imperialism. Cocaine can deaden the spirit, drain the strength of their people, of their society, make it easier to bring them down. Is it not so?"

Negrete nodded gravely.

"I am not asking you to smuggle cocaine into the United States."

"What are you asking?"

"You know where the coca fields are. You know the men who work the fields, who harvest the coca leaf. They trust you. Buy their leaves, see to their refinement, pay everyone a fair price."

"And send the cocaine to you?"

"Exactly. I will take all the cocaine you can deliver."

Negrete thought it over. Napoleon was making sense. His revolution was a deceit, a handful of men roaming the hills doing mild damage to a remote police outpost or a small army patrol, getting no closer to victory. It was time he made a strong move forward.

"All this, it will take a lot of money. Where will it come from?"

"From me." Napoleon cleared his throat. "This is the way it will work. You will be the supplier, Juan-Manuel. A friend of mine will do the selling. The profits will be divided, fifty percent for me, twenty-five for my friend, twenty-five percent for you. Can you find us a chemist?" Negrete nodded. "The stuff will be stepped on, ten times, more if necessary. I want only good stuff; better than good. The chemist must be reliable. I will pay him a generous salary." Napoleon leaned forward. "Also, I will need an enforcer. I look for no trouble, I wish evil to no one. But if someone gets in our way, he must be blown away, and blown away fast. Especially the first time. Early lessons are well learned."

"It sounds as if you are connected already?"

"Not exactly," Napoleon said.

"How then—about the money? Believe me, my friend, I am for the plan one hundred percent. But I must pay the campesinos in cash. And I have none."

Napoleon began to pace. "That is why I have called you here. I will explain. Soon we will be rich." And he began to talk fast and earnestly.

When he was through, Negrete said, "It's a good plan. So simple nothing should go wrong."

"Something can always go wrong."

"Personally I can't be part of this. Too many people know me."

"I understand," Napoleon said, "and I respect your decision. But your people . . ."

"They are all excellent."

"Bring them to me," Napoleon said. "Tell them nothing. The less they know the better."

Negrete rose. "When do we start?"

"We start now. We will execute tomorrow." He waved his hand. "Now, I must meet these people of yours."

"And my surprise."

"Ah, yes," Napoleon drawled, "the surprise."

Ten minutes later Juan-Manuel Negrete returned, leading three people into the room. Two men and, to Napoleon's startlement, a woman.

"What do you think of my surprise?" Negrete asked with a sly grin.

Napoleon maintained his composure. What a woman, he thought, of such beauty as he had never before encountered. Tall and slender, with a poised, animal grace and a fall of shining black hair that descended her back almost to her waist. She stared at Napoleon out of luminous eyes that revealed nothing and missed nothing. Napoleon turned back to Negrete.

"In this matter, I have no need of a woman," he said in a thin, disapproving voice. "I told you to bring three men."

"I will be better for you than any man," the woman said, without emphasis. "Whatever a man can do, I can do it better."

That drew a loud approving laugh from Juan-Manuel Negrete. "She speaks the truth, Little Fish," he said, massaging one hand against the other. "This one is called Nina Fuentes, Napoleon."

The woman nodded slowly.

Napoleon motioned her into a chair. "*Mi casa es su casa*," he said grandly, before turning his attention to the two men. First there was Antonio. Squat and muscular, slightly hump-backed, with thin lips and a mustache to match. He answered Napoleon's handshake with a powerful grip that made it clear he was no one to be trifled with.

"And last is Jesus," Negrete said, introducing a young man only a year or two older than Napoleon. His face still retained some of its baby fat and his deep dark eyes were without life. When he spoke, his lips hardly moved.

"I am honored, Napoleon."

"The honor is mine." He got the men seated and looked around; Nina Fuentes, erect and unmoving in her chair, feet flat on the floor, her gaze fixed on Napoleon, dominated the room. She would, he understood, have to be dealt with first.

"What does she do for you?"

Negrete smiled. "She's my right arm. Please understand, my friend. Nina is my comrade, a colleague, not my woman."

Nina rose from her chair. "I do what has to be done." Her voice was low, uninflected.

Negrete said, "She is good. She can be relied on. She is better than most men. I have found this to be so."

Napoleon ran it all through his mind, put it up against his plan, what was needed, what had to be done, the difficulties that might arise.

"You tell me these are good people?" he said to Negrete.

The guerrilla chieftain answered with great solemnity. "My best. All of them have been with me for more than a little while. All have conducted themselves with courage and dignity, no matter the risks. Each with special skills. I depend on them, you can depend on them."

Napoleon made up his mind. "Very well. Then this is what the plan is." He spent the next five minutes explaining what he had in mind, how it worked, what the risks were, what assignment each of them would have.

When he finished, no one spoke until Juan-Manuel broke the silence. "This all must be done before the soldiers arrive. A dozen soldiers with automatic weapons against the four of you, that is not a good way to go."

"I told you," Napoleon said. "By the time the soldiers appear, we will be away from there and safe."

"And if the plan does not work?" Jesus said without feeling.

It was Nina Fuentes who answered in a voice flat and full of threat. "We will make it work with our weapons. That is why we are here."

"Yes," Napoleon said, increasingly impressed with her. "Are there any other questions?"

"When will we be paid?" Jesus wanted to know.

Antonio grimaced and averted his face. Negrete lowered his eyes, as if embarrassed by the question. Nina Fuentes stared at Jesus. They waited for Napoleon to answer.

"When the job is done, each of you will be paid, each the same amount. Is there any objection?" There was none. "Very well, then we begin. Antonio, you will find us a car—steal it—to serve our purposes. Juan-Manuel, the weapons . . . ?"

"They are in a safe place."

"Good. Then we meet at El Banco Grande at the appointed hour tomorrow. Until then—*vaya con Dios, mi amigos*."

He watched them file out of the room, Negrete lingering behind to take his hand. "Be patient, Little Fish, and all will be well. I know these people."

"Yes, my friend," he said with a confidence he did not feel. "And after the job, you will meet with us here?"

"Depend on me."

That was the trouble, Napoleon thought. He had to depend on too many people—strangers, and one of them a woman. It made him uneasy, aware of the flaws in the plan he had concocted, aware that it was almost too easy. Something was bound to go wrong, of that he was convinced. And when it did, it would be up to him alone to make it right.

The unimportant plaza was still in the waning minutes of siesta. Here and there, a shopkeeper opened his establishment early. A boy of nine or ten kicked a soccer ball along one side of the plaza, dodging back and forth among the outdoor food stands. A mongrel dog slunk along the building line and out of sight around a corner. As if to take the place of the mongrel, Jesus appeared, walking slowly, looking awkward in a jacket too small for his body, a campesino out of place in the city. From his place on an iron bench in the shade of a tree in the plaza, Napoleon took it all in. He sat back on his spine, legs extended, crossed at the ankles, hands folded across his flat belly. The .38-caliber revolver dug into the small of his back, its presence more comforting than painful. Then the fat uniformed guard appeared and opened the front doors of El Banco Grande. He gazed up and down the street as if looking for customers before withdrawing into the musty building.

The time had come.

Napoleon strolled unhurriedly across a diagonal path that traversed the plaza and descended a few worn steps to the street that fronted the bank building. An ancient American car of indeterminate make came rolling toward him, its engine remarkably quiet. He watched the car pull up to the curb and Nina Fuentes climbed out. Dressed in finely tailored slacks and a dark blouse, and carrying an expensive purse, she seemed out of place in this unfashionable plaza.

Napoleon entered the bank. Nina and Jesus followed, leaving Antonio behind the wheel of the American car. They spread out, taking up previously agreed upon positions. Napoleon approached the teller in the first cage. He leaned forward and spoke intimately.

"Where are the canvas bags?" he asked conversationally.

"What?" the teller said, a faint professional smile on his face.

"The bags of money. The money the soldiers take away. Where are they kept?"

"What . . . ?" the teller said. "Why . . . ?" he stuttered. The blood drained out of his face. "Are you *loco,* asking about such things?" He gestured to the fat guard. "Miguelito! This one wants to know about the bags of money. He is mad, yes. Get him away from me."

Without alarm, the fat guard trundled forward. "You! Out of here! What do you think you are doing?"

"Holding up the bank," Napoleon said, matter-of-factly.

That stopped the fat guard. The answer confused more than

alarmed him. "You are loco. Nobody robs this bank. Get out of here, at once."

"You see the woman, that man," Napoleon said. "They are with me. We are robbing the bank, I tell you."

The guard looked around, assimilating the words. Then, having made up his mind, he went for the pistol on his hip. His movements were slow and clumsy and the pistol hadn't yet cleared its holster when Nine Fuentes, from ten feet away, shot him, his fat head disintegrating in a mist of skin, bone and blood. The guard's great body fell to the floor with a great crash. One of the other tellers cried out in alarm.

"Quiet!" Nina Fuentes commanded. "Unless you too wish to die."

"Now," Napoleon said to the first teller. "The bags."

"I will show you." It was the woman teller who had spoken. Napoleon, the .38 in hand, went after her, followed by Jesus. Nina Fuentes herded the team of tellers along, trying to keep them from collapsing in fear.

At the rear of the bank there was a small room containing safe deposit boxes and a huge iron safe. The safe was tall as a man, and as wide. "In there," the teller said in a whisper. "In there. The bags are in there."

Jesus knelt down and laughed. "This is a joke," he said to Napoleon. "It must be seventy-five years old. Not even a combination lock." He brought forth some tools and went to work. Seconds later he twisted the handle of the door of the safe, and it opened silently. Four green duffles were stacked inside.

"Mother of God!" Jesus said. "Look at these, stuffed with money. We are rich!"

"Enough talk!" Napoleon snapped. "Get the bags into the car!" He shoved his gun in his belt and lifted one of the duffles to his shoulder, carrying it outside. Jesus came up behind him. Then they returned for the last two bags. "All right," he said. "Let's go!"

"Everyone, down on the floor," Nina Fuentes said. The tellers obeyed. "You will not move until the soldiers get here. Is that clear?"

"Clear," someone mumbled.

Satisfied they would follow her instructions, Nina backed out of the bank and slid into the back seat of the American car, which sped away under the sure hands of Antonio.

Juan-Manuel was waiting in Napoleon's room when they arrived, puffing nervously on a cigarette. "Well?" he said. "How did it go? My God, are those bags filled with money? Did it go well? Was there any trouble? Where is Antonio? Is he dead?"

Napoleon answered calmly. "Antonio disposes of the car, as planned. He will come up the back stairs as we did soon enough. Then we shall complete our business."

"You did it!" Juan-Manuel cried out. "You did it!"

"There was never any question," Napoleon said.

"Let's open the bags," Jesus said. "Let's see the money."

Napoleon nodded in assent and the thin man opened one of the duffles and emptied its contents onto the bed. American money in neat bundles bound with rubber bands came tumbling into view.

"Madre de Dios! What a fortune!"

Nina picked up a packet of money, counting quickly. "These are twenty-dollar bills, all used, untraceable. One hundred to a stack. That's two thousand dollars."

"There must be two hundred packages in that duffle," Jesus said.

"Check the other bags," Napoleon said.

Jesus hurried to obey. Again he exclaimed over what he had found. "I told you, a fortune!"

"The last two bags," Nina said in a businesslike manner, "contain only ten-dollar bills. That's a thousand dollars for each bundle."

"How many bundles in each duffle?" Napoleon said.

"Without counting," she answered, "I can only guess. About two hundred."

"How much altogether, would you say?"

She answered deliberately, her eyes tilted at the corners, fixed on his. "Approximately one million, two hundred thousand dollars, American."

"Aieee!" Jesus burst out. "We have become millionaires!"

"Be still," Napoleon said. "I have to think."

A knock at the door signaled Antonio's return. He assessed the pile of bills on the bed. "We have put in a good day's work, I think."

"There's something wrong," Nina said.

"We did the job," Jesus said angrily. "We have the money. What can be wrong?"

"Only money," Napoleon muttered. "Only paper money."

Nina agreed with him. "Why no paper? No bonds. No stock certificates. Nothing but cash."

They stared at the pile of money, nobody speaking, until Napoleon said, "The job is done and you all deserve to be paid." He counted out three stacks of ten thousand dollars each. "This is payment for you, Antonio, and you, Jesus, and you, Nina. You all did well."

"And the rest of it?" Jesus wanted to know. "There is so much. If I had known how much, perhaps I would not have agreed . . ."

"Be still," Juan-Manuel bit off. "If you have a complaint, make it to me when we are alone. Now, one at a time, you will each leave. Antonio, you first."

Minutes later, Jesus departed.

"That one will make trouble," Napoleon said to Juan-Manuel.

"If there is trouble," Negrete answered, "it will be my trouble. Now, Nina, it is time for you to go."

The tall woman turned to Napoleon. "We shall meet again, yes."

"Yes. You did well. I thank you."

"I do what must be done." She left without a backward glance.

"Was I right about her?" Negrete said when he and Napoleon were alone.

"She is some woman."

"Yes, unlike any other I have known. Now, what about the rest of our business?"

"All this money, I want to think about it. What does it mean?"

"You need someone who knows about such things."

"I know such a man, but I don't know where he is or how to contact him."

Juan-Manuel shrugged. "We meet again tomorrow, then?"

"Yes, in front of the Ascension Cathedral. There is a small plaza there. At noon."

"You did well today, Little Fish. Very well."

But Napoleon, drifting into his own thoughts, was not as sure.

In the morning, Napoleon's worst fears were confirmed. He went through *La Prensa,* the only daily newspaper in Chiriqui, and found no mention of the robbery of El Banco Grande. Births and deaths were reported in profusion. Four drunken brawls were reported. Three car accidents. The robbery of a meat market of two hundred pounds of beef was mentioned, but nothing about the bank. It was, he decided, cause for real concern.

An hour later, his phone rang. It was Juan-Manuel, canceling their meeting. "I must return to my camp at once," he declared.

"There is trouble?"

"There is always trouble everywhere, yes. I am unable to keep the remainder of our arrangement, Little Fish. For that I am genuinely sorry. But my revolutionary fighters, they must come first, you understand?"

Napoleon did not understand, and he said so. "What shall I do with your share of the money?"

"I want no part of it, not now, not ever."

"Again I don't understand. What are you afraid of?"

"If you were wise, you would be afraid, also. Leave this place, Little Fish. There are forces at work here neither of us can deal with. Go with God, my friend." Negrete hung up.

Napoleon dropped the dead receiver back in its cradle. What was happening? Negrete had sounded terrified. But of what? Of whom? He tried to address the mystery when the phone rang a second time.

"Napoleon?"

"Who is this?"

"Willie Hatcher, Napoleon. It's important that we talk . . ."

A mixed tide of emotion swept through Napoleon. He was glad to hear again from Hatcher, but the tone of his friend's voice made him apprehensive. Even more, it startled him that Willie should call at the precise moment when his mind was awash with questions and problems and fears. Certainly this call could not be put down to coincidence.

"Why are you calling at this moment?"

"It is vital that we talk."

"Tomorrow. . ."

"Now!" Hatcher shouted into the phone. Napoleon could hear his hoarse breathing. He spoke again, more quietly this time. "Now, Napoleon. At once."

Napoleon's eyes passed over the great green mount of gringo money on his bed. "There is a cantina . . ."

"No. Privately. In your room. I'll be there in fifteen minutes."

Napoleon stuffed the money back into the duffles and the duffles into the closet. He had just finished when there was a firm knock at the door. He checked his .38 before shoving it into his belt at the small of his back. Only then did he open the door. Willie Hatcher, fat as ever, was sweating profusely, an agitated expression on his large oval face. He went past Napoleon into the room, looking around.

Napoleon spread his hands. "No abrazo, mi amigo? No friendly greeting? Is this the way a friend acts?"

Hatcher snorted and put himself into a chair. "It was you, wasn't it?"

"I am so glad to see you," Napoleon said, ignoring the question. "I wondered where you were, if I would ever see you again. I have many questions to ask . . ."

"Answer mine."

"I don't know what you mean," Napoleon said slowly.

Hatcher drew a sheet of small photographs out of his pocket and handed it over. Napoleon studied it briefly, then swore.

"Where did these come from?"

"El Banco Grande, my friend. You did not see the cameras?"

"I did not know about cameras. I did not notice . . ."

"Now they know what you look like . . ."

"They?"

"They have men out looking for you, all over this town. Sooner or later, someone will show up at this hotel and speak to the desk clerk, the porter. Someone will identify you as the man in these pictures. Then they will send someone after you, someone who is very good at his job . . ."

"*They*. Who the hell are *they?*"

"You still don't get it, do you? El Banco Grande belongs to them. It is their laundry. Drug money comes down from the United States and ends up here in Chiriqui, much of it in that bank. It is the final step in the laundering process . . ."

"A laundry, for money?"

"You still don't understand? Very well. I will explain. El Banco Grande belongs to the Regents. To men called Salazar, Vega, Uribe. The most powerful of all the drug dealers. They own the bank, they own this city, someday I believe they will own this country. And you, in your immense wisdom, have ripped off their bank. Their money. Now do you understand?"

"Ah," Napoleon said with surprising tranquility. "I sensed something was wrong."

"Very wrong for you."

"It seemed so easy."

"So what are we to do?"

Willie Hatcher, wide-eyed in disbelief, said, "We! I am no part of this. It is you they are after. And when they find you, someone will put a bullet in the back of your head."

"Tell me, Willie, how is it you have those pictures?"

"They know me, you fool. They know everyone. They showed the photos to everyone. Half the town is out hunting you."

"But they don't know of me yet?"

"They will soon enough, and then . . ."

"Until then there is time to make things better."

"My God, Napoleon! This is insane. I am talking to a dead man and he thinks he can make things better. I'll tell you what you can do—run. Hide. Pray that you are able to make good your escape."

"And if I do all that, what is left for me? To be a little fish again in the sea, to be eaten by the bigger fish. No, I will not go backwards. I cannot." Napoleon fell silent. "I looked in *La Prensa,* I saw nothing about the robbery."

"They own the paper. They own just about everything."

"The soldiers . . . ?"

"Much of the army. Much of the police force. Most of the government. They don't advertise their failures, they correct them. They will erase you the way a child erases his scribbles on a piece of paper. Run, I tell you."

"You know these men," Napoleon said carefully. "You've known them a long time."

Willie nodded.

"What if I return their money to them?"

"Use your head. They will find you, and take back the money you have stolen. Then they will punish you. Tear out your eyes, maybe, or cut off your balls. Make you weep with anguish and cry out for the mercy of a quick death. Oh, yes, they will torture you, as a lesson to others, and you will die slowly. Perhaps in a hundred years another fool just off the ranch will rob such a bank, but not until then."

"They will never find the money."

"You underestimate them."

"Listen to me, El Gordo. The money is in a safe place, safe from their hands. It is booby trapped. Let me fail to make certain phone calls each day and the money is gone. Blown up. Nothing but ashes."

"I don't believe you."

"But will they? I think so. Can you reach them?"

Willie shrugged. "I can try," he said.

Willie looked at Napoleon. Never had he looked more Indian, standing straight and ominous, his eyes two dark stones in his head.

"Now," Napoleon said.

Hatcher dialed the phone, spoke quietly behind his cupped hand. After a while, his manner grew more intense, agitated, and Napoleon understood that the fat man was arguing his case. Finally, Hatcher swung around, handed the phone to Napoleon. "He'll talk to you," he said.

"Señor?"

"This is Salazar," came the thin, wheezing voice. "Who is this?"

"I wish to apologize for my mistake. I did not know."

"The money is safe, my son?"

"Safe," Napoleon said. "As long as I can call every hour. If not, it is wired. It will vanish in a small explosion. Unless we can make a deal, señor. Can we meet?"

The old voice said, "You wish to preserve your life? That would be a beginning. We want our collections back. The money is ours, not yours. Shooting and killing," the old voice went on, "these are bad and unnecessary things to do. Stealing is bad, too. Stealing from us is the worst, my son. The worst thing you can ever do."

"I have no wish to die, Señor Salazar."

"Then you must return to us what is rightfully ours. Of course, there is still the matter of the bank guard you killed. He leaves a widow, some children. A pension must be arranged. So you can see, this is no simple affair. What do you say, my son?"

"I say there is much to discuss, much to arrange."

"Ah, yes. I hear no fear in your voice. I like that. But a man without fear is a fool."

"I am afraid, señor."

"Good. Then you shall join me for *comida* and see what arrangement is possible. Today, at La Caverna. Señor Hatcher will bring you. And you will bring our money."

"My apologies, señor. But I am doing this in order to live, not insure my death. When we have talked, made arrangements suitable to us both, when I am convinced I am protected, then I will see that the money is delivered back to the bank."

The old man cleared his throat, and the sound of his thin cackle sounded over the wire. "I like you, my son. You make it sound as if you are doing Raphael Salazar a favor, a very big favor. Very well. We shall eat and drink and talk and see what comes of it. Until then...."

The phone went dead in Napoleon's hand. He swung around to face Willie Hatcher. "There, it is done. I am meeting him for lunch. All will be well."

"I hope so," the fat man said. "For both our sakes."

* * *

La Caverna was on a narrow street lined with high stone walls. The narrow cobblestoned way had been designed for small carts and burros, not for modern automobiles. Behind the walls were the houses of Chiriqui's wealthiest and most important families; members of the government, ranking colonels of the army, the mayor and the chief of police. For them, La Caverna was a neighborhood restaurant and they could often be seen dining there with their wives and children. When such men went out with their mistresses, they patronized the flashier establishments at the southern edge of the city.

A small man in an elegant business suit greeted Napoleon and Willie Hatcher, bowing and rubbing his hands together. "You are the guests of Señor Salazar, no? This way, please."

"How did he know?" Napoleon whispered to Hatcher as they trailed behind the small man up a flight of narrow steps. "It's his business to know," came the unsatisfying answer. A short corridor brought them into a cheerful room with a long, polished wooden table. At the far end of the table an old man sipped red wine and smoked a thin, brown cigar. Behind them, the door closed.

"Sit," the old man said. "I am Salazar."

Through another door, two waiters appeared with trays of food which they laid out on the table. They poured wine for Napoleon and Willie Hatcher and asked if there was anything else they could do, before withdrawing on silent feet.

"Eat." Salazar said, and suited action to word.

Napoleon watched him with interest. He might have been seventy years old. Or eighty. Or perhaps younger, it was hard to tell. The long, aristocratic face was hollow at cheek and temple, with a hawkish nose set between alert, dry eyes. His movements, as he served himself, were elegant, without wasted gestures. He put a small triangle of roast chicken in his mouth and chewed deliberately. Only after he swallowed did he look up again.

"Eat," he said again, this time directing himself to Napoleon. He allowed himself a small smile that was without warmth or humor. He waited until Napoleon began to eat. "Good," he said. "Now, tell me, why did you come?"

The tightness of Salazar's voice, the chilling effect of his words, made Napoleon shiver, and he could think of nothing except how much he wanted to destroy this old man.

"To make a deal," he said.

"A deal. You stole my money. You killed my bank guard. You embarrassed me and my compatriots in front of all of the people of Chiriqui, and now you want to make a deal. Very well. Give me your terms."

"I will return all the money. Well, not quite all. There were expenses..."

"Two men and a woman."

"They must not be harmed."

"What else?"

"I want to be permitted to operate here in Chiriqui."

"Operate?"

"To buy and sell cocaine. I wish to become part of your organization."

"What an impudent puppy you are. I owe you nothing."

"I can be good for you, señor, good for your partners. I can make more money for you than any other of your dealers."

"We have done all right without you, Impudent Puppy." The old man pushed his plate aside. "You have taken away my appetite. Tell me, Señor Napoleon, why should I not have you killed at once? My men are everywhere. There is no escape for you. You and those who helped you in that obscenity at the bank. You and your fat friend here."

"The money," Napoleon said.

"Oh, yes, it will be blown up if you do not make certain phone calls. Why is it that I do not believe that story?"

Napoleon placed his knife and fork down on the edge of his plate. He wiped his lips with the napkin and slowly shoved himself erect.

"Believe it or not, as you wish. I did not come here to be called a liar. Or to be threatened. I did the robbery. I am capable of doing much more. With or without your cooperation."

Salazar eyed him from out of hooded eyes. "Is it possible, you are not afraid of me?"

"I am afraid, señor."

"Perhaps you are too dull to be afraid."

"I am not stupid, señor."

"Perhaps it is only that you are too soon off the ranch and you have yet to learn anything worthwhile." He lifted his wine glass, made a face and put it aside. "You're right, of course. You can't buy or sell in Chiriqui without us." He sighed and that small fugitive smile returned. "What precisely is it you want?"

The old man rested his chin on the knuckles of his right hand and stared into space. The seconds became minutes until he lifted those feral eyes to Napoleon.

"No," he said. "You are not afraid. And neither are you a fool. Perhaps you are mad, we shall see. Very well, you have made a deal. You may buy and sell cocaine, from my organization, of course. And you will be allowed to borrow, *borrow*, one hundred thousand of those American dollars to launch your new business."

"What about Vega and Uribe?"

"We speak in one voice in this affair. But be warned. Another such mistake and it will be your last. We shall watch you carefully, young Señor Napoleon. Step out of line again and there will be no more meetings, no more deals, only swift retribution. It is understood?"

"Understood."

The old man looked down at his plate and addressed Willie Hatcher. "Take him out of here, gringo, before I change my mind and eliminate both of you. This comida has given me a sour stomach that I shall never forget..."

The ride back to the hotel was made in silence, Napoleon listening to the small, triumphant voices that were speaking for his ears only. Certainty swelled up in his gut, and he was caressed by a spreading warmth, penetrating and golden. He felt as the girl, Joan of Orleans, must have felt when she first heard her voices. Great saints and great sinners, both are irrevocably convinced of their destinies.

* * *

Napoleon showed no surprise when he discovered Nina Fuentes waiting in his room. She rose, as remarkably beautiful as he remembered her.

"I did not go with Juan-Manuel."

"He told you to stay?"

"It was my own idea. To come to you, to stay with you, to work with you. Until you tire of me."

"Has any man ever tired of you?"

"No one." She didn't smile. Then she said, "Juan-Manuel told me about the bank, what was wrong."

"I have already put it right."

"You're sure?"

"No, I am not sure. But I will make sure."

"I will help you."

"Yes, you will help. In many ways."

She crossed to where he stood, touched his smooth cheek with her finely manicured nails. "First there is this thing between us, this passion . . ."

"Yes," he murmured, his mouth finding hers. "First the passion . . ."

FOURTEEN

IT WAS A SHINING SPRING DAY, FULL OF LIGHT AND shadows, good spirits and an abundance of tourists. It was the day of Jack Keveney's first visit to Washington, D.C. The city had the grand, imperial look of a national capital, history deliberately etched into its gardens and monuments.

Keveney visited the Lincoln Memorial and the Washington Monument and at the appointed hour made his way to one of the solid, everlasting buildings on Constitution Avenue, feeling a vague unease in this bastion of politics and power.

A marble corridor brought him to a suite of offices behind a tall, dark door. A receptionist spoke his name into an intercom, then ushered him into another chamber where a man slightly younger than Keveney waited. He offered his hand and inspected Keveney with the swift competence of someone accustomed to making snap judgments.

"I'm Jim Donnelly."

"The one who called me."

"Yes. Glad you were able to make it. The secretary is anxious to meet you. You had no trouble getting away?"

Trouble, no. At Narco Division, he was virtually his own boss. At home, a few lies sufficed. Lie and deny, the twin foundations on which his married life was based.

"No trouble," he told Donnelly.

"You've certainly got all the right credentials. I thought you'd be older."

141

"Give it time." Keveney wondered why he'd come. There was nothing here for him. He'd worked with the F.B.I. from time to time, the Drug Enforcement Agency, and one or two other Federal bureaus. Always the same, haltered by red tape and arrogance, a great deal promised and little accomplished. The Feds, he'd decided, were okay when it came to extracting money from Congress and creating headlines. Less good at putting bad guys away. He waved an encompassing hand. "All this, it's not my scene."

"Let's not make hasty judgments, John. May I call you John?"

"It's Jack."

"Jack, then. Call me Jim. Wait until you hear what we've got to offer. The secretary is free now. Shall we?"

Through another tall, dark door along a narrow passageway and into the private office of the secretary of the interior. The secretary possessed a broad body, powerfully built, with a face wily and dour and a voice that rumbled irascibly out of a wide, fleshy mouth.

"I thought you'd be older."

"Give it time, Mr. Secretary."

The secretary turned to Donnelly. "How much did you tell him, James?"

"Enough to get him down here, that's all."

The secretary considered that before addressing Keveney. "They tell me you're one hell of a cop." When he received no reply, he went on. "They tell me you're the youngest captain in the New York P.D." Keveney said nothing. The secretary glanced at Donnelly, cleared his throat and said, "Not much of a talker, are you?"

"Donnelly said you wanted to talk to me."

"Yes, well. Still do, I guess. There's a job down here needs doing. Calls for a cop, a good cop. Imaginative, daring, innovative. Computer threw up your name, along with a dozen others. Most of them won't do. Got to admit, your file intrigued me. What do you say to that?"

"I think I'll listen a little bit more before I say anything."

"Sounds to me like you lack daring. Sounds to me like you're too damned cautious."

"The old-timers say—there are bold cops and there are old cops. There are no bold, old cops."

"And you want to be an old cop?"

"I want to listen. I don't know the game I'm in. I don't know the rules. I don't know the players. A little caution seems to be in order."

"Makes sense, I suppose. James, why don't you tell Captain Keveney what we have in mind."

"As you know, Jack," Donnelly began in a pedagogic lilt, "an epidemic is sweeping our country. I am talking about the importation, distribution and use of illegal drugs. Narcotics. Heroin is being brought into the country from the Orient via the West Coast. Marijuana comes up from Mexico and points south. Cocaine from Colombia, Sixaola and other places. This administration," Donnelly went on, "is committed to protecting the American people from this creeping disaster. The president, as the secretary will attest, has dedicated himself to victory over this insidious enemy. To that end, a new, highly efficient, independent organization is in the process of being established."

The secretary spoke in a slow, subdued tone, each syllable clearly enunciated. "Captain Keveney, we are talking about a body of specialists combating the drug traffickers. People, dedicated people, who will have great latitude in their charter and the most up-to-date equipment available to accomplish their ends." His voice faded and he lowered his long chin to his chest.

James Donnelly said, "So there you have it, a high-tech, high-impact drug team working outside established police bureaus and with access to all of the in-house assets. Should extra personnel be needed, it will be supplied. Ditto extra equipment, funds, etcetera. We call the team D-Group." Donnelly smiled at Keveney. "What do you think, Jack?"

"Catchy name," Keveney said flatly.

"Well, are you interested?"

"In what?"

"In running the show, Captain," the Secretary muttered with some annoyance. "Why'n hell do you think we had you come down here? We are talking about accomplishing great things here. We intend to put an end to the drug trade."

Keveney gathered his thoughts and spoke directly to the secretary. "I'm willing to give you good marks for intentions, Mr. Secretary, but all the cops, the DEA, customs, the Border Patrol—all of us and our intentions don't cut off more'n ten percent of the stuff that comes into the country each year. The demand is there. The profits are there. People willing to do the job are there. So much for intentions."

"Does that mean you won't take the job?" Donnelly said.

"It means the whole damned country is spinning its wheels. Unless—"

The secretary inched forward. "Unless, Captain Keveney?"

"There are two ways to do it."

"And they are?"

"Wipe out the pot plantations, destroy the poppy fields, burn coca where it grows."

"That requires the active and public cooperation of other sovereign countries which don't always see eye to eye with us. The second way . . . ?"

"Rip out head, body and tail in one swift move, Mr. Secretary."

"Explain, please."

"Each drug organization has its own sources of supply, its executive officer, administration, its own chain of command, its own distribution and sales people and security force. Zero in on an entire operation, go after them all, top to bottom, arrest and convict. To hell with picking up street guys pushing dime bags of coke."

"But how?" Donnelly said.

"Any way you can. Harass them at every level. Disrupt, destroy, locate the weak spots and turn them around. Interrupt the flow of drugs into the country and the flow of money out. Get 'em on collusion and conspiracy, if nothing else. Whatever will stick. The way Internal Revenue got Capone in the old days."

"That would require a worldwide force of people," the secretary said.

"You fight a war wherever you find the enemy."

The secretary waited a long time before he spoke again in that low, slow way of his. "Assuming the job were yours, Keveney, what would you need?"

"Money."

"That part's easy."

"The right people."

"You'd have the power to hire and fire as you saw fit."

"And independence."

Now it was Donnelly's turn to break in. "We all have to answer to higher authority. You take too much upon yourself."

"The people I'd hire would answer only to me."

"And you, sir," the secretary said, "would answer to me, only to me. And I answer to the president. That's the way it is. Now, do you want the position?"

Keveney hesitated. The job was tempting. If it proved to be all it was painted to be, he would be able to make a major dent in the international drug trade. He would be able to hit the *peses gordo,* as the Latinos called them, where they were most vulnerable. Make truly serious busts.

"Well, sir," the secretary intoned. "I am offering you a position."

Keveney formulated his answer carefully before replying.

A driving rain was falling when Jack Keveney reached the house in Queens. It was late and the house was still and he hoped Rosie and Patrick were all asleep, as he was in no mood for conversation.

He shrugged out of his jacket and loosened his tie and went after a beer. In the kitchen, he sat at the old English pine table that Rosie was so fond of and took a long pull on the Bud. He lit a cigarette and began reviewing the events of the day in his mind. Soon he heard footsteps coming up behind him, but he kept himself from turning.

"Didn't mean to wake you," he said.

Rosie sat opposite him. Her hair hung loose across her shoulders and for a brief interlude she looked as young and vulnerable as she had when he saw her for the first time. She was, he conceded silently, a remarkably handsome woman; he wished she had remained in bed, asleep. He wasn't ready to talk, he needed time to reflect, to weigh his decision and the ramifications of that decision.

"How did your day go?" It was the sort of question his mother would have asked.

He emptied his lungs of air. "Interesting." He shrugged as if to acknowledge the inadequacy of the answer. "They offered me a job."

She inclined her head and waited.

That too reminded him of his mother. The same silent patience —no, endurance, Christian endurance—as if any reaction to his news would at least be a venial sin. When he'd told his mother he was joining the cops, she had simply examined his face as if seeing it for the first time, saying nothing...

"You outta your mind?"

That was his father speaking. Mike Keveney, a street laborer with an impoverished past, a bleak future and a present that offered few rewards, held the police to be the workingman's natural enemy. Next to the bosses, of course. The wiseguys on Eleventh Avenue, the Democratic District Leader, the boyos drinking beer at the local Irish bar, those were his intimates and allies.

"You wanna job, I'll talk to McSorley. Charlie'll arrange something fine for you."

"I want to be a cop," Keveney had insisted, and in that tense family moment, he understood that it was true. Becoming a cop was the most important thing in the world, and nothing would change that for him.

He brought his eyes up to meet his wife's unwavering stare. "A new agency, working out of Washington. They call it D-Group. The idea is to go after a drug organization from top to bottom."

"They want you to leave the cops?"

"They want me to run the whole ball of wax." His mouth

curled, less a smile than a grimace. "No more surprise calls in the night."

The words were a mistake. They made him think of Officer Nicholson, and so did she, though she had never learned the name of her husband's lover.

He was graying around the edges, and the boyish cast of his face was tempered by a fan of laugh lines at the corners of his eyes and the deep creases around his mouth. A faintly shadowed beard made him appear slightly disreputable, dyspeptic almost, as if he'd recently swallowed something distasteful.

He was changing in ways she did not understand. Her husband, her lover, father of her son; he had become a stranger to her and she to him. So many agonies, she reminded herself, so many separate pleasures. So many singular victories and defeats. Still sleeping in the same bed, they existed apart from each other, sharing nothing of importance, neither fears nor hopes nor the small necessary vicissitudes of daily life.

"They'll plant you behind a desk," she warned.

"I'll be able to get out into the field whenever I choose. My own boss, I'll be my own boss. What am I now, just a paper cop, getting nowhere."

She made no reply.

He felt compelled to convince. "More than twice the pay. A job like this one, I'll be able to make things happen. Take out the big fish."

"Sounds like you've made up your mind."

"It's the chance of a lifetime." Then, after a moment: "It means moving to Washington."

She thought about that. "What about my job, Patrick's school, his friends."

"We're a family."

She brought herself around in her chair in a succession of small, awkward adjustments until she faced him squarely. "We haven't been a proper family for a long time."

He wished she had remained in bed, asleep or feigning sleep. There was much to be said for deception in the name of peace. Hypocrisy made life bearable, eliminated so many conflicts, allowed angers to recede, allowed the flat, tasteless daily routine to go on.

"What are you saying to me?"

"When was the last time you spent an evening at home? Helping Patrick with his homework. Playing basketball with him. Watching TV together. When was the last time you and I went to a movie or restaurant? When was the last time you touched me?"

"I thought you didn't want me . . ."

"I didn't. I don't. You and your life away from here. The cops, being with your friends, the danger. You love all of it. And the women."

"I told you, that's over, been over for a long time."

"Why don't I believe you, Jack? It was a mistake, our getting married. I should never have married you, Jack."

"You don't mean that."

"Damn it, yes I do. Damn your being a cop, damn all cops. Damn that secret male loyalty of yours. Damn the nights you spent drinking with cops, leaving me alone. Damn the women who hang around cops as if they were rock stars. Damn, damn all of you."

"You don't know what you're saying."

"You don't want me to know. You come home. You're so careless with our needs, our feelings, our lives. Announcing you've become a fed. 'We're moving to Washington, Rosie. Pack up, pack up our son.' Who the hell do I know in Washington? Does Patrick have friends there? Do I? What kind of a life will we lead? But here I have a life, not perfect, not full, but in many ways rewarding. My son, my friends, my job. Did you ever stop to consider my hopes, my dreams about the future? Washington, that's your life." She paused, struggling not to weep, to keep her voice under control. "I am not going to Washington."

"Okay," he answered after an interval. "I'll phone 'em tomorrow, tell 'em I changed my mind. They can find another boy."

A tormented wail died in her mouth and she hugged herself as if in pain. "No! It's where you belong. It's your *work*. Your life, your duty."

He considered her words. "Okay. Maybe that's the best way. I'll

get a small apartment down there and come up here on week-
ends. That way—"

"No!" she hissed with renewed frustration. How could a man so
aggressive, violent even, a man daring and determined beyond
other men, a man able to walk into a street brawl or a gun fight,
be so passive, so lacking in emotion? The betrayal, his betrayal of
her, was complete. "No weekend marriage, Jack. No commuting.
No marriage anymore."

"What the hell are you saying?"

"That it's over, Jack, all of it." She spoke weakly, all energy
suddenly drained away. "I want us to get a divorce."

In the morning, Jack Keveney headed out. He felt youthful and
cheerful, vibrating with anticipation, all excess luggage left behind. From now on, he vowed, nothing would be permitted to
come between him and his work. He couldn't have been happier.

FIFTEEN

AT AGE TWENTY-TWO, NAPOLEON CRUZ CUT A DIS-
tinctive figure in Chiriqui. He towered over most of his country-
men—he carried his six feet, four inches of height with the stiff
bearing of a military cadet. His shoulders were wide and bony, his
long body sinewy, lean, deceptively strong. When he moved it
was with spidery grace and delicacy that made him seem almost
weightless—and ominous.

His face, too, was long, the bones in clear outline under his
swart, taut skin. His eyes, set deep under arching black brows,
were flint-hard and opaque, and his mouth was mobile, slow to
smile, as if he carried within him the racial melancholy of every
one of his Indian ancestors. His thick black hair was cut close to
his scalp in a vaguely military style.

Other men were wary and fearful of his power, as if sensing the
swift move to violence of which he was capable. Women were
drawn to him, saw him as mysterious and dangerous, a threat to
their nesting instincts; yet few women who met him were prepared to refuse him anything. He made few male friends and ignored most women; except Nina Fuentes, of course.

This day, this bright, high April morning, was one of the best
days of his young life. For it was on this day that he was going to
move into his new house. To term it merely a house was to do the
structure Napoleon had caused to be built on a hillside north of
Chiriqui a severe injustice. For so long a hallucination, an amal-
gam of dreams and fantasies entertained throughout his years,
stone by carved stone it had at last been brought into being.

151

It began with rough drawings made by Napoleon himself, childish scrawls that provided naked hints of what grandiose ideas simmered in his imagination. An architect imported from Buenos
Aires—a man trained in the United States and heralded for his
unique designs—was provided with those odd squares and rec-
tangles, those misshapen ovals and rounds that signified Napoleon's deepest longings for a home of his own.

"Everything," he instructed the architect, "must be perfect."

The architect, dazzled by a fee twice the amount he would have
dared asked for, conceded that perfection was what he had in
mind.

"Money is no object," Napoleon pointed out. "I have deposited
two million dollars in a special account for the building of the
house. When more is required, it will be made available. Are my
drawings clear to you?"

"Clear," the architect retorted. Equally clear were the unstated
cravings of his peon drug dealer for a permanent base, for the
security of a home of his own to cloak himself and his nefarious
activities with the appearance of respectability. Everything was
entirely clear. He tapped one piece of paper and the drawing it
represented. "Except this, what is this?"

"A wall," Napoleon replied.

"It will obstruct the view. A house on that hill, you will be able
to see to the horizon . . . but this . . ." He searched for a word to
express his revulsion at the peon's limitations and lack of good
taste. "This thing . . ."

"There is nothing to see, some trees, the fields, the city to the
south. I have seen them all. The wall is a necessity. It should be
three meters in height at least with shards of sharp glass imbedded in concrete at the top. That way no one will dare enter . . ."

"No one," the architect agreed. "This will take at least a year to
build."

"The wall?"

"The house."

"Employ as many men as you need. The best workers, the best
craftsmen."

"All this space, I make it out to be thirty-two rooms."

"Exactly."

"Are you sure—and seventeen bathrooms?"

"You think there should be more?"

"Seventeen seems sufficient. And the garage. You will have the only underground garage in Sixaola."

"Yes,'" Napoleon gloated. "I learned of such a thing in an American magazine."

The architect sighed; if only he needed the money less he would have refused this crass, vulgar man as a client. Instead he accepted the job and went to work. And now, one year, one month later, the house stood ready for Napoleon and his entourage to move in.

A large black Mercedes limousine drove through the immense, hand-carved wooden gates on this April morning, and as it pulled to a stop the gates swung noiselessly back into place, enclosing Napoleon's private world from any possible threat.

Napoleon led the way out of the Mercedes. Next came Nina Fuentes, then Willie Hatcher. Behind Willie came a short, stout woman who planted herself some distance from the others, arms folded across her ample breasts, surveying the scene with a stoic face. At her shoulder stood an adolescent boy.

"Well?" Napoleon said, gesturing. "Have you ever seen anything like it?"

An uneasy silence was broken finally by Willie Hatcher. "No," he said honestly. "Nothing like it."

"What do you think, Nina?" Napoleon said.

She answered slowly. "It is like a fortress."

Napoleon clapped his hands together as if in approval. "Exactly. It is my fortress, my hacienda. From here I will conduct my business affairs. Entertain when necessary. Here my friends and associates can live or visit. They will find everything they require. There is a swimming pool in the back, the water purified and heated. And I have my own movie theatre. Every bedroom has its own bathroom—you must see the bathrooms. Special marble was imported from Italy and carved into sinks and tubs and toilets. Only hand-painted tiles were used. And special woods." His voice rose with excitement. "We make our own electricity so that when the city loses power, here there shall be light. And hot water. Nothing has been overlooked..." He swung around to the short, stout woman. "Well, Rosa, have you nothing to say?"

"It is the finest hacienda I have ever seen, Señor Cruz."

"The kitchen is such as you will not believe, Rosa. Stainless steel and polished tile, of an immense size. Entire cold rooms to store meat and other things. You will be able to feed an army from such a kitchen, Rosa."

"Si, señor." Her face was closed with that traditional campesino clench that allows no hidden thought to be read.

"There will be parties here, Rosa, of such grandness as you have never imagined."

"Si, señor."

"And you will be in charge of everything. The kitchen. The house. All of it."

"It is large," the woman said stolidly. "Such an establishment, no woman alone can run such an establishment."

"Hire people. All that you need. You are in charge."

"It will cost a great deal."

"The money, you need only say how much you need and it will be there, yes."

"Si, señor."

"Good. Begin at once. Today. When you decide what you need, tell me. All shall be as you wish, Rosa. Here you and your son—" For the first time he glanced at the boy and a deliberate smile curled his wide, Indian mouth. "You and Carlito shall have your own apartment, a bedroom for you each. As this is my home, so shall it be yours. Agreed?"

Rosa nodded solemnly. The decision, she acknowledged silently, had been made long before this morning. Made as much by Señorita Nina as by herself. She was committed, and at the end of five years, when she had accumulated money enough to live for the rest of her life, she would be allowed to leave, if that was her desire. So she would live the lie she had agreed to, keep her mouth shut and her eyes averted and do the job she was hired to do. Aloud, in a subservient voice, she said, "Agreed, señor."

Satisfied, Napoleon turned again to Carlito. At fifteen, the boy possessed an air of self-control, of inner authority, as if he had already determined his worth in the world and his rightful place in it. He wore a white shirt, open at the neck, and white trousers. On his feet were a pair of huaraches. Of medium height, he wore his dark hair long, almost to his shoulders. His cheeks were brown and smooth, with a faint flush of youth and good health. His eyes were very much like Napoleon's eyes, obsidian, unforgiving, hidden. When he smiled, his teeth were white, small and regular. He was beautiful standing in the sunlight, and his hair sparkled when he moved his head.

"You like your new home, little one?"

"I do not yet know, señor. It is a very grand house, the hacienda of a god."

Napoleon accepted the compliment in silent modesty. "Come," he said. "I will show you all my house."

The entrance foyer was dark and cool, with a dome of red brick fashioned to form a perfect arch about their heads. On one white wall, an elaborate Cristus, larger than life, looked down on them from the massive cross on which he hung. The face of Jesus was serene, his nose long and aquiline, his mouth in repose.

His agony seemed remote. Yet his white robe was dotted with crimson drops of blood, and a circle of thorns had been painstakingly carved and gold-leafed around his pale forehead. He seemed unapproachable, a Christ made only for the great of the world.

"He blessed this house," Nina Fuentes said, uncharacteristically, her voice echoing in the vaulted dimness of the foyer. They moved on. Next, the kitchen, and even Rosa, with her frozen face, gasped at the huge space with its restaurant stove, walk-in cold rooms, pastry room, butler's pantry, and row upon row of shelves upon which platters and glasses were neatly arranged. "I can cook for three hundred people here," she said.

"You will," Napoleon promised her.

They moved on through room after room. Napoleon, drawn inexorably to Carlito, beckoned him to his side, and the two of them led the way.

Napoleon's suite was in the rear of the house, isolated from the rest. It consisted of two adjacent bedrooms, and a relatively small living room, with a fireplace. One of the bedrooms was for Nina. Each bedroom had its private bathroom complete with a whirlpool tub and a separate shower. There were towel warmers, a bidet in Nina's quarters, the walls lined with mirrors, some of which concealed medicine cabinets.

At last they ended up in the underground garage, which had been built into the side of the hill beneath the house. Two immense steel doors opened to the outside, each operated independently by a radio signal, the transmitter for which had been built into each of Napoleon's five cars. There was the black Mercedes 600S which had carried them to the hacienda; and in the garage itself, a Maserati, two Rolls Royces and a spotless white Cadillac.

"This garage," Napoleon pointed out, "will accommodate ten automobiles, at least." He turned to Carlito, his arm resting lightly across the boy's shoulders. "Well, have you nothing to say?"

"Impressive, señor."

Napoleon displayed his gleaming teeth in what passed for a smile, shifting his glance to Nina. "And you, my dear, you also are impressed?"

"Very much so, Napoleon. It is all very grand, a proper setting for a man of such wealth and such power."

"Willie?" Napoleon said softly.

Hatcher rolled his thick shoulders. "It is indeed as much a fortress as a home."

"Exactly," Napoleon replied, pleased with himself.

"There is just one thing," Carlito said gravely, his glance bold and steady.

"And that is?"

"The house is on a hill, good. All the approaches are covered from behind the wall, also good. But there is one more thing that might have been done."

Napoleon frowned. "And that is?"

"Señor, I would have provided a way out, an escape, just in case. The house is magnificent. But it could become as much a prison for those within as it is a fortress to those without."

Napoleon made a snap decision. "Show him," he said to Willie.

Hatcher pressed a button on the near wall. A six-foot section of the back wall lifted up, revealing a narrow passage. Fluorescent tubes lit the way.

"The tunnel runs through the hill," Napoleon said, "and it ends at the helicopter pad below. Soon a plane will be there. Always fueled, always manned. Twenty-four hours a day, ready for take-off." The door slid back into place.

Carlito nodded his beautiful head. "Excellent," he said.

"Aiee," Napoleon said softly. "How like me you are, little one. You know what they used to call me. Little Fish."

"Then I am a minnow," Carlito said.

"Minnow. That is a good name too."

Abruptly, Napoleon was in high good humor. "It's a beautiful day," he said. "I feel like driving." He looked at Nina. "We'll go in the Maserati. The rest of you can drive back in the Mercedes."

He was halfway to the car when he heard Carlito calling. "Permit me, señor."

"Yes?"

"Let your chauffeur drive the Maserati out of the garage."

"Why?"

"Permit me, señor. When a man is rich and powerful, he has many friends. But he also has many enemies. Let the chauffeur start it. It is his job."

Napoleon nodded. "Little Minnow, you are invaluable." He sent for Antonio, the revolutionary, now his chauffeur.

The little man inspected the Maserati. Very gently he opened the hood. He ran his hands over the enormous motor and shone a flashlight into its guts. Satisfied, he closed the hood of the car and crept underneath it. They could hear him moving about. At last he reappeared and said briefly, "It is clean, señor."

"You will check them all routinely," Napoleon said.

Antonio jerked his head in assent. On orders from the Señorita Nina, he had already begun a routine inspection of each vehicle before it was put into use. But he saw no need to mention that, no need to in any way fuel a competition that might erupt among Napoleon's followers.

He watched Napoleon and Nina climb into the Maserati. A deep satisfying roar of the engine and the sports car screeched as

it sped out of the garage. With a suitable amount of obsequious-
ness, the little chauffeur led the others back to where the Mercedes waited, staid, solid and reassuring.

Napoleon drove the Maserati along the winding road back toward Chiriqui, thick clouds of dust trailing behind. A silent laugh
broke out of him and Nina marked it as one of the few times she
had seen him laugh. His face in profile, as handsome and perfect
as ever, had taken on a thickening air of authority. Despite his
youth, he had truly matured and become a man in all things, in all
ways.

"Carlito," Napoleon said, speaking above the roar of the Maserati. "A special boy, no?"

"Very special," she agreed, putting her eyes back on the narrow
road. Off to the left, a peon worked a wooden plow behind a team
of plodding oxen. He paused to watch the speeding car. How to
reconcile the two, Nina thought; Napoleon was a man of this time,
and the farmer still existed in the eighteenth century.

"How fortunate," Napoleon said, "that you were able to find
Rosa to run my house for me. How fortunate she has a son like
Carlito."

"How fortunate," she mused, her mind reaching backward and
forward in time. Her intricate scheme, the extended search she
had made, the careful planning and rehearsal, all of it had worked.
And there was no reason for it not to continue to work to Napoleon's benefit and her own.

Napoleon, she told herself, though he was unaware of it himself, was in love for the second time in his life. A kind of love
Napoleon did not entirely understand. A kind of love he might
have mocked and scorned before Carlito came along.

Nina gave a quiet sigh of resignation and relief. So much of
herself had gone into the scheme, so much depended on it. It had
taken nearly three months to discover Rosa, cooking for a family of
norteamericanos in Bogotá. And it had taken the promise of immense amounts of money to win Rosa away from them. She was
worth every *centavo;* Rosa was smart and reliable, and she understood that only a secret never spoken aloud could remain a secret.

Carlito, on the other hand, came from Mexico City where he had run errands for the girls in a fancy brothel that catered to the men of the upper classes. He, too, was smart and dependable and understood that Nina was offering him a rich and exciting future that he could never otherwise hope to achieve.

So Nina brought them together, Rosa and Carlito, and rehearsed them in the requirements of their respective jobs. Mother and son; she insisted they believe their roles for only in that way would Napoleon believe it. Both exceeded her expectations and no one would ever have thought to question their relationship.

Why had she brought Carlito to Chiriqui, offered him to her employer, her master, her lover? She had sensed a need in Napoleon that even he was unaware of, a need that could not be spoken about until Napoleon was ready to address it.

After a few years of living with Napoleon, she came to understand that she would never be able to fulfill him completely. No woman could. But she had managed to figure out his sexual mix, his inconsistent needs, needs that he had yet to recognize. It was vital, therefore, that he be kept content, that his frustrations not be allowed to spill over and work against her. She intended to be a part of Napoleon's world for as long as possible; it was too satisfying, too enriching, to allow anything to spoil her chances.

So it was that Nina insinuated Carlito into Napoleon's life, into *their* life together. Oh, yes, she had become aware of Napoleon's diminishing interest in her. With decreasing frequency did he invite her into his bed. And when he did, the imagination and passion that fired his lovemaking was often lacking; he merely went through the motions. That very indifference excited her more, made her want him more, made her yearn to please him. She began bringing him gifts. A heavy gold chain that he wore around his neck. A gold Rolex watch studded with diamonds. A massive linked bracket for his wrist, also solid gold. But the greatest gift of all—Carlito.

Beautiful to look at. Unpredictable and cunning. With the promise of a smoldering adolescent sexuality that would provoke and gratify a man or a woman.

It was her dream. That Carlito would bring her and Napoleon closer together, create a rejuvenated passion, a renewed intimacy. And if Carlito was required to bring that about, so be it. As long as she was a partner to it all.

Carlito understood what was required of him and was committed to fulfilling his part of the bargain, to winning Napoleon's admiration and interest and affection. Nina was convinced of that; she had recognized the hard, hot gleam in the boy's eye for what it was. Napoleon was not the only one falling in love.

"Bustamente must go," Napoleon said, his voice without emotion. Telephones evoked a strong feeling of distrust in him, and he suspected that unfriendly ears were always listening in. He preferred face-to-face conversations, particularly when such important and delicate matters as Sixaola's chief justice were concerned. "He gives me no choice," he ended flatly.

Raphael Salazar's tremulous voice replied diffidently, which Napoleon took as a sign of the old man's faltering strength.

"There is always a choice in such matters. There are always ways..."

Napoleon broke in, a rudeness that would have been out of the question only a few months earlier. "I have tried all the ways. My emissaries have spoken to the man. He has been offered money, large amounts of money. All efforts fail. Bustamente is incorruptible and unafraid."

"Ah," Salazar breathed softly. "A brave and honest man—what a terrible liability."

"Bustamente hands out prison terms to my people..."

"And mine, my son. Still—"

"Some of my best men are in jail."

"Ours is a harsh business with many risks. Nevertheless, the rewards are great."

"Bustamente must go," Napoleon repeated.

"There is one thing," Salazar said. "The man has a weakness for beautiful women. Perhaps blackmail... A man in his high office, married, with children of his own. How can a society be strong when its leaders act like moral pygmies? I am concerned for the future . . ."

Napoleon's impatience increased. "Do I have your permission, señor? To deal with Bustamente as I must?"

"Let me consider this matter."

"There is not so much time . . ."

"We will work out something."

"Soon?"

"Oh," Salazar answered without urgency. "Soon enough."

Napoleon swore silently at the dead phone. Salazar was old, losing the sharp edge that had made him the power he was in Sixaola. Once he was a man of strong convictions, able to act on those convictions. Recently he seemed to postpone action—no matter how necessary—a man locked into his dotage and unable any longer to assert himself. But Napoleon was young and strong and decisive; he could do whatever was required.

Bustamente. Chief justice of the federal court. His removal would have three results: a sharp prod would be removed from Napoleon's professional side, a greater fear would be instilled in the hearts of the judiciary and the police of the nation and an important job would open that Napoleon himself might be able to fill with a man of his own choosing.

Oh, yes, Bustamente must go, he said to himself. He repeated the words aloud, lifting his eyes to where Carlito sat in a comfortable chair across the room. The boy was reading a comic book.

"What do you think, Little Minnow?"

Carlito looked up, face and voice without expression. "You have never hesitated before to remove an obstacle from your path, why now?"

Napoleon shook his head. "You do not understand—Salazar, the other Regents. They work with me. They tolerate me. They say I am their equal. Yet I sense that to them I am still an outsider, not quite on their level. It is necessary to give them no cause . . ."

"You are afraid of them?"

Napoleon said, "No one else dares speak to me that way."

Carlito stood up. "You want me to leave?"

"Sit down." Carlito obeyed. "What there is between us is between us. But never forget who I am, and what I am."

"Shall I tell you that I am sorry?"

"That is not necessary. Instead tell me what you believe I should do."

The boy said, "Bustamente, it can be done quietly. . ."

"No. People should know that Napoleon did the job."

"Señor, getting rid of Bustamente is second only to getting rid of the president himself. Everybody will know. You are very powerful, you do not have to advertise your power, it is part of everything you do. Do it quietly. Talk to Nina. It will be more frightening if the chief justice is removed without fuss, without bother." Carlito snapped his fingers. "As you would kill a fly."

Napoleon remembered what Salazar had said: "The man has a weakness for beautiful women." "Yes," he said. "Nina . . ."

He found Nina standing at the edge of the outdoor living room looking to the west. The afternoon sun bathed her face in light and outlined her exquisite figure under the thin white dress she wore. She was, Napoleon reminded himself, the most beautiful and special of women. For a long interval he stood watching her, making no sound, not wanting to shatter the tranquil moment. She spoke without turning.

"The sea is beyond the mountains." She turned to face him. "The ocean is restful, its rhythms strangely stirring. It excites me to listen to the waves and calms me at the same time. A paradox, no?" Her smile was languorous. "You wish to speak with me, Napoleon?"

"There is a man named Bustamente."

"The chief justice?"

"He is troublesome in so many ways. He refuses to change, resists my offers of friendship."

"He is your enemy."

"My enemy, yes."

"You wish me to—eliminate your enemy?"

"With discretion. Yet in such a way that all will understand who is responsible. A lesson must be learned."

"Trust me."

"With my life, *chiquita*." He crossed to where she stood and took her hand in his. "I will be away for a few days. To visit Negrete. To see to business."

"Business?" She laughed. "Whatever happened to Juan-Manuel's political dedication? Where is the revolution he was going to make? That all of us were going to make?"

"Negrete plans and his army grows. He has nearly eight hundred men under arms. He gets stronger every week. When the time is right, I shall give him the word, and he will strike. The revolution will begin."

"*Your* revolution."

"Yes, mine. My army. My revolution. And one day, who knows, this may become my country."

"You have large ambitions, dear Napoleon. Already you are one of the wealthiest, most powerful men in the country. But that is not enough, is it?"

He released her hand and looked out beyond the stone wall surrounding the house. It occurred to him that perhaps there would never be enough. Not for him.

Chavoya's was by far the best restaurant in the capital city of Sixaola. It was expensive—and the food and drink was worthy of the cost—and the expense limited the clientele to a sedate, select company. Only those who could afford the exorbitant prices came here; only those who required quiet and privacy bothered to come. Chavoya's was divided into a succession of intimate dining rooms, each one served by attentive and skilled waiters, all overseen by the owner himself, a sleek, soft-spoken man named Hernandez. He knew all his guests by name, greeting each as an old friend and seeing to his comfort. Here meals were prepared to order and no order was too outlandish, no demand could not be fulfilled. Unlike most restaurants in Sixaola, Chavoya's welcomed women alone. Each night a handful of them could be seen dining by themselves, although seldom did they leave alone. A discrete introduction was Hernandez's speciality, and when he informed an interested man that a certain woman was not for him, that man accepted Hernandez's judgment without question; Hernandez was known for his impeccable taste.

Thus, on this night, Hernandez displayed no surprise when one of his honored guests, Chief Justice Eduardo Bustamente, displayed a great deal of interest in the dark-haired young beauty who sat alone at a small table near the fireplace in the rear dining room.

"Who is she?" Bustamente wanted to know.

"The mistress of an American businessman who comes and goes, señor. At this time he is gone and she is very much alone."

"And lonely?"

"In my opinion," Hernandez allowed quietly.

Bustamente, a fleshy man in a conservative suit, rubbed his thick hands together. "Lonely and alone. How fortunate for me, my friend. Or is it?"

"Shall I speak to her on your behalf, señor?"

"It would give me great pleasure to dine with her. She would be my guest, of course."

"Of course." Hernandez backed away. He made his way to the back dining room, pausing here and there to exchange pleasantries with his guests, finally pausing at Nina Fuentes's side.

"Señorita," he began, with a half bow. He knew that the chief justice was watching from his place in the adjoining dining room.

"Señor Hernandez," she replied. "Would you fill my wine glass again?"

"With pleasure. But may I suggest that you might enjoy your wine even more with Chief Justice Bustamente. He would appreciate your company..."

"He sent you to say so?"

"Indeed, Señorita."

She smiled up at the man. "You do your job very well, Hernandez. I will mention that to Napoleon."

"Señor Cruz should know that I am always at his service. And yours, Señorita."

"Of course." She rose and spoke for his ears only. "This meeting never took place, Hernandez. I am not here. I have never been here. I have never dined with Bustamente."

"I understand."

"Your continued good health depends on your understanding."

He grew pale under her gaze and ushered her over to Busta-mente, made the introductions and hurried away. She presented a faintly shy, faintly breathless visage to Bustamente, her remark-able eyes wide, the pupils limned with white, her full lips parted, moist and inviting.

"Señor, it is such an honor to meet a man of your importance. I am so excited..."

Bustamente silently agreed; he was one of the most important men in all of Sixaola. Powerful, wealthy, still handsome with a full head of shining black hair. Yes, why wouldn't a young woman be honored? Why wouldn't she be excited? He meant to do his best to further provoke that excitement, rouse it to new heights, be-stow upon her all his manliness and manly power. He took her delicate hand in his.

"You, my dear, are a uniquely beautiful child and it is I who should be honored."

Nina lowered her eyes modestly and after a moment withdrew her hand. Fingertips lingering against his. Now. she told herself, came the hard part, the long boring hours listening to this fat fool trying to seduce her. Listening to his inane talk about himself, his career, his achievements, his conquests. But listen she did, and she nibbled delicately at the dishes Bustamente insisted she try, and she sipped his wine and allowed his knee to make contact with her own, to linger in place.

She listened faintly to the rush of seductive words he sent her way, remarking silently on his lack of imagination, the absence of spontaneity and sensual warmth; the chief justice was a performer and his act was well-rehearsed. How ardent his attention, how eager his demeanor, how hard he strove to win what she had already decided to bestow. How boring he was. She removed her-self from the present, opened herself to the past, and people who cast no shadows wandered through her mind, memories as incor-poreal as angels. How far she had come. How far, how far. How very damned far.

*   *   *

Nina Fuentes became a sinner of monumental proportions in the eyes of God, the Holy Roman Church and in her own fevered imagination when she was only eleven years old. Her father, Hector Fuentes, was the perverted device chosen to make her know the depth and seriousness of her depravity and wicked ways.

Hector was a minor civil servant in the administration of the town of Celaya in the hill country in the west of Sixaola, not far from the capital city.

Having been graduated from the regional branch of the national university, Hector considered himself an intellectual, a man destined to do great things with his life. Unhappily, his natural gifts were minimal, his tolerance for hard work small and his interest in the cantinas of Celaya overwhelming. Hector was a confirmed drunk, a chronic critic of life around him and a dedicated adulterer. He grew more and more bitter as men of lesser talents were promoted over him, as fewer and fewer women responded to his drunken advances, as he watched his life dissolving into an alcoholic mist.

On the night of Nina's fall from grace, Hector returned home drunk and abusive. He complained about the dinner his wife, Nina's mother, Dolores, had prepared. He told her she was a poor cook, an extravagant woman who squandered his hard-earned money in secret ways; he accused her of being an adulteress. When Dolores denied everything, he struck her and continued to beat her until, sobbing and bleeding, Dolores fled their tiny adobe house. Hector, his rage unabated, directed himself toward his daughter, accusing her of being just as bad a female child as her mother was a wife and a woman.

"Oh, no, Papa, I am a good girl. Mama is a good woman."

Infuriated at such defiance, he slapped the child, sending her stumbling to the floor. He followed, both fists swinging. She shielded her face behind crossed arms and, frustrated in his efforts to punish her, his anger increased. He pushed her arms aside, pinning her to the floor, held her in place by the weight of his own body. He cursed her, cursed her mother, cursed all women for ruining his life, and then with a startling suddenness he pressed his mouth down upon hers. How quickly it all happened, as if in a dream. He forced her legs apart, situating himself between her young thighs, his penis hard and painful as he thrust it unmercifully into her vagina, beating her down against the floor. And through the pain, through her anguish and guilt, there was born in her a direct link between violence and pleasure.

"It is all your fault," Hector accused her afterwards, striking her once more. "You made me do this thing. And should you speak of it to anyone, you will have to be punished. By God in heaven and by me. Do you understand?"

"Yes, Papa. I will tell no one."

"No one."

"Yes, Papa," she wept.

"And who can say," he ended. "I may be nice to you again . . ."

Hector Fuentes slept with his daughter whenever the opportunity presented itself after that. He insisted she do those things that pleased him and in return he gave her his attention and his love, as he put it. And each time, while Hector was inside her, she imagined she was killing him, that his life's blood was emptying into her belly.

It went on for nearly a year, until the afternoon her mother returned from her job as a school teacher to find her husband and her daughter in bed together. There was considerable shouting and crying, accusations and vows of renewed fidelity and passion. Until, in the end, Nina was banished from the house, packed off to live with a distant cousin in the capital city.

Six months later, when Nina learned that her father had been run down and killed by a truck, she went into the nearest cantina and offered herself in celebration to a man who looked very much like Hector. She shed no tears for the dead man.

By then many other men had been struck by her blossoming beauty and had used her. Among them was the son of her cousin, a muscular retard with bloated muscles and oversized genitals. He too beat her and in a moment of uncharacteristic generosity, gave her to four of his *compadres* who kept her locked in a room for forty-eight hours, using her when they wished. While in that room, she plotted her revenge.

When finally they released her, she went back to her cousin's

house and cleansed herself and treated her wounds. She packed
what few belongings she owned and went out into the streets. For
two nights she tracked her cousin's son from place to place. Finally she confronted him in a poorly lit and narrow street that
separated a police barracks from a string of tiny shops, all closed at
this hour.

"Hola, Pedro!" she greeted her cousin's son.

"Hola, Nina! where have you been? I have been thinking about
you." He clutched his genitals in grinning emphasis. "My friends
have been thinking of you. You get better looking all the time and
I think your tits have grown. Here, let me see." His coarse hands
reached out for her.

She submitted to his touch, one hand clutching at his belt. In
her right hand, hanging at her side, was a serrated cutting knife
she had removed from his mother's kitchen. He kissed her, his
huge flaccid tongue penetrating deep into her mouth. She drew
him in and then plunged the knife into his belly with all the force
she could muster. He grunted and fell back, eyes wide in surprise
and pain. She struck a second time, higher between his ribs, aiming directly for his heart.

"Aieee!" he cried. "You have killed me! Why have you killed
me? Why . . . ?"

She left him in the narrow street, aware of the immense satisfaction she felt, aware of her rising excitement, of her need for a
man.

Nina learned to survive in the capital city. To survive with guile,
with wisdom, with a certain developing style. She worked in a
shop selling Sixaolan crafts to foreign tourists. She worked as a
waitress. She worked for a member of the American embassy,
cleaning and doing the laundry, and it was here that she learned
to speak English the way Americans spoke it. La Señora took a
liking to the girl and taught her to read and write in English and
filled her head with glorious tales of life in the United States.
Then, without warning one day, La Señora announced that her
husband had been transferred, that they were leaving the capital
city, leaving Sixaola, and that Nina and the other servants were

out of work. Two weeks later Nina went to work as a cook in one of the most exclusive brothels in the city.

It was here that she met Alexandro, who was a professor of political science at the National University. Enamored of the beautiful young girl, Alexandro made arrangements to see her away from the brothel. He took her to the movies, to the theater, to concerts. He gave her books to read and introduced her to Marx and Lenin, spoke in glowing terms about Mao Tse-tung and Fidel Castro, spun romantic stories about Che Guevera, about his betrayal and death in the mountains of Bolivia. Alexandro convinced her that power indeed came out of the barrel of a gun, that only those with power would change the world, that only a Marxist revolution could create a new man, a new life for all peoples.

So, when the time came, a few years later, Nina Fuentes, by then in the full flower of her youth and beauty, made her way into the mountains behind El Arbolito where she joined the revolutionary band of fighters led by Juan-Manuel Negrete. But not until she met Napoleon Cruz did she realize where the true power in her country lay, who the true revolutionary was, which man would truly change the world. And she came to love and respect Napoleon as much for that as for his shrewdness and determination and ruthless efficiency. Where other men made empty talk, Napoleon acted. What other men dreamed about, Napoleon accomplished. He was, she decided, unique in all ways, worthy of her loyalty, her trust and her love. There was nothing she would not do for him. And in his service, she would ride to earthly glory.

". . . Will you honor me?"

The words brought her back. Bustamente leaned across the table, stroking her hand, gazing longingly into her eyes. He had invited her to return to his apartment—for a last drink in comfort and privacy, was the way he put it. She returned his anxious smile with a reassuring one. "The pleasure will be mine, Eduardo."

A taxi took them to his apartment. She sat close to him, her hand in his, thigh to thigh, hip to hip, and she began to tingle in anticipation. She felt warm and moist, caught up by a rising excitement.

Once inside the apartment, Bustamente turned her way, offering a drink. To his surprise and pleasure, she fitted her superb body up against his, her arms circling his considerable girth. "We both want the same thing, Eduardo, and more liquor can only numb our passion."

"Oh, yes," he answered breathlessly. "Yes, my dear, yes." He guided her toward the bedroom.

She disengaged. "Allow me a moment of privacy, dearest Eduardo. And then come to me. When you do, I shall be in your bed waiting."

In the bedroom, Nina undressed swiftly. She removed the nickel-plated, .25-caliber automatic from her purse, slid it under the pillow nearest her, then got into bed. She allowed her eyes to flutter shut, aware of the tremor of her limbs, the tightness in her middle. Mother of God, how much she wanted him now, *now*. . .

"Come to me, Eduardo," she said aloud.

The chief justice appeared, innocent in his nakedness, trailing his partly engorged cock to the bed. He slid in beside her.

"Perhaps you would like some champagne first. . . ?" Her beauty, the perfection of her sleek body, made him dizzy with desire. Never had he been with such a woman, the tawny skin glowing in the semidarkness, as if hewn from polished stone.

Nine took hold of his cock. She caressed it, stroked it, tickled his heavy testicles. He moaned and groaned, he writhed and rolled. He squeezed her breasts and shoved his hand between her legs.

"This is everything I want," she said between gritted teeth. "You, Eduardo, this hard cannon of yours inside me."

"Oh, yes, my darling, my pigeon, oh beautiful child. . ."

And in that moment Nina experienced a tide of desire such as she had not known in years. "Now," she commanded.

She mounted him, guiding the swollen cannon, tugging and shoving, putting him inside her, rolling her hips to accommodate him. He rose up, driving deeper. She gasped and called out his name, spoke of his impressive size, the hardness of him, the force and power that he possessed. He grunted and shoved harder and she met his every move with one of her own. She rocked this way and that, she encompassed him, and sought to take more of him inside her, until she felt his body stiffen, his legs lock under her, the great cannon poised to fire.

"Ah," he cried. "Ah, ah, ah."

She rode him in a desperate gallop until he collapsed under her, flesh twitching, limp and weak, thinking vaguely that at his age he could not survive many more such encounters. Greatest fuck in the world.

"Never," he muttered.

"Of course, my darling." She slid off her own side of the bed, his semen seeping like a cool stream along the inside of her thigh. Her hand closed on the shining automatic.

"You have worn me out," Bustamente said without complaint.

"Rest, Eduardo. You have done your best."

"The best is still to come, my dear." He lay spread-eagled on his back, his breathing rapid and harsh, his eyes closed. He longed to sleep. He barely noticed the cold muzzle of the .25-caliber automatic when it was pressed up against his ear. "The best," he repeated, before his world dissolved in pain and blood and endless blackness.

Nina felt Bustamente's body jerk, already dead. She took his cock in her hand and, as she knew it would be, it was pumped up in terminal tumescence. She pressed forward, her long, strong legs wrapped around the still warm corpse, pounding insistently against the curve of his hip, caught up by an excitement such as she had never before known. Spasm after extended spasm left her shaken and drained, still embracing Bustamente. Electric impulses made her flesh twitch and blinding lights went off behind her closed eyes, until she rested contentedly.

Ten minutes later she went into the bathroom and showered and dressed. Without a backward glance, she left Bustamente's apartment. Nothing remained there of any interest to her.

Napoleon's hacienda was still and dark when Nina Fuentes returned the next night. A single soft lamp brought her to the spacious living room where she discovered Carlito dozing, a movie fan magazine in his lap. He woke as soon as she entered the room and watched her come closer. She put herself in a chair opposite him.

"You've been waiting for me?" A faint taunt underlined the words. He ignored it.

"How did it go?"

She stared at him. Had Napoleon spoken of her mission to the boy? Not that it mattered, not really.

"It went well."

"Napoleon will be pleased."

She resented his intrusion into this matter, preferring it to remain between Napoleon and herself. "And how do you know that?"

"I know many things, my sister. Was it difficult for you?"

This one, Nina warned herself, is the spawn of Death; he *is* Death. And like Death, he had no smell, no lingering humanness.

"It went well," she repeated.

He considered her answer before he spoke again. "And you, how was it for you?"

There was no doubt in her mind that he knew, *knew* what the experience with Bustamente had meant to her, what it had done for her, to her. He knew, and she loathed him for knowing, and she feared him, too. There was something preternatural about this catamite, and at once he seemed both smaller and larger than life.

Carlito smiled a lovely smile. "How many times did you shoot him?"

"Madre de Dios. Leave me be."

For a moment she was embarrassed by their intimacy, ashamed of what bound her and Napoleon and Carlito together, and yet it had been her plan, her idea. She, who was never afraid, was afraid of this child.

She pulled away, unable any longer to meet his unflinching gaze. "I'm tired. I am going to bed." She paused at the door and looked back. "Be careful, Little Minnow. Sometimes it is not good to know so much."

"I do not know what you mean."

"I think you do. I think you know everything and that is too much of a burden for anyone to carry."

In the morning Napoleon greeted her with an abrazo and a kiss on each cheek. He handed her a packet of American money. "Twenty-five thousand dollars," he said. "In appreciation of your good deed."

"Whatever you wish."

"Tonight you shall dine with me. Willie Hatcher will be there. I have certain plans I wish to discuss with you, that deeply involve you. You will be doing considerable traveling in the next few months."

"Leave here?"

"Exactly. I am expanding my operations and I need your help."

"I would prefer to remain here, with you."

"This is important to me. However, if you choose not to take the assignment . . ."

"Whatever you wish Napoleon. You can depend on me."

"More than anyone else," he purred.

"More than anyone . . ."

SIXTEEN

OUT OF UNIFORM, FRANK ABERNATHY, JR.'S PARTS failed to match. A Harris tweed jacket and designer jeans clashed with the aggressive, alert posture that bespoke a man cocked for battle. He was lean and tall, with burnished good looks, a man who took care of his body with the earnest commitment of a religious novice. His hands were large and long, his wrists corded, his deep-set eyes surveying the urban landscape.

He wished he were back in the field commanding a combat battalion, planning to fight, getting his men ready for war. War was what it was all about, ultimately. The final act that decided differences between nations. If not that, he could certainly be profoundly valuable in the Pentagon or as a member of the National Security staff. It was, after all, the NSC advisor who had sent him on this mission, on orders, Abernathy was convinced, from much higher in the chain of command. Well, he was a soldier and he would carry out his mission no matter how distasteful or disappointing it might be.

He sat at a small round table in a cafe on the Via Veneto, sipping cappucino. He scanned the avenue of chic shops and fashionable hotels in a vain effort to distinguish friends from enemies. Down the street, protestors, complete with painted signs and Italian chants, were picketing in front of the American Embassy, causing Abernathy's brain to inflame and his muscles to swell in barely suppressed animosity. "Red bastards," he muttered aloud.

Across the table from him sat Plato Papageorge, delicately constructed, with gentle features and a plump crimson mouth. He

175

wore a neat black beard and quizzical eyebrows to match. Amused by Abernathy's discomfort, he dismissed the source of it with a wave of one tastefully manicured hand.

"Pay them no mind, my friend. Politics in Italy are nothing but a lunchtime entertainment this time of year. As long as the weather holds, protestors abound. Yesterday they marched against the French."

"The French," Abernathy said, glowering. "I can understand that. But the United States. People don't appreciate my country, God bless her."

"As you say, God bless her," Papageorge agreed readily. He was not a political person, his interests and loyalties engaged completely by whoever could afford to purchase his services. "So. Shall we return to business. Do we have a deal, as you Americans like to say?"

Abernathy brought his attention back to the bearded Greek. Too swarthy and too smarmy for his taste. But vital to the mission at hand—either Papageorge or someone very much like him.

"Can you meet my specifications?"

"Four thousand AK-47 rifles. Two thousand RPG-7 rocket launchers, yes."

"Keep your voice down. Also the mortars and the antitank weapons."

"In Rome no one pays attention. They are all too busy making deals of their own." Papageorge laughed, a shrill, rising laugh. "Plus suitable supplies of ammunition, of course. You will supply the waybills and end-user certificates and so on and so forth."

"Don't sweat it."

"I beg your pardon!"

"Yes, all that will be taken care of."

"Excellent. Initial assembly point will be in one of the Greek islands. From there the package will be transported via leased British transport planes—DC-9s, I expect—to Ethiopia, ostensibly for subsequent transfer to North Korea. Once airborne, however, the planes will head for Florida with a refueling stop in Angola. Arrival is planned for the twenty-fourth."

Abernathy made no attempt to conceal his irritation. "Forget it, Papageorge. That won't cut it."

"Cut it?"

"I told you, the package has to be in Honduras no later than the fourteenth for delivery in Sixaola ten days later. No room for tardiness."

Papageorge fingered his beard and rolled his eyes. "So many items. They must be gathered from various sources. The Middle East, certain African nations, Czechoslovakia. You know how ponderous those bureaucracies can be."

"If you can't meet my requirements, I'll go to Teddy Prendergast."

"Prendergast! The Englishman is a gonnif, as my Jewish friends would say. A thief. A swindler. His markups are outrageous."

"So that's what this is all about, you want more money."

"Ah, Major, you have my word. A twenty percent markup, I said, and I stand by my word. And I'll do my upmost to meet your schedule."

"Secrecy is vital."

"Keeping secrets is what I do best, let me assure you. Well, one of the things. Tell me, Major, this is a Central Intelligence operation, no?"

"Everything's on a-need-to-know basis. My authority is from the highest level. That's all you need to know."

"Naturally. Better to know less than more, is it not? Look at Watergate."

"Why bring up Watergate? That's ancient history."

"Of course. Iran-Contra then. The parallel is more clear. Shall we discuss recompense, Major?"

"Money."

"You Americans are so forthright, so direct, so businesslike. Except when you are devious. Yes, money."

"Where—?"

"The Cayman Islands, I think. A certain bank account the number and code of which I will supply you. A straightforward deposit, in dollars, if you don't mind."

"Dollars. I'll alert Geneva at the propitious moment and the money will be transferred to London's World Finance bank and then to your account in the Caymans."

"Transfer completed by. . ."

"When the shipment is delivered in Sixaola."

"Pardon me for even suggesting this, but some indication of goodwill is in order."

"Twenty percent. . ."

"Fifty percent would be more to my liking."

"Split the difference and that's that."

"Thirty-five percent, very well. Within forty-eight hours."

"Done." Abernathy inspected the other man's eyes as if searching for some reassurance otherwise lacking. He shook his head and sat back in his chair. "I can depend on you, Papageorge?"

"As surely as I can depend on you, sir."

"Perhaps we should meet again?"

Papageorge was startled. "Is it not all settled?" He answered his own question. "Yes it is settled. So meeting another time would produce only risks unseemly and self-defeating."

"I suppose you're right."

"I am certainly right." Papageorge rose, offering his delicate hand in a swift, limp handshake; and he left the American, his cappucino cold and bitter, his confidence diluted, to pay the bill.

Templo Mayor rose out of the earth only a single block north of the *Zocalo*, Mexico City's central plaza. The principle temple of the Aztecs, it had been unearthed by accident during construction of the subway back in 1979. Vargas escorted Jack Keveney to see the excavation site and they stood next to each other on the balustrade surrounding the dig, watching the men at work, hoping to uncover new treasures left behind by their golden ancestors.

"To understand this country," Vargas said pensively in English, "you must recognize the significance of its Indian heritage. The Spanish ruled here and the French. You Americans invaded Mexico. But to know the people it is vital to remember the Indian past. It is there that everything of value is ultimately revealed."

"Vargas," Keveney said. "You have the makings of a philosopher, I think."

"A minor league historian is all."

Vargas was a thick-bodied man with a massive head and high, round shoulders. His mustache was incredibly dark and thick, drooping over the corners of his mouth, giving him the rough, unfinished look of someone just off the ranch. In contrast were his finely tailored gabardine suit and the leather attache case in his hand. He was, in fact, an American of Mexican parentage, formerly a Border Patrolman working along the Rio Grande and now one of Keveney's undercover agents.

It was a cool, bright morning, unusually clear for Mexico City, the yellow fog of pollutants that was so much a part of the valley that had once been the capital of the Aztec nation having been washed away by recent spring rains. To the southeast rose up Popocatepetl and Ixteacihautl, the twin volcanoes, those splendid guardians of the city.

Keveney would have preferred a gray, gloomy day full of mist to cloud the vision of passersby. He wanted no one to notice him, no one to recognize him, no one to record this meeting. But Vargas had agreed with the prison officials: the confrontation must take place in a public setting so that a small army of men could keep watch on the prisoner. Keveney, given no choice in the matter, had agreed.

Keveney checked his watch. "They're late."

"We are in Mexico, señor," Vargas reminded him pleasantly. He looked around. "Ah, here they are now."

Three men were marching in cadence. Two of them were Latinos, dark of skin, flat-faced, with the muscular swagger of policemen everywhere. Between them was Willie Hatcher. Closer now, an expression of surprise and delight lit up Hatcher's round face. "Hey!" he began. "I remember you. Keveney, isn't it? You made captain, that's great."

"Don't be too sure, Willie. I want to talk to him alone," Keveney said to Vargas, who spoke to the guards in Spanish. One of them answered with a few hard words.

Vargas addressed Hatcher. "He says run for it and he'll put a bullet up your ass."

Hatcher made a face and fell into step alongside Keveney. A few yards behind, his two watchdogs kept pace, Vargas to one side of them.

"You lost weight, Willie," Keveney said.

"Where they got me, it ain't exactly gourmet cooking. I heard you'd given up the cop business."

"I'm in Washington these days, a couple of years now."

"Politics." Hatcher laughed. "A man can always turn a profit in politics."

"The word is you have a severe problem, Willie. A kilo of cocaine, that was dumb, carrying yourself. You'll be an old man when you get out."

"A friend of mine is working on it."

"No one can help you, Willie. The joint they're sending you to gives hard time a bad name."

"Oh, yeah."

"Believe it."

"You're after something, right?"

"Information, Willie. It's what I deal in. I hear you're well-connected. You help me, I help you. Simple as that."

"I don't talk about my friends with cops."

They had come to the rim of the Zocalo, oblivious to the traffic rushing past. Behind them, the Mexican guards positioned themselves strategically, at the same time reaching under their jackets. Their dark, sharp eyes raked the great open space suspiciously.

"Don't shit me, Willie. I've got a file this big on you and your pals. Napoleon Cruz, your friend. I hear he's on the way up in the world. And Nina Fuentes, well, she's his woman, yes?"

Willie let the air out of his lungs in a silent whistle. "Ah, man, you know how it is, some women . . . If you saw her you'd understand. There's magic in that female. Just thinking about her can make a man crazy."

"Make you crazy, you mean. Only she belongs to Napoleon."

"That's over."

"The way I hear it, with Napoleon nothing is ever over. You belong to him once, you belong to him forever."

"It's been over for a long time."

"She works for him still?"

"Who says so? I say anybody works for anybody?"

"You're Napoleon's man, Willie. The computer keeps putting your name next to his."

"Computers. Technology's taking all the fun out've life." He shot a glance at Keveney as if trying to reach a decision. "It's over between Nina and Napoleon."

"Unless Napoleon changes his mind."

"Go to hell, Keveney."

Keveney laughed and then Hatcher laughed. "Look at you, Willie, just twitching at the idea of her being back with Napoleon. He snaps his fingers, she does him good, whatever he wants."

"Ah, man. We are talking about designer merchandise. You don't know."

"Is she for you, Willie? Look at you—thirty pounds overweight and your hair going fast. You're what—fifteen years older than Napoleon, beholden to him or to someone like him. Nina looks your way and it makes your day. Napoleon gets a notion about you, and it's goodbye Willie."

Hatcher made a small lonely sound in his throat.

Keveney said matter-of-factly, "Is it true she's a killer, Willie? That she functioned as Napoleon's hit man? How about that, your boss finds out about this conversation, Willie, he has Nina blow you away." Hatcher groaned. "Just trying to inject a shot of reality into your life. Napoleon, you're just another slave to him. And Nina, you got the hots for her and her eye's always checking out Napoleon. Wise up, Willie."

"If you saw her . . ."

"Arrange it, pal."

"You ask too much. Nina and Napoleon, they're my friends."

"I'm the only friend you got, Willie. You're charged with possession with intent to sell. Transporting. Bribery of a federal officer. Using a deadly weapon with intent to kill. What're you, a hard guy, Willie? I don't think so. They put you away down here, they bury you. Those Mexican cons will use every orifice you got. You think Napoleon cares? You think Nina's out there waiting? You'll die in the joint, Willie, while Napoleon gets richer, and whenever he has a hard-on, there she is, Nina, ready to service him."

"Bastard."

"Think about it." Keveney gestured and the Mexicans hurried to join them. "Change your mind, Willie, I'll be at the Hotel Geneva in the Zona Rosa. Say the right word, Willie, and you're a free man again. Forty-eight hours and then I'm gone so you ain't got a lot of time. Think about it."

"Fuck you," Willie drawled with more force than he felt. He waddled off between his two guards, a forlorn droop to his shoulders.

Word came the following evening. Keveney had a light supper in the dining room of the hotel: enchiladas Suisa, refried beans, yellow rice and Dos Equis beer. Willie Hatcher had asked to meet with him again.

Arrangements were made and Keveney took a taxi to the Polanco district, to a modern home of glass and steel constructed behind a traditional colonial stone wall. A servant led him down a tiled passageway past the same pair of *federales* who had been with Hatcher the previous day. Double doors slid open to bring him into a comfortable living room with a glass wall that looked out on a flowered garden, complete with a running fountain. Hatcher was waiting.

He was bruised around the face, his mouth swollen, his nose out of line.

"Jesus, Willie."

"They beat shit outta me, four of 'em."

"Guards?"

"Prisoners. All because I was a gringo . . ."

"National pride . . ."

"They took my money."

"Greed is everywhere."

"They raped me."

"Men without women—a bad scene."

"If I talk to you . . ."

"Become one of my agents. Covertly, of course. Your name on no rolls, your identity known only to me. You'd be safe."

"I'll never be safe, not as long as I'm alive. What do I get out of it?"

"Freedom from prosecution. And a modest government stipend."

Hatcher knew what would happen to him should anyone learn of his defection. Let Napoleon even suspect he was bent and he would be killed. As for Nina . . . he didn't want to think about Nina, not now.

He said, almost pleading. "I can't go back to that place, not even for an hour."

"I'll make a phone call or two."

"Make them, dammit, and then we'll talk."

The American Embassy on the *Reforma* resembled an impregnable fortress. A black iron fence circled the building and armed U.S. Marines guarded the entrance. Mexican police were always on duty and visible on the streets and in their radio cars, ready to summon help, if needed.

Keveney and Hatcher were admitted to the Embassy that same night through a private entrance. They were provided with sleeping quarters and, in the morning after breakfast, they were brought to a spacious room with comfortable leather couches and a professional quality tape recorder.

"Is that necessary?" Hatcher wanted to know.

"I need a verbatim record of everything you tell me."

Hatcher conceded the practicality of the machine but he still didn't like it. "Where," he said, "should I begin?"

"Napoleon . . ."

Hatcher clucked once. "Nobody can bring him down."

"You talk," Keveney replied. "I'll listen."

He cleared his throat and began to speak: "He was a child when I met him. In Chiriqui, in Sixaola. He was about fifteen and he'd gotten hold of a kilo of coke. Good stuff, too. I never did find out where it came from. Not that I asked. Even then you had to be careful with Napoleon. He was slender and soft looking, but he went from zero to a hundred in seconds and all of a sudden there was a knife or a gun in his hand."

"You ever see him kill anybody?"

"Let's just say that he's no stranger to killing."

"Tell me about the kilo."

"I helped him sell the stuff and we've been tight since. He parlayed the profit into other buys and other sales and by the time he was seventeen he had an organization of his own."

"How old is he now?"

"Middle twenties, no more than that."

"Keep talking."

"He's a millionaire many times over. Growers work for him, distributors, muscle, couriers, dealers, bankers. He owns homes in four or five countries, maybe, even the U.S. of A. He's got a layout in the Bahamas. An airport of his own. He owns ranches, thousands of hectarès of land. He grows pot in Mexico, coca in Colombia and Sixaola. He refines some himself, transports it to the U.S. for sale. He's a king, one of the four."

"Four kings?"

"Regents, if you prefer. Raphael Salazar, Rene Vega, Pablo Uribe. You've heard of them?" Keveney nodded. "These men run the drug business in Sixaola. From grower to plant to user, they control it."

"Napoleon too?"

"Napoleon too. He's half their age. But in a dozen years he's accomplished as much as any of them, more even."

"They are equals?"

"More or less. Each has his own interests. Each his own constituency, you could say. Each emphasizes different things, each has different specialities. Uribe's a peon, blunt, cruel. Vega was born on a farm and to him land is precious. Salazar, he's an aristocrat, he owns many factories. He refines more coca than the others."

"And Napoleon?"

"He dips his toe into many different ponds. He buys, he invests, he refines and ships and sells. The man likes variety."

Keveney phrased the question carefully. "How do the other Regents look upon Napoleon?"

"Necessity brings them close. Common causes. Otherwise, each goes his own way. I believe there is a certain amount of nervousness, even suspicion. Napoleon has a drive, a hunger, that the others may have lost. He is a constant prod to them, he raises questions to which they seldom have answers, he raises doubts in their hearts. He makes them uneasy and therefore distrustful. They don't appreciate it when he goes off on his own. They—the older ones, they have become more conservative—they do not wish to attract unnecessary attention. But Napoleon takes risks, acts on impulse, stirs up the waters. In certain ways he has usurped the authority of the others and become, I think, a threat to them."

"Go on."

"You have heard of the Ché Brigade? Well, it is a band of Marxist revolutionaries. They hope to bring down the government of Sixaola and establish a Leninist state. The Brigade operates in the mountains and the jungles of Sixaola. Napoleon is close to the leader of the Brigade, Juan-Manuel Negrete. When it makes sense, they help each other to achieve certain goals.

"The Brigade. Well, they attack army outposts, they kill policemen and murder government officials from time to time. Once in awhile they kidnap a member of the oligarchy for ransom. The thing about the Brigade you have to know is its relative weakness. If the government were strong, the Brigade would have been destroyed long ago. But the government is indecisive, shaky in its exercise and power, and monumentally corrupt, as is every other institution in Sixaola. The point is, the Brigade functions under Negrete as Napoleon's private army. All in addition to his other people."

"Tell me about the other Regents. How does the government deal with them?"

"Wrong question. It should be—How do the Regents deal with the government? Answer: They buy, they kill, they kidnap. Negrete's influence, and therefore Napoleon's, extends into the high-

est offices, El Presidente's included. An occasional drug raid results in abandoned refining plants or fields long-ago harvested, a
few small-time pushers. Not so different than in the U.S. of A.,
my friend. The Regents control everything. And before too long
that also will change."

"Meaning?"

"Meaning Napoleon has vast ambitions. He has been buying up
weapons, ammunition, strengthening the Ché Brigade, as well as
his own people. Napoleon lusts for more. More money. More
power. More—everything. To know him you would do well to
consider his namesake . . ."

Keveney stiffened in place. This Napoleon, with his fantast's
dreams and megalomaniacal ambitions, his unsatisfied lust for
power, Keveney could almost taste the man's searing ambition in
his own mouth. He had to find Napoleon, had to attack and con-
quer him. More than any of the Regents, it was Napoleon he
wanted . . .

The film had the usual poor quality of one shot out of the back
of the disguised police van. The light faded and grew stronger. It
was grainy and the figures moved in quick, nervous ways that
made them appear to be comic characters in an early black-and-
white movie.

But there was no mistaking the startling beauty and femininity
of the woman in the film. She carried herself with a kind of ances-
tral arrogance. Tall and well-formed, she owned a long, easy athletic stride. Her shining black hair was pulled back from a high,
smooth brow and held in place at the nape of her graceful neck by
what might have been a rubber band, flaring across her shoulders
in a feathery fall. There was a regal set to her face, the cheekbones
prominent, the mouth voluptuous and wide, the nostrils slightly
flared, defiant almost.

But her eyes captured Keveney's attention. Large and steady,
they were set in a vaguely Oriental cast, the dark pupils limned
by irises pale and cool, in vivid contrast to the satiny velvet that
was her skin. A woman of parts and aspects that would tantalize
and delight the most sophisticated and jaded of men, she was,

Keveney conceded grudgingly, more beautiful than anyone he had ever seen. Even more, he perceived a challenge in those remarkable eyes, the challenge of someone who would never allow herself to be made subordinate to another human being; and a threat, the threat of a woman capable of the most outrageous acts in pursuit of her private aspirations. This was a woman sensual and strong, passionate and deliberate, a woman intelligent and committed. All that he saw and dwelt upon and grew afraid of and finally obsessed with.

"Who is she?" he demanded of the D-Group agent running the camera. Keveney was seated in the small screening room in D-Group's Washington headquarters, studying film shot by his undercover operatives worldwide. Listening to verbal reports. Entertaining suggestions and plans submitted by his associates. Until this last piece of film, none of it amounted to very much. Until this woman appeared on the screen, so clearly a special human creature.

"Her name is Silvia Gutierrez. She was spotted for the first time about ten months ago in San Ysidro, across the line from Tijuana. A few weeks after that, there she was again in El Paso. Then in Eagle Pass. This time in Laredo."

"Always along the border," Keveney remarked.

"All the time. These pictures were taken less than a week ago."

"Run it again."

The street in the background paralleled Interstate 35 and was lined with shabby motels and fast-food restaurants. Cars and pedestrians moved lazily under a high Texas sun. Palm trees cast elongated shadows. A silver Mercedes sedan drew up to the curb on the far side of the street and Silvia Gutierrez climbed out with a flash of fine, long legs. A soft-sided overnight bag in hand, she disappeared into a freestanding building bearing a hand painted sign:

Texacali
Money Exchange

The film kept running for nearly five minutes before she reappeared. The overnight bag was gone. She climbed back into the Mercedes and drove away.

"Enough," Keveney said. The projector switched off and the lights came on. "She's washing money."

"I'd say so, sir. It's the same each time. She shows up at these *casas de cambios* with some kind've luggage and leaves without it. We put a watch on the people who work the Texacali. They carry the dough to a local bank where it is deposited."

"Yeah," Keveney drawled. "And twenty-four hours later it's transferred overseas. Say to Panama or the Bahamas."

"Yes, sir. Down there it's a cinch for a drug guy to pick up his cash and walk away, no questions asked."

"Okay," Keveney said. "I want a trace on the money. Where it goes. Who accepts delivery. Ownership of the banks involved. Where majority control lies. Get me names, records, the works."

"Yes, sir."

"As for Gutierrez, I want to know everything about her. Who she works for. What's her base. Is she married? Lovers? Get me names, addresses, phone numbers. The Mercedes—who owns it, who paid for it?"

Keveney rose to leave when his secretary appeared, a somber expression on her face. She handed him a typed message. He read it and swore, falling back in his seat.

"Something wrong?" the agent said.

"It's Tom Vargas," Keveney muttered. "Somebody blew him away."

Hotel Jalapa was in the Alameda District of Chiriqui. It was in a restored seventeenth-century colonial mansion with wide, high-ceilinged corridors and stone patios. Broad tiled stairs led from the dark, cool lobby to the floors above. Keveney's room was large, shadowed, a ladder of sunlight falling to the polished wood floor through ancient wood shutters. A ceiling fan whirred creakily, stirring up very little air. Keveney, in khakis and a short-sleeved white shirt, drank ice water from a tall glass and eyed the telephone impatiently. At last it rang.

"Yes?" he said.

"Señor Keveney?" The speaker put a note of deference into his voice, the voice of a man used to bowing his head when circumstance dictated.

"Speaking."

"I am Colonel Xavier Rubio Santana, at your service, señor."

Rubio was chief of the Sixaolan federal police who were headquartered in the nation's capital city. He had come to Chiriqui at Keveney's request.

"I called your local office three hours ago." Keveney made no effort to mask his annoyance. Given the same situation in the U.S., Keveney would have been more responsive.

Colonel Rubio was unused to being criticized, especially by strangers, especially by gringos. Still, this Keveney was a personage of considerable importance, of considerable power, a power that reached into the highest echelons of Sixaolan society. Many millions of American dollars were fed into the budget of the federales each year, and a harsh word from Keveney might interrupt that stream of funding, certainly cause it to be squeezed down to a mere trickle. Rubio had learned early on in life how to adjust rapidly to a changing situation.

"Ah, señor, you know how it is with all Latinos. Two-hour siestas. We are the mañana people, yes. I have only just arrived at my office." What Rubio failed to say was that he had spent the time with one of his mistresses, a fifteen-year-old girl of remarkable sexual sophistication and an insatiable appetite for more, more of everything. What was a man to do?

Keveney said, "Let's get together, Colonel. As soon as possible."

"Of course. What has occurred, it is horrible, a blow to all who wear the badge and the gun. You would honor me by being my guest for dinner, señor. At the best restaurant in Chiriqui, naturally. We will talk and—"

Keveney broke in. "Let's get started right away. I want to know what went wrong. Tom Vargas was a good man, a good cop, he wasn't easy to kill."

"But he was killed, señor." Rubio said mournfully. "Each of us is vulnerable."

Keveney hesitated; was that a threat? All he said was, "I want to interview the detectives. The witnesses. Whatever you've got so far..."

"At your convenience, señor." Rubio sighed. His young mistress had worn him out, though he would never admit it. He required a good, leisurely comida, some solitary, quiet time in which to recuperate. But like all gringos, this one was in a hurry to do things..."

"Now," Keveney said.

Rubio said grandly, "I will present myself to you in twenty minutes, señor, if it pleases you."

"Twenty minutes," Keveney answered, before he hung up.

They met in the hotel lobby. Colonel Rubio was of medium height and build with a neat black mustache squared off at the ends, and eyebrows to match. He had a prim mouth that gave him the stiff, artificial look of a wax fixture brought recently to life. His handshake was firm and lingering, as if testing the American, his narrow eyes searching Keveney's face for some hint of exploitable weakness. A flash of white teeth came and went.

"I'm honored to at last meet you, Señor Keveney. In Sixaola we know of your good works..."

"Let's move it, Colonel, okay?"

Rubio's laugh was a hiccupping gasp, thin and forced. His words, when he spoke, were sliced off between small sharp teeth.

"You Yanquis, how rapido you must do everything. How eternally efficient. Well, why not? Yours is a great and powerful nation. You will wish to examine the scene of the crime?"

They left the hotel and entered a world of humid, blinding sunlight. A cab driver offered transportation, but Rubio refused. "It is only a short walk from here and this will allow you to inspect our city, establish your own view of what took place..."

"What do you know about Vargas?" Keveney said.

The colonel ushered him around a corner, and here the streets were narrow, the ancient, painted buildings closing out the sunlight. The air was stagnant and hotter. Some children were kicking a soccer ball, and young men leaned against walls splashed with revolutionary slogans, speaking in guarded tones. One block later the pavement ended and the street ran on, hardened dirt with deep ditches along either side. Some chickens crossed their path and a scrawny dog kept pace with them for a while. The colonel, as if responding at last to Keveney's query, spoke.

"A melancholy affair. Vargas was a very great man."

"You knew him?"

"Alas, no, señor. Such good fortune was not to be mine. But I have been informed he was a man of immense dedication and serious bravery. In this line of work, could a man be otherwise and survive for very long?"

Keveney was in no mood for empty answers. He said, "Vargas didn't survive."

Rubio peered straight ahead, lips purposefully pursed.

"Why do you think he was killed?" Keveney said presently.

"Motive, opportunity, means." Rubio recited the words as if by rote. "Provide answers to those questions and we solve the crime, yes."

"Someone found out he was working for me, for D-Group. They blew him away. Drugs is at the bottom of it."

Rubio considered his answer at length. "Possibly, but I think not, if you do not mind my saying so. We are inclined to believe this unfortunate matter was simply an affair of the heart."

"Explain, please."

"A crime of passion, señor." He made a slight gesture. "See, we have arrived. We are here."

Here the street was only a rutted dirt path with low sun-bleached walls made of adobe brick behind which cactus loomed up like tall, spiked guardians. Rubio pushed open a splintered wooden door and they left the street behind. A wooden structure with a corrugated metal roof leaned precariously against the back wall, and three cats darted for safety at the appearance of the two men.

"In there," Rubio said, pointing. "This is where he died." Rubio led the way into the shack. A single room, dank and dark, confronted them. The floor was dirt and there was no running water, no toilet facilities. A soiled mattress rested in another corner of the room. "There, señor. There is where we found Vargas . . ."

"What was he doing here?" Keveney walked over to the mattress. Dried bloodstains were visible. "Where was Vargas?"

"On the far side, señor, near the wall, the woman at his side. His clothes were scattered about and he was naked. Both of them were naked."

"Tell me exactly how he died."

"Shot twice, señor. In the stomach the first time, I believe. That wound disabled him and made it impossible for him to resist. A second shot to the back of the head finished him off."

"And the woman?"

"More or less the same. A shot to the body and another in the head. Very efficient."

Keveney glanced around. "The woman lived here?"

"Oh, no, señor. She owned a very fine apartment in the Santa Felicidad district. She lived very comfortably."

"Then why were they here? Dammit, it doesn't make any sense."

"You must understand, señor, the woman was married. Perhaps this was the only place where they believed they would be safe from her *esposo,* her husband. As you can see, they found no safety."

Keveney searched the room for the slightest hint of what had transpired only three nights earlier. Vargas, he knew, was a man of delicate tastes, mannerly and fastidious, a man of refined appetites. There was more to Vargas than Colonel Rubio had discovered.

"You've arrested the husband, then?"

"Ah, no. We have questioned him. He claims innocence, no knowledge of his wife's transgressions. Besides, señor, his was not the finger on the trigger. Oh, no. Two men were involved. Witnesses reported seeing two men flee on a motorbike. But no one will admit to seeing their faces. In Chiriqui, people are extremely cautious. Death by strange and violent means is a daily occurrence."

"Saturday night in the Wild West."

Rubio laughed cheerfully. "Ah, you are so right, señor. Life here is like a cowboy movie, except that every night is Saturday night."

"Any signs of a struggle?"

"None."

"Vargas was not the kind've man to give up without a fight. Had his gun been fired?"

"There was no weapon. Perhaps the killers took it with them."

"You say a jealous husband. Why not drug dealers?"

"Logic dictates . . ."

"The witnesses . . . ?"

"No one saw the actual shooting, señor. Some people said they heard the shots and believed them to be the backfiring of a car. In our poor country, there are many old automobiles which do not function as efficiently as they should. No, no witnesses. So you see, logic . . ."

Keveney wondered what had brought Vargas to this depressing place. To this abrupt and unexplained end?

"Let's go," he said. "I've seen enough."

"I understand." Outside the sun had begun to set and the air was cooling rapidly. They began to walk. "Be my guest for dinner, señor. A fine meal will take your mind away from the unfortunate affair. There are good times to be found in Chiriqui, good food, good things to drink."

Purple shadows stretched across the narrow streets, and the acrid smell of cooking fires drifted from behind the adobe walls. Perhaps Rubio was right; perhaps it was time to stop thinking about Vargas's death.

"Sure," he said abruptly. "Let's do it."

Cafe Convento was at the end of a dead-end street in what once had been a convent. Arches and candlelight and heavy wooden tables provided a traditional Sixaolan ambiance. Straw sombreros and striped serapes were pinned to whitewashed walls and brightly painted ceramic bean pots decorated the mantel of a huge, empty fireplace. Once seated, Rubio issued instructions to the waiter in rapid Spanish, and the man soon returned with two mugs of strong dark beer and a platter of bite-sized *quesadillas* and *pelizcadas* to take the edge off their appetities.

"The food here is excellent and the tables are far apart enough so that a private conversation may be carried on."

Keveney looked around the half-empty room. Older men with young women were the primary clientele. "There are places like this in my country, the same sort of couples."

"Youth," Rubio said with a smile. "It has increasing appeal as a man grows older. It takes a little extra to heat aging flesh, to bring the flames up high again, if even for a little while." He was amused at his own wit. "You are married, señor?"

"I was."

"Ah. Divorce in my country is forbidden by law. The ways of the Church are extremely influential here. We are an excessively moral people."

Keveney nibbled at the quesadilla, the cheese hardening swiftly into rubbery yellow. Flakes of red pepper heated the lining of his mouth. He emptied his mug and the waiter brought another beer at once.

"How many shots?" he said quietly. "At least four."

Rubio produced a soft moan. He despaired of enjoying a full, pleasant evening; the gringo policeman was a fanatic about his work. "Six, señor. We discovered two slugs imbedded in the wall."

"Six shots, the sound of the motorbike, and no witnesses to make an identification."

"None willing to provide useful information. There is too much crime in Chiriqui. Too much shooting and killing. People have learned to mind their own business. Not to get involved is better, safer, a wise man's avenue to a long and peaceful life." He glanced slyly Keveney's way. "Is it so different in the cities of your country?"

"Which way did they go?"

"Back to the center of the city. A corner turned and they were out of sight, gone forever. Two hours passed before the police were notified."

"I'd like to talk to the husband."

"The man has disappeared, señor."

Convenient, Keveney thought. "What about Vargas's clothing, his belongings? And the woman's? Have they disappeared, too?"

"Oh, no, señor. They are at headquarters."

"I'll want to look them over."

"I will arrange it for you."

Keveney was about to ask another question when the arrival of a large, noisy party drew his attention. Twelve people in all entered, with considerable laughter and talking in raised voices. The owner of El Convento materialized to greet the group with much bowing and shaking of hands, obsequious in word and gesture, ushering the man and his friends toward a long table at the far side of the dining room.

Now the leader of the party took over, seating his friends with a word or a gesture. He was a tall man and straight, with a face that reminded Keveney of a statue he had seen at the Anthropological Museum in Mexico City of an Aztec lord chipped out of dark, mottled stone. He was lithe, with a feline grace, each movement sure and steady, his step quick and light. Only when everyone else was seated did he assume his place at the head of the table.

Waiters brought drinks and baskets of warm tortillas and containers filled with red hot and green sauces, and the tall man issued orders to the owner of the restaurant for the meal to come. It was, Keveney conceded, an impressive performance. Reluctantly he brought his eyes away from the handsome man at the head of the table and examined the rest of his party. A small smile appeared on his mouth.

"Yes?" Rubio said. "Something amuses you?"

"A private joke." Keveney's eyes held on the eyes of one of the men at the long table. Even from this distance, it was clear that Willie Hatcher had begun to sweat.

Keveney watched the telephone.

A glass of Scotch in one hand and a cigarette in the other, his collar open and his sleeves rolled back to expose his corded forearms, Keveney slumped in a chair that didn't fit his body and waited.

He willed the telephone to ring.

He waited most of the night and the next morning, into the
afternoon. He ate two meals in his room and smoked nearly two
packs of Camels; he read that week's *Time* magazine and an old
copy of *National Geographic;* he drank two-thirds of a fifth of
Johnny Walker Red; he showered three times and shaved once.
He thought about Patrick, his son, missing the boy, and wondered
if Rosie might take him back if he quit this damned job and went
to work in something more respectable, say head of security for a
museum or one of the automobile companies. He decided that she
wouldn't have him, that marrying her in the first place had been a
mistake, that he wasn't cut out to be a husband or a father. He
wished Officer Denise Nicholson were in town; God, what a piece
of work she was. Sister Asumpta would not have approved of the
life he lived, of the man he had become. "Remember who made
you," she would've scolded. "And pray for forgiveness for your
sins."

Oh, boy, have I sinned . . .

The phone rang a few minutes after seven that evening. He
lifted the instrument gingerly.

"What took you so long?"

"Jesus H. Christ!" Willie Hatcher declared in a voice lined with
self-pity. "Are you trying to get me killed? Trying to get the both
of us killed? You got any idea what you're doing?"

"Get your fat ass over here."

"Thanks a lot. What are you doing here? In this country? In this
town? You have lost your marbles! Taken leave of your senses.
Gone completely south, you have."

"Pronto," Keveney said.

"Certifiable, that's what you are."

"You're wasting time."

"Impossible. There are no straight lines."

"What you're doing, you're babbling is what."

"You think it's like Manhattan, all neat and clean, streets running east and west, north and south, uptown and down? What'sa
matter with you, Keveney? Everybody in this town is paranoid.
Nobody trusts nobody. Nothing is what it appears to be."

"When will you get here?"

"When I get there, is when."

"Make it quick."

"You ain't heard a word I said. Not a friggin' word," he ended gloomily and hung up.

"I knew I could depend on you," Keveney began.

Hatcher minced into the room and looked around. "You alone?"

Keveney made a face. "What took you so long?"

"I took a bus, two cabs, I walked for a while. I had to make sure I wasn't followed. Those buses, you wouldn't believe 'em. Guy next to me was carrying two chickens upside down. Live chickens."

"Why would anyone follow you, Willie? You that important down here?"

Hatcher settled into the biggest chair in the room, his ample body slack and spreading. Keveney was in a foul mood, and that portended no profit for him. "I don't approve of mixing," he muttered.

"What?"

"Mixing worlds. You belong in New York . . ."

"I work in Washington now, remember?"

"Yeah." The reminder made Hatcher's mood grow darker. The world was closing in on him, wiping away all the protective barriers he had so carefully erected. He felt vulnerable, fragile, suspectible to pain, betrayal and sudden death.

"What do you know about Vargas?" Keveney said.

"Who's that?"

"One of my agents, he was murdered three days ago. Along with a woman."

"So that was his name, Vargas. I heard about that."

"Tell me what you know."

"I don't know a thing. People are always getting killed in Chiriqui. The locals play rough games. It pays to be careful, to have the right friends. You can't do him any good now."

"You know who killed Vargas?"

"Hell, no!"

"Ask around, Willie?"

"Oh, sure! Ask around, Willie. 'Hey, any've you hombres know who took down the gringo drug agent? My friend, Jack Keveney wants to know.' What're you crazy, Keveney? I don't know nothing, I don't want to know nothing. I ain't asking any questions."

"Your pal, Napoleon, he might know something."

Hatcher lifted his eyes as if seeking divine intervention. When he received no communication, he spoke to Keveney as if instructing a small, ignorant child. "Yes, Napoleon. Maybe he knows something, maybe. Maybe not. Only how long do you think he will remain my friend if I ask too many questions? The wrong questions, at that. Man gets shot dead down here, nobody says, 'Who did it?' That's a dumb question here, Keveney. That's what I need, Napoleon on my case. He finds out I'm having this tête-à-tête with you, he'd snuff the both of us in about a minute and a half."

Hatcher worked to slow his breathing, his heartbeat. A man of his bulk, it wasn't good to let himself get too excited. His blood pressure was probably up around two hundred already. He unclenched his fingers and made himself smile in Keveney's direction.

"You think I'm exaggerating, Keveney? I'm not. Leave Sixaola. Go home. Back to New York. Washington, wherever. Settle in behind a desk. Work regular hours. Eat good. Get your sleep. Leave this to me and whatever agents of yours who're still alive. I get something for you, you'll be the first to know."

"About Vargas?"

"You never give up, do you? What was in the papers, what guys say, that's all I know. Two characters took him out, him and a dame. Big deal, it goes on all the time."

"Colonel Rubio, he's chief of—"

"I know the slimeball."

"Rubio says it was a jealous husband."

Hatcher tried to look inside his head. "Why not?"

"You don't buy that?"

"What do I know?"

"I don't buy it either." Keveney leaned forward, elbows on his knees, hands spread. "The thing about Vargas is, he would never have been with a woman like that. He had no use for women that way. Vargas was gay, a serious homosexual. He told me, not once in his life had he ever made love to a woman."

"Maybe he decided to change his luck."

"Vargas lived with a woman once. In Mexico City. An entire year with this woman and he never laid a glove on her. Never could, he told me. Never had the urge. A woman's body, it turned the guy off."

Hatcher leered at Keveney. "Leaves more for the rest of us."

"Explain to me why he was found with the woman. Why in that crumby shack on some nowhere street? The hit was too clean for a jealous husband. Professionals do that kind've work, not feverish husbands with blood in their eyes. A couple of pros is what they were."

"I guess so," Hatcher said sadly.

"Tell me something, Willie. Tell me anything."

"The word," Hatcher said in a low, slow voice, "is that the woman was a puta, a common whore. Snatched up off the street and put in there to make it look like a jealousy killing."

"And the husband?"

"Who knows? Maybe a pimp, if there was a pimp."

"But not likely?"

"Not likely. Thing was, your man was cuffed, I hear."

"Handcuffed when he was shot?"

"Wrists and ankles."

"Rubio never mentioned that."

"I guess not."

"No wonder he didn't fight back."

"The shooters might've been cops, some people say."

"Rubio's people?"

"Nobody is saying."

"Damn Rubio. No wonder he's not hot to trot. He was part of it."

"Maybe." Hatcher avoided Keveney's eyes.

"Willie, you holding out on me? What are you holding out? Come on, Willie."

"You're gonna get me killed."

"What'd'ya know?"

"I'm not sure."

"What?"

"There's talk. That's all it is, talk."

"What talk?"

"That—it may have been—well, Napoleon."

"Cruz ordered the hit?"

"Maybe. Maybe somebody got wise to Vargas, that he was a narc. If Napoleon found out, he'd've had him hit."

"That sonofabitch, how I want him. Willie, you show him to me, Napoleon. I'll do the rest. Point me his way, so I can see him with my own eyes . . ."

Hatcher stared at Keveney. "You already have."

"What?"

"The other night, at the Cafe Convento. The tall one, the one at the head of the table—that was Napoleon Cruz."

SEVENTEEN

EL NEGRO'S SKIN WAS ALMOST BLACK, SCARCELY THE skin of a man, so leathery and hard was its integument. His face was almost as broad as it was long, the features bold and rough. He stood six-feet-four and weighed almost four hundred pounds. His belly hung over his belt in folds. But beneath the blubber, there were enormous muscles. His hands were as outsized as the rest of him. He was a man of immense appetites, too often able to be satisfied only by incredible amounts of food and outrageous acts.

Shrewd and suspicious, he possessed a precognitive sense of personal danger. His mind crackled with the electric precision of a computer, but the program was set for death. Death was his response to danger and to doubt. He dealt death calmly, took great pleasure in killing. El Negro was the Regents' man, had been for fifteen years. He was Chiriqui's chief of police.

It was this outsized and threatening creature who presented himself at Napoleon's hacienda in the still, early morning cool of the day, clad in police blue, a cap too small for his huge head tilted forward over his baleful yellow eyes, and a .357 Magnum hanging from his belt in a quick-draw holster.

Antonio, the chauffeur, admitted him. El Negro stared down at the shorter man.

"You know who I am, little one?" There was a wide spread of lip displaying his large stained teeth.

"I know," Antonio conceded.

"Good. Tell Cruz I am here to speak with him. I carry a mes-

201

sage of some importance to him and his future welfare."

Antonio rolled his stocky shoulders in the peon's traditional gesture of helplessness and acceptance. "El Señor still sleeps."

"Wake him, say that I am here."

"I will tell him."

"And while I wait—I am hungry." El Negro rubbed his great growling gut.

Without a word, Antonio led the dark giant into the smallest of the three dining rooms. "Wait here, food will be brought." He vanished into the kitchen. To Rosa he said, "It's El Negro. The Regents' enforcer. He is come with a message for the Señor. And he is hungry."

Rosa rolled her eyes. "I know that one, with the appetite of an elephant. Very well. I will feed him."

Antonio went to wake Napoleon. He did so in fear and trembling, but all Napoleon said from his bed was, "Tell him I will be with him shortly."

El Negro had downed a monstrous portion of *huevos rancheros*, a half dozen warm *bolillos* and butter and a pot of hot coffee by the time Napoleon appeared wearing a red dressing gown made of Chinese silk and appropriately decorated. He placed himself in a chair some distance from El Negro and watched him eat. Rosa brought him coffee and went back to her kitchen.

El Negro stuffed half a buttered bolillo into his mouth, chewing with relish. He and Napoleon were neither friends nor business associates, but their paths had crossed many times. Their exchanges were always polite and wary, each careful not to give offense.

"Well," Napoleon said. "Welcome to my house."

El Negro dragged his hand across his mouth, then wiped it ostentatiously on the Belgian linen tablecloth. His stomach rumbled. He belched. He farted. He grinned at Napoleon.

"Señor Salazar is angry," El Negro drawled. "He was extremely fond of Chief Justice Bustamente. As were Vega and Uribe. They have prayed for the poor man's soul. They have lit candles for him. They have visited his widow. They did not expect him to die so suddenly."

"Death comes in its own time to all men."

El Negro filled his cup with coffee and emptied it in one great gulp. He lit a huge black cigar that gave off a penetrating stench. He grinned once again.

"It is the wish of Salazar and the others that the murderer of Bustamene be delivered into the hands of the authorities by the end of siesta today. That means my hands, since I am chief of police, no? In this way justice will be served."

There was a brief silence before Napoleon responded. "What makes them think I know who killed Bustamente?"

El Negro grinned.

"Do they believe I shot the man myself, perhaps?"

El Negro's grin widened. He shoved himself erect and stepped away from the table. "Such questions are of no concern to me. In this affair, I am only delivering a message. I will be in my office at police headquarters after siesta. *Hasta la vista,* señor."

Napoleon waited until the big man was gone, then summoned Antonio. "El Negro brought me a message and it requires an answer. You will deliver it once. Take the Maserati, overtake El Negro, and give him my answer. Loudly, painfully, so there can be no doubt of its meaning. You understand?"

Antonio grunted. "El Negro is an abomination. He called me 'little man'. Only my compadres call me that. I will deliver your reply, Napoleon, at once."

El Negro's great bulk filled the cockpit of the Mercedes 450 SEL. He drove without haste along the dirt road leading through the countryside, sucking on his cigar, pleasantly satisfied. His belly was full, he had done his job well and—as the results would inevitably show—he had further ingratiated himself into the favor of the Regents, thus insuring his future. El Negro understood that he operated as he did and profited as he did solely due to the Regents' beneficence. At the end of the siesta, the murderer of Bustamente would be delivered to him and he would question the man, determine who had ordered the killing and, after seeing to the hit man's suicide, would tend to the ultimate culprit. There was, El Negro had long ago decided, something eminently gratifying about being a police chief.

He barely noticed when the red Maserati went speeding past, kicking up a storm of dust. He swore at the driver of the other car, slowed to avoid the swirling pale clouds, and put his mind forward to the woman he would be visiting in no more than an hour. What a prize she was, so beautiful, so willing, so very, very young. Pleased with himself, he drove a little faster.

As he approached the crossroads—one road led to town, the other south into the hill country—El Negro slowed the Mercedes. All at once alarms were unloosed throughout his massive body. His skin twitched, his nose sniffed the fine, clear air, his eyes raked the scene ahead. But he saw nothing, heard nothing, smelled nothing.

He swung onto the road to Chiriqui and there in a stand of trees spotted the Maserati. There was movement to one side of the red car. El Negro swore and pressed the accelerator to the floor, at the same time reaching for the .357 Magnum. The tires of the heavy car spun in the dust, fighting for traction, and it fishtailed as El Negro took evasive action. It did no good.

Antonio, in full sight now, held a Mac-11 pistol complete with a silencer in his hands, the weapon on full automatic. The first burst shattered the windshield. El Negro was hit in the neck and shoulders and the chest. A second burst stitched a line of crimson from the policeman's jaw to his hairline. He screamed out his agony and rage and fired wildly in return. The Mercedes swerved and headed off the road, ending up on its side in the ditch.

Antonio approached with care, looking in. El Negro jerked reflexively behind the steering wheel, the .357 clutched in one massive hand. Antonio shoved the Mac-11 through the shattered windshield and sent a half dozen rounds into the great black head.

El Negro had delivered his message; and Napoleon had answered loudly and painfully, so there could be no doubt of its meaning. Antonio drove back to the hacienda; it was his day to clean and polish all the fine cars belonging to Napoleon Cruz.

They marked the death of El Negro with a feast, Napoleon, Nina and Carlito. They toasted Antonio's competence and courage with fine French wines and champagne. They stuffed themselves with food and drink, little noticing what it was they swallowed, each lost in the celebratory nature of the evening. Napoleon gloated over the removal of one of the Regents' key allies.

"They won't take this without offense," Nina pointed out. "First Bustamente and now El Negro."

"They won't dare strike back at Napoleon," Carlito boasted.

Napoleon reveled in the boy's pride in him, the respect, the homage he perceived in those youthful eyes. "Never underestimate those three. They are always dangerous, cunning, and unrestrained in the exercise of their power. But we shall watch them closely." He raised a glass. "To more and greater victories."

They drank and drank some more, declared their undying allegiance to each other.

"To the best friends I have in all the world," Carlito said. "I love you both."

Napoleon drank to that, then embraced the boy. "Come," he said, voice thick with wine and sentiment. "Come with me, Little Minnow..."

At the door of the dining room, he swung back to where Nina still sat at the table. "And you, my beautiful one, will you join us...?"

Nina hesitated only briefly. She could deny Napoleon nothing. Nodding, she said, "In a few minutes, Napoleon, I will be with you..."

When she made it to Napoleon's bedroom, Nina discovered the tall man on the bed with Carlito. Each of them was naked, and despite the cool dimness of the room, both men shone with a thin coating of perspiration. Both were slender, almost fragile, as if lighter than air, creatures meant to dance and float beyond the reach of ordinary mortals.

They were on the bed, locked in mock combat, wrestling. First one prevailed, then the other. And Nina soon understood that had Napoleon wished it, he could have pinned the smaller boy at any time. At last the bout ended, the two men on their backs and breathing hard, limbs akimbo, as if displaying their proud, dark genitals for Nina's admiration and approval.

She said nothing.

Napoleon reached out for Carlito, drew him close, kissed him lovingly on the mouth. Their embrace was long and passionate and when they separated it was Napoleon who spoke to Nina.

"Come," he said. "Come here. Now."

She climbed on the bed, feeling their eyes travel over her flesh.

"What a woman!" Napoleon said. "Have you ever seen one more beautiful, niño. I think not."

"Never, Napoleon."

"And you, Nina. Look at this boy. Is he not the handsomest creature in all the world?"

Creature was the correct word. Despite his rigid cock, the heaviness of his testicles, there was a silky, androgynous quality about Carlito, half-boy, half-girl. Not the slightest imperfection marred the polish of his skin. His limbs managed to appear soft and graceful, his buttocks round and almost childish. His teeth gleamed when he smiled but his eyes were still and lifeless. He frightened her more than any man she had ever encountered.

Napoleon beckoned and she went to him. He kissed her on the lips and then Carlito did the same. He squeezed her breast until she gasped in pain and he laughed, falling back on his elbows. He shoved his hand roughly between her thighs, fingers spreading, thrusting.

Now it was Napoleon who sucked her breast and at the same time reached out for Carlito. For his buttocks, for his young cock.

There was constant movement now, hands and mouths touching, stroking, licking, sucking. She was on her back suddenly, Napoleon riding her in deep, long strokes. She kissed him on the mouth and, as if repelled, he rolled away.

When she rose up it was to see him entering Carlito from behind, penetrating those sweet round buttocks, the two men grunting in pain and pleasure. Then Napoleon was on his back once more and Carlito's svelte form was bent over him prayerfully, his mouth at Napoleon's cock. Napoleon rose and fell in ancient rhythms and Nina, on some silent command, lowered herself between his thighs, lips soft and warm at the base of his shaft, her tongue probing.

Carlito and Nina, worshipping at the shrine of Napoleon's

power and his glory, paying homage to their employer, their lover, their liege.

Then Carlito withdrew and positioned himself on top of Nina, entering her from behind, and almost at once both men went into violent spasm after spasm, each crying out in relief and dismay, and Nina was drenched with the hot essence of each.

Later, she lay apart from them both, untouched, unnoticed, nostrils clogged with the musky scent of the room. Was this all there was ever to be for her? This hard, demanding sex, careless with affection, devoid of any permanence? That was when she knew that it was time for her to leave the hacienda, time for her to expand Napoleon's empire to another, distant place.

EIGHTEEN

"MI CASA ES SU CASA."

Jorge Ponce Guerrero, Sixaola's minister of internal affairs, greeted Frank Abernathy, Jr., with a brisk handshake and an *abrazo* worthy of a blood relative. A limousine hired for the occasion had carried Abernathy from the Hilton Sixaola to this house in a district known as *Los Balcones,* spreading out as it did over seven hills and looking down on the rest of the capital city. A pair of armed guards had checked Abernathy's identity outside the black stone wall that enclosed the minister's house before admitting him. A servant, short and swarthy, had led the American through a lush tropical garden and across a tiled patio past potted palms and wicker furniture, around a reflecting pool with a fountain from which water fell in gentle cascades, into a low, sprawling structure the minister called home. In a comfortable living room, four men sipped tall drinks and smoked Cuban *supremos*.

"Mi casa es su casa."

With a sweep of one arm, the minister indicated the other men. "Allow me to introduce my colleagues," he said in excellent English. One man, bent and wizened, advanced in a crablike shuffle, eyes concealed behind folds of brown skin—the look of lurking evil.

"Señor Raphael Salazar," the minister said with some pride.

The old man's smile was highlighted by a pair of gold incisors. "Your name is familiar to me, Major Abernathy."

"And yours to me, sir," Abernathy said at once. He found it hard to believe that this wrinkled old man could possess the power ascribed to him in those secret government reports he had read.

"Señor Rene Vega," the minister went on.

Vega was a short man with the tight, muscular body of a veteran jockey. His movements were quick and abrupt, as if ended before they could be completed. He bowed.

"And my good friend, Pablo Uribe," the minister said.

Uribe bowed. He had a peasant's powerful body and the face of an Oriental potentate. His eyes were black, lifeless, still; the face of a scoundrel, Abernathy remarked to himself.

Three of the four Regents, he noted, the men who controlled at least eighty percent of all the drugs that entered the United States from Latin America. Men of power and wealth; and in Sixaola, men who were widely feared and respected.

The fourth man in the room was willowy, diffident, almost foppish in the way he held himself. "Señor Ismael Moreno-Diaz," the minister intoned.

Abernathy was impressed. Moreno-Diaz was Sixaola's minister of defense, brother-in-law of el presidente, leader of one of the six families that had controlled the country since the days of the Spanish conquistadors. The government was well represented in this room, along with the narcotics elite. Optimistic now about the results this meeting would produce, Abernathy offered his hand. "I am honored, sir."

Moreno-Diaz ignored the extended hand. "I, too, Major." He made it sound like an insult.

"Shall we sit and begin?" Ponce Guerrero said swiftly, bridging what might otherwise have been an uncomfortable interlude.

"The matter before us leaves every man present vulnerable and, it should be admitted, with a certain growing apprehension. We live in a changing world, gentlemen, and it is necessary to acknowledge those changes and alter our ways." He inclined his handsome head toward the American. "It is for you to commence, Señor."

Abernathy decided to waste no time on small talk. These men were pragmatists and anxious to get to the heart of the matter.

"My government," he said, "is uneasy about the insurrection in

Sixaola. My president is fearful that it may succeed."

Rene Vega raised a long, strong forefinger, as if requesting permission to speak. "Does that mean that your president has authorized this meeting? If so, is he willing—"

Abernathy broke in. "It means only that I express what I believe to be United States policy. It does not follow that any particular individual in Washington is aware of my presence here."

Vega sighed and sat back in his seat. The others attended to their drinks and their cigars. So much was being asked of them to accept on faith, and faith—outside of the confines of the Church —had never been the accepted currency in Sixaola.

When no one spoke, Abernathy continued. "The Ché Brigade grows stronger by the day, and Central Intelligence insists that Negrete intends to mount a massive attack soon. The key question becomes, can the military repulse such an attack and will the political system withstand such a violent shock?"

The Regents and the Ministers busied themselves in the way of men who had something to conceal. This time it was Salazar who replied.

"Your intelligence estimates give us how much time?"

"Two weeks at the most."

Rene Vega spoke. "If only we had weapons enough. Our soldiers will fight, if they believe they have a chance to win."

Moreno-Diaz, in a musical voice, said, "I was informed that a certain shipment of arms was on the way. Has there been some difficulty with delivery?"

Abernathy shifted around in his chair. He felt ill at ease out of uniform, as if civilian dress brought him down to a lesser level, deprived him of authority and purpose. What was it his commanding officer had said? "Let's get something in return from those Spic bastards . . ."

"The arms," Vega insisted.

"Quid pro quo," Abernathy said.

"What?" Vega grunted. "What does he say?" he said in Spanish.

"Something for something," Moreno-Diaz answered with a smile. Then in English, he went on. "What do you have in mind, Mr. Abernathy?"

Abernathy spoke with conviction and force. After all, for the moment at least, he was the forward arm of American Foreign Policy. He was about to create that policy, put it firmly in place, make sure that it would be carried out. Not bad for a man who wore only gold oak leaves on his shoulders.

"Drugs are doing great damage to our people," he said.

"Drugs," Uribe muttered, his annoyance clear. He had not come to discuss his business with this pale gringo. "Let's talk about guns."

"What drugs?" Vega said mildly. "What drugs is he talking about?" He turned to Salazar.

The old man bared his teeth in what passed for a smile. "Coca, sí, Major? Coca is on your mind?"

"There is nothing to talk about," Vega gritted out.

"The poor of our nation cannot exist without coca," Uribe said.

"It is their only cash crop," Moreno-Diaz explained. "The center of their lives."

Abernathy made his disapproval evident. His eyes flashed, his lip curled, his voice grew heavy with sarcasm. "And does not coca make all of you rich and powerful—or am I wrong?"

Ponce Guerrero answered. His manner was smooth, a slight smile curling his finely etched mouth, his eyes glittering and showing nothing. "Coca is the economic base of Sixaola. Oh, yes, it does make certain people wealthy. But is that not the way of capitalism? For the few to grow fat off the labor of the many? Please, allow me to continue. Without some wealth this nation would not be able to pay the exorbitant interest rates your American banks charge on the twelve billion dollars they have insisted we borrow..."

"Insisted!" Abernathy sputtered.

"Indeed," Ponce Guerrero went on. "Money dangled until our people, in the manner of weak and underprivileged people everywhere, could not resist. Money that promised relief for our people from starvation and disease, money that would modernize our economy, educate our children. Sadly it has not happened that way. The poverty is everywhere around us. Diseases kill the people. Too many of us wake up hungry and go to bed hungry. Without the coca leaf, what will the peons have left?"

"The United States is not responsible for the corruption—"

Ponce Guerrero went on without pause. "This talk of halting the coca business is an exercise in futility, señor. It will not happen. Not under this government. Not under a revolutionary government. Never. The oligarchy will not and cannot permit it. Never. The Marxists—Negrete—he speaks openly of cocaine as the weapon that will ultimately bring down the norteamericanos, that will topple the giant at last. No, Señor Abernathy, coca is with us to stay."

"And if I say we will allow Sixaola to go under?"

Moreno-Diaz spread his hands. "Then I will say to you, what will happen to your twelve billion dollars? An impoverished people cannot pay such a cruel debt. Consider what will then take place. How many banks will fail in your country should that happen? How many fortunes will be lost? How far will the stock market crash? How many businesses with investments in my country will collapse? And what will be the fate of an administration that allows such a calamity to take place? What of it?"

It was Salazar, gold teeth twinkling as he spoke, who summed up. "We shall do what has to be done. We will contact Negrete and make whatever arrangements are possible with him and his men. It will not be as congenial as it could have been with the Americans, but in time it will work to our benefit. Napoleon deals with Negrete, and so can we."

"Will Negrete deal with us?"

"Of course. He is a patriot. He is of our blood, our culture, he thinks as we do. All differences are negotiable."

Abernathy saw his mission sliding into disaster, his career ruined, his reputation shattered. These men had prepared for any eventuality. They expected the worst of every situation and so were prepared always to deal from a position of strength. His eyes skittered from one to another, his pale skin mottled, his mouth taut.

"Let's keep on talking," he implored.

"What is left to talk about?" Salazar said. "What you want we cannot provide. What we need, you will not give. So be it."

"So be it," Uribe echoed.

Abernathy leaned forward, gesturing to include them all. "Tell me—what is possible and what is not? From there, we may proceed." He smiled placatingly. "After all, we are all reasonable men."

Uribe said, "The required arms must reach our military forces as discussed. That is not negotiable. Along with the arms, experts who can teach our soldiers to use such advanced weaponry."

Ponce Guerrero agreed. "For our part, we shall create a situation where Negrete and his bandits can be neutralized. The revolution will be contained, the government will stand, the relationship between our countries will continue as before. Allies and neighbors, friends in all matters."

"Sounds okay to me."

"As for the coca," Salazar said, "it will be permitted to continue as it is. No special operations, such as your military launched in Columbia in 1986. Intercepts at the border as before, conceded. Arrests of low-level personnel in Central America, of course. On-going aggression against dealers within U.S. territory, naturally. These are expected costs of doing business, we understand that. But no one will be allowed to interfere severely with operations here or with the lives or financial concerns of any man in this room."

"My superiors may not agree that this is an equitable arrangement."

"Let your superiors consider this," Salazar said in a low, firm voice. "Let them consider another Marxist state in Latin America. Cuba, Nicaragua and possibly Sixaola. Is that what your people want? I think not."

Abernathy was desperate to come out of this meeting with some small prize. Otherwise—

"You must try to give me something substantial," he said. "I cannot return empty-handed."

The Regents conferred among themselves. Bustamente's murder was mentioned. And the death of El Negro. The tenuous future of Napoleon Cruz.

"Something that will produce a dramatic effect in my country." Abernathy continued. "Create favorable headlines. Editorials. That sort of thing. There's a Congressional election upcoming, you see. It would help if the administration could claim a substantive victory in the war against drugs."

Salazar looked up, his ancient face expressionless. "It may be that we can supply what you need. Certain complicated arrangements must be put in place, however. You will be informed."

"Soon?"

"Oh, yes, very soon."

NINETEEN

THREE DAYS AFTER HIS RETURN FROM SIXAOLA, JACK
Keveney looked again at the film taken of Silvia Gutierrez. Her
beauty was stunning, as was the quiet, implicit authority that
emanated from her. There was an animal grace to her movements
and a regal set to her chin and an imperious shift in those
strangely pale eyes set in that tawny face, all angles and shadows.
She was, he decided, the most exciting women he'd ever seen.

"Who the hell is she?" he said aloud, not expecting an answer.
The agent with him repeated her name. Keveney went on as if the
other man hadn't spoken. "She appears on the scene out've nowhere. Handling big sums of money. She bounced along the
border, then drops out've sight. What've we got on her so far?"

"Nothing yet."

"Well, that's great. Next time she surfaces, I want her followed.
Where does she live? Who puts up the dough? Find out everything there is to know about her. Her age, her height, her weight.
Where's she from? What's she do in her spare time? Is she married? Have a lover? Whatever there is. Run her through the
D.E.A. computer. Check the F.B.I. I want surveillance kept on
every one of those border laundering operations. This Silvia, I got
a hunch she's the key to something big..."

If so, Silvia refused to open the lock of the secrecy that surrounded her. Government files revealed no information about
her. And the team tracking her was frustrated when she faded
from view in rush-hour traffic in San Diego. She was gone.

Until nine days later when she turned up at a Hudson River

217

pier in Manhattan. A D.E.A. agent, shooting film out of the back of a truck of the disembarking crew of a Panamanian flag freighter, aimed his camera on a man greeted by a stunning woman in black leather slacks and jacket. The film was not brought to Keveney's attention until a week later. The woman, of course, was Silvia Gutierrez.

"And the guy?" he demanded.

"Name of Raul Cepeda. A Columbian chemist."

A flush of excitement took hold of him; a courier for large sums of drug money and a chemist. "What've we got on Cepeda?" he said.

"Cepeda is believed to have set up cocaine processing plants in Colombia, in Sixaola and in Bolivia. Three times the plants were hit by the good guys and each time Cepeda got away. He's smart, he's good, he's slippery. Last time he surfaced, he was cooking for a character in Chiriqui."

"You get a name?" Keveney said, knowing the answer.

"You'll get a kick out of this. Calls himself Napoleon. Napoleon Cruz. Word is he's a comer."

"What else?"

"Not much. Cepeda and Gutierrez drink some coffee in a Times Square greasy spoon. They talk for about an hour before they split up. He checks into the Waldorf, stays in his room for a couple of hours, has dinner alone in a steak joint on Lexington Avenue. He walks back to the hotel, goes up to his room and, get this, has never been seen again."

"He checked out?"

"No check out. Nothing. Just gone. Left his suitcase in the room. A change of underwear, toilet articles, like that."

"And Silvia?"

"That's interesting. She books a flight on Eastern to Miami . . ."

"You had your people pick her up when she landed?"

"That's just it, instead she hops a shuttle for Boston. One of my people went along. In Boston, she boards a plane for Chicago where she changes planes and flies on to San Francisco."

"And then?"

"We lost her. The lady is very good at what she does. What do you make of it, Mr. Keveney?"

Keveney went over it all in his mind before answering. "Somebody is about to change his M.O.," he said deliberately. "Somebody is about to start shipping coca paste into the States, process it here."

"Set up a lab and cook the stuff?"

"Exactly."

"It doesn't make sense."

"The hell it doesn't," Keveney shot back. "Look at it this way, our people, the D.E.A, we're all trained to look for the White Lady. Nobody thinks paste. Nobody even knows what the stuff looks like. While we're retraining our personnel, the paste comes in unnoticed."

"Shit. It's a whole new ball game."

"Not yet, but soon. We've got to locate that chemist. Wherever the man is, that's where the lab will be—"

"Dumb luck is what," Art Brennan, D-Group's number one man in Los Angeles, spoke over the long distance wire. "We were tracking a pair of Colombian importers out at the airport when the lady makes her entrance."

"Gutierrez?" Keveney said, unable to control his excitement.

"The one and only. What a prize she is. You want me to pick her up?"

"What I want is for you to put a tail on her. She goes to the john, I want to know when and where, what she did. Who she spoke to, the works. Don't lose her, Brennan."

"You got it, Boss."

Two days later, Brennan called back. "The lady's in the market for real estate."

"Like what?" Keveney asked.

"Factory buildings mostly. Industrial sites. She checked out one location and visited it a second time, walked around the neighborhood. I put a call in to the real estate guy, said I was interested. He told me it was rented, just today."

"What other businesses are in the building?"

"An electrical appliance outfit, a carpentry shop, a plastics factory and, would you believe it, a fertilizer plant. Place smells like a chemistry class..."

"Perfect for a coke lab. Noisy, smelly. Nobody's gonna pay much attention to the stink of the sulphuric acid they use to cook the paste." Keveney tried to sort out what he knew; this could be the breakthrough he had been hoping for. Once Cepeda put the laboratory together, once it was operative, he would be able to hit them hard, sweeping up Silvia Gutierrez at the same time. "Keep a watch on that site," he said. "Give me daily reports, daily. I want to know what equipment they bring in. We'll put out an alert to D.E.A., to customs, to the Border Patrol, to watch for coca paste."

"How do you think they'll bring it in?"

"When I know, you'll know."

The surveillance of Silvia Gutierrez continued. Men and women drinking lukewarm coffee in unmarked cars and smoking more than was good for them. Others on foot, ducking in and out of doorways. Waiting while she shopped for clothes on Rodeo Drive. And always there was the peripatetic van with its hidden cameras grinding away. And thus did Arky Garrett come into the picture.

"A player," Aaron Marks said. Marks was an agent with a rare skill at analyzing evidence, with linking events and suspects. A dark-haired man with moist eyes and a thoughtful way of speaking, he had been a street cop in Detroit before joining D-Group. "Garrett is in the trucking business in St. Louis, which gives him a good reason to run around the country making deals, making connections. Check him out."

Film flickered across the screen, and there was Arky Garrett standing in front of a Mexican restaurant in East Los Angeles. He looked at his watch, lit a cigarette, then tossed it away. He looked at his watch again.

"Nervous," Keveney remarked.

"Man doesn't like to be kept waiting. This time it's worth it. Look at what we have here..."

Joining Garrett on the street, Silvia Gutierrez, sleek and shining in designer jeans, boots and a red leather bomber jacket. She greeted Garrett with a generous smile and a brisk handshake before leading the way into the restaurant.

"A deal," Aaron Marks said. "Arky the buyer, Silvia the seller."

"Has it gone down?"

"Two days after these pictures were taken. In Oakland. A pilot for Sixaolan Airlines flew into Kennedy on a direct flight. Breezed through customs without a looksee. Two hours later he was on his way west, carrying a blue Samsonite weekender. He gave it to Silvia in the Oakland airport and she gave him a brown paper bag in return."

"Drugs for dough."

"Exactly."

"And then?"

"Silvia connects with Arky Garrett in the lobby of the Mark Hopkins Hotel an hour or so later, delivers the blue bag to him and collects an airline shoulder bag for her trouble."

"This time she gets the money."

"You got that right. Next thing, she's back in L.A. and her apartment, taking a long swim in the pool."

"And Arky Garrett?"

Aaron Marks grinned. "Stuck in an isolation cell in the city jail in Oakland."

"I'd like to talk to him."

"Figured you might. I made a plane reservation for you tonight. Art Brennan will meet you..."

Arky Garrett's expensively tailored suit was stained and wrinkled, and his equally expensive haircut was no longer a thing of beauty. Behind thick glasses with wide black rims his eyes resembled hard-boiled eggs, frantically jerking around, seeking a safe and restful place to light. He had been chewing on his manicured nails and dried blood seeped out of one wounded cuticle.

"You look real shitty to me, Arky." Art Brennan was a tall man, dour and reserved, with immense hands and feet and a Lincolnesque visage. He shook his head in disapproval. "Think of it, Arky, if you had to pull some truly hard time. Not your way at all, not at all."

Garrett had the faded look of a man who had once considered himself tough. He was a workingman who'd managed to bring himself up to a loftier economic state, losing too much of his essential self in the process. His voice was shrill when he spoke.

"This is crazy, holding me this way. I'm a citizen, I'm entitled. To a phone call. To a lawyer. I got rights, y'know. Why can't I call my lawyer?"

Brennan gestured and Garrett flinched. "Meet Jack Keveney, Arky. He came all the way from Washington, D.C., to talk to you, Arky. Mr. Keveney wants to ask you some questions."

Garrett met Keveney's gaze for a beat or two before turning away. The man in front of him might have gone unnoticed in a crowd. But here, up close, there was a disturbing element about Keveney, a silent intimidation. The set of his mouth, the bright sheen in those steady accusing eyes from which Garrett found no escape, no relief. How, he wondered, had he come to this?

"I don't know anything," he said, almost to himself. "I'm a businessman."

Keveney lowered himself to the edge of the narrow cot in the narrow cell and continued to examine Garrett. Silence, he had long ago learned, was a fearsome weapon to use against a man without a hard core of self-confidence. Most men preferred bluster and threats; Garrett, Keveney believed, was such a man. He let Garrett wait a little while longer.

"Listen," Garrett wailed. "You guys have no right."

Brennan cracked the swollen knuckles of his right hand. Finished, he did the same to his other hand; they sounded like gunshots. Garrett jerked around, looking to Keveney for relief.

"There's the Constitution, the Bill of Rights. What you're doing, it isn't right. It isn't legal."

Keveney leaned this way. "Silvia," he said, almost inaudibly. "Silvia Gutierrez?"

Garrett's hard-boiled eyes rolled in their sockets and a low moan dribbled across his lips. "I think I'm gonna be sick. You gotta get me to a doctor."

"The stuff is in the blue bag," Brennan said. "Fifty percent cocaine. How much you pay Silvia? Two hundred thousand? A quarter of a million? Arky's right," he said to Keveney. "About being a businessman? A trucking magnate . . ."

"It's just a small business," Garrett protested.

"He gets around, travels a lot. Even goes out on a run by himself now and then. Arky's well-connected in the street and all've a sudden he is moving some prime Sixaolan coke."

"No, no, it's a mistake. I'm a married man with a wife and a house, three kids."

Brennan produced a down and dirty laugh. "Arky even owns a boat. Nice, sweet job, she is. After six months in the slammer, Arky, that good-looking wife of yours will be running that boat out on the river with some sleek young stud, getting it from him three times a day while you get banged around in the joint. Not so nice for your kids, Arky. Not so nice for you."

"Go to hell, you guys, go to hell . . ." Garrett's voice weakened and ended in a tight, dry sob. "I was going under," he cried. "I expanded too fast and had to borrow. I owed the local sharks just over a million. You know what those creeps do if you don't keep up the vigorish. They break legs, shoulders . . . I had to find a way."

"Which is where Silvia came in," Keveney said gently.

"She came to me. Like she knew what trouble I was in, that I had the shorts. Her people had some problems around St. Louis, she needed distribution. She supplied the names and all I had to do was make the drops . . ."

"Perfect for a trucking outfit," Brennan said.

"She helped me pay off the sharks. She covered my ass. She said it would only be until she could line up somebody else."

"Once she had her hooks in you, Arky, you were her boy. Besides, you liked the dough."

"Oh, Jesus God! I don't want to go to jail."

"You a Catholic, Arky?" Keveney said.

"What? Oh, yeah . . . maybe I oughta talk to a priest, make my confession."

"Get it off your conscience, Arky," Keveney said. "Put right what you did wrong. Be a good citizen, a good Christian." Keveney edged closer to the other man and took hold of his hand, gently but firmly. He smiled, and the smile terrified Garrett more than anything that had been said. These awful men, Silvia, the sharks—none of them cared about Arky Garrett. None of them were concerned with his problems. Living and dying, that was up to him now. It was time to take care of himself, good care, to protect his family, to keep himself alive. And then Keveney provided the chance.

"Talk to me, Arky. You'll feel much better."

"What do you want to know?"

"Everything," Brennan rasped.

"And then," Keveney added simply, "you're going to put me on to Silvia Gutierrez . . ."

"Surprised?" Brennan said.

"The lady breaks patterns," Keveney conceded.

"You figured a fancy house up in the hills of Hollywood. Or on the beach at Malibu. The pool, the tennis court, the houseboy, the works. Not this bimbo. Plays it safe. Quiet. Strictly bourgeois. Fit in. Don't attract attention. Which is hard when you got a body that don't quit." Brennan laughed, Keveney didn't. He stared straight ahead.

Rainbow Apartments was a complex of two-story buildings not far from the glitz and grubbiness of the Sunset Strip. Once sleek and modern, the buildings showed signs of age and neglect. Erected around a liver-shaped swimming pool, the complex contained small units occupied for the most part by stewardesses and young actors, and a few low-level executives. It was a pleasant enough place to live friendly, and the rents were manageable.

"Lots of fine looking young quiff," Brennan pointed out. "So Silvia can fade into the background, just another one of the girls. Could be a few of them are part-time hookers, but not our Silvia.

Office furniture, that's her cover. A traveling saleslady, which lets her put in a lot of time on the road."

"Men?" Keveney said without emphasis.

"Nobody that we know about. She keeps her distance from the studs around the pool. Fact is, nobody gets close to Silvia."

The two men were seated in a battered Chevy, Art Brennan behind the wheel, across the street from the Rainbow Apartments. "You're moving in tomorrow morning," Brennan said. "Furniture, TV, the works. You're office manager for Satellite Import-Export, a New York firm, establishing a Los Angeles office for the first time. We rented space downtown and some of our people will be on duty there all the time. Your name is John Abruzzi. Italian father, Irish mother, an only child. Here's your biography, names, dates, everything, and all the necessary paper —Social Security card, company I.D., credit cards, driver's license, the works."

"Looks good."

"If Silvia has you checked out, the calls will be fed into our New York office and they're all set up to handle it, special operator and all. I still think you should've let me assign a man to this. What if—"

"This one belongs to me. Now let's split. I got work to do before tomorrow comes..."

Keveney could find no satisfactory answer. To put himself on the line this way, to submit himself to possible exposure, to danger, even death, as if demanding to be found out. Yet he was profoundly unable to assign Silvia Gutierrez to another man in D-Group: She rightfully belonged to him.

Since watching the surveillance film of Silvia in Laredo, hardly a day had passed without his thinking about her. It went beyond thinking. Conjuring up visions of the black-haired woman in motion, that undulating stride, incredibly graceful and erotically provocative. Her beauty, her easy confidence, her ability to fade in and out of sight no matter how many people he assigned to watch her, enhanced her appeal and enlarged her importance to him as a cop. She was the key piece of the puzzle, Keveney kept telling

himself, and to control her meant to make the other pieces fall
into place. Where had she come from? How had she managed to
advance to such a responsible position in the drug world? Who
did she work for? Who did she shield from public view? All questions only she could answer, for she was clearly no ordinary street
dealer.

Yet deal she did. As she had with Arky Garrett. As she had with
others, Keveney was convinced.

Why not take her now? Charge her. Arky Garrett, already
turned, would bear witness against Silvia sufficiently to put her
away for the best ten to twenty years of her life. Her organization
would be destroyed—certainly dealt a major blow from which it
would take a long time to recover. The cooking plant she intended
to set up would never become operative. The chemist, Cepeda,
could be sent away. It would be a major coup for D-Group; it
would justify their continued existence.

But Keveney wanted more. He knew with an irresistible certainty that behind Gutierrez existed a complex and thoroughly
professional organization that reached deep into Latin America.
Through Medellín, the drug capital of Colombia. Or Chiriqui, in
Sixaola. To the hundreds of thousands of coca-growing acres in
Peru and Paraguay. He yearned to penetrate the chain of supply,
to break the distribution links, the labs, to arrest the couriers and
the mules, the murderous muscle that made such an organization
work. Most of all, he longed to identify the head of the organization, the man, or men, who functioned with such impunity,
whether in their own lands or in the United States. He wanted to
cut off the head, destroy it forever.

Gutierrez could give it all to him. Names, places, avenues the
smugglers used to bring their grim product into the country,
methods of communication, schedules, a roster of peripheral
workers. She knew it all. She could provide it all. To Keveney.

And why not to another man?

Why risk leaving his command desk in Washington? A thousand
details could go wrong, and if only one or two did, his position
within D-Group would be subverted, his career left in shambles.
Despite this, he refused to let go.

Silvia Gutierrez was his.

Why?

The answer came rushing at him with unseemly haste, frightening him even as he mocked his own shortcomings and laughed at his private failings and the absurdity of the twisted need that drove him.

Silvia Gutierrez could return to him something precious, now lost. Those marvelous days of his young manhood when he worked undercover, amidst unforeseen threats and dangers. She could supply the stimulation and excitement that these days eluded him, leaving his life sapped of purpose. Ambition had carried him to a high position in his profession, only to leave him professionally emasculated; the cop he had once prided himself for being had failed to survive. He had been transformed into a paper shuffler, dispensing orders to better, more vigorous men, men deeply enmeshed in the rigors of the real world. Without family, without friends, without the minute-by-minute thrills and satisfactions the job once provided, he had receded into impotence as a cop and as a man.

He had to become part of it again.

To breathe new life into his aging flesh. To revive his flagging vigor. To experience once more the lust for life he had once reveled in.

Silvia, and all she represented, belonged to him alone.

He would bring her down.

Keveney and Silvia. They were, he understood, a match made in hell.

Every morning Keveney left the Rainbow Apartments dressed to do battle in the world outside. And every afternoon he returned, looking a little the worse for wear, a man barely holding his own against the forces of commerce. And when the hot California sun dipped toward the Pacific Ocean, Keveney went out to the livershaped pool and swam laps. He swam without urgency, not keeping count, continuing until, arms and shoulders exhausted, he climbed up to the edge of the pool. He rested in a lounge chair, he smoked, he read a biography of Peter the Great.

Occasionally some of the tenants set up a charcoal grill and broiled steaks at poolside or hot dogs and hamburgers. Twice Keveney was invited to join them and each time he declined, choosing to maintain a strategic distance. Nevertheless, he allowed himself to be drawn into conversations from time to time, and soon word spread throughout the complex: John Abruzzi was in the import-export business, he was unmarried—divorced—a loner who talked openly about certain easily verifiable details of his life. Yet he allowed no one to peer into the shadowed portions where every man carried his secret self.

There were some tenants who—their imaginations shaped by movies and TV—made subdued jokes about Abruzzi, linking him to the Mafia, making him out to be on some deadly assignment. No one dared raise the question with him, however. The men who congregated around the pool each evening were vaguely intimidated by the muscular man with the shaggy, graying hair; and the women found him oddly appealing.

Silvia Gutierrez eventually heard all the talk. She identified the object of the gossip but displayed no interest in him. Each evening, when she was at home, she too swam laps. But she gave no indication that she was aware of his presence, even when they were in the water at the same time.

More than once, having completed his swim before her, he watched her lift herself out of the water, body sleek and lush, shining in the purple light of dusk. It occurred to him that to see her without clothes on would be like looking at a naked woman for the first time. She would be different, unique, in ways he was unable to fathom. To look her way was to experience sensual promises that he could neither describe nor anticipate, magical rewards she alone could bestow.

Thinking about her made him edgy and aware of the weakness of his flesh, his character. And he began to believe that he had committed some massive, indescribable blunder in taking on this assignment; he vowed one night to correct the mistake by assigning another agent to Silvia Gutierrez. But the next evening he was back in the pool, swimming laps with renewed energy. Smoking his cigarettes. Trying to concentrate on Peter the Great and failing. Waiting anxiously for Silvia to appear again.

Without warning the weather turned bad. It rained steadily for three days and three nights. Confined to his new apartment, Keveney periodically looked out at the deserted pool, wondering whether Silvia was at home or out consummating some drug deal or, worse, lying somewhere in the arms of another man. He rejected the idea at once, refusing to consider that possibility.

During the day, Keveney spent his time at the Satellite Import-Export Company, where he received reports from local agents as well as from his headquarters in Washington. He realized that by remaining in the field he was neglecting his executive duties. But if Silvia was the conduit to the large and well-organized drug operation he believed her to be, it would be worth it.

Twice in the last week his men had watched her carry dirty money to her contacts along the Mexican border. And twice more they had seen her exchange packets—drugs, Keveney was certain—with buyers. These activities had Keveney convinced that Silvia was merely a cog—though an important one—in a much larger operation. Whoever was at the top would never risk his personal safety as she did.

Art Brennan reported no progress in the search for the chemist, Cepeda. "The man has dropped out of sight."

"He's buying. Equipment to cook the stuff. Ether and sulphuric acid. Keep me abreast of every incoming shipment your men apprehend. Every suspicious plane or boat. That first load of coca paste will show up soon."

"And if we're wrong, if there's no coca paste?"

Keveney gave no answer; the presence of the chemist in the equation made him sure that a shipment of coca paste was inevitable.

The rain ceased around noon that day and the sun soon appeared. The air grew thick and sluggish, the heat suddenly oppressive. Keveney left work early, anxious to cool his fevered skin in the pool. He had just finished his laps when Silvia appeared.

She dropped her towel and headed toward the pool. Keveney decided it was time to make his move.

"Miss Gutierrez," he began, giving her his best smile.

She turned a haughty gaze his way. "Yes?" There was a slight sibilance in the way she spoke the word, extending the sound, making Keveney feel that in her presence he was one of God's lesser creatures.

"I understand you're in the furniture business." He waited for her to respond but she said nothing, those tipped eyes of hers flat and unyielding. "I've opened an office in Los Angeles and..."

"You wish to do business with me." It was a declaration, with neither concern nor interest.

"The coincidence of both of us living here. I thought—"

"You have a card?"

"Back in my apartment." Keveney saw a chance to move the relationship forward. "I'll deliver it to you this evening. Better yet, why don't you let me buy you dinner? I can outline my requirements and—"

"Drop your card in my mailbox, Mister..."

"Abruzzi."

"Yes, Abruzzi. I'll get back to you when I can."

Before he could reply, she executed a flat racing dive, advancing through the water with clean effortless strokes. Keveney watched for a while, admiring her style.

Three mornings later Silvia Gutierrez presented herself at Keveney's office. He guided her through the various spaces, saying little, watching her take measurements, make notes, draw designs on her pad. Her inspection completed, they returned to Keveney's private office.

Seated, she refused his offer of coffee and began asking questions about the nature of his business, the projected number of employees, their functions, and the placement of telephone and computer lines. She seemed to know what she was talking about. Keveney, having been carefully rehearsed, was able to provide answers to her questions, answers that seemed to satisfy her.

"Well, then," she said finally. "This is what you require." She spoke in a manner that allowed for no contradiction, referring seldom to her notes. Keveney listened from behind his desk, fascinated by the slow play of her wide mouth. Once her glance met his and those pale irises seemed to flicker—a momentary crack in her professional demeanor, quickly gone—then she hurried on, discussing square footage, computer stations, sliding divider panels. When she was finished, she put the yellow unlined pad in her lap and crossed her legs. "Well?"

"Sounds good. Let's go with your suggestions."

She showed no surprise at his easy acceptance. She turned to a price list, presenting a total cost. "I require a twenty percent down payment, Mr. Abruzzi."

"Call me John. I'll write you a check."

She read it carefully before folding it and depositing it in her purse. "Delivery for most items within ten days. Some of the larger pieces will take a week or so longer." She rose and offered her hand.

He took it.

"A pleasure doing business with you, Mr. Abruzzi."

"John," he corrected, still clinging to her hand. "It's almost time for lunch. I know a good restaurant and—"

"I think not." No excuses, no explanations, no coquettishness. Just a flat turndown.

"How about dinner then?"

She gazed at him for a moment, and he imagined he saw a flicker of interest—or was it merely amusement?—in her eyes. "I'm sure we'll meet again at the pool, Mr. Abruzzi." She reclaimed her hand and was gone.

The faint, disturbing scent of her lingered for the rest of the day.

Exactly ten days later the first shipment of furniture was delivered to Keveney's office. Workmen arranged the panels, dividing the large central space into cubbyholes, and that afternoon a cadre of "employees" materialized. They were, of course, agents of D-Group, detached to this special assignment. By noon the next day, the telephones and computers were hooked up and the place looked and sounded like a business office. And that evening, when he returned to the Rainbow Apartments, Keveney discovered Silvia Gutierrez already in the pool, steadily swimming laps.

When at last she climbed out of the water, skin shining, looking tender to the touch, Keveney was waiting. He handed her a towel and she dried herself. She lowered herself onto a lounge chair, legs stretched out, put her head back and closed her eyes.

"You're staring," she said.

He laughed and arranged himself in a chair facing her. "I won't deny it. But you're used to being stared at, I'm sure."

After a brief interval, she said, "Are you satisfied, Mr. Abruzzi?"

The question startled him. "Satisfied?"

"You did receive your delivery yesterday?"

"Oh, yes. Very satisfied."

"Good. Perhaps we'll be able to do business again sometime, Mr. Abruzzi."

"What must I do to get you to call me John?"

She chose her words carefully. "We do business, Mr. Abruzzi. We both swim in the same pool. Hardly the basis for a personal relationship."

"I'm just trying to be friendly."

"We Latinos are more reticent about making friends. We are—a bit more cautious about allowing strangers into our lives. It is our Spanish heritage, I suppose. Stiff-necked and proud."

"Admirable qualities," he said with a smile.

"I amuse you, Mr. Abruzzi?"

"You please me in many ways, Miss Gutierrez."

A quick glance and she looked away. He took in the smooth line of her throat, the graceful fall of her breasts. He imagined he could smell her, delicate and womanly, and knew that her skin would be incredibly soft and smooth. How would she taste, he wondered. Sweet, with a subtle pungency flavored by dark, foreign spices. At that moment he hungered for her more than any other woman he had ever known, and with the hunger came a rush of guilt as he remembered Rosie, the vows they had taken that, in the eyes of the One True Church, bound them as one for eternity.

She brought her eyes around to meet his. "You are a married man," she said, as if reading his mind.

"Divorced."

"We Catholics don't believe in divorce."

He could not contain his surprise. "You go to church?"

She appraised him solemnly. "I no longer am a practicing Christian, Mr. Abruzzi. But when you are raised Catholic—" She shrugged and her breasts rose and fell under the thin dark fabric of her bathing suit. "Abruzzi," she went on. "Italians are Catholic?"

"Lapsed," he said, adding lightly, "like you."

She did not respond to his smile. "You don't ask if I have a husband. Is it that you do not care? Perhaps you prefer the company of married women. That would be safer in one way, even as it is dangerous."

"No," he responded. "No husband, not you."

"In my country a woman without a man is considered incomplete. Unfinished. Still to be fulfilled."

"These days, in America, such ideas are considered old-fashioned. Out of date."

"Ah." Her eyes closed again. "The women's movement, as you call it. I have never required a community of my sisters to set me free."

The truth resonated in her voice. She enlisted in no cause other than her own. She would never subordinate her ambitions to any group. If she gave her loyalty, it was for reasons she alone determined, that much was clear to Keveney. She was, he conceded, a full load for anyone foolhardy enough to attempt to subdue her.

"You are," he said with admiration, "one fine piece of work."

"Piece of work?" The phrase was strange to her.

"A bundle. One hell of a woman."

Her eyes traveled over his face, as if seeing him for the first time, lingering over significant details that might reveal more about him than he would freely confess.

"You're right, Mr. Abruzzi. I have no husband."

"Bingo. Then we can have dinner together."

"But there is a man."

"Serious?" The word was out before he could cut it off. He felt dismay and despair, denial, unable to accept what she was telling him.

Again that hint of mockery. "Serious, yes. But not solemn, Mr. Abruzzi. As you Americans like to say—can you handle that?"

He wasn't sure how to answer.

She was full of surprises.

She kept him at a distance, at the same time provoking his interest in ways he could not always identify. It was as if he had been turned by her, was being controlled and manipulated. She was in his thoughts always and danced mockingly through his dreams at night. She came and went like a wraith, disappearing for days at a time, only to surface again where one of his agents could catch her. Their reports told of her efforts to sell office furniture, of business lunches and professional meetings. No drugs were delivered. No money exchanged hands. No indication was given of lab equipment being shipped, and there was no sign of Raul Cepeda. Keveney became more and more frustrated and began to consider confronting her directly.

Until she surprised him once again.

After a three-day absence, Silvia returned to her apartment. And that evening she presented herself at Keveney's door, looking delicate and almost girlish in a flimsy green flowered skirt that matched her eyes and a blouse without sleeves. Her raven-colored hair shone as it tumbled freely across her shoulders, and her tawny cheeks were scrubbed. There was a taunting tilt to her mouth and it occurred to Keveney that she hardly ever smiled and he had never heard her laugh.

"For you," she said in greeting, offering him a single long-stemmed rose.

Startled, Keveney almost dropped the flower. "No one's ever given me a flower before."

"No woman, you mean? How sad for you, Abruzzi."

He noted the new familiarity; some progress had been made. He invited her in. "I'll put this in water." There was no vase in the apartment, nothing suitable, and he looked around the small kitchen helplessly.

"American men," she said disparagingly, but without malice. From the refrigerator she removed a half-empty carton of milk, emptying it into the sink. Using a serrated knife, she cut away the top of the carton, rinsed it, the filled it halfway with water. She placed the rose with a flourish. "How beautiful," she said. "In my country, flowers are a part of our lives. Every house, no matter how poor, has its garden. Jasmine, bougainvillea, jacaranda trees; there are color and sweet smells everywhere."

He led her back into the living room. "May I offer you a drink?"

She took up a position in the center of the room, as if claiming her own space, looking at him steadily. "I have been away," she declared after a while.

"I know. I missed you."

She hesitated. "You don't know me well enough to miss me, Abruzzi."

An adolescent awkwardness made him uneasy, as if he were a boy again confronting the prettiest girl in school and unable to make a move in her direction. As if anticipating him, she took a single sinuous stride, closing the gap which separated them, searching his eyes. His knees locked and a debilitating weakness settled in behind his navel. She swayed his way and her lips touched his, the caress of a butterfly's wings. She spoke in a whisper.

"Well, Abruzzi, is that the best you can do . . . ?"

Her words, her nearness, gave birth to a rising mist that raised him up, thrusting him into a warmly inviting environment that was, at the same time, frightening and without familiar checkpoints. From afar he observed her gestures, caresses, all familiar even as they were new.

They shed their clothes and made for his bed, with pauses here and there, sensual stations of the cross, the exquisite agony of his flesh transporting him out of time and place.

She was never still. Squirming, twisting, humping without pause, each part of her giving and extracting elusive rewards, tantalizing beyond his reach. Her breasts, her warm belly, her shapely arms so strong for someone so slender, her fingers in performance across his skin. The weighted female scent of her, hot and honeyed, clogged the cavities of his skull, made him tremble, helpless before her, craving more. Her thighs were wondrous and strong, a pulsating vise around his waist, forming a fleshy cushion against his cheeks. Sounds back in her throat, echoing, muffled, unrecognizable as being made by her.

Her mouth never paused, an unintelligible mix of Spanish and English. Her lips were hot and moist, her tongue a wet probe into heretofore forbidden orifices. Sated at last, he fell back exhausted and enfeebled, heart pounding, eyes rolling back in his head.

She allowed no respite. There was a directness to her lovemaking, a completeness, a singularity that launched him deep into inner space until, by means not yet revealed to him, she drew him back.

It went on. Seamlessly. From crest to valley and back to crest again. Without interruption—and if they stopped to rest or drink or talk, he could not remember any of it later when he tried. All that remained afterward was the hot, physical smell of her that clung like some magical female emission in the hollows behind his knees and below his genitals and renewed his excitement and made him believe he might die were he to experience her even once more. And certainly die if he failed to.

He was asleep when she came out of the bathroom fully dressed, as fresh and as magnificently simple as before, saying, "Soon it will be dawn, Abruzzi, and we each have work to do."

"I want to see you again," he heard himself say. "Soon. Tonight. We'll have dinner..."

A long silence ensued and he feared he'd committed some terrible, irrevocable blunder. Until she spoke, saying, "Whenever. Who knows?"

He knew better than to press the issue. "Whenever," he repeated.

She nodded agreeably and went to the door. She looked back over her shoulder, then was gone.

Before he fell asleep, Keveney remembered that she didn't

truly know him. Who he was. What his name was. His real name. And that left him incomplete and sad.

She failed to appear at the pool. The men keeping surveillance lost her when she went shopping at Nieman-Marcus on Rodeo Drive and managed to evade her watchers and get out of the store unseen. A week went by and Keveney alerted his people up and down the West Coast; a watch was put on the airports, bus stops and railroad terminals. But Silvia Gutierrez had dropped out of sight. Eight days later she appeared at the door to his apartment at eleven o'clock at night with a bottle of Moet in one hand and some caviar in the other. They made love and he wondered how he had survived without her.

They spent five consecutive nights together, and Keveney confessed to himself that he had lost his soul and was going mad. She was never the same, enticing him along dangerous sentient paths, testing his seriousness, daring him to refuse her anything, and elevating his passion to terrifying heights.

She dared him, she mocked him, she questioned his maleness in word and deed. Nothing satisfied her completely. Do this do that, put your hand here, your cock there. Harder, faster, deeper. He felt himself sliding into a ghastly subservience, his pride and respect for himself stripped away. She made him go beyond prior limits, until all sense of himself fled, leaving him trembling and afraid.

Struggling to mount her in the warm, blurred hours just before one dawn, her body became elusive, a humping, squirming taunt that avoided his hard thrusts. Her sharp, painted nails raked his flanks, dug into his buttocks, danced over his scrotum, a confusing set of signals.

She presented her back. The soft round cushion of her behind heated his groin and he moved forward, trying to turn her.

"That way," she hissed. "The way I am . . ."

"What?" His brain, dizzy and slow with the insane craving he felt for her, could not assimilate her meaning. She took his penis in her hand, guiding him.

"What?" he repeated, unholy images flickering through his mind, a lifetime of defenses crumbling before her physical and emotional onslaught.

"Go in me from behind."

Her buttocks spread, she positioned him; or had he done it by himself? She pulled him onto her, and with grunts and tiny screams into her pillow, she made him aware of the debased and obsessive pleasures the moment provided.

And after he exploded inside her, she said, "Has anyone ever . . . ?"

He responded with a groan of despair. "Not ever . . ."

". . . done for you what I do?"

"No one. Never."

They never spoke of the incident again, nor repeated it. As if all those black, transient needs had been satisfied in that one encounter. He began to believe he was insatiable—as she was— that they were engaged in a wild, rebellious march toward some great and singular love that would exalt them both even as it left him empty and miserable.

"You make me crazy," he told her.

"We're lovers only," she said. A line of his semen streaked her inner thigh. She wiped it with her forefinger, licked at it, all the while looking into his eyes. She offered him the finger, slowly, slowly inserting it into his mouth. "Now," she murmured. "Now you know what I know, the taste of you."

"You make me crazy, the things we do." It was only a matter of time until he spoke of it, he knew, spoke of *him*. The need to know swelled within him like a living creature. "This other man," he said, avoiding those penetrating, pale eyes. "The one with whom it is serious but not solemn."

She stirred until she was above him, looking down almost maternally. "Are you sure that you wish to know?"

"Do you make him crazy?"

She sighed. "Such a simple question, such a complex answer. Why do you want to know?"

"I keep thinking about him, about him with you. Maybe it's how I get my kicks."

Another sigh and, diffidently, she answered. "He makes me crazy. All women are like that with him. He is unreal, a fantasy come alive, the despair of every mother for her female child, the secret longing of that child."

"You're no longer a child."

"No. I ended being a child when—I was still a child. You could not know that, either."

He grew troubled; how separate and different they were. How many barriers kept them apart. How desperately he needed her and how compelled he was to destroy her. But that was still in an uncharted future. For now, she was real and with him, and that was all that mattered.

"Listen to me, Abruzzi," she was saying, bringing him back to her side. "We come from conflicting worlds, you and I."

"Conflicting?" he said, finding it difficult to breathe suddenly. How much did she actually know about him? How vulnerable had he allowed himself to become to her sharp intelligence and finely honed intuition?

She brushed the question aside. "Different, then. Alien. If we were trains on a single track we'd be heading in opposite directions."

"Sounds like a serious breach."

"I am serious. You are a businessman and I . . ." She lapsed into a morose silence.

"What about you?"

Again that dismissive gesture and an answer too practiced, too glib. "Take what is here, Abruzzi. Nothing else matters, it has no connection to you."

He reached for the pack of Camels on the night table. "Smoking may be hazardous to your health." Her tone of voice startled him and he dropped the lighted tube to his chest. He retrieved the cigarette and smelled the acrid scent of scorched hair. He massaged his chest absently and inhaled. "The surgeon general says so," she added. Then she laughed, a big, womanly laugh that roused his interest; he could not recall her ever laughing aloud.

"I'm more likely to burn myself to death while smoking in bed."

"Another hazard of the filthy habit." She was inadvertently

funny, he decided, unaware of the pointed irony of her words. She went on with pedagogic solemnity. "Sometimes to know too much about another person is like a fire that consumes you."

Was that a warning? A threat? Lying in bed with her, drained of energy, his reflexes dulled, his pistol taped beneath the tall chest against the wall, made him aware of how dangerous Silvia Gutierrez could be. He came up on one elbow. "I want . . ."

She cut him off, placing that same finger across his lips. She kissed his chest where the burned hairs were curled and blackened. Her tongue played with his nipples, dispatching circles of passion into his gut, into his cock, which shifted and thickened and began to swell again. Mother of God, he thought. Never, never before, had it been like this for him.

She was gone by the next day, managing once more to elude the agents assigned to follow her. Keveney, disgusted with the inability of his trained men to stay on the trail of a single woman, blasted them for their continued failures. And secretly admired Silvia for the skilled professional she was. Her ability to shed her pursuers, did that mean she was on to them? Did she *know* she was being watched? If so, did that mean someone on his team was also on her payroll? He refused to believe that, putting it all down to her natural caution and refusal to travel in a straight line. With her gone, Keveney opted to tend to neglected business. He caught the first available flight to Washington.

There were administrative decisions to make. Calls to be returned. Reports from around the world to read and digest. He was given an appointment with the secretary of the interior, to bring that man up-to-date on his progress. The secretary seemed more pleased with the results obtained so far than Keveney himself was, and he concluded that nobody in government knew a damned thing about the narco business. Nobody, that is, but he and his men.

One evening he phoned Rosie in New York, inquired about her health and asked to speak with his son, Patrick. Patrick was out, staying at a friend's house.

"Isn't he awful young for that?" he said, annoyed by the boy's absence.

"He starts high school next year, Jack. He's growing up fast."

Keveney recognized the implied rebuke in her voice but said nothing. He wondered if he would even recognize his son should they pass in the street. Had he sacrificed too much for the job? He chose not to linger over the question.

"Well, tell him I called . . ."

"I'll tell him. Are you all right, Jack?"

"Sure, why wouldn't I be?"

"No reason. Is there someone in your life, Jack?"

"You mean a woman? No," he lied, able almost to taste Silvia, the residual smell of her leaving him slightly dizzy. "Nobody," he added.

Rosie had to laugh, had to answer. "Oh, I don't believe that for a second. A man like you, you were never without a woman for very long, Jack."

"Well," he said. "I've got to go now. I've got paperwork that needs doing."

"You always did give too much to the job, Jack. I'll tell Patrick you called, give him your love."

"Yes. You do that."

"Remember, you're in our prayers, Jack," she said before she hung up, leaving him irritable and unable to concentrate on the work at hand. There was that about Rosie, her ability to get under his skin, to arouse his defenses, to get him pissed off at her, at her world, at the Church. Damn woman should've become a nun, a sister of silence and solitude, living a cloistered existence, removed from the sinful, fleshly life of ordinary mortals.

He flew back to Los Angeles that night and was back at his desk at Satellite Import-Export the next morning. Art Brennan caught him up on the activities of his field agents. But Keveney was concerned with only one case.

"Any word on Gutierrez?"

"Nothing. Dame's faded into the woodwork. I gotta admit, she's as good as anyone I ever saw."

Before Keveney could reply, his secretary appeared. "There's a call for you. He refuses to give his name."

Keveney picked up the telephone. "Jack Keveney here, who is this?"

"Hey, Jack, recognize my voice? No need to say my name unnecessarily on an open wire, is there?"

It was Willie Hatcher. "Come talk to me," Keveney said.

"No way. Meet me someplace where nobody knows either of us."

Keveney named a downtown bar. Hatcher laughed mockingly. "You got no taste, Jack. Let's say the Polo Lounge in an hour. It's in the Beverly Hills Hotel, okay?"

"I know where it is. One hour."

Willie Hatcher looked like he belonged to the Polo Lounge. Tieless, his black silk shirt open at the collar, wearing a lime green linen jacket and two-tone wingtips that looked brand new. He grinned cheerfully when Keveney appeared and waved him to a table. A waiter materialized. Hatcher asked for a lightly salted margarita and Keveney had a beer. The detective felt out of place in a gabardine suit and a black knit tie.

"Classy, this place," Hatcher said. "Lookit, is that Tom Selleck in the corner with those guys? I hear he's leaving 'Magnum,' gonna make feature films. How you been, Jack?"

"You've been out in the sun, Willie, and you put on some more weight."

"Handsome and healthy, that's me. You're a little peaked, Jack. Working too hard, are you?" He turned a cherubic smile toward Keveney, who realized how glad he was to see the round man once more.

"I missed you, Willie."

"I missed you, too, Jack." He laughed aloud. "Enough of this lovemaking, let's get down to business."

"That's why you're in L.A., business?"

"On the button."

"Yours, mine, or Napoleon's?"

"All of the above. In my position, I wear a number of hats and it's vital to my continued good health that none of them get knocked off."

"What have you got for me?"

"Would you be interested in a shipment of coca paste?"

Keveney straightened in his chair. "Keep talking."

"Let's say, two thousand pounds of the stuff."

"Jesus!"

"Yeah." Willie grinned, a fleshy arc of tooth and gum. "I figured that might get to you. Cook it and cut it by—let's say eighty percent, and you get fifteen, maybe sixteen hundred pounds of pure white."

Keveney did some rapid calculations. "You're talking about two and a half million dollars on the street." Hatcher nodded gravely and Keveney leaned his way. "When's it coming in, Willie? How? Stop jerking me around and let's have it."

"Hey," Hatcher protested, an ingenuous expression fading across his tanned round face. "I'm with you, all the way. . ."

The customs inspector at the Laredo crossing felt his sensitized antennae began to quiver alarmingly. There was something wrong with the truck—a somewhat battered old army two-and-a-half-ton that had been paneled and repainted. The drivers were too well dressed, too clean, too perfect. He was in his mid-twenties, smooth-shaven and cheerful, his studious blue eyes looking everywhere. She was one of those cover girl types, with incredible legs and a sexy mouth and a ready smile. Too eager, the customs inspector decided. Both of them were too comfortable with themselves, with the situation; most young people coming back from Mexico were always a little tight at the border, made edgy by the natural guilt of the young, whether they've transgressed or not. Not these two; they were well-rehearsed with their answers to his questions, ready to give him easy access to the contents of the truck.

The inspector asked for the manifest. A load of Mexican crafts; painted horses made out of red clay, shining black pottery, a couple dozen two-headed pots for plants and flowers, each with the exaggerated head of a goat and the head of a rooster; there were

piñatas, serapes, handworked tin ashtrays and table lamps, some
heavy, carved furniture, thickly paneled with dark iron drawer
pulls. Part of the shipment was ticketed for a shop in Chicago, the
black pottery and the tinwork for Aspen, the rest to a wholesaler
in San Mateo, California. Everything was in order, except for the
uneasy sensation that lodged itself in the inspector's stomach. But
the sensation could not be permitted to supersede the orders of
his supervisor, who had alerted him to the coming of the truck, to
the specifics of the load it carried . . .

"Pass it along," the supervisor had said. "Keep it routine."

The customs inspector was young and enthusiastic, only seven
months on the job. "Any particular reason?" he asked.

The supervisor glared. He was six feet six inches in height and
weighed close to three hundred pounds. He reminded the young
inspector of John Wayne, only more so; better looking and more
intimidating. Not a man to argue with.

"Son," the supervisor had drawled, pure Texas menace. "I say
do something, you do something. I say don't, you don't. You want
reasons, come see me later. Come to think've it, you come see me
later anyway. Clear?"

"Clear."

The customs inspector waved the truck on through. Minutes
later it groaned its way up the short ramp onto Interstate 35,
heading north to San Antonio, the young driver and his companion singing a Johnny Cash number about the glories of life
on the open road. They were optimistic people, graduates of Ivy
League universities, accustomed to succeeding in whatever task
they chose to do, and convinced of their natural superiority,
especially when it came to some dumb cops. Neither of them
noticed the dusty Chevy that kept pace with them about a
quarter mile to their rear. Nor did they notice when the Chevy
left the highway north of Austin to be replaced by a battered
but smooth-running Ford wagon, nor when the wagon was replaced by a Toyota sedan. It never occurred to them that they
had failed to beat the system. It never occurred to them that
anything could go wrong.

* * *

"Tell me about him," Keveney said, in the half light of the new day. Silvia Gutierrez had returned to the Rainbow Apartments the night before and, to his surprise, had cooked dinner for him. Of her many gifts, real and suspected, this was one he had never attributed to her. Domesticity in any of its aspects hardy seemed her style.

First there was a fresh *guacamole* along with margaritas, then a superbly flavored *ceviche*, containing an assortment of lime-marinated raw fish and, for a main dish, chicken *chipotle* in a hot sauce made with ground, smoked chilies that left a not-so-mild aftertaste on Keveney's palate. All with a dark, strong Mexican beer.

Afterwards, there was black, bitter coffee and flan, which they took on her sofa, sitting side by side, talking intermittently.

But now in her bed, after a prolonged bout of lovemaking, their bodies still damp and drained, Keveney was compelled to talk, to learn more about her private life. Her secretlife.

"Who?" she replied absently, knowing what he desired of her, anxious to fulfill his needs and her own, yet at the same time protect that which she was required to protect.

"The Serious Lover," he said, smoking a Camel, blowing smoke toward the ceiling in a long, gossamer cone. "Serious but not solemn, you said."

She said nothing at first and he wasn't sure she would respond at all. She left the bed and returned with a bottle of chilled white wine and two glasses and poured them each some. Keveney put his glass aside. She sat propped up on pillows and dipped her tongue into the white wine.

"He is unlike any man I have ever known," she said at last.

The answer depressed him, made him question his own masculinity, his value to her as a man. He felt uncertain, as he had as an adolescent, convinced he did not deserve the sweet, passionate attention of this magnificent woman.

"As a lover, you mean?"

"Listen to me, gringo," she said with an exaggerated Hispanic accent, "you Yanquis are such a simple people. You compartmentalize everything. A man is an entity, okay, complete in every way. *He* is a special hombre, okay."

Keveney struggled to hold back the question and failed. "He's better for you than I am?" A low-burning rage simmered in his gut, jealousy and a kind of madness that caused him to pursue the matter. "Whatever he does, I'll do for you. However he does it. Is he bigger than I am? Is he more patient, stronger, does he last longer? What is it that makes him better?"

"Special is what I said. Different from you, different from anybody else I have known. As you are different from him, from any of the others."

How many lovers had she had? Visions of her with other men, doing what they had done, saying what she had said to him, feeling what she must have felt, ignited the madness again and he began to feel slightly ill, slightly feeble. But he couldn't stop.

"Tell me about him," Keveney said again.

She sipped some of her wine, not looking at Keveney, eyes fixed on some point in memory. "He transformed me from a girl into a woman. He aroused me, sharpened my senses, made me understand that I need not fear my passions, allowed me to release all that was in me. No man before has affected me so profoundly..."

"Nor since?" Keveney insisted.

Now she did look over at him. There was a softness in the planes of her face Keveney had never before noticed, a compassion and affection and for a moment he thought she would touch him, softly caress him. Assure him. Lie to him. But that was not her way.

"I'm here with you, Abruzzi. That should be enough."

"Why? Why are you with me?"

She considered the question, and enough time passed so that he feared she might not reply. "You intrigue me, Abruzzi. You are a strong man. You are clever and I sense that there are parts of you you keep to yourself. Mystery fascinates me, makes a man more interesting than he may in fact be, makes him more devious and inaccessible, and also more desirable. You are a beautiful lover, Abruzzi, you can be tender and thoughtful, rough and demanding, nervous and desperate to prove yourself. I like it all. To be with you pleases me."

"Do I make you happy?"

"Ah, happy. When I am with you, yes, I am happy. But I am not always happy."

"No one is."

She laughed softly. "Truth, my darling, it is the beginning of wisdom."

Keveney wanted to believe that he mattered to Silvia, that he had become a necessary part of her life. Until he reminded himself why he was with her, reminded himself that he was a cop, that he was after her, that she was one of the really bad guys.

Later, they made love again, and even as she cried out in pleasure, even as he felt himself dissolving into her warm flesh, he feared it was the Serious Lover who occupied her mind, and Keveney wanted desperately to destroy him.

"He is unlike any man I have ever known."

"You keep saying that."

"Isn't that what you want to hear, Abruzzi? About my Serious Lover?"

"To hell with him."

"If only he could be dismissed that easily."

Each time they were together after that, they spoke about her Serious Lover. At first, Silvia made him an adjunct to their lovemaking, as calming and as stimulating as the fine grade marijuana she often smoked before having sex. Gradually she expanded her descriptions of the Serious Lover, detailed his physical appearance, his personality, and finally his varied skills as a lover.

"His imagination is never still, there are always surprises."

He protested that he'd heard enough, but when she stopped Keveney asked another question, provoked her to go on. Images of the Serious Lover accompanied him wherever he went, whatever he did, tormenting and pleasing at the same time, making him want to know more.

She obliged him. "He skips along the peaks of life, taking what he wants, risking everything to gain his victories. He started out as the son of a whore . . ."

Keveney reached back for an image of his mother cooking. Or scrubbing the floor. Or in the street gossiping with neighbors. How different he and the Serious Lover were. And yet . . .

"He stole."

As Keveney had. Lifting fruit off a vendor's cart. Taking cheap toy soldiers out of the Five-and-Dime. Snatching penny candy off the counter of Mr. Maloney's corner store.

"And he killed," Silvia told him one night. "Murdered when he was only fifteen years old. So that he and his mother could survive, make a better life . . ."

The line between the Serious Lover and himself was thin, Keveney admitted to himself. More than one cop had used the badge to hide behind while he stole and extorted, even killed, growing rich while pretending to a morality that left him unsullied. He himself had killed. More than once. But always in the name of law and order. Always, after firing a fatal shot, he had silently debated the necessity for taking a life. Could he not have traveled another route in the cause of justice, whatever that might be? Each shooting had left him glad he had survived the ultimate test, the ultimate confrontation, but he came away always with the searing knowledge that he was a killer.

Silvia was speaking, her voice an insinuating caress behind which lay danger and death. "He became rich and powerful. Power emanates from him. Authority. And his touch makes my flesh tingle. I long for him to be inside me. To give me his strength, to absorb his magical power. Can you understand that, Abruzzi?"

He almost denied the name, desperate for her to know him for who and what he was. His real name echoed inside his skull and he was forced to clamp his teeth shut against the crippling urge to say it aloud.

"He," she said, recognizing the anguish in his face, "begins where other men stop. There is no softness in him. No loving weakness. He is tireless, insistent, and mean. For him love is a tool. A weapon with which he punishes you for daring to love him. Am I making sense to you?"

"I understand him very well."

"No woman has ever refused him. None can."

"He fucks the world," Keveney said harshly, full of rage and envy.

Her laugh was truncated, without mirth. "In more ways than you can know." She faced him, breasts sagging as if weighted abruptly by age, that once magnificent body gone slack and soft. She was, he was convinced, the ultimate whore. She too fucked her way through life, marking her path with the White Lady. A glint of recognition came into those remarkable green eyes and she mounted him, holding tightly to his shaft, forcing herself down on him, mouth frozen in a thin mad rictus. "There," she cried. "There is where he's been and will be again. Fuck me where he has fucked me. Know him as I know him. Fuck me and through me you fuck him. Yes, fuck me . . ."

Unbearable tensions gathered in him and he opened his mouth and screamed and so did she as they pounded against each other. Her head went back, mouth agape, eyes bulging, a massive exhalation forming, desperate to be expelled. And when it was, the single name she spoke clattered around the inner slopes of his skull. And he understood that she had given him all she was capable of giving . . .

"Napoleon!"

The Foodmobile was parked in the middle of the block, dispensing coffee and Danish to men and women on their midmorning break. Some of the men sat on the sidewalk and smoked and talked; others carried refreshments back to the job. No one paid much attention to the old Army two-and-a-half-ton truck with its new panels and fresh paint unloading goods in front of the corner building. Ceramics packed in straw inside wooden boxes, stacks of serapes and handwoven blankets, some carved furniture. The stuff sat on the side until workers appeared and began carrying it inside. A man in a white shirt signed the young trucker's manifest and he and the trucker laughed and shook hands before they parted.

It was nearly three o'clock—with the lunchtime rush ended—when the operator of the Foodmobile closed up and drove away. He located a pay phone outside the factory district, within sight of the Harbor Freeway and made his call.

"Mr. Keveney, please."

A moment later, Keveney answered.

"Myles Young, Mr. Keveney. Delivery was made about four hours ago."

"I know. The surveillance team picked up the couple and the truck. What's your status?"

"They brought the stuff into Latino Arts and Crafts, Inc., that's on the first floor rear of the building. The perfume outfit is in the front. The way I make it, the lab is on the second floor."

"Has Cepeda shown up?"

"Not yet. We got a couple of guys on stakeout posing as telephone linemen."

"Okay. Same schedule tomorrow. When Cepeda shows, you get word to me quick."

"Yes, sir."

Willie Hatcher lowered himself into a seat in the small screening room Keveney had hired for the occasion. "Nice," Willie cooed. "I like it, free movies in the middle of the day. Hope it's something I haven't seen before."

"Funny," Keveney said, signaling the projectionist. The lights dimmed and the screen lit up. Grainy pictures began to flicker into view. "Pay attention, Willie, this is business."

Silvia Gutierrez appeared on screen, tall and confident, moving with an easy gracefulness, long black hair falling across her wide shoulders in a shining flair. Willie hunched down in his seat, chin resting on the backs of his clasped hands. Keveney could hear him breathing. Silvia went inside a border money exchange and Keveney ordered the lights brought up, the film cut off. He said to Willie Hatcher: "Silvia Gutierrez. She fronts a bigtime drug operation out of L.A. Launders money along the border using certain banks in Panama and in the Bahamas. She's got contacts in Chi-

cago, New York, a number of other cities. She's in touch with a
Colombian chemist name of Raul Cepeda. Maybe you've heard've
him?"

"Yeah. They say he's the best."

"He's in L.A. now, or soon will be. About Silvia—what do you
know about her?"

Hatcher cleared his throat and sat straight in his seat, avoiding
Keveney, hating what he was about to do. "First thing, Silvia,
that's not her name . . ."

"I never believed it was." Keveney set himself against whatever
Willie Hatcher had to tell him. "Who is she then?"

Hatcher jerked around in his seat, grinning malevolently. "As if
you didn't know, that's Nina Fuentes."

It was late in the afternoon when the call came.

"He showed, ten minutes ago, the chemist."

"Cepeda? You're sure it's him?"

"It's him, awright. There's someone with him, a dame."

Keveney's heart began to fibrillate. He wanted it not to be Nina
Fuentes. "Tell me about her."

"World class, Mr. Keveney. Tall with black hair and the kind've
figure makes you want to cry, if you know what I mean."

"She's in there now?"

"Both of them, sir."

"Okay. I'll have the team there inside of thirty minutes. Cover
the back and the front."

"Consider it done, Mr. Keveney."

D-Group's people—augmented by a team of local police—
were in place at ten minutes before the hour. Keveney nodded to
the officer in charge and he gave the order over his hand-held
radio:

"Hit 'em now!"

Seconds later Keveney's men entered the drug lab and the police burst into Latino Arts and Crafts, Inc. In the lab, they discovered the chemist, Cepeda, plus four helpers busily at work

cooking coca paste with sulphuric acid. The place reeked of rotten eggs, reminding Keveney of the chemistry class he had suffered through in high school. Along the wall, five-gallon containers of ether plus gallon jugs of a clear liquid that Keveney knew to be Acetone and kerosene. Bricks of the cream-colored coca paste, which had been concealed in the piñatas, were stacked neatly on a long table. A brown slurry of the treated paste was being processed through plastic tubing into filtered gauze soaked with ether and kerosene.

"One more step," Keveney remarked, and they'd have turned this batch into cocaine, one hundred percent pure and lethal."

His men began to drift in. Four Spanish-speaking illegals had been found in Latino Crafts.

"Just workers," Art Brennan said. "Only thing they know is they're scared of being deported."

"What nationality?"

"Sixaolan."

Keveney exhaled. "They may not be as innocent as they claim. Take 'em in and question them."

"Right."

"What about the woman?"

"Gone," Brennan said, with an apologetic spread of his hands.

Keveney swore. "How can that be? We had the place covered..."

"In the basement," Brennan explained. "There's a passage to the adjoining building. All she needed was a couple of seconds warning and she was on her way, walking right past our people in the street."

"Damn," Keveney said.

"Nobody paid her any attention, most likely. Not while the raid was in progress."

"Search the neighborhood," Keveney ordered. "Send some men over to the Rainbow Apartments. I want the airport and bus stations covered, roadblocks set up."

"Sure, Jack. But if she's running, it may already be too late. The lady is smart, she'd've had her escape routes all worked out..."

"Damn," Keveney said again. "Damn, damn." But in the shadowed recesses of his mind he felt a grudging admiration for Nina Fuentes, was pleased that she'd managed to escape, and he wondered sadly if he would ever see her again.

She fled. Driven by a spreading fear, aware of how close she had come to personal disaster, to arrest and imprisonment in a gringo jail. On the edge of panic, she nevertheless felt a flood of gratitude for the alternate escape routes Napoleon had insisted she establish. All she had to do was make her choices.

She went north by car along Route 1, the scenic route, to San Francisco, certain the police would expect her to head toward Mexico. That, too, was Napoleon's teaching; always do the unexpected. From San Francisco she flew to Denver, where she bought a secondhand Chevrolet. She waited a week and drove by a roundabout route to San Diego, and then San Ysidro, where she called a certain number and arranged to be flown into Baja.

It took nearly three days to make her next contact, for money to be passed and arrangements concluded. At midnight, on a moonless Thursday, she was taken to a fishing village and ferried out to a Panamanian freighter that was heading south.

She was put ashore in Managua and spent two days waiting for a phone call. This led her to another ship, a fishing vessel that brought her to a small town on the northwest coast of Colombia. On to Bogotá, where she boarded a commercial flight to the capital city of Sixaola. A Mercedes sedan was waiting and she was driven to Chiriqui and the security of the complex Napoleon Cruz called home. Even then she could not rid herself of the notion that she was still being pursued, that her pursuer would eventually catch up and harm her irrevocably. Not since her mother had died had she felt so unsafe, so alone, and it occurred to her that no one, not even Napoleon, could protect her from the dangers now closing in.

She longed for Abruzzi. For the reassurance of his strong arms, his soft, caressing voice in her ear. She needed his strength and his certainty. Twice she almost picked up the phone to call him, but she knew it was too dangerous; she was cut off forever from the world of Silvia Gutierrez, cut off from John Abruzzi.

In bed at night, visions of Abruzzi floated into her mind and tears came into her eyes. She grew angry at herself for this show of weakness; tears were for other women, not for Nina Fuentes. She was too strong for that. Too proud. Too much in charge of her emotions and her destiny. But the tears refused to cease flowing and the need for John Abruzzi grew stronger. And she understood that he had made a place inside her that would always belong to him.

TWENTY

D-GROUP, NOURISHED BY ITS SUCCESSES, GREW steadily. Agents operated with increased efficiency throughout the drug world: in Turkey, in the Middle East, in the Orient, in France and Italy, along the northern tier of Africa, in Nigeria, in all of Latin America and on many islands of the Caribbean, and in the United States itself. They burrowed into the drug organizations, feeding information out when possible, their lives in constant jeopardy. They worked as teams—lawyers, accountants, chemists—inspecting income tax returns, business records of companies and individuals; they checked passports and mounted surveillances, they interviewed, reviewed, consulted. Files were opened depicting each new operation, growers were spotted and linked to buyers, labs were located and marked, smuggling routes into the U.S. were entered onto a large wall map in Keveney's office. Reports, rumors, facts, lies, a jumble of information from agents and informers: Keveney's office was the magnet for them all.

Fact and fancy, all of it went into D-Group's information bank and much of it became the basis for a number of major drug busts made by the D.E.A., as well as various law enforcement groups. In every case credit went to the local police, D-Group remaining a largely unknown entity. But the narcotics confiscated and the men and women arrested were a small portion of the known quantity of narcotics entering the country. Summoned to testify before the Senate Oversight Committee in Executive Session,

Jack Keveney pointed out the shortcomings, the inefficiencies, the contradictions of national policy.

"At the highest levels of government," he declared, "we call for an end to drug use and vow to get tough with the dealers. At the same time, we provide diminished funds and resources to the organizations on the front line. Our customs people are over-worked. The Border Patrol is badly understaffed. Municipal police forces lack the training and manpower to get the job done in our towns and cities. War may have been declared on drugs, but there has been no proper commitment to that war. We are losing the war, gentlemen, and losing it badly, no matter the occasional victories we manage to achieve . . ."

The Committee chairman promised future cooperation. He spoke about larger budgetary commitments. Of more intensive diplomatic pressure on those countries where the drugs originated. He complimented Keveney on the fine work he and his men were doing. But nothing concrete came out of the meeting.

Keveney continued to study reports and to look at surveillance films, hoping for the one break that would allow him to shatter the cohesiveness of a major drug organization. It came one day in mid-morning. One of his agents—Marco Fried, who had worked undercover in Colombia and in Sixaola and was currently assigned to the Miami area—called with a morsel of information that set off intuitive alarms in Keveney.

"Give me your best shot," Fried, a hale, happy man, began. "Who do you think just stepped off a flight at Miami International?"

Keveney was in a foul mood and said so. "I wanna play games, Marco, I'll hit the basketball court. What's on your mind?"

Fried was chastened only briefly. "Raphael Salazar," he reported, pleased with himself. "Traveling under a phony name on an Argentine passport. The old man in the flesh."

"Salazar." Keveney breathed the name as if savoring it, running what he knew about the dean of the Sixaolan traffickers through his mind, asking questions. What was Salazar doing in the U.S., risking arrest and a long stretch in a federal prison? Salazar was a

cautious man by nature, conservative, commanding his drug empire with Machiavellian viciousness, holding himself aloof from
the seamier sides of the work. It fit his quiet personality and his
social background.

Salazar, unlike the other Sixaolan Regents, was the product of a
middle-class family of education and culture. Though never
wealthy, they never lacked for anything, either. Salazar, it was
known, had studied at universities in Madrid and in France. He
was well-traveled, experienced in the ways of the world, a man
who collected fine art, listened to Mozart and Bach, enjoyed good
food, good wines, and in his earlier years, the company of beautiful women. It was rumored that he looked upon his colleagues
Uribe, Vega and Cruz as lesser creatures without the human refinements that Salazar prized so greatly.

"Salazar," Keveney said again. "In Florida. What's it mean?"

Fried said, "It makes no sense."

Keveney almost agreed. "Maybe it does. For him to risk his
freedom—Marco, something big is going on."

"Salazar would never carry himself."

"Of course not. But I'll bet my badge a major transaction is in
the works."

"He hasn't passed through customs yet. Want me to have the
bastard detained?"

Keveney thought that one over before replying. "Do nothing.
He's not to get a hint that you're onto him. Just watch him. Where
he goes, who he talks to. Lose him, Marco, and I'll fry your butt."

"Sure," Fried purred over the long distance wire. "It's great to
be appreciated."

"I'm on my way to Miami. Stay in touch with your people and
meet my flight . . ."

"Sure, Boss, but what if . . . ?"

"No ifs. No buts. No maybes. Just stay on Salazar's tail." He
hung up.

Out of a locked drawer in his desk, Keveney brought a small
address book. He located Willie Hatcher's name and began calling. He dialed four different numbers in the United States, two in

Central America and one in Canada before he located Hatcher at a house owned by a wealthy German widow who made her home in Zihuatenejo on the Pacific Coast of Mexico.

"Having fun, Willie?" Keveney began in a voice larded with disapproval. It seemed fundamentally wrong to him that in a world so crowded with sin and sinners Willie was taking his ease in a semitropical paradise. Once the Sisters of the Sacred Heart got their blessed hands on you, injected you with a full dose of their moral certainty, like a pack of holy bulldogs, they never let go.

"Hey, Jack, how'd you find me?"

"I'm looking for some answers, Willie."

"And the questions?"

"Raphael Salazar." Keveney spoke louder than he had to, as if to bridge the distance. "He's in Florida. What's going on, Willie?"

"Beats me. First I heard of it."

"Maybe you call somebody?"

"Sure, the way you call me. Why'n't I ring up Napoleon and ask him? 'Hey, Napoleon, what's Salazar got going in the States?' Is that what you mean?"

It occurred to Keveney that Hatcher no longer feared him. Or at the very least feared him less than he feared certain other men. Namely Napoleon Cruz. "Okay," he said softly. "So you don't know. Calling was just a reach on my part."

Silence ensued before Hatcher spoke again. "Hey, Jack, Napoleon sent me a message, too. Wants me in Chiriqui. I'm due back in a couple of days."

Keveney heard the fear in the round man's voice and understood that this was no ordinary summons. Hatcher's fear was palpable, and Keveney almost suggested that he not go, that he return to the States where Keveney could protect him. But Hatcher was his connection to the Regents, a source Keveney had to risk, had to keep open for as long as possible. "Stay in touch," he said, making his voice casual. "You learn anything, you let me know."

"Sure, Jack. I'll do that."

The connection broken, Keveney returned the address book to its place and locked the drawer. He refused to allow himself to worry about Willie Hatcher; the informer could take care of himself. He would have to. As for Keveney, he had more important things on his mind. He made arrangements for a seat on a military flight leaving for Miami that afternoon.

When Keveney landed in Miami, Marco Fried, in his embracing, avuncular way, greeted him with a powerful clap on the back and a toothy grin. The agent was a cheerful man with the thick body of a fullback and a face that spoke of many battles won and lost. Lidded eyes and a nose broken many times gave him the look of a sad sheep. He led Keveney to a waiting car.

"Tell me about Salazar," Keveney began.

"Like I said, he's on an Argentine passport, claims to be in the construction business in Buenos Aires. Up here to get financing for a new design in pipe scaffolding. Gonna revolutionize the building industry, he told the customs guy."

"Where is he now?"

"He was driven to a house in North Miami. Turns out the place is owned by someone named Ismael Moreno-Diaz. Who is Moreno-Diaz, you ask? I will tell you—he is the Minister of Defense for Sixaola."

Keveney whistled through his teeth. "A couple of heavy hitters," he said. "Where are they now?"

"Still at the house, far as I know."

As if provoked, the CB radio crackled and Fried answered. A voice faded in. "They're on the way out, Mr. Fried. Salazar and Moreno-Diaz, plus a couple of other dudes. All Latinos, carrying a couple of big suitcases."

"That's it!" Fried exulted. "A major shipment. This Moreno-Diaz was holding for Salazar . . ."

"I don't think so," Keveney said, trying to make sense of all this. "When did Moreno-Diaz show up in Miami?"

"Near as we can make out, two days ago."

"Carrying what?"

"Nothing much personally. But there were two crates—diplomatic luggage. I figure that's how the shit was brought in, the diplomatic pouch."

"Maybe. In any case, we can't touch this guy if he's on a diplomatic passport."

Fried swore. "But there's Salazar, we can take the bastard."

"I suppose so." He indicated the radio. "What's going on now?"

Fried spoke into the microphone. "Santiago, you still there? Talk to me."

The radio crackled. "Car coming out of the estate, Mr. Fried, black Caddy with tinted windows."

"Figures," Fried growled.

"Heading toward Interstate 95."

"Stay with 'em."

Two minutes later, Santiago was back. "The Caddy's going north on the highway."

"Okay, stay cool, y'hear."

"I got four cars leapfrogging."

"We're coming along behind you."

They drove for nearly three hours before the car carrying Salazar and Moreno-Diaz left the highway, turning west across the flat midlands. They went past cattle ranches and through citrus groves, arriving finally at a private airfield.

By the time Fried and Keveney caught up, D-Group's agents had taken up positions within sight of an unmarked hangar. Santiago, a handsome man with wide shoulders and long arms, reported. "Subject's inside, along with some other guys. Maybe three or four more, I'd say."

"It's a deal," Fried said. "A big deal. Otherwise why would Salazar be here? Why Moreno-Diaz? We take those characters, Mr. Keveney, we can shake up the entire Sixaolan establishment. They're making it easy for us."

Keveney massaged his cheek. "Too easy, maybe."

Fried grew worried. "We're going in, aren't we?"

What choice did they have, Keveney asked himself. And if they did go in, what would they find? Cocaine? Pot? Heroin? Once the meeting ended, once the participants separated, Moreno-Diaz would be off the hook—his high governmental status protecting him from harm. As for Salazar, that pernicious old man would disappear, fade into the protected world from whence he had come. If they were going to act, the time was now.

"We hit 'em," he said aloud. "Is there a back exit?"

"One door."

"Okay, Santiago, take four men and cover the back. Fried, the rest of your people go with me. In exactly three minutes we go in. And for Christ's sake, be careful." They were, he feared, outmanned and outgunned. Drug dealers could be expected to be heavily armed—AK47s, Uzis, M-16s. He and his men carried only handguns. They would be severely tested if shooting broke out. But there wasn't time to wait for reinforcements.

At the appointed moment, Keveney went through the front door of the hangar. To his surprise, it was unlocked. No guards greeted them. Fried and the other agents fanned out across the great, gloomy open space of the hangar. From the rear, Santiago and the others moved in.

Midway along, a mountain of crates and boxes loomed up, reaching almost to the ceiling. Nearby stood half a dozen men. Startled by the appearance of the agents, there were some hoarse cries and protests to Keveney's command that they raise their hands above their heads.

"This is a mistake, señor," one of the men said, his cultivated English marked by only a slight accent. He wore an expensive suit with a muted stripe and a white shirt and a conservative tie.

"Moreno-Diaz," Fried informed Keveney.

"Frisk 'em all," Keveney ordered.

Keveney identified himself and his authority, watching as his agents searched each man. Another surprise—none of the men were armed.

"Señor. . ." Moreno-Diaz tried again.

"When I'm ready for you, Mister," Keveney snapped. The two suitcases stood on the concrete floor to one side. Keveney ordered them opened.

Moreno-Diaz objected. Despite his willowy frame and soft voice, he possessed a certain authority, a man used to life at the top of the pyramid, a man used to having his orders obeyed. "I am an official of the government of Sixaola, señor. These cases are shielded by diplomatic immunity. . ."

"Open 'em," Keveney said.

A small crowbar was produced and the locks were jammed open, the lids of the cases flipped back. Neatly arranged in each case were three layers of plastic bags, each filled with a fine white powder. Keveney hefted one of the plastic bags.

"Tell him," Salazar hissed in Moreno-Diaz's ear. "Insist. This will damage all of us."

"Yes," the minister agreed, stepping forward. "Whatever my luggage contains, señor, is protected by my diplomatic status. You see I—"

Keveney interrupted. "You are a minister of the government of Sixaola. But you are not in this country on official business. You are not a member of your government's embassy staff. You are not an ambassador. No, this is some private affair. Besides, drugs are my business and unless I'm badly mistaken, what we have here is enough cocaine to bring in about two and a half, maybe three hundred million dollars retail. . ." He motioned to Fried. "This stuff is confiscated."

Salazar, his wrinkled face screwed up in rage and frustration, shuffled forward. "You cannot do this. We have rights. As guests in your country. . ."

Keveney stared in curiosity and admiration. "Señor Salazar, I take it?"

The old man fell back as if struck. "No, no. I am Hernandez. Roberto Hernandez. I am an Argentine. My business is construction. You have me confused. . ."

"You are Raphael Salazar," Keveney said, showing his teeth in a lifeless grin. "You traffic in narcotics. Your business is to cheat and steal and murder. Okay," he said to Santiago. "Check I.D.s on everyone while I take a look into this pile of—what, Señor Moreno-Diaz? What am I going to find in these boxes?"

Fried opened the nearest box. Inside were four metal tubes painted military green, each about two feet in length. "Lookit this," he said.

Keveney took one quick glance. "Sonofabitch, what we have here are shoulder-fired antiaircraft missile launchers."

"Stingers, I make 'em out to be," Fried said.

They opened three more crates to reveal automatic rifles, grenade launchers and mortars.

"Combat weapons," Keveney said.

Moreno-Diaz tried once more. "As I told you, señor, you are making a mistake."

Keveney ignored the minister. He was puzzled; he had anticipated the narcotics, he had not expected armaments. Could Moreno-Diaz be right; was he indeed making a mistake?

As if in confirmation, a lean, athletic man with a military bearing came forward. He offered himself with confidence, even a touch of arrogance.

"The minister is right, Keveney. You are making a mistake. But it's not too late to put matters right with nobody the worse for this unfortunate incident. What you've stumbled into here is none of your affair."

Keveney looked him over. "Who in the hell are you?"

"Abernathy, Frank, Jr., major, United States Army. And I am telling you that you are out of your element here."

Fried, having gone through the collection of identification cards, handed one over. Keveney gave it a quick glance.

"Okay, so you're an army major. That doesn't cut much ice around here."

"I'm advising you, Keveney. I'm warning you, get your men out of here. Before it's too late."

"You ever been in the army, Fried?"

"Three tours in 'Nam."

"Whataya think of majors who give warnings, make threats?"

"Not much."

"Me too," Keveney said. He considered his next move.

"Okay. Cuff 'em all," he said finally. "Take 'em in and we'll sort it all out later."

"Dammit, Keveney, don't you get it? You are intruding on official federal business..." Abernathy broke off and scribbled on a small white pad he drew from his pocket. "Call this phone number. It's a private line and you'll be put right through."

It was as if Abernathy had somehow managed to usurp his position. His command of the situation had been passed on to the major without a shot being fired.

"I don't think so," he said, starting to turn away.

"Dammit, Keveney, at least make the call!"

There was a phone in a small office at the rear of the hangar. Keveney dialed the number. It rang twice and a calm male voice answered. "Office of the president of the United States. Who is calling, please . . . ?"

Fear and guilt were the twin companions of Jack Keveney's childhood. Imbedded in his heart by a mother who attended mass twice daily and perceived only sin and sinners everywhere in the soiled and spoiled human condition, as she liked to put it.

At Our Savior School, on the West Side of Manhattan, his mother's values were hammered home by the Sisters of the Sacred Heart with all the subtlety of true believers down through the ages. Sister Asumpta was the worst of the lot.

Behind round, steel-rimmed glasses, her tiny eyes were inflamed, giving off terrifying pinpoints of holy light. She spoke God's truth in a voice that permitted a recalcitrant boy no room to dissemble or equivocate, the words snapping out of her in a brisk military cadence. Keveney had always been fascinated by the thin mustache on her upper lip.

"Who made you?" No matter which of God's commandments or the school's prohibitions a boy may have committed, Sister Asumpta started him out with the first question of the Baltimore Catechism and a crack across the knuckles with her yardstick.

"God made me," was the quick answer in the hope that it might bring relief from the by-now-pervasive fear and terrible guilt that pulsated out from a boy's heart. But that was not to be. On this occasion, there was no absolution. No way to avoid the consequence of his actions. No escape from the Eternal Damnation that he understood was justly his due. Off he went to Father Gregory's office, the good father being headmaster of Our Savior.

Sister Asumpta herself delivered the quaking twelve-year-old, along with the awful evidence of his crime against God's natural law—an unrolled, unused condom, already yellowing with age. Sister Asumpta tossed the offending item onto Father Gregory's desk with a pious flourish that dared him to ignore this felonious assault upon the Church's good teaching at peril to his immortal soul. For his part, Father Gregory stared at the condom with considerable alarm, since it reminded him of the weaknesses of his own mortal flesh. Pink-cheeked and paunchy, Father Gregory was a man of few words. He knew his duty when he saw it. He delivered fifteen mean strokes with a wooden paddle to Jack Keveney's bottom, with the boy in a suitably humiliating position.

"And I'll see your mother at eight o'clock in the morning, young man . . ."

The fear was the same now. And the guilt. The spreading helplessness, the deep sense of inadequacy, the knowledge that he had intruded onto sacred territory. But replacing Father Gregory was the long Protestant visage of the secretary of the interior, the fleshy mouth sealed in prim disapproval. The secretary was authoritatively ensconced behind a big, antique desk and at his shoulder, ramrod straight in the uniform of an army major, replete with battle ribbons and other symbols of his dedication and derring-do, stood Abernathy, Frank, Jr.

"You've met Major Abernathy." It was a declaration designed to recall that low moment when Keveney had dared to transgress. Abernathy wore his contempt for Keveney as if it were another medal.

"We've met," Keveney said.

"Your office is in this city," the secretary said in that booming voice of his.

"I was in Florida for less than twelve hours."

"And weeks in Los Angeles."

"That was our deal, I'd go where the job was."

"There are those in the administration, men close to the president, who feel D-Group is a mistake."

Fuck 'em, Keveney longed to say. Instead, he shrugged, and replied matter-of-factly, "These things take time."

"Tell me about Los Angeles."

The guilt boiled up. Dark memories of Silvia—no, Nina Fuentes—came into focus. The overheated sensuality of her was reborn in his nostrils and his genitals shifted and swelled. Damn that woman. "It's all connected. L.A. and Florida. One of the largest and deadliest of the drug kings."

"Kings." Abernathy made his disdain clear.

"Salazar is a king. One of four who control nearly eighty percent of the drugs that enter this country. Salazar, and the others, they're killing our people."

"Back off," Abernathy said.

Keveney felt the weight of the soldier's eyes. Lacking color and life, they masked off the inner man. There was nothing to see in them and that worried Keveney; he preferred men of passion and impulse.

Abernathy executed a half-right turn, directing his words to the secretary. "What took place in Florida is none of Keveney's business. Outside of D-Group's scope. What we have here is a jurisdictional dispute, Mr. Secretary."

"Salazar is my business."

"Obey orders, Mister," Abernathy snapped out. "Like the rest of us."

Keveney drew air into his lungs, meeting those lifeless eyes and speaking in a still voice. "Kiss my Irish ass, soldierboy."

The secretary spoke, the long melancholy face drooping. "The major's right, Keveney. You've stumbled into matters that have nothing to do with your charter, so to speak."

"Three hundred million dollars worth of coke, that is my business."

"Not this time," Abernathy said.

"That's the way it has to be," the secretary added.

"Oh, I get it. The coke pays for those guns, those stingers, those mortars. That's why Moreno-Diaz was in on it. His government gets Salazar to put up the drugs as payment for weapons and our government makes the swap. But why are we—" His heart began to beat irregularly and for a long moment he went weak, limbs slack, and he feared he might go to his knees. He gathered strength. "This piss-ant army major is running the show and the rest of our government—and you, Mr. Secretary, are protecting his ass. All this talk about a war on drugs—so much bullshit. Jesus God almighty, I should've seen it. We're peddling arms to those bastards for coke, straight up . . ."

"You're a good man, Mr. Keveney. Righteous and courageous." The secretary spoke with all the certainty of his Puritan ancestors; "Business," he said, "is business."

Keveney heaved himself erect, his face pinched and pugnacious. Betrayed again. He had been in his last year at Our Savior when word got out about Father Gregory and Sister Maria Theresa; they had been discovered in the janitor's supply closet locked in carnal embrace. Nothing and no one ever was what it appeared to be. Betrayal was the name of the game.

"That coke, it goes up the noses and into the arms of our people. They'll turn it into crack and kill our kids on the streets. You guys are gonna let it happen. You guys are making it happen. And the thing is, nobody in this town truly gives a fuck . . ."

Abernathy sputtered.

The secretary sighed. "Do your job, you're good at it. Forget what you've seen. Forget what you think you have discovered. This time you're in over your head, Mr. Keveney, so put it behind you and get on with your life."

"You're telling me the U.S. Government is involved with Raphael Salazar in a major drug deal. You're telling me that . . ."

The secretary leaned forward. "What I am telling you, sir, and for the last time, is to return to your desk and to mind your own damned business."

Silvia Gutierrez was the name that fit her. In fact and in the undulating memories that served still to arouse him. Nina Fuentes, that was a name for a senior in high school. A bouncy creature with jiggling breasts under a cheerleader's sweater and thighs still smooth and chunky. It was Silvia, the woman, who made that tantalizing sweet crawl back into his consciousness.

Memories abound.

She had been so full of surprise and a challenging caprice, eyes sliding his way, lush mouth spread in silent laughter, daring him to discover what she was all about. Full of secrets and denial that left him edgy and suspicious but unwilling to do anything that might drive her away.

She had taken possession of him. And he was properly worshipful. He had learned to anticipate her needs, her unexpected, unspoken demands. On his knees, he paid homage to her flesh. To the heavy womanly breasts, to the glowing skin, to the lush black triangle into which he thrust his face, lips working feverishly, his tongue entering her, caught up in fantasies of his own destruction. Never able to get enough.

And always the surprises. The newness she brought to each of their meetings, each an adventure, as if she had profited from other encounters with other lovers. That possibility made Keveney plumb some subterranean source for a passion more driving and imaginative, anything to please her.

There were the rough times, Nina slapping at him with abandon until he seized her wrists and pinned her down; she would plead to be hit, to be hurt, to be spanked. Caught up in her wastrel games, he obliged with a vigor that surprised and frightened him. And more than once he pulled back for fear of doing real damage to her. And to himself.

Her tenderness surfaced without warning. A surge of disarming affection, moist and seductive, assuring him of her lasting devotion. He feared the softness most of all, feared giving too much credence to anything she said. Except when she spoke of Napoleon. Always in a voice sly and derisive, skittering around the edges allowing him only a glimpse of the man, making him desperate to learn more.

No, Napoleon had been no surprise. Even before she'd uttered his name in the sensual fever of that night, he'd known. Prodding at him in that most private of private places, there could be no doubt. Napoleon had to be her Serious Lover.

Oh, yes, he had known, all right, had known always. Since he'd first viewed her flickering across that grainy film in those border towns, so regal and special, deserving of someone equally regal, equally special.

Napoleon.

Visions of the drug enterpreneur pounding his wiry body against Nina crashed into Keveney's consciousness with pile-driving force. He could see the gleam on the tobacco-colored skin, he could hear Nina's choked cries for release, for the rewards that Napoleon alone could bestow.

"There is no one like Napoleon," Keveney heard her say.

Or were the words his own, born of a searing rage, of knowing that he could never replace Napoleon in Nina's imagination. He vowed to gain his revenge on each of them for the torment he felt. The lingering anguish. The lost love.

There remained the truth of his job. Truth distorted, distorting his existence, lending unreal proportions to the way he viewed himself as a man and as a cop. That was the worst of it; the secretary and the major—every governmental department and bureau, every level and cranny of the Federal establishment—had been designed to effectively slice away his authority. To diminish his sense of himself. Transformed him into a front man for masters seen and unseen. All that he had tried to do—had indeed accomplished—was a charade. Providing headlines when headlines made sense to the body poetic.

MAJOR DRUG RING CRACKED:
We're Winning the War, says Prez

Horseshit.

Nobody cared. Not the secretary. Not the president. Not any of the powerful men in or out of government. Each of them pursued an agenda of his own, aiming to satisfy his own constituency. Plucking Jack Keveney out of the municipal small-time to put on a show. A hired busker complete with stunts and gags to clown around in pursuit of a few cheap laughs. No star turn this.

On impulse, he hopped an Amtrak liner for New York, the tug of those familiar sights and smells too strong to resist. He prowled the nighttime streets, muggers and whores giving way before him. They sensed the ferociousness in Keveney and kept their distance. The mean streets were no threat to him; it was in the muted corridors of political power that he was outmatched, out-smarted, outfought, outside.

He sought out his roots in Hell's Kitchen. What he found was some crap players under a street lamp. Boys shooting baskets in a darkened schoolyard. A man and a woman flinging imprecations at each other on a tenement stoop, both drunk and bloodied, each lost without the other. All of it was familiar and a breach of his private peace. Whatever he was looking for no longer existed in the old neighborhood.

A lighted phone booth drew his eye. He fumbled for a dime and learned that a New York call now went for a quarter. He swore at the concealed forces of change and the rising price they extracted in the false name of progress. Wonder of wonders, the phone worked.

"Yes?" she began, making the one word symptomatic of her displeasure with things as they were.

"It's Jack."

It took her a little while to assimilate the information, fitting him into her present circumstances. He imagined her slipping into her most accepting Christian visage.

"Jack, what a nice surprise."

"I'm in the city."

"New York?" It was as if he had somehow broken through the invisible defense system with which she surrounded herself, a vaguely disturbing prospect. "On business?"

What a question! As if cop's work could be equated with any commercial enterprise. "I'm pushing penny stocks on unwary housewives," he declared in a mocking manner. "Get a lot of everything that way."

She ignored the insinuation, her silence extensive. He had never gotten used to her silences, so eloquent and disapproving.

"How's Patrick?"

"Why don't you speak to him yourself?"

He blurted out, "Can I come over?"

"Now?"

Questions with very few answers, it was how they communicated. All was implication. Suggestion. Sarcasm and irony. Christ-almighty, no wonder they were no longer husband and wife.

Except in the wise eyes of the Holy Roman Church.

"Unless it's a problem."

"Why would it be a problem?" Pause. Sigh. A forced but cheerful response. "If that's what you want."

Such enthusiasm. "I don't know what I want."

"Have you eaten? Dinner, I mean."

"Don't worry about me."

"It's just a simple casserole, nothing fancy."

She had never prepared a simple meal in her adult life. Her library of cookbooks spanned the continents, the nations, the cultures, from Tibetan steamed dumplings to couscous.

"Whatever," he said.

"Give you a chance to talk to Patrick. It's been a long time since you saw him."

Properly chastised, he wanted to know if he could bring anything.

"Some wine, if you'd like to. Something white, I think, and not too sweet."

Dry, he almost shouted into the phone. The word is dry. He said, "Sure," and hung up instead, remembering that a glass or two of *vin ordinaire* used to make her inordinately sexy. He supposed she'd since strengthened her immunity to such a fundamental aphrodisiac. He bought two bottles of Chablis. Expensive and very dry.

The casserole was delicious, and Keveney said so.

The wine was super, and Rosie said so.

The conversation was desultory, sporadic, with a series of awkward silences.

"You're lucky," Keveney told Patrick. "Your mother's one fine cook."

Rosie thanked him, Patrick ducked his head in assent.

"How's school?" Keveney asked.

"It's okay," his son said. The boy was tall for his age, with wide bony shoulders and surprisingly muscular arms. His early adolescence had marked his chin with a smattering of red zits and a lowering, defensive expression in his eyes.

"Doing okay, are you?"

"I get along."

It occurred to Keveney that he had no idea how to talk to a teenager. His son was a stranger to him and he could think of nothing to say that would provoke the boy's interest. In lieu of conversation, he asked another question.

"How're your grades?"

Rosie answered with some pride. "Mostly As and Bs."

"You study hard?" Keveney didn't want his son to be a wimp. He looked for some indication that the boy was involved in sports; no athletic equipment showed up anywhere.

"Not so hard."

"What about sports?"

The defensive look returned. "What about them? I fool around with the guys sometimes."

"You don't play on a regular team."

"You think I should, I guess."

"No," Keveney shot back. "Just wondering is all. You've got the look of an athlete."

Patrick turned his head and they finished the meal in relative silence and Rosie excused the boy, saying he had to do his homework. Keveney was disappointed when he left and relieved at the same time; fatherhood left him feeling awkward, with a swift rush of subterranean anger.

Rosie served coffee in the living room. The furniture was familiar. Irish Catholic ordinary, Keveney used to call it. Protective fabric on the arms of the sofa and lace doilies on the coffee table. A wooden crucifix hung over the entrance and there was a glazed painting of the Holy Mother on the wall. He made a gesture.

"You're getting more Catholic every day," laughing to take the sting out of the words.

A stiffness came into her once beautiful face. "There's His truth in the Church and the word of God is for us all to hear."

Oh, Jesus, he almost said, but knew how she'd respond: "I'm glad you're calling on Him at last."

Humor was not Rosie's strongest point, he reminded himself. "You're looking well," he managed.

"And you're still the best-looking man I've ever known."

"Is that an invitation?" He knew better than that.

She blinked. "To what, Jack? To use my body for your private pleasure?"

"And yours, too, maybe." One mistake after another, he told himself. What if she accepted? The biggest mistake of them all.

"I think not. But thank you for thinking of me."

"Oh, Jesus!"

"I'm glad you're calling on Him at last."

It was time for him to leave. He lied about an appointment, someone he had to speak with. "An informer..."

"Always working, you never change." Then, as he shoved himself to his feet, as if reluctant to allow him to leave, "How is the job in Washington?"

"A bitch," he heard himself say. "There's no honor down there. No one to depend on. Politicians feed off betrayal, worse there than anywhere else."

That drew a benevolent expression. "I'm sure you'll work things out."

"Sure," he muttered.

"I know everything will be all right. You're the best at what you do, you always had to be the best."

He longed to strike out at her, to let his frustration and anger wash over her, to make her understand that he was caught in a vise of his own making.

"Yes," he said. "Things work out. Tell Patrick goodnight for me, I don't want to disturb his homework. And you take care."

"I'm a child of God," she said with a satisfied smile. "He will look after me. You're in my prayers, Jack."

"Sure," he said, on his way out. "I never doubted it."

TWENTY-ONE

"IT HAS BEEN A LONG TIME, WILLIE," NINA FUENTES said, inspecting his face unhurriedly as if seeking indications of change.

Hatcher took her hand. "I missed you."

"And I you." Her smile was cool and she removed her hand with a controlled, graceful gesture. "Friends should never be apart so long."

What, he thought, if he told her of his secret longings for her? That she was in his thoughts all day and in his dreams by night? A mistake, certainly. A woman like Nina, how magnificent she was —she would mock the romantic yearnings of a man so plain and ineffectual. Only a man like Napoleon could win her, someone handsome, daring, unpredictable. Someone like Jack Keveney, intense and single-minded, a man of heroic proportions.

The memory of seeing Nina on Keveney's surveillance film made him tremble. His duty to Keveney and D-Group was clear. But his friendship for Nina conflicted with that duty and he was not sure how to reconcile the two. No matter what happened, Nina must not be hurt; a beautiful flower, she would wilt and soon expire behind bars.

"Napoleon keeps both of us busy," Hatcher said.

A servant appeared with breakfast. Tall glasses of freshly squeezed orange juice, eggs *rancheros*, hot tortillas and sticks of sweet butter and a pot of strong coffee.

They were seated at a round table topped with brightly colored tiles on the covered patio of Napoleon's house just outside Chiri-

275

qui. Behind them, the rising sun cast long shadows; to the front, the morning mist still attached to the valley stretching out to the west. The view, Willie believed, was the most beautiful in all of Sixaola.

They ate silently for a while, each picking through his or her own thoughts as they picked at the food. Until Nina sat back, looking at Hatcher over her coffee cup, which she held in both hands. "You heard about Salazar?" she offered.

Hatcher attended to his breakfast, deciding what to say, how much information he could safely claim without giving away his source, Jack Keveney. "Only that he went north for a while."

"The Regents," she said, still watching him in that closed, probing way of hers. "They arranged for a large shipment of guns for the army."

He chose not to reply.

She went on. "You would think the government could buy guns without help from Salazar."

"You would think so," he answered carefully.

She tasted the coffee in her cup with the tip of her tongue, pink and moist. Hatcher, fascinated, watched, banking images of her for later review.

"The government is without funds, fearful of an uprising..."

"The Ché Brigade?"

"They grow stronger, the government grows weaker by the day. The Regents, with the cooperation of the Americanos, are trying to keep Negrete and his people in their place. So, cocaine pays for weapons, a fair enough trade."

Hatcher made himself laugh. "That puts the people in Washington in bed with Salazar, dealing just like us."

"Exactly. Only the deal almost fell through. A new agency that calls itself D-Group. You've heard of them?"

Hatcher managed a small nod; how much could he safely admit? When to deny, when to reveal that he was on top of things. Keveney and D-Group, it was his business to know about them. Or was it?

"This D-Group," Nina said, "according to our informants, it almost spoiled the deal."

Hatcher attended to the egg on his plate. Did Jack Keveney know that Napoleon's long reach extended into D-Group's operations? Someone had to be feeding information to Nina, to Napoleon.

"Imagine," she said cheerfully. "Moreno-Diaz was on the scene along with Salazar and a few of his people. Imagine if he ended up in a gringo prison."

"Not a pleasant prospect."

She pronounced a thin laugh. "This Jack Keveney—he is the leader of D-Group—he might have done us a favor. You know of him?"

Hatcher looked out across the valley. The mist was lifting and the sun's rays had reached the green fields below. In the distance, a campesino worked his small plot of land with a wooden hand plow behind a team of oxen. It was a scene out of an earlier century.

"The name is familiar. A cop in New York working narcotics, I think. He's the only one of that name I know."

"The same man."

"I remember, he was supposed to be very good at what he does."

"Oh, yes, very good. He came very close to busting me, which I would not have found amusing." She lapsed into thoughtful silence. "Certain American men..."

"Yes?"

"There is one in California—*es un tipo extraordinario*—he goes by the name of John Abruzzi."

Hatcher's heartbeat increased and he set himself against the resentment and envy he felt. He existed in a hostile world that never fully recognized his gifts, never would, he had come to believe. Would any woman ever say that about him, es un tipo extraordinario? Not likely.

His eyes came around to her, revealing nothing of what he felt. "You are in love with this extraordinary man?"

Her Latino smile was humorless, complex, tinged with self-mockery. "Love? What I felt for him was profound, and he is often in my mind, but love, who knows? When I left, it was hurried.

There was no opportunity to speak to him, to explain how it was with me."

"This Americano, he does not know about Napoleon, of course?"

She avoided his gaze and chose her words carefully, anxious to paint a proper picture of John Abruzzi and her connection to him. "He understands that I have an attachment. That it is only occasional. That it is a unique matter."

"I see."

She perceived an implied criticism in the words and responded with a flash of anger. "Abruzzi accepted what I told him. He is a real man, sophisticated and worldly, he understands how it can be sometimes between men and women."

"Of course," Hatcher said without expression.

"He was interested," she went on tonelessly. "He asked questions."

"And you answered?"

"Naturally, I was discreet."

"Naturally."

She put her coffee cup back on the table. "This Keveney," she said, moving on briskly, "we must know more about him, about this D-Group. Check your sources, Willie, find out what you can."

"Done."

"This arms deal of Salazar's. Napoleon is convinced it is only the first of many. He has had to change his plans, speed up his schedule."

"I don't understand."

"Napoleon has certain ambitions."

"Part of his charm."

"He has a secret dream, our Napoleon. It is a dream of monumental proportions."

"Nothing he does will surprise me."

She leaned his way, her voice soft, caressing, a suggestion of wonder on her face. "He intends to rule . . ."

Hatcher interrupted, as if his words could change anything. "To rule? To rule what, the world? Others had that dream—Alexander the great, the first Napoleon, Hitler. They all failed."

"Napoleon is no fool. He recognizes his limitations . . ."

"I never noticed."

"Then look more closely, my dear friend," she said, not disguising the serrated edge in her voice. "It is Sixaola only he is after. Oh, no, he is no fool . . ."

Hatcher slumped in his chair. When put that way, it seemed so reasonable and logical, so alarmingly possible. "The Americans . . ."

She waved that objection aside. "The United States will do nothing. Napoleon has the weapon that will weaken and drain the Americans of their purpose and will, a weapon that no other leader ever owned—cocaine. Cocaine as a weapon, Willie, consider it. So insidious in its effect. Subtle, doing its damage gradually and, for the most part, invisibly, eating away at the nation's youth, its future, its soul. Oh, yes, cocaine, as a weapon, it is more dangerous than a nuclear bomb. And we have it."

"Coke will make Napoleon King of the World, is that it?"

"Of Sixaola, I told you."

"And the other *narcotrafficantes?* They too have money, influence, power. What do they say to all this?"

She hesitated, but was unable to stop, unable to keep it all to herself. "Soon Napoleon will be alone at the top."

"What are you saying? The other Regents, once they find out, they'll destroy Napoleon."

"They know nothing, they'll learn nothing, unless you tell them, Willie."

Her words made him quiver. "You know better than that, Nina. You know I can be trusted."

She stared at him for a long time and then the tension went out of her face. "For the sake of us all, it better be so." She allowed herself a warming smile. "It is all worked out, my darling. At a certain time on a certain day, Juan-Manuel Negrete will lead the Ché Brigade out of the hills in a surprise attack at the federales. First the army posts on the outskirts of the capital city. At the same moment, forces already infiltrated into the city will attack the military barracks behind the Palace of Justice. Police headquarters will be taken and key federal buildings will be occupied. Within a few hours it will all be over."

"Impossible," Hatcher heard himself say, aghast at the enormity of the scheme, at its daring. This was nothing less than a political revolution launched from a base of narcotics profits and the insane ambitions of one man.

"What flaws are there?" Nina said. "Where are the weak spots? Convince Napoleon that we have erred and corrections will be made. But, no, nothing has been overlooked."

Hatcher could not confront her. Nina was as much a part of this mad enterprise as Napoleon, was privy to it from its inception, wanted it as much as he did. "The Army," Hatcher said. "With their new arms . . ."

"Before they can learn to use them effectively, the attack will take place. Besides, Negrete has placed men in every unit. Many are leaders, sergeants or officers. Men in positions to dictate what ordinary soldiers do and do not do. Certain districts will surrender without a shot being fired. Confusion will spread as contradictory orders are given. Units will be transferred on the day of the attack to noncombat areas. Reinforcements will arrive too late. I tell you it will work . . ."

"This is crazy."

"In the first hour, el presidente, the cabinet, the justices of the courts, the generals, all will be assassinated. Victory is inevitable."

"The Regents?"

"By noon of the appointed day, the Regents will be dead. Boom, boom, boom, shot down by members of their own body-guards."

"And then?" Hatcher was unable to answer his own question. Napoleon Cruz, whore's brat from El Arbolito, would have an army of his own, a nation of his own. A drug industry of his own. He would spend time solidifying his position before moving ahead with his grand plan.

Sixaola only? Oh, no. Napoleon's ambitions transcended borders, it climbed mountains, it spanned the seas. Napoleon truly dreamed of ruling the world, as his namesake must've done, as Hitler and Stalin must've dreamed, as Alexander had. Hatcher was charged with reluctant admiration and terror; and always a jealousy that kept him an arm's length away from the true center of power. "When does all this occur?" he dared to ask. "And what will my role be in this great adventure?"

"To do exactly as you are told to do," that familiar resonant voice said from close behind.

Willie came to his feet a little too quickly, swinging around with that top-heavy gracefulness so many fat men possess. Napoleon stood at arm's length away, tall and willowy, deceptively soft, looking as young as ever and as handsome, yet somehow different. The fine tobacco-colored skin remained taut over his cheekbones and the long, lean jaw; but in those dark, sapient eyes there was a duality Hatcher had never noticed before.

He's crazy, Hatcher thought. Mad as a hatter and all the more dangerous for being so. And in that instant he knew that everything Nina had told him was true, that Napoleon thirsted for power—absolute power—with the blind craving of a madman. Nothing less would satisfy him; and in his drive to slake that terrible thirst, he would destroy the world, if he had to.

He flung his arms around Napoleon in a brotherly abrazo and was instantly aware of the other man's stiff withdrawal. He stepped away at once.

"El Gordo," Napoleon said in a mannerly, fastidious way, the words without affection. "You're putting on weight again, too satisfied with yourself."

"You haven't changed a bit." Hatcher felt himself to be in the presence of a stranger.

Napoleon settled into a chair, his movements gracefully feline, ending up low on his spine, those tapered fingers touching at the tips in a steeple over which he studied Hatcher.

"And when you're told what to do, mi amigo, in what way will you respond?" He spoke in a dark, gloomy voice as if the demon in him had unloosened some hellish argument.

Hatcher shifted from one foot to another, struggling to calm himself. Too much was happening too fast, too much that he either didn't know about or didn't comprehend.

"As always, *jefe*," he said, his manner more subservient than he liked. "I obey in your service."

Napoleon's lips tightened as if holding back sardonic laughter. "Of course. Now. About this man, Keveney, he begins to offend me. He could be a threat to our operations."

Hatcher felt his sphincter contract and his awareness of Jack Keveney increased sharply. A sense of comradeship, of connection, of loyalty. Oh, yes, Keveney used him for his own purposes as did Napoleon. But unlike the druglord, he could trust Keveney, find in him the sanctuary he was convinced he would shortly require. Keveney alone could keep him alive when the shaky structure on which his life was erected came tumbling down, as it inevitably must do one day soon.

"My sources tell me he is clever. After all, he almost arrested our little Nina, and only a very clever man could do that. You know him, Willie?"

A chill settled in Hatcher's middle and he held himself still, stiff, fearful his body might reveal to Napoleon the extent of his relationships with Keveney. "I have heard of him."

"You have heard of him." Napoleon spoke intimately, as if he and Hatcher shared a bitter secret. "Have you ever seen this gringo?"

Hatcher shook his head.

"No, naturally not. I told you he was clever, too clever to allow my people to see his face. But it is vital that I know who my enemies are in order that I may deal with them. Fortunately, I have in my service people who not only can be trusted but who are highly efficient..."

Willie, possessed by an almost juvenile rush of guilt and fear, opened his mouth to protest; he was unable to speak. He waited helplessly.

Napoleon placed a white envelope on the table with an imperious little motion. "This Keveney is there, in the envelope, all that needs to be known about him. You will locate this gringo who makes so much trouble for me. He must be eliminated. Killed quickly so that the Yanquis will spend their time searching for his murderer and pay no attention to my operations there and here."

Napoleon, his face in repose now, measured Hatcher with faint amusement. "Can you do the job for me, Willie?"

"No!" Hatcher heard himself say, appalled at his poverty of judgment. He tried to soften his reaction. "This Keveney, the way I hear it, he can smell a trap. Avoid danger where others take the bait. It is said that he cannot be killed."

"Is there any man who cannot be killed, Nina?"

"There is no one, Napoleon."

To Hatcher, it seemed the woman was mesmerized by Napoleon's presence, his personal force, the long history they possessed in common. She gazed steadily into that ancient Aztec face.

"No one can get close enough to him," Hatcher said.

"Are you with me," Napoleon said, "or with Keveney?"

"I have always been with you, Napoleon, I always will be. But I do not want any of our people to be put in jeopardy."

Napoleon permitted himself a flat smile. "Willie says no one can get close enough to kill this Keveney, Nina."

"I will get close enough," she said.

Napoleon said, "Every man is vulnerable. Look at our Nina, Willie, at how beautiful she is, how seductive in the morning sunlight. No man can resist such beauty, so much sensual promise. Not even a paranoid gringo policeman. Oh, yes, our Nina will get close enough. She will disarm him, leave him weak, his senses dulled, sinking into the false comfort of the well-loved. Then she will blow his brains out." The words, the manner of their delivery, rendered Hatcher fearful and uncertain. "Nina will do this for me. And it will be a clear message to all Americano drug agents that none of them may safely trespass on Napoleon's great crusade."

"I will kill him," Nina said.

"Still," Napoleon went on, "it would be wrong to underestimate this man. I would not want this assignment to turn out badly."

"I will not fail."

"We shall take no chances. I will send along a backup, someone to protect you and make sure Keveney is dealt with. Antonio will go with you."

Nina protested. "I do better by myself."

Napoleon left no room for debate. "With Antonio at your back

you will be safe. In that envelope is information about this Keveney. Where he works. Where he loves. There are photographs.
Find him and kill him. And when you have done so, come back to
me. I want you at my side when the day of my greatness comes."
He turned to leave, pausing to speak to Hatcher. "I will talk to
you again later. . ."

Nina withdrew a folded sheet of white paper from the envelope,
committing the typed information to memory. Then she turned
the envelope over; a color photograph fell onto the table. Somehow it came as no surprise that the man she had agreed to kill was
John Abruzzi.

TWENTY-TWO

KEVENEY RETREATED BEHIND THE PROTECTIVE
hedges of memory, safe against the rough intrusions of reality. He
struggled to isolate his victories, to give them a weighted value
that overshadowed his defeats. He viewed the past as a wastrel
smog of futility and failure. The future was dim, a frightening
black hole. He longed to feel again as he had when he was a young
cop undercover, energized by the daily challenges of the job,
cheered and encouraged by the succession of small victories. Instead, he had become ponderous and clumsy, without goals, fighting to hold on.

He lived with hypocrisy and deceit; lies and betrayal were the
currency of his existence. Nothing was as it appeared to be; he
was without friends or family, without love or lovers. He wearied
of being alone.

Then the telephone on his office desk began to ring, pulling
him back to the present. After the fifth ring, he picked it up and
said his name. Willie Hatcher, conspiratorial and anxious, was on
the other end of the wire.

"Remember what I told you about Napoleon . . . ?"

Napoleon Cruz. The focal point of his pain, the most important
man in his life. *The symbol of his failure.*

"You still there, Jack?"

"I'm listening."

"Well, it's arrived. The big day. Napoleon intends to take them
all out—Salazar, Uribe, Vega, all of them. With the backing of the

285

Ché Brigade, he is going to pull off a quick military strike against
the capital city."

"You lead a rich fantasy life."

"You don't understand. Napoleon's fantasies, he's making them
real."

"Kill the Regents?"

"And take over the entire Sixaolan drug business, take over the
country itself. Name himself king, president, whatever."

Keveney sat straighter in his chair, all faculties suddenly alert.
He permitted himself a short burst of laughter, a mocking, almost
satisfied laugh. "Beautiful. So we get a government run by a drug
peddler and a Marxist-Leninist revolutionary."

"Sounds nuts, right?" Hatcher said, voice lowering. "Only it's
not. You can guess their agenda, Keveney. . ."

"Pushing coke into the U.S. and spreading the revolution."

"You got that right. They're already talking about Paraguay and
maybe Brazil, who knows what else."

Keveney allowed his mind to drift backward. The arms shipment in that Florida airport hangar. And the narcotics that paid
for them. The Regents had their own agenda and it was operative,
tied in to whatever plans the U.S. had for Sixaola. Secret, dirty
little schemes were on everybody's mind; sometimes the fucking
you got was not worth the fucking you gave.

"How'd you know all this?" he said into the phone.

Willie answered in a whisper. "Nina and Napoleon himself.
There's a lot going on down here."

A surge of emotion rocked Keveney. The pungent taste of her
was in his mouth, the hot, physical smell of her flesh in his nostrils. As if it had a will of its own, his body began to respond.

"How's she doing?" he heard himself ask and almost cried out in
protest against his own lack of pride, his weakness. Would he ever
be separated from Nina Fuentes? "Never mind . . ."

"They're going to hit you, Jack. Nina and—"

The words made no sense to him; Nina—Silvia—would never
do anything to hurt him, he was convinced of that. Besides, she
had no idea what his real identity was.

"Even if she knew who I was, Nina would never..."

"The fuck she wouldn't!" Hatcher dared to say. He was flooded by fear, for himself and for Keveney. He craved a safe haven, an end to existing with danger and death, an end to working both sides of a dangerous street. His commitment to Keveney was total, unwavering, and he was determined to make the other man understand exactly how vulnerable each of them was.

"She's a killer, Nina is! Napoleon's best. That judge, Busta-mente, that was Nina. And there have been others. Many of them. She'll take you off guard, Jack. Put a bullet in your head. Napoleon, he put the finger on you. Name. Photo. The works."

"I can take care of myself." It was juvenile bravado, too loud and empty. Anybody could be taken out, if the hit man was smart and patient. He didn't want to think about it. Not yet, not now. "Where are you, Willie?"

"Napoleon's ranch, outside Chiriqui."

"I don't like it."

"Neither do I. But I had to warn you, I had to..."

"Okay. You get out of there. Today."

"As soon as I can."

"Get in touch, when you're clear."

"Depend on it, Keveney."

Hatcher dropped the receiver back into its cradle and consid-ered Keveney's advice; certainly it was time to leave, to sever his connection to Napoleon and his world. And leave he would, first chance he had. He turned and there, less than ten feet away, stood Nina Fuentes.

Never had she appeared more beautiful. That finely featured face, a study in perfection, the blessed visage of a madonna, framed by the magnificent fall of shining black hair. Her remark-able eyes, pale and still, were luminous. Her lips were slightly parted, moist and voluptuous. What, he wondered, all joints lock-ing, his sphincter tightening, his muscles taut, what would it be like to possess her? To experience all that warmth and passion, that velvety skin beneath his hands, to explore every orifice, to plunge his face into the most mysterious and fulfilling part of her? How he loved her, had always loved her, and she would never be his.

She pointed a nickel-plated revolver at Hatcher's navel in a grip strong and unwavering. She cursed him. "Chinga su madre." Her voice was thin, vibrating with rage and frustration. "You are a spy."

"No, no. You don't understand."

"You betrayed us. With this Keveney. You did not know him, you said. You had only heard of him, you said. You lied to Napoleon. You lied to me . . ."

He was desperate. "You know him, Keveney, what kind of a man he is. Es un tipo extraordinario, you said, He is extraordinary. Yes, I warned him. Do you want to see him killed?"

"You betrayed us."

"Nina, please, we have been friends."

"You betrayed me." Visions of Abruzzi—Keveney—rose up before her eyes, that strangely boyish face contorted in mocking laughter; laughing at her. Madre de Dios, how he had used her! Used her flesh, caused her to talk about Napoleon so that he knew, knew that she was with *him*. Used her body and used her mind, her spirit, all that she was, degraded and corrupted for his base purposes. "I hate what you have done, fat man . . ." Her arm straightened, the revolver pointing. "You are a traitor . . ."

All blood drained out of Hatcher's face and his knees began to shake. He raised a pudgy hand—so inadequate—as if to ward off her anger, as if to deflect the killing bullet she was about to send his way. "Don't," he whimpered. "Please, don't . . ."

She brought the revolver to full cock and he could find no mercy in those magnificent eyes.

At that moment, the world erupted. The floor under them seemed to rise up as if the earth everywhere were in motion, the walls shifted and the ceiling cracked, unloosing a fall of plaster. Hatcher ducked instinctively, and Nina, struggling to maintain her balance, brought the gun back to where he crouched.

"Madre de Dios!" she cried, "what is it?"

The roar of engines came and went and she was able to isolate the distinctive whoosh of air-to-ground missiles and the rhythmic crump of small cannon. She heard men crying out in surprise and fear and anguish and the higher pitch of automatic weapons.

"Jesus God Almighty Christ!" Hatcher shouted, less afraid of Nina's wrath now.

The door to the room burst open and Carlito appeared, a nine-millimeter automatic in his hand. His eyes were wide, less in fear than excitement, and he shouted out the news.

"They are attacking the hacienda. The army. Helicopters. They are everywhere. Soon they will be inside the walls. We must fight . . ." His sharp dark eyes took in the scene in the room, the tension between Hatcher and Nina. "Que pasa?"

"This one," Nina said. "This one is a spy. He works for the gringos, for Keveney. He has given us all away."

"Is that so?" Carlito said, his voice equable. "Are you sure?"

"I am sure," Nina said. "I heard him on the telephone."

"You don't understand," Hatcher said, trying to buy time, trying to find a way out of his worsening predicament. Carlito was cruel and without mercy; he enjoyed dispensing death. "I must talk to Napoleon . . ." It was his only hope.

"I will kill you first, traitor," Nina said.

Carlito, in a tranquilizing monotone, said, "You've heard nothing of what I told you—the army, the troopers. We are under attack, all of us. This is no time to be killing each other."

Nina, her rage tempered by disappointment, slowly, very slowly, lowered the hammer of her revolver back into place. "Play the horses, Willie, you are a very lucky man. For now. But this is not finished yet."

Carlito allowed himself a small smile of satisfaction. His glance went from Hatcher to Nina. Not so much those stony black eyes, as his entire body shifting awkwardly from right to left, his joints locked, his muscles taut. "You are a good and loyal friend of Napoleon," he murmured, "of us all." And then he shot Nina in the chest. She fell to the floor, face up, those remarkable eyes wide, lips working soundlessly.

"My God!" Hatcher yelled, rushing forward.

Carlito brought the fat man to a halt with a small, menacing gesture of his pistol. He stepped closer to the wounded woman and put another bullet into her skull. "There," he said to no one in particular. "It had to be done. She was a serious danger while she lived." He looked at Hatcher, an open, innocent, boyish expression on his face. "Now, who knows, we may yet survive, you and I. If one of those stupid soldiers doesn't kill us first..."

Hatcher, eyes fixed on Nina's corpse, said, "She was my friend. I loved her. Why did you kill her?"

"Listen to me, gringo, and understand what I say. All of us may be dead in a few minutes. Napoleon, Antonio, the others, are fighting. But they don't have a chance. The hacienda would be a fortress if those were banditos attacking. Instead, it is a trap. That is the army with heavy weapons. What good will it do for us all to die out there? Listen to me, gringo, and do as I say. Follow me to the garage, we shall hide in the tunnel. When the fighting is over, we'll come out. Surrender. Perhaps then we can retrieve something from this chaos..."

"Are you going to kill me, too?"

The question caught Carlito by surprise. "Only if you do something monumentally stupid. Now, let's go." He directed the fat man toward the narrow staircase near the kitchen that led to the underground garage.

Outside, the sounds of battle came closer. The shadow of a passing helicopter flitted across the windows in the west wall and a quick glance revealed men in combat gear firing automatic weapons as they advanced on the house. "Go," the boy ordered. "Go faster, if you want to live..."

Hatcher could make no sense out of all this, but he understood that, for reasons of his own, Carlito intended to keep him alive. It was the only good thing in this day of death and despair.

They made it through the garage into the tunnel and Hatcher fell back against one cold wall, fighting for breath, trying to calm himself. Less than three feet away, Carlito, the pistol in hand, was amazingly composed and unafraid.

"Will you tell me what in hell is going on?" Hatcher said.

Carlito indicated the outside sound and fury. "A small war. The government has decided to do something about Napoleon Cruz, at last."

"The government? I thought the Regents owned the government."

"Naturally. Which raises a number of questions. Who ordered the attack? And why at this particular time? No matter. Meanwhile, the important thing is to stay alive, no?"

"Did you have to shoot Nina?"

"Either I shot her or she shot you." He pointed his pistol at Hatcher. "If you are so anxious to die, I can accommodate you, El Gordo." He produced a thin, mirthless sound, more a cough than a laugh. "It is very simple, I am a practical man. Those crimes Nina accused you of doing—they are all true. No, no, do not lie to me. It offends me to be lied to. You betrayed Napoleon. Well, I too have betrayed him. Or I shall, when I get the chance. Napoleon has everything I want. He is everything I want to be.

"Why did I save your life? For one reason only—I need you. You will remain alive only as long as I do need you. Never forget that, gringo. You live by my will, mine alone. Listen," he ended.

"The shooting is heavier now."

"Yes. The small war will be over before long, I think. Until it is, wait here. Let their nerves grow steadier. Let their fears settle. Let peace reign once more. Then you and I will climb out of this rat's nest and make our arrangements with the victors, whoever they may be . . ."

TWENTY-THREE

NAPOLEON SPRAWLED COMFORTABLY ON A WICKER-
and-leather lounge veranda at the rear of the hacienda, drinking
hot coffee out of a ceramic mug, inspecting the close horizon
beyond the wall to the north. The hills undulated from east to
west, the first line of defense for the stone complex Napoleon had
erected. His mind, as ever, was active, going over the plans he
had made, seeking flaws that could be corrected, and finding
money. Soon the arms his agents were purchasing around the
world would be delivered to Juan-Manual Negrete and the revolution, *his* revolution—*La Causa,* as Negrete had taken to calling
it—would be launched. Police barracks would be overrun. Army
positions would be destroyed. High-ranking officers would be assassinated by teams of guerrillas. The presidential palace would be
attacked. In a matter of days, the government would fall. Negrete
would declare victory in the name of La Causa, appointing himself
el presidente for life. The mopping up would begin.

The Regents—Salazar, Uribe, Vega—would be sought out.
They and their men would be killed, their properties confiscated,
their fields of coca appropriated; and Napoleon Cruz would control them all. He would be the ultimate authority in Sixaola, the
manipulating force behind the scene, the most powerful man in all
of Sixaola. And should Juan-Manuel's ambition become too great,
should he at any time challenge Napoleon's dominance or fail to
respond to his commands, then he too would be eliminated.

His mind reached into the future. And the undulating hills
seemed to blur as he allowed himself to dream even greater

293

dreams of eventual glory. So it was, that when the first of the helicopters rose up like a spidery apparition from behind the hills, it registered only dimly.

The machine hung almost motionless in the slow afternoon air, black and ominous against the sun-washed blue of the sky. Soon a second helicopter appeared, and a third, flanking the first in a tight military V, floating forward in ghostly silence.

Napoleon shoved all dreams aside. He blinked and brought the hills into sharp relief. The helicopters lost their ghostly status, a reality that gave birth to a certain cold knowledge; he had been betrayed.

The coffee cup fell out of his hand as he came to his feet, alert. He swung around; to the south, a second flight of helicopters was coming swiftly. To the west, to the east, they were everywhere, a dozen planes in all. The stuttering roar of their engines reached out before them, a warning come too late.

"Carlito!" he shouted.

But it was Antonio who appeared, an automatic rifle in each hand. He tossed one at Napoleon. "We are under attack!" he cried, almost happily. "It is the military."

"Order the men into position. We will fight them off."

"I've done so," the little man said. "But we have only a dozen security men. If this is a major assault . . ."

In counterpoint, the gunships began to fire. First, the whoosh of rockets and explosions of red and orange ringed Napoleon's wall, and that precious, impregnable wall was shattered, breached in four or five different places.

Cannon fire, a metronomic thump of airborne weaponry, was next. The great carved double doors of the house of which Napoleon had been so proud, burst into a jumble of torn wood and splinters. Mortar shells, fired from behind the line of hills, began to land in the courtyard and gardens. Beyond the wall, beyond the fields and out of the woods, advanced a squadron of armored vehicles, and behind that were hundreds of foot soldiers, shooting as they came.

Inside the complex, Antonio's men fought back. But their weapons were no match for the army's might, and most of them were killed in the first onslaught. Others were wounded and unable to continue the battle.

A mortar shell exploded near the main gate and pieces of stone whistled overhead. Trees were flung to one side and a giant cactus was blown apart. Another mortar round sent the bricked *bovida* of Napoleon's foyer crashing down. And finally the troops came pouring through the gaps in the wall.

Napoleon's men fought back until they died. Antonio, crazed by combat, was nearly sliced in half by the fire from an automatic weapon.

A helicopter landed in the courtyard, not far from where Napoleon crouched behind a low interior wall, still shooting. Soldiers came leaping to the ground, strong, stocky men, spraying the hacienda with bullets, looking for someone to kill. They worked in teams, smart, aggressive, protective of each other. And Napoleon, watching them advance with wild eyes, understood that everything was over: the battle, his dreams of glory. His empire was torn down before it was fully formed.

Carlito!

Where was the boy? Had he managed to make it through the carnage? Napoleon rose as if to run, thinking he might make it down to the garage and into the escape tunnel. He never had a chance. A half dozen soldiers surrounded him, weapons leveled, their faces grim and serious. Napoleon dropped his weapon and raised his hands above his head. He produced his most charming smile.

"I must talk with your commander," he said. "Someone has made a terrible mistake."

Quiet returned to the hacienda. In the kitchen, Rosa had taken refuge under a heavy work table. Trembling with fright, she emerged under the watchful gaze of two soldiers. They led her outside.

Three of the dozen men who provided security for the hacienda were brought before an army colonel who materialized polished and proud in a meticuously tailored uniform. He barely glanced at the three prisoners. "They are already dead," he muttered. "They were killed during the fighting. See to it," he ordered. The men were taken away. Moments later a burst of gunfire, and another. The colonel turned his attention to other matters.

A Mercedes limousine rolled up the winding road that led to the hacienda, drawing to a stop inside the shattered gate. Raphael Salazar, bent and fragile, stepped out, surveying the scene with obvious disapproval.

"Such a waste," he murmured. "Such a waste." He addressed the colonel. "Napoleon, he has been killed?"

"Not even a scratch, señor. He is our prisoner." The officer gestured and Napoleon was brought out of the house. His face brightened at the sight of the old man.

"Raphael, tell them to release me. They are making a mistake."

Salazar inspected the young man. "It would have been more accommodating had you allowed yourself to be shot, Napoleon. This way there will only be anguish for you and embarrassment for the rest of us."

"Are you insane, old man? To treat Napoleon in this manner! You shall pay for what you have done, all of you shall pay."

"Arrangements have been made," Salazar said without regret. He addressed the colonel. "Everything is ready?"

"Arrangements!" Napoleon blustered. "What arrangements? Nobody makes arrangements for Napoleon, except Napoleon."

"The helicopter is waiting," the colonel answered.

Salazar's chin drooped, more in sadness than assent. His breathing was audible and he licked spittle from the corner of his mouth.

"Good. Then take him out of my sight."

"Wait!" Napoleon cried, struggling against the soldiers who held him. "Wait!"

The soldiers led him away, still protesting, still issuing demands, still threatening. When he was gone, the colonel said, "It is still not too late for the army to attack the guerrilla, Negrete, and eliminate his force."

"To what end? The campesinos require a dream to cling to, an eventual victory to dream about. We will control Negrete, limit his activities. Should it become necessary—with the help of our American friends—we can always wipe him out."

"Whatever you say, señor." The colonel saluted, stepped back and said, "There are still two more prisoners . . . the fat gringo and the boy."

"Oh, yes," Salazar breathed. "Bring them to me."

A sergeant and two soldiers escorted Carlito and Hatcher to where Salazar waited. The sergeant spoke with considerable deference in his manner. "We found them hiding in a tunnel under the house, señor. They surrendered without a fight."

Salazar clucked remorsefully. "There is no reason for either of these two to continue to live. Shoot them both."

"Hold on!" Hatcher cried.

Carlito displayed no emotion. "Señor Raphael, may I speak to you in private?"

"To what end, niño? There is nothing more to say."

"A moment of your time?"

Salazar shuffled back in the direction of the Mercedes. "Very well. Speak to me."

Carlito caught up to the old man. "Napoleon is dead, yes?"

"No, not dead. Sent to America where he will be brought to trial like an ordinary criminal, placed in jail for the rest of his life. He would have done better to have put a bullet in his brain."

Carlito swallowed his surprise. He said, "No matter, there still must be a Napoleon. The men who work for him, the campesinos who grow and harvest the coca, the chemists in the laboratories, even Negrete—he brought to life in them a certain loyalty, even love. He was special. Think of how much he accomplished and in so very short a time. The distribution network. The money laundering. The banks. The shippers. The police on his payroll, the politicians. They have never worked for the Regents, Señor Salazar, only for Napoleon."

"Good point, Little Minnow, but our arrangement with the norteamericanos is solid. Napoleon belongs to them now. Eloquence cannot save him."

Carlito ducked his head in boyish shyness. "Oh, that is not my intention, señor. I wish only to save his organization, to keep it in place and working."

"Yes, that might be desirable. But Napoleon is gone, his empire finished. All empires pass, turn to dust—the Greeks, the Romans. The Third Reich was destined to last for a thousand years, Hitler said. How insignificant are the dreams of men in the hindsight of history."

Carlito shook his head. "What Napoleon built need not fall. It can continue being productive."

A slight, sardonic smile curled its way across Salazar's dry lips. "With a new emperor, yes?"

"Someone must lead."

"And you are that someone, I take it?"

"Why not?" the boy spit out in challenge. "I know as much about the organization as Napoleon. Was I not always at his side? He taught me. He told me everything. I know where the laboratories are, the fields of coca, the rendezvous points for our goods. I know how to manage the money, I know the banks and the men who manage them. With me at its head, the organization would go on as before. Only one thing would be different—no more Napoleon. No one else can do it, señor."

Salazar grew thoughtful. "What about the woman, Nina? She too was close to your master."

Carlito shrugged. "She died in the fighting, señor." He made the sign of the cross. "Loyal to the death, isn't that so, Willie?"

Hatcher, pale and fearful, could not bring himself to speak.

Salazar chuckled, a thin, dry cackle. "You could almost be Napoleon, except younger, of course."

"Napoleon was the glue that held the organization together, señor. And I was always with him. Without him, without me, it will shatter and come apart. The entire structure. Yes, you and the others can take over, but make it work as efficiently? As profitably? Never. Napoleon's business. His people. His plans. Every element in the organization. It makes no sense to let it die. All that money! What a waste."

"Yes," Salazar said, "you are like him. Perhaps more so."

"I alone can guarantee continuity, Señor Salazar. No one else can do it. Not even you, with all my respect, not even the other Regents." He discovered he was breathing hard, and he paused and smiled a boyish smile before he went on. "I will do what Napoleon was doing—only I will do it better. There will be more profit."

"We do not wish to risk another Napoleon."

"Señor," Carlito said with dignity, "Whatever I have been, I will work for you, not against you. I will be your loyal servant."

"In return for what?"

"I dip my beak a little. You tell me how much. All of us must live. But the business goes on without interruption."

"And the profits?"

"Directly to you. Once they are in your hands, you pay me."

"You would be an employee, nothing more."

"I understand."

"Your condition would never change. You would never be allowed to accumulate power, as Napoleon did."

"I understand."

"Why is it I find you less than convincing, niño?"

"I am always loyal to my employers. Ask Napoleon."

"Ah, yes, Napoleon. How sad that he did not die in the battle, fighting to the end. He is a man of such inventiveness, a man persistent and cunning. I fear he may someday make his way out of the gringo prison . . ."

"Leave Napoleon to me, señor," Carlito said in a hushed voice. "He will never return to disturb you and your friends."

The old man shuddered. There was a chilliness to the boy's voice, such a deep emptiness in his black eyes that Salazar wondered how safe he was, how safe any of them would be with this Carlito around. Still—

"Napoleon," he said. "I wish to have nothing more to do with him. Whatever his fate, it should not involve me or my friends. Is that clear?"

"Clear. I will arrange everything. If we have a deal."

"Yes," Salazar answered presently. "A deal. We shall try it. For a month or two. Then we will decide if it is in our interest to continue. Is that clear?"

"You can depend on me. Oh, one thing, señor. El Gordo, this gringo, Hatcher. He could be valuable to me."

"You want him, he is yours."

"Thank you, señor."

Nodding, Salazar climbed back into the dark confines of the limousine and drove away.

Carlito waited until he was out of sight before turning back to the half-wrecked hacienda. It would take time to rebuild the house, he thought, to rebuild all of Napoleon's empire. To make it—and himself—stronger than even Napoleon had been. And unlike his predecessor, Carlito was convinced he would do it right. No more mistakes.

TWENTY-FOUR

THE TRANSPORT PLANE CAME TO A STOP IN A REMOTE corner of Andrews Air Force Base. Workers wheeled a portable staircase into place and the doorway swung open to reveal a military policeman, a sidearm strapped to his waist. He surveyed the area around the plane with a baleful curiosity before speaking to the officer in charge of the M.P. detail on the ground.

"Who're those guys?" he yelled. "Nobody tole me nothin' about civilians, Lieutenant."

"It's okay, Sergeant. They're official, here to take charge of the prisoner."

The sergeant thought it over before nodding. He disappeared back in the belly of the plane. Some minutes passed before he returned to his place in the doorway, still skeptical, still looking for trouble. When none materialized, he started down the stairs. Behind him were two more M.P.s armed with automatic weapons. Behind them, shackled hand and foot, came Napoleon Cruz, an M.P. at either side helping him down the stairs.

Keveney stood with his back to the limousine, watching. From this distance, Napoleon looked no different than he had that evening in El Convento. He was tall and stood straighter than other men, moving with a feline grace despite his chains. His face was darkly handsome and slightly flattened, and he gazed around with imperious disdain. But as he came closer, it was clear that changes had taken place. Shadows cupped those black eyes and the mottled Aztec face had begun to show the wear and tear of the years and was now lined at the mouth and the eyes.

301

Keveney's satisfaction was tempered by a faint regret that he had not been the one to bust the trafficker. This was an empty moment, anticlimactic, laced with regret and despair. Had the secretary of the interior not ordered him to take Napoleon personally into custody, he would not have come. For Keveney, his entire career seemed to have come to a grinding halt. He was unproductive, fraudulent, a front man for the governmental hoax that had yet to reach its climax.

"Take him," Keveney said to the agent at his side. "I'll be in the car."

Minutes later Napoleon was seated alongside Keveney, shifting around to face the head of D-Group. There was no fear in those dark eyes, no doubts etched on that impassive visage. He smiled a slow, sweet smile.

"Keveney," he said in accented English.

"You know who I am?" There was surprise in the words.

Napoleon produced a short, metallic laugh. "Perhaps more than you know about me, señor. Although I suppose Nina told you a great deal. Ah, yes, the beautiful Nina—how sad an end."

Keveney stared without speaking as the limousine, one of his men at the wheel, began to roll ahead.

"She's dead, you know. Shot in the confusion of the attack. You played an important role in that attack, did you not, Señor Keveney? Therefore, it is possible to say that it was you who killed her, you who pulled the trigger..."

The pile of arms in that Florida hangar, Keveney thought. Which one of those weapons was used to destroy Nina, to put an end to all that life, all that beauty? He could have stopped it then, put an end to the treachery and the madness, this conspiracy between governments and drug runners. He refused to believe that Nina was dead.

"You're lying," he said.

Napoleon gazed out the window. "This is wrong, you know. Stealing me away from my own country. I have committed no crime in America. I have never been here before. So many laws you gringos break to get your way. Laws of my country and your own."

"Who did it?" Keveney said, a desperate note creeping into his voice.

He answered with regret. "Does it matter? It happened. A terrible waste, no? Nina was a woman of exceptional attributes, wouldn't you agree, señor?" A smile displayed perfect large white teeth. "Think what you will miss, señor, what both of us shall miss . . ."

Keveney's fist drew back and he cursed.

The agent on the jump seat, facing them both, intervened. He said nothing, waiting until he felt the tension diminish in Keveney's arm before releasing him.

Napoleon produced a small, sage laugh. "You gringos, you take life too seriously. How soon before I am free again, señor? How long will it take? No matter the bail—my lawyers will see to it."

"For you, Napoleon," Keveney said, through the pain, "there will be no bail. You'll be brought to trial, you'll be found guilty, you'll be sentenced. You'll be an old man before you see daylight again . . ."

This time a disdainful look. "Señor Keveney, even as we speak, my friends are at work on my behalf . . ."

"If you're thinking about Salazar, Uribe, Vega, forget it. They're why you're here."

"Sons of putas, each of them. Of course not. Even as we speak, my little Carlito labors to free me. He knows what to do. He has access to the necessary funds. The political connections here and in my country. Oh, yes, señor, soon I will be free again . . ."

It occured to Keveney that Napoleon might just be right.

TWENTY-FIVE

THE PRISON HAD BEEN SET DOWN WITH MATHEMATI-cal precision at the center of a military training camp for the special forces, which, in turn, had been built at what was almost the geographical center of the United States. The prison was circled by high brick walls, complete with watchtowers and electrified metal fences topped with barbed wire. Brutish men in green uniforms carrying automatic pistols patrolled the perimeter of the complex with leashed attack dogs. No one had ever escaped from this prison. No one dared to try. No one ever would.

This was where Napoleon was brought. He was placed in a cell in C Block, at the virtual center of the prison in an eight-by-twelve cubicle without windows that was lit by a single glaring bulb recessed into the high ceiling behind a metal guard. The walls and floor of the cell were made of reinforced concrete fourteen inches thick, and the door had been fashioned out of solid steel, as impregnable as a bank vault.

Twice a day Napoleon was removed from his cell and taken to the exercise yard where he walked in a slow circle, often gazing up at the high blue sky of middle America. The sky made him think of Sixaola, of Chiriqui, of the hacienda before the attack, of Carlito. Somewhere, he was convinced, Carlito was making a mighty effort to free him from this gringo prison.

Three times a day Napoleon was taken, under guard, to the cafeteria. He sat alone at a table and nibbled tasteless Yanqui food, remembering fondly the culinary skills possessed by Rosa. Soon he would be out of this place, brought back where he belonged, living with all the style and comfort he had grown accustomed to.

He spoke only to his guards, and they never responded, those hard-eyed men with thin lips and big, meaty hands. In the exercise yard, in the cafeteria, the other prisoners barely noticed him. If they knew who he was, how important a man he was, they gave no sign.

Isolated in that cell, out of touch with the world he was familiar with, with *anyone*, Napoleon began to wonder if he had been abandoned. Surely Carlito must be working on his behalf, calling in his political debts, making new contacts, spending money in whatever amounts were necessary. Gringo officials were as susceptible to bribery as those in Sixaola. So he sat in the cell and waited. He grew bored, he grew bitter, corrupted by rising doubts and a small sick anger.

One day, without warning, Jim Struthers appeared. Tall and rawboned, he resembled a movie cowboy more than the attorney he was.

"Carlito sent you?" Napoleon said, with a rare display of cheerfulness. Certainly Little Minnow has not deserted him, that was clear now.

Struthers pursed his pale lips. "Don't know any Carlito, Mr. Cruz. Court-appointed attorney, that's what I am. 'Course, if I don't satisfy you, there's no sayin' you can't dump me and try again. But I'm here to tell you I'm as good as you're likely to get, specially at these prices."

"I can afford the best, the best."

Struthers tugged at his long, strong nose. "The way I hear it, you are destitute, without access to funds."

Napoleon opened his mouth to speak, then clamped his teeth together hard. Why allow this gringo to know anything about his affairs? There were accounts in Switzerland containing more than thirty million dollars. Another twelve million was safe in the Bahamas. And still another seventeen million in Panama. Money was certainly no problem, if only he could get to it.

"Get me out of here," he ordered Struthers.

"There's the problem, Mr. Cruz. Y'see, you've been denied

bail. No roots in the community, and such as that. Court's worried you jes might skip the country. Yessiree, this is home for you for a while. A formal arraignment that'll take place in a week or so, charges brought, and so on and so on. Trial should come up in no more'n six months. Less if I can manage it. Jes thought I'd drop by and let you in on how things are progressin'. I'll be back in a few days and we can begin putting together your defense; unless there's somethin' you want to say to me now?"

Struthers's visit aroused very little optimism in Napoleon. He perceived the tall lawyer as a bumbler, without sophistication or skill, yet he remained Napoleon's only link to the outside. He made up his mind to take the risk; he would send a message through Struthers to Carlito, insisting that efforts in his behalf be expedited. It was time to get him out of this repulsive gringo prison. He spent hours composing the message, printing it crudely on coarse toilet tissue. Finished, he read what he had written and began all over again. The message required had to be brief and powerful enough to galvanize Carlito into speedy action.

When he wasn't writing, his mind reached back inexplicably to El Arbolito and his boyhood among the stilted shacks, to his life in the narrow streets and back alleys, in the cantinas. And into his memories his mother's painted, powdered face appeared again and again. Ah, yes, she would have been proud of him, had she lived. Proud of his accomplishments. Of the fortune he had collected. The power he had achieved. The influence he possessed in high places in Sixaola and elsewhere.

She would have had an apartment of her own, complete with a luxurious bathroom, a television set in every room and an expensive stereo so that she might enjoy again the romantic music of her own girlhood.

Poor little mother...

He put her out of his mind and began to plan his revenge. Over the slow, lonely days and nights in the cell, he had come to understand how completely and in what a complicated fashion his betrayal had come about. Salazar, naturally, had been at the forefront; his great age and experience, his aristocratic background, provided him with a special place in the hierarchy of Sixaola's drug traffickers. He was a shrewd, cunning old man, charged with meanness, pitiless, and willing to do anything in pursuit of his own gain. Then, or course, there were Pablo Uribe and Rene Vega. Oh, yes, he would extract sweet revenge from each of them when the time came, from their fortunes, their families, their disgusting flesh. And from whoever else was involved. He would track all of them down and make them pay in pain and terror, providing only the slowest, cruelest of deaths.

And, he thought, glancing at the small radio, the president's tinny words echoing inside his skull, he would extract vengeance on the Americans. Those treacherous gringos had done this to him through Jack Keveney. And through Keveney he would have his revenge. He would find Keveney and kill him, destroy him and destroy all that was good about his country. Yes, he would do these things. He, of all men, was able to do them. With a word, a gesture, a single command.

Adios, Keveney.

Adios to all of his enemies.

A metal clanging jerked him back to his present condition. The electric bolts on his cell door withdrew into their stainless steel sheaths. The door was unlocked; an icy premonition held Napoleon in place on his narrow cot. Then the familiar confident smile lifted the corners of his wide mouth. The gringo lawyer— Struthers. Come to begin planning his defense. Well, why not? It was a way to pass the time until Carlito reached out to him, as he certainly would, once he received Napoleon's message. He rose to greet the lawyer.

The door swung open and three men crowded into the cell. Prisoners, like himself. Heavily muscled, wide-bodied men, with large, bony faces. Napoleon fell back a step, unafraid but wary. Men like these, men with faces like these, they were the destroyers that men like himself hired to do rough jobs. They were without sentiment, without intelligence; single-minded men who, for a price, would commit any act, perform any abomination. The smallest of the three brought the solid steel door silently back into place.

"Carlito sent us," the oldest of the men said, with no change of expression.

Napoleon's hopes rose. Little Minnow had not forgotten him after all. Naturally not. He had been working, spending money, doing whatever was necessary. Until he was able to reach into this Yanqui prison, into this very cell. These coarse gorillas were, when you thought about it, in his employ, come to carry him back to freedom.

"Ah," he breathed, with all his old insouciance. "What are your orders?"

The biggest of the men displayed a bottle of Coca Cola. "This is for you," he said, taking a step forward.

Without thinking, Napoleon reached for it.

The big man drove his fist into Napoleon's chest, sending him back against the wall, gasping for breath. They were at him, all three of them, pounding away. Each blow gave pain and he felt the ribs on his right side bend and crack. One big fist broke his nose. His head was rocked back and forth and a dizziness took hold, traveling quickly into his stomach. A knee to the crotch made him retch and he fell forward.

"No more," he muttered. A cracked plea, echoes of despair and defeat, and a shot of awful, penetrating terror such as he had never known. His strength was stripped away, his power; helpless and debased, he had become one of the victims he had always mocked and scorned. Demeaned and full of shame, he had to try again. "I will pay . . ."

The big man was amused. He ran his great hand through Napoleon's black hair. He caressed his smooth cheek. "Too late, my friend. Payment has already been made. To us, to so many others. From top to bottom, you might say. All that's left to do—is to finish the job . . ."

"Hurry up!" a thick whisper demanded. "We ain't got all day."

Hands stripped off his trousers, his shorts, and he was heaved onto the cot, face down. When he tried to resist, he was beaten again. The chilled bottle of Coca-Cola came to rest on his bare buttocks and he understood what they were about. He cried out, struggled; it was no use. The bottle was shoved hard into Napoleon's rectum and he was sure he was being torn apart.

When he cried out, he was beaten into silent submission. A mocking vision of Carlito came dancing onto the shifting screen of his mind. He never knew when the bottle was withdrawn and the big man put himself in its place. Gradually he became aware of the muscular pounding, the whispered oaths in his ear, and he fought back out of the dark agony. A fist smashed into his jaw and through the pain, he knew that his jaw had been broken. The second of his attackers used him, and then the third. At last the oppressive weight was lifted off his body, but he experienced no relief, no gratitude.

"Carlito," a voice said from afar.

"Ah, Carlito," Napoleon replied silently. "You have come to me at last. To help me. To save me from the savagery. Take me, Little Minnow. Take me home. Behind the wall, only there will we be safe..."

"From Carlito..." a voice said.

And the sharpened point of a screwdriver stolen from the machine shop plunged into Napoleon's, penetrating his heart. In one extended, rattling spasm, unable to believe that this could happen to him, Napoleon died.

TWENTY-SIX

JACK KEVENEY MARKED THE DEATH OF NAPOLEON Cruz with a drink. And another. He drank in fashionable hotel bars not far from the White House, among the great and the near great of the capital city of America. He drank for two days with a senator from the West Coast, commiserating with him over the dismal state of the Union. He drank with a secretary in the Bureau of Labor Statistics until they collapsed into bed together, each too drunk to do more than fall asleep. He drank with a black lobbyist from New York who lectured him about the shortcomings of a capitalistic system. And finally, he drank alone, at his desk in his office, holding fast to a bottle of Jack Daniels.

There, in institutionalized solitude, he summoned up a vision of Napoleon. The handsome Aztec face wore a deep look of disbelief and regret. The eyes, large and dark, glittered with a practiced irony and were full of challenge. Accusation, almost. As if Keveney had conspired with his other enemies to bring him down.

Keveney toasted silently the ghost of his dead antagonist and swallowed Jack Daniels out of the bottle. A part of himself, a vital part, a part he had never dared to explore, had died when Napoleon had died. Violated, punished, and finally murdered by his *friends*. Could a man like Napoleon ever truly have a friend?

How little he knew about the dead man, Keveney thought: Willie Hatcher had sketched a figure in vague outline and Nina Fuentes had delivered bits and pieces, catering to Keveney's obsessive curiosity. Yet Napoleon remained a ghostly image, elusive and beyond his reach.

311

Gradually Keveney came to understand that Napoleon's ruth-lessness, his driving greed, his lust for power were little more than reflections in a cracked glass of his own needs and ambitions, obverse sides of the same battered coin. Without Napoleon's world of disorder and anarchy, Keveney's own world of law and order would have no reason to exist. Each of them fed off the other, making each other possible and real, and each of them ended up without gratification or hope. No hope, Keveney cried silently. No hope at all.

For the first time in his life he felt diminished, defeated by events, by implacable and unreachable enemies. Everything he had ever believed had been called into question; a rush of envy caused him to stagger and he clutched at the bottle for support. Napoleon, at least, was dead, and death after all was the final certitude. And comfort.

Keveney despaired; he had somehow been transformed into the man he'd never wanted to be—a twentieth-century Quixote, tilt-ing at contemporary windmills, mounting a flashy show without substance, accomplishing nothing, gaining nothing. A minor player in a game without winners.

"What now?" he dared to ask himself, knowing there was no good answer. "What do we do now? What do I do?"

As if in reply, the telephone on his desk began to ring. He stared at the instrument for some time before lifting it to his ear and answering.

"I've been trying to get hold of you for two days," Rosie de-clared, that special pontifical mix of displeasure and beguiling charm in her voice. "Are you all right?"

"All right?" That was one to think over. Why wasn't he sur-prised at her call? Displeased at the familiar lack of approval that lined her words? Neither surprised nor displeased, he confessed to himself that of all the people he had ever known, Rosie alone understood him.

"Not so good," he answered.

"Isn't it wonderful?" His response failed to register.

"What?"

"The returns are coming in and the president is certain to win both houses of Congress. Isn't it wonderful?"

Her politics, he acknowledged, had become steadily more conservative as she slid deeper into the religious life. She was a pious moth trapped forever in plastic, an icon of a hollow belief.

"And you did it, Jack. You deserve so much credit. The president was right, Jack—it's men like you who make this country what it is . . ."

Oh, shit, he almost said aloud, knowing she would lapse into that awful judgmental silence she had learned to cultivate, so patient and Christlike.

"You've made Patrick and me so proud, Jack. You have so much to be proud of, catching that terrible man . . ."

"He's dead."

"Let him burn in the fires of hell for eternity, his punishment is God's will. What was he—nothing but a common criminal."

Criminal, yes, Keveney reminded himself. But nothing about Napoleon Cruz was common. He was unique, a man who might have been an emperor or a king, a president or a pope, if only his gifts had been less twisted. He had been the most uncommon of men.

"He's dead, Rosie."

"What?" she cried softly into the phone, aware that something she had never before encountered was taking place. Keveney— her Jack, her husband in the eyes of God and Holy Mother Church—had undergone some dark and secret transformation. "What?" she said again. "What, Jack?"

"He's dead," Keveney repeated.

"I know."

Such certitude made him uneasy, such immutable piety raised unanswerable questions. Rosie was able to separate evil from good, and like the simplistic bleatings of a campaigning politician, she always came down on the side of home, motherhood, and the national anthem. How sweet, he told himself, and how reassuring, never to be wrong.

Such was the difference between them; for so long Keveney had struggled to ally himself with goodness, to remove himself from evil, to seek out evildoers, to deliver justice. The word was a pointed sliver of bone in the lining of his conscience, a prod that allowed him no relief from reality.

His naivete could no longer protect him from the truth, from the memories of his own contributions to corruption and deceit; his innocence had been violated, raped and destroyed as convincingly as Napoleon's flesh had been violated and destroyed.

His sense of separation expanded. He longed for what could now never be his. The bizarre fixation on Napoleon, more real to him in death than in life, and his eternal obsession with Nina Fuentes spanned the grave and left him feeling a loss acute and profound. Isolated in a crowd, he felt himself to be without friends or family, purposeless, the most meager of his dreams wiped away. "There is no one to talk to,," he muttered.

"You can talk to me, Jack."

His eyes fluttered shut and he struggled to set himself against the weakness and the loneliness, the endless horror of his failure; and he failed once again. "You think so?"

"Come home, Jack."

"Now?"

"As soon as you can. No matter when. I'll be waiting. Jack! Are you still there, Jack?"

"Yes."

"Why don't you come home, Jack?"

He recognized the plea in her voice, and the demand, and he was too weary to oppose such righteous authority for very long. He wanted so much to forget, to rest, to allow the numbness to take hold and to shield him, to give himself over to someone else's care.

"Sure," he managed to say at last. "Why not?"